THE
REFLECTING
POOL

THE REFLECTING POOL

A MARKO ZORN NOVEL

OTHO ESKIN

OCEANVIEW (PUBLISHING

SARASOTA, FLORIDA

ISBN 978-1-60809-411-0

Published in the United States of America by Oceanview Publishing

Sarasota, Florida

www.oceanviewpub.com

10 9 8 7 6 5 4 3 2 1

PRINTED IN THE UNITED STATES OF AMERICA

For Therese

ACKNOWLEDGEMENTS

I would like to thank Judith Ehrlich, my literary agent, for her patient and invaluable guidance and advice; the late Richard Marek for his thoughtful editing suggestions; and Gregory Murphy, novelist and playwright, and Ludovica Villar-Hauser, theater producer and director, for their encouragement and support.

THE REFLECTING POOL

CHAPTER ONE

SHE LOOKS AT me through three feet of water. Rose? I ask.

As a homicide detective I see the faces of the dead all the time. This one is different. I remember those blue eyes. But that can't be possible.

"On my count of three," the EMS man shouts. Four of us have waded into the Pool to retrieve the body. Her hair moves softly.

"One. Two. Three." We stagger from the unexpected weight and lift the body to the surface. Her clothes are heavy with water. We wade to the lip of the Reflecting Pool where we gently place her on the granite edge. I haul myself out of the Pool and stand to one side while two medics examine the body. We're too late, of course. There's nothing we can do. There's nothing anyone can do.

It's dawn and morning shadows rake across the Mall. The Lincoln Memorial looms at the far end of the Pool and Lincoln watches us from his marble throne. I think about the girl with the blue eyes.

"She's dead," a medic announces, getting to her feet. "I call it at zero seven twenty-two. She's all yours, Detective."

She is dressed in a gray pants suit and white blouse. She has dark brown hair, cut short, and wears what looks like a watch on her left wrist—a watch with no numbers. She wears no jewelry and has no wallet or purse and no cell phone. She has no shoes.

I call for the medical examiner staff and crime scene techs and for uniforms to secure the area then walk along the edge of the Pool, looking for signs of what happened during the night. I kneel down to examine faint marks on the granite ledge.

"We'll take it from here," a loud voice announces from over my shoulder. A tall man in a police uniform stands above me.

"Who are you?" I ask as I get to my feet and face him.

"Captain Darryl Fletcher. United States Park Police," he replies. "This is my jurisdiction." His voice is loud, meant to intimidate. Park Police troopers gather behind their senior officer. "Who are you?" he demands.

"My name's Zorn. Detective Marko Zorn, Washington DC Metropolitan Police. Homicide." How in hell had the Park Police gotten here so fast? There's something seriously wrong going on here.

"You and your people must leave," the captain tells me, loudly. "My men will take over the investigation of this incident."

"This is a homicide," I say, keeping my voice calm and professional. "That means the Metropolitan Police has jurisdiction. That means I have jurisdiction."

"Who says it's a homicide?" the Park Police guy asks. He has a couple of inches on me. Stands maybe six two. He has broad shoulders and his brass buttons and belt buckle sparkle in the morning sun. Even his shoes glow. Obviously, Captain Fletcher spends a lot of time polishing things. He wears aviator sunglasses even in the dawn half-light, so I can't see his eyes. I don't like it when I can't see the opposition's eyes.

"I say it's homicide."

"By whose authority?" Fletcher demands.

I show him my DC Police shield. "By this authority."

"We're on the National Mall, one of the crown jewels of the National Park system," the captain announces officiously. "This incident took place in the Reflecting Pool, a site revered by millions of visitors. Events that occur in the nation's National Parks are the responsibility of the National Park Service. You have no business trespassing on my park."

"This is not an *event*. This is murder," I say, firmly. "That gives me jurisdiction." I have no idea who has legal jurisdiction here. But then neither does this Park Police joker.

"Right now this part of the National Mall is a crime scene," I announce. "It belongs to me." This captain is getting on my nerves. I haven't had my morning coffee. My feet are wet. And I badly need a cigarette. "Get your people out of here, Smokey," I say, real calm like, "and let me do my job."

"What did you just call me?" Fletcher asks. "Did you just call me *Smokey*?"

In the distance there is the sound of multiple sirens. A fleet of DC Police cruisers and vans and ambulances is sweeping up to the edge of the Mall and disgorging teams of uniformed police officers and crime scene investigators. Fletcher becomes aware of the oncoming mob.

"What did you say your name was?" Captain Fletcher demands angrily, trying to preserve as much dignity as he can.

"Marko Zorn."

"I've heard of you, Zorn!" He doesn't make it sound like that's a good thing.

"Then you should know to stay out of my way."

Fletcher spins around, and I think for a moment he's going to charge my guys. Fletcher probably feels a bit like George Custer.

"You'll hear about this, Zorn," Fletcher announces, looking back at me over his shoulder. "I guarantee! You've not seen the last of me!" With that he storms off across the Mall, followed by his crestfallen troops.

The medical team moves in quickly to make a preliminary examination of the body. Members of the tech teams begin their investigation of the scene, spooling out yellow tape that reads "POLICE LINE DO NOT CROSS" to cordon off the area. Others photograph the body and the area around the Pool, their camera flashes lighting the Mall.

As I walk away through the grass, my shoes squelch. My pants, soaked through, stick to my shins.

One of the crime scene techs, a guy named Carl Nash, calls to me. He's crouched in the grass about twenty feet from the Pool. "I've got something, sir." He's found a single woman's shoe lying on its side in the damp grass—an Ecco loafer. Left foot.

"Where's the other shoe?" I ask.

Carl shrugs. "Haven't found it."

"And why so far from the Pool?" It's a rhetorical question. I don't expect an answer.

Somebody takes a flash photo and I see a bright glint in the grass on a slight rise among a cluster of elm trees. There's another flash and the glint is about twenty feet ahead of me and to my right. I head toward it.

I get down on one knee and put on my glasses. The object appears to be a metal bracelet consisting of a small medallion and chain. I remove a pen from my jacket breast pocket, slip it through the chain, and lift it up. The medallion is engraved, but in the dim light I can't read it.

I call Carl over and he places the bracelet into an evidence envelope, marks the envelope with the time, date, and location, and seals the envelope with evidence tape. He presses a red evidence marker into the ground, imprinted with the number "8." I put the evidence envelope in my inside jacket pocket. Strictly against police rules, of course. But then, I'm not big on rules.

There's no more I can do here. It's up to the crime scene technicians to search for the woman's identity and any evidence about what happened to her. I walk back toward my Jag where I left it parked at the edge of the Mall when I arrived in response to the 911 call.

The cops and techs are spreading out in search patterns. The medical team lifts the body, now covered with a heavy blanket, onto a gurney. The National Mall is filling with early morning light. At one end stands the Lincoln Memorial. A quarter of a mile to the east, the Washington Monument rises five hundred feet above the Mall, a brilliant white obelisk. Beyond, at the far end of the Mall, the United States Capitol dome gleams in the morning sun. The White House is just visible through a gap in the trees.

In the distance, curious early morning joggers stop to look at the police activity. The sky is turning bright blue with thin cloud streamers tinged with pink. The American flags on the government and museum buildings stir in the wind. It looks to be a fine day.

I take a crumpled pack of cigarettes from my coat pocket along with my silver lighter. I'm trying to quit smoking and normally don't have my first cigarette until late in the afternoon but I feel strangely affected by the death of the young woman in the Reflecting Pool—a woman I've never met, whose name I don't know. I light the cigarette and inhale the poison and wonder vaguely whether the US National Parks are "No Smoking" areas and half expect Captain Fletcher to arrest me for desecrating public land.

A man leans against the front fender of my Jag, arms crossed, watching me intently. He's an African American with handsome features, tall and slender, wearing a double-breasted Italian silk suit.

He calls himself Cloud.

I've arrested Cloud several times—most recently about a year ago for attempted murder. Mine. Thanks to him, I carry a fragment of a .38 caliber bullet about half an inch from my spleen. Every time I see

Cloud, I feel a pain in my midsection. I think it's the bullet fragment twisting. My doctors tell me it's my imagination. I know better. Cloud and I go way back.

A few feet away stands another young African American I recognize from mug shots as Cloud's number two—a man named Lamont, Cloud's bodyguard and driver. He is short and muscular and
has bright orange hair.

"Yo, my man," I say to Cloud. "You better not mess up my car."

Cloud moves slowly away from my Jag.

"I don't want any scratches," I say. "I like to keep the car looking
sharp."

"Your car got no scratches, man." Cloud stops directly in front of
me, close and menacing. "You may scare a lot of folks in this town
but you don't scare me."

"That's your first mistake of the day, Cloud."

"Sister Grace wants to see you. This morning. Nine sharp."

"I'm busy."

"Don't fuck with me, Detective. Be there!"

"I'm investigating a murder."

Cloud shakes his head. "Your stiff can wait. Sister Grace can't.
You don' want to keep her waiting, know what I mean? You disappoint Sister Grace, you die. That be the rules. You of all people
should know that." Cloud glances at the police activity on the Mall.
"That your new murder?"

"That's the victim," I tell him.

"You tag a brother?"

I shake my head as I open the door to my car.

"Better not," Cloud says to me. "Remember, Sister Grace expec-
tin' you at nine. Don' be late." He walks away, followed by Lamont.
They climb into a gleaming black Lincoln Town Car parked in a
"no-parking zone" on Constitution Avenue, Cloud in back, Lamont
at the wheel. They drive away.

CHAPTER TWO

My Fennix Italian oxfords are ruined. When the EMS team and I, along with the two uniformed cops, responding to the 911 call, arrived at the Reflecting Pool we plunged right in, hoping whoever was in the pool might still be saved. Naturally, we gave no thought to what the water would do to our shoes. It's a shame though; I was particularly fond of those oxfords. I wonder, vaguely, whether I can put the cost of new shoes on my expense account but decide that's not a good idea. The department would probably give me grief about the price and it would not be a good idea to draw attention to the cost of my wardrobe. At least I had the presence of mind to take off my Vacheron Constantin watch before reaching into the water. That would have been a major loss.

After changing into dry clothes and new shoes, I go to the kitchen to make myself a dark Sumatra espresso. My kitchen faces east and, at this hour, is filled with cheerful morning sunlight. Through the window I can see the trees of Rock Creek Park swaying in the morning breeze.

I start up the espresso machine then turn on a small television set that sits on the black stainless-steel countertop and I half listen to the morning news while the machine does its thing. A perky young woman stands in front of a weather map pointing at numbers showing temperatures and wind directions and humidity. "The fourteenth day without rain," she announces cheerfully. The program shifts to national news and a story about the death of a former Army general and prominent political figure. I switch off the TV. I have no interest in dead generals.

I put the evidence envelope on the counter and study the bracelet through the transparent plastic. The bracelet is a slender, rather delicate, affair, with a metal link chain and a medallion with an inscription that reads:

Sandra Wilcox
Peanut/Tree Nut

This is followed by a telephone number beginning with a 202 area code.

There are three miniscule red dots on the medallion. Using my cell phone, I dial the number on the bracelet. It's picked up before the second ring. A man's voice repeats the number I've just called.

"My name is Marko Zorn," I announce. "District of Columbia Metropolitan Police Department. Homicide Division. Who am I speaking to?"

"I am not at liberty to provide that information."

"What is the name of your organization?" I ask.

"I am not at liberty to provide that information."

Okay, I think. I'm dealing with some kind of high-level security organization whose employees are trained to be sphinxlike. So I say: "Please pass along this message. One of your employees was found dead this morning. The name of the employee is Sandra Wilcox. If your organization has an interest in this individual, call me." I gave the voice my cell number.

"That is not the number of the Metropolitan Police," the voice informs me.

"You are quite correct." I cut the connection.

I place a small porcelain cup under the brass nozzle of the espresso machine and pull a shot. While the steaming, black liquid flows, my cell phone rings. A woman's voice says: "I want to speak to Detective Zorn."

"You're in luck. You've reached him."

"I'm told you have information about a Miss Sandra Wilcox."

"That's possible," I say. "Who are you?" I take a sip of coffee. It's very hot and strong.

"I am not at liberty—"

"I know," I say. "What's your connection to Sandra Wilcox?"

"Can we meet at your office, Detective? Say in half an hour?"

Someone's in a hurry, I think. "Make it eleven," I say. "I have an appointment at nine."

"Can't your appointment wait? This is important."

"My appointment at nine is important."

There's an impatient sigh at the other end. "Very well. Eleven."

"My office is at police headquarters," I start to explain. "Homicide Division. That's at—"

"I know where your office is, Detective Zorn. We know all about you."

CHAPTER THREE

MY 1971 LIME green Jaguar drop top is kind of conspicuous—probably the only one in the city—and I don't like parking it on the street in this part of town. It's not that I'm afraid it will be lifted—there are those here who know it belongs to me and will see that it is not touched. But I prefer not to advertise I'm visiting Sister Grace. A taxi or Uber would leave an electronic trail I can't risk being traced so I drive.

The street seems empty except for a young African American wearing fierce dreadlocks. A Lincoln Town Car with low-number DC tags is parked in front of a liquor store. I park the Jag behind the Lincoln.

"Haven't seen you around this neighborhood," the man in dreadlocks says to me. "You sellin' or buyin'?"

"I'm here to see Sister Grace."

"Ain't no one here by that name."

"That's too bad." I enter the liquor store, its doors and windows covered with heavy steel mesh. It sells cheap booze, cigarettes, and lottery tickets. An elderly black man with white hair sits behind the counter. He looks up at me, smiles pleasantly, and gestures toward the back door. I remember the same gentleman from my last visits, nod in a friendly way, and walk past racks of vodka and wine bottles out the back door into a narrow alley. A basketball hoop has been set up at one end. Two large dumpsters are at the other. Four CCTV cameras cover the length of the alley.

A boy of about ten or eleven wearing a gray hoodie stands in the alley waiting for me. "I'll take you in," the kid says.

"I know the way," I say.

"I'll take you."

We cross the alley and go through a steel door marked in stencil "Do Not Enter" and into a small entryway. The kid punches the keys to a cyber lock and pushes open a second heavy metal door. We step into a room that might once have been a commercial showroom. There are a dozen or so unmatched chairs scattered around the room, a regulation-size pool table at the far end, and a large plasma TV set on one wall showing a college basketball game.

A dozen armed men intercept me at the door. One is Cloud. I vaguely recognize one of the others who, I'm pretty sure, is wanted for murder and drug trafficking. There is no sign of Cloud's number two, Lamont. Almost tangible tension fills the room. In all the times I've been here, I've never before seen so many armed guards. Something big is going down. Or is about to happen. Something bad and dangerous.

Cloud pats me down, very smooth, very professional and practiced, and I feel a pain in my midsection but try not to wince. I don't want to give Cloud the satisfaction.

Cloud leads me through an inner door, and we step into a small, cozy room furnished with old, but comfortable, furniture: a floral chintz-covered sofa; several large, overstuffed armchairs with lots of poufy cushions; and two side tables on which are vases filled with African violets. The walls are covered with wallpaper with images of roses, once bright red, now faded. There is a faint smell of lavender mixed with Marlboro cigarettes in the room. There are no windows;

the only light comes in from two floor lamps on either side of the sofa. A picture on one wall shows Jesus Christ surrounded by adoring children.

This is Sister Grace's parlor—some would say the most dangerous place in the city of Washington.

A tiny African American woman sits on the chintz sofa holding a seriously overweight ginger cat on her lap. Part of the cat's left ear is missing. A green tote bag with the words "Smithsonian" printed on the side rests on the couch next to her.

The old woman gestures with one ancient hand for me to approach. "Good morning, Detective Zorn," she croaks.

"You look lovelier than ever, Sister Grace."

"Don't try your sweet talk on me. I be a very old lady and in no mood for crap. Especially your kind of crap." She gestures at Cloud and the boy waiting by the door. "You! Get out! Both of you."

Cloud and the boy slowly back out the room, Cloud with obvious reluctance. They stop at the door and Cloud is about to say something. "Out! Now!" the old woman yells. Cloud moves through the door, eyes on the old woman. The boy watches me intently. "Out!" the old woman yells. They leave, closing the door firmly behind them.

"Sit down, Detective," the old woman orders.

I sit in one of the armchairs across from her. She is older and smaller, even more dried up, than last time. Nobody knows how old Sister Grace is. Some believe she's over one hundred. I'd guess she's in her nineties.

She's dressed in a simple cotton ankle-length housedress with a delicate white-lace collar at her throat. Her white hair is cut short. She scratches the head of her cat who watches me suspiciously. Sister Grace picks up a crumpled pack of Marlboro cigarettes and I lean forward and offer a light from my lighter. She inhales deeply, coughs, then takes my lighter in one of her arthritic hands.

It's an old-fashioned, sterling silver, art-deco lighter made in Scandinavia. Sister Grace turns the lighter over slowly and examines the inscription. She smiles but that may be my imagination. "Pretty," she says. I don't know whether she means the lighter or the inscription. "Must have cost a lot."

"A gift from an admirer," I say.

Sister Grace coughs. "My doctors say smokin's not good for my health. So far, I've buried 'em all, so fuck 'em."

"Cloud said you want to see me, Sister Grace."

"That a fact. I have a problem I need you to fix."

"I've been thinking of going into a different line of work," I say.

"Mercy, Mr. Detective, ain't you a caution." She rubs the cat's head. "You will go into a different line of work when I tell you to." She takes a drag on her cigarette. "Besides, I have reason to believe you have need of money."

"I'm doing just fine, thank you," I say.

"I know that not to be the case. You got expensive tastes. Like that lighter." She passes it back to me.

"I told you, it was a gift."

"That watch you wearin'—I bet that cost a pretty penny. How you afford that on a city employee salary?"

I'm silent. She holds her cigarette in her left hand while she caresses the cat with her right. The ash on her cigarette is getting long, but she seems not to notice.

"I unnerstand you just bought yourself an expensive painting," she says.

"What do you know about my painting, Sister Grace?"

"They tell me it's by some Frenchman named Melisa or somethin'. Knowin' you, it probably of some naked lady."

"It's not a naked lady." I can't seem to take my eyes off the ash at the end of her cigarette.

"How you afford fancy pictures by a no-account French painter?"

"It's a beautiful painting. I've been waiting for it to come on the market for two years. And the name's Soutine, not Melisa."

"Never heard of him . . . Musta cost a fortune. How you gonna pay for that?"

"How do you know about that painting?" I ask. "It was a private sale. Supposed to be confidential."

"I keep an eye on my people."

"I'm not *your people*."

"You are when I say you are. And that car you drive. What kind of damn fool thing is that, I ask? A Jag-u-are car. That no car to be drivin' in this neighborhood. You the biggest damn fool I ever did meet."

"I thought we had an understanding," I say.

"My boys will leave you and yor' fancy car be so long as I say so," the old woman says. "And I say so, so long as you of use to me. But if that should happen to change, you have no protection. And there'll be nothin' left of your car but one hubcap. If Jag-u-ares have hubcaps. I don' know."

"How come you know so much about me?"

"My boys, they look and they listen. You understand? I have eyes an' ears everwhere. I know everthing that happens in this town."

"What is it you want me to fix?" I ask.

"You know Cloud?"

"I know Cloud. He tried to kill me," I say.

"I recollect that involved a woman. Cloud's woman, Mariana. You got involved with her. Damn fool thing to do. French pictures and fancy cars and fancy women. That means trouble. Messing with one of Cloud's women—that be fatal."

"So I learned." The .38 fragment twists in my gut.

A few years ago, I'd been assigned to a security detail at a concert featuring The Rolling Stones. I was standing near the entrance watching the crowd pushing and shoving to get in and I found myself staring into the eyes of a woman whose beauty still takes my breath away—tall and willowy, with olive skin, large brown eyes, and a warm, moist, seductive mouth. A woman who will arouse any man's erotic longings and suppressed desires. And probably every woman's, too. She looked frightened and lost so I slipped under the rope and went to her. "Can I help you, miss?"

"I'm supposed to meet Cloud in the VIP lounge," she whispers. She speaks with a slight accent. "I got lost."

"Come with me," I say. "I'll take you to Cloud."

I pulled her out of the surging line, and we ducked under the rope barricade. She slid her arm under mine in the possessive way beautiful women do.

Mariana was a celebrity in Washington. Born in Argentina, she'd gone to New York as a teenager and become a celebrated model. She did gigs in Paris and Milan and her picture appears in glossy fashion magazines. Photographers love her and she loves the camera.

I also knew this: She was Cloud's woman and her smile will destroy people.

A year before, a lawyer from a downtown firm took her out to dinner at some posh restaurant. Two days later he was stopped in front of his Georgetown town house and beaten by two thugs. This was in the middle of the day and there were witnesses. His attackers left the man, broken and bleeding, on the sidewalk.

The lawyer died of internal injuries two days later. I was assigned the case, but it was hopeless. Although a dozen people witnessed the beating, no one would identify the attackers. Why would they? It doesn't pay to annoy Cloud. As I've learned at my cost.

I escorted Mariana to the VIP lounge where a cluster of security guards was gathered.

"Thank you, sir," Mariana whispered. "You saved my life. It proves there are still gentlemen."

She squeezed my hand. Even though we were surrounded by dozens of people, the moment felt exquisitely intimate. The door to the VIP lounge opened, and Mariana swept in. There was applause and I heard Cloud yelling: "Where the fuck you been, girl?"

That should have been the end, but I couldn't get Mariana out of my blood. As Sister Grace said to me, when it comes to women, I'm a damn fool. So it wasn't the end. I couldn't stay away from her and that ended up with a bullet in my gut.

The cigarette ash finally falls onto Sister Grace's lap and she brushes the ashes impatiently away. "I've told Cloud to stay away from you," Sister Grace says to me, yanking a fresh cigarette from her pack. "That why you still breathin' regular. Cloud my grandkid, you know."

"I didn't know that," I say, offering her my lighter. "What's Cloud's real name?"

"I don' know." She drags deeply on her cigarette,

"Of course you know."

"Why do you care?" she asks. "Is it important?"

"Probably not. I'd just like to know."

"I can't remember," she says. She looks once again at my lighter, then returns it to me. "It was a long time ago. When Cloud was just a cute little boy."

"Of course you remember," I say. "You just don't want to tell me."

She drags on her cigarette. "Tyrone. His name was Tyrone."

"Tyrone," I repeat.

"It *was* Tyrone," she says. "It's Cloud now. Satisfied?" Sister Grace stares for a moment into the middle distance.

"Why am I here?" I ask.

"I got a problem," she replies. "One that takes special talent to fix. You get a substantial fee for this job. Fifty thousand dollars. Maybe you can buy a frame for yor' new picture. Twenty-five thousand up front." She pats the tote bag on the couch next to her. "The final twenty-five thousand when you fix my problem."

"What is it you want me to fix?"

"I try to keep things under control 'round here, but Cloud becomin' a serious problem. He has his young thugs. Like that Lamont boy. Lamont itchin' to kill people." She takes a drag on her cigarette. "Four people shot. In a schoolyard. Just this mornin'. One of 'em a little girl, itty, bitty thing. That just don' sit right with me. I gotta put a stop to that. Before the police and politicians get serious and roll up the gangs and put me out of business."

"You've survived worse."

"The police ain't the worst of it. I got enemies. All 'round. I know what they say 'bout me. I be old an' weak. I losin' my mind. But I'm not that far gone I can't see danger. Cloud want to take over my organization. He want me out of the way. He becomin' real impatient with me. Cloud be my Calvary. You be the fixer. Fix Cloud!"

"Get someone else."

"It got to be you. For this kind of problem I can't use my usual crack-head just out of lockup lookin' for some pocket money. It got to be a professional job. You the professional." She picks up the tote bag and hands it to me. "This your down payment. Do the job in the next couple of days. Cloud gettin' tired of me naggin' at him. Any day now he gonna put a bullet in my head." She drags on her cigarette.

"What exactly do you want me to do?"

"I want you should kill my Tyrone."

"I don't do that kind of work."

"You suddenly got a conscience? I go to church ever' Sunday. I tithe and I pray regular. I doubt you ever pray. Do the job. You done a lot a' wicked things for me in the past. This is no different."

"You've never asked me to murder someone."

"I have a serious problem. Just fix it so Cloud no threat to me."

CHAPTER FOUR

SY HOLLAND PULLS a plastic mask from his face and nods toward the four bodies stretched out on steel examination tables. "Came in just now. Another expected any moment. I don't know where I'm going to put them." Across the lab, Laura Kennedy, one of Holland's assistants, is prepping a body for examination. There's something by Santana playing on the sound system. "That's in addition to yours."

"Some kind of accident?" I ask.

"The investigating officers tell me it was a gang drive-by shooting. At a schoolyard in Southeast. Can you believe? Some young kids shot. One was a girl—she can't be over eight." He gestures toward the bodies. "What with the drug overdoses, it's getting worse every day."

The woman I've come to see lies motionless on the steel slab. Laura Kennedy gently removes a plastic sheet from her face. Again, I have the shock of recognition. False recognition. I know this woman, but the girl I knew died over twenty years ago. When I last saw her, the girl I once knew had deep slashes in her chest, her abdomen was cut open. The woman lying on the metal slab in front of me today shows no signs of physical violence. Is this how Rose would look had she never met Clyde Fenton? I turn away, angry. I can't look into her blue eyes and I gesture for Laura to cover her.

"Female," Holland says to me, his voice expressing no emotion. He never does. "Mid-thirties."

"She looks younger than that," I say. *Am I thinking of Rose?*

Holland shrugs. "Some people age well. She'll never grow old now."

"What can you tell me?"

"Five foot seven and a quarter. One twenty-eight pounds. In good physical condition. Looks like she worked out a lot."

"Time of death?" I ask.

"Between one and three."

"Cause of death?"

"Probably drowned. Can't say for sure until I open her up."

"Any signs of sexual assault?"

"None."

"How about drugs? Alcohol?"

"I won't know until we get the tox results and that won't be for several days. We're kind of backed up here, as you can see."

"Anything else I should know?"

"Scar on lower right leg. Very old. Probably a childhood scar. A recent minor wound on the left wrist. Abrasions on the knees."

"Show me the abrasions," I say.

Holland gently pulls the cover from the woman's feet, revealing her legs. There are dark marks around her kneecaps.

"Just these abrasions?" I ask. "Nowhere else?"

"Just on the knees. I thought that unusual myself."

"You said there's a cut."

Holland lifts the woman's left hand. There's a raw, red scratch, about two inches long, on her wrist.

"When did this happen?" I ask.

"Very recently. Definitely before death."

"Look at this." I take the plastic evidence envelope containing the bracelet from my pocket.

"It's a medical ID bracelet," Holland says. "The wearer was allergic to peanuts."

"Do you see the small red spots on the bracelet?" I ask.

"Of course I see them," Holland answers impatiently.

"Could they be blood?"

"I'll find out, Marko. And, before you ask, I'll match them to the victim's blood."

"I need to look at the clothes," I say.

Holland leads me to an examination table on the far side of the autopsy room on which has been placed a clear plastic evidence bag containing clothing, neatly folded. I put on a pair of green vinyl evidence gloves and go through the contents. Inside the plastic bag are the gray pants suit, underwear, and a plain, white blouse. According to the labels, the clothes mostly came from Ann Taylor.

"These look like workday clothes," I say.

"So?" Holland shrugs.

"Why would she be wearing workday clothes in the middle of the night?"

"I don't know. I know nothing about women or women's clothes. You're the detective. You're the expert on women. You tell me."

There is one shoe in the evidence bag—the one I saw lying in the grass. It's been tagged by the forensic tech showing date, time, and location. Lying next to the clothes is a plastic evidence bag containing the device I'd seen on the woman's wrist when we pulled her from the Pool.

"I need to take this," I say, picking up the evidence bag.

"Isn't this supposed to go to forensics?" Holland asks.

"Of course it's supposed to go to forensics. I'll see they get it as soon as I'm finished."

* * *

I wave the evidence envelope in front of Malcolm Wu, the senior IT guy in the police department who knows every electronic gadget and device ever invented.

"Do you know what this is?" I ask.

Malcolm grudgingly looks away from his array of computer screens and focuses on the plastic envelope. "It seems to be one of those gadgets people wear to monitor their activity. You know, people concerned about their weight, keeping in shape. That kind of thing." Malcolm is at least forty pounds overweight and has probably never seen the inside of a gym.

"Tell me what's on it."

"You want me to open it up?"

"That's exactly what I want you to do."

"You will need a password."

"I don't have a password."

"Ask the owner."

"The owner is dead, Malcolm. She's in the morgue I've just come from and where I stole this device. I need to know what time the wearer died and what she was doing the last few hours of her life."

"Don't you need a court order for something like that?"

"Let's not involve the lawyers, shall we? Why do you think I came to you? If I send it to forensics, they'd feel obliged to consult with counsel and that would lead to endless talk about laws and statutes and legal precedents. I don't have time for that. Just sneak a peek and tell me what she was doing just before she died."

"This is totally illegal, you know."

"Are you saying you can't open the device?"

"Of course I can open it. Just saying it's against the law. You'll never be able to use what you learn in court."

"Whatever makes you think I expect this case to go to court? When can you give me a readout?"

"Is it urgent?"

"Very."

"You owe me a beer."

*   *   *

"You hear about what happened this morning?" Frank Townsend asks as I sit in a wooden chair across from his desk. "The playground shooting?"

Townsend, the chief of the Homicide Division, holds a large mug inscribed "World's Greatest Detective" in bright red letters. A birthday gift, I assume, from some dutiful grandchild.

"I just came from the medical examiner's lab," I tell him. "I saw."

"There were kids there. Little kids, you hear! One girl dead. Another ten-year-old girl critically wounded. She's still in surgery. And that's on top of several other street shootings last night. Not to mention the drug plague we're having. This shit has got to stop!"

"Do we know who did the shooting at the playground?"

"Yes, as it happens, we do. A thug named Lamont Jones."

The mention of the name Lamont Jones gives me a visceral jolt, but I decide not to tell Townsend I'd seen Lamont earlier this morning, presumably not long before he went on his rampage. Frank would just want to know about my encounter and I don't want to go there.

"The gang division is working that case," Frank says. "They tell me this Lamont was after a local dealer who works for Cloud. I think you know Cloud."

"Why would this guy Lamont try to shoot down one of Cloud's people. They both work for Cloud?"

"Beats me. There were several eyewitnesses. Lamont's hard to miss what with his orange hair. The mayor's giving a press conference this morning. He'll make all kinds of promises to bring this gang violence to an end. All bullshit."

Townsend takes a drink of coffee and makes a face. "I have some good news, Marko."

My heart sinks. Townsend has called me to his office because he has something important to tell me. Never a good thing.

"I've found you a new partner," Townsend says.

"I don't want a partner."

"You have a partner. It wasn't easy."

"Who is this lunatic?"

"A young officer. Recently graduated from the Police Academy. Name of Kenneth Blake. I'm sure he'll be a great asset to the division. He's very enthusiastic."

"I don't want a new partner," I say. "Least of all one who's enthusiastic."

"He's in HR right now finishing up his paperwork then he'll look for you. Don't scare this one too much on his first day. Teach him the trade. Mentor him. Look after him. Try to keep this one."

I'm silent.

Townsend searches nervously among the papers on his desk. "I've already received a complaint about you." He glances at his wristwatch. "And we're barely into the workday."

"Who's complaining this time?" I ask.

"The Feds. Seems you offended the Department of Interior. Some undersecretary named Torrance called a few minutes ago." Frank glances at his notes. "Overreaching your authority," he reads from the memo. "Showing disrespect to a superior officer."

"You want details?"

"Certainly not," Townsend says. "I told him you've been severely reprimanded. Consider yourself reprimanded. Why were you out in the middle of the Mall this morning harassing federal employees anyway?"

"There was an incident."

"What kind of incident?"

"Somebody called 911 around six thirty and reported seeing what looked like a body in the Reflecting Pool. I got the call at home and went to the scene. We discovered the body of a young woman in the water."

"The Reflecting Pool? Really?"

"Really."

"Could this have been an accident? Maybe the victim was drunk or something and fell in."

"This was no accident."

"Could she have drowned herself?"

"The Reflecting Pool is three feet deep. You don't commit suicide in three feet of water."

"You think it was murder?"

"I know it was murder."

"How can you be so sure?"

I hesitate, picking my words carefully. I can't tell Frank my real reason. "The victim had no ID," I say. "No cell phone. No young woman would be out in the middle of the night without a phone."

Townsend looks skeptical. "Maybe. She could have been robbed. Who was the victim?"

"She had no ID but I found a bracelet—one of those medical ID bracelets—near the scene. The name on the bracelet is Sandra Wilcox."

"Who's she?"

"I have no idea," I say. "But my guess is Sandra Wilcox is our victim. I've been in touch with an organization she worked for. I'm meeting with somebody from that organization in my office in just a few minutes. I'll learn more then."

"Anything else?"

"I need help searching the area for the victim's ID and phone."

Townsend scowls.

"The murderer may have thrown these items into one of the trash containers on the Mall," I say, patiently. "I need men to help search the containers."

"Do you have any idea how many trash containers there are on the Mall?"

"I imagine there are a lot."

"Hundreds. I can't spare anybody. This seems like a routine homicide. If it's even a homicide at all. I can assign the case to Taylor or Warren. Or some other junior officer. I've got more important things to deal with. The city is facing a gang war and we need all our resources on the streets. I can't waste a senior investigator."

"I want this case, Frank."

"How sure are you this is murder?"

"I'm sure." I can't explain to Frank why I'm sure. But I know two things happened this morning that are seriously wrong. Two things that make me think this case is a lot more complicated than it looks. And I know that it will take me a long time before I will be able to get this woman's blue eyes out of my mind.

Townsend's obviously overwhelmed by the gang wars and drug plague going on in his city, pressured by the mayor and the politicians on one side and the violence in the streets on the other. He'll have no patience for my fantasies.

And I certainly can't tell him the real reason I know it was murder. The victim told me.

CHAPTER FIVE

A WOMAN STANDS impatiently in front of my desk. I've just spread out a map of the National Mall—one of those tourist maps they give away to visitors showing monuments and interesting sites in the Nation's Capital. It's eleven sharp.

The woman is middle aged and dressed in matronly tweeds, her dress extends to her ankles and her feet are encased in sensible brown shoes. Her hair is gray and cut short. She carries a cavernous brown handbag and there is no smile on her thin lips. I take an instant dislike to her. "Jessica Kirkland," she announces. "I'm here to see Detective Zorn. I have an appointment."

I remove my reading glasses. I'm vain about wearing glasses when I'm in the presence of a woman. Even a middle-aged woman I don't like. I hold out my hand and we shake. Given her age, this old-fashioned courtesy seems called for.

"Marko Zorn," I say.

The chair next to my desk is filled with unread police department memos. I requisition one of Sergeant Foster's chairs, place it next to my desk, and the lady takes a seat. Primly.

"Your police identification, please," she says. Very firmly. It's not a question.

I pass her my shield and ID. She removes a cell phone from the subterranean regions of her handbag, photographs my shield and

ID, and punches info into her cell, pursing her thin lips in concentration. She's silent the better part of a minute, waiting for some kind of response. She frowns when she sees the response then returns my shield and ID to me without a word.

"May I see your identification, Mrs. Kirkland?"

She hesitates, annoyed, then reaches deep into the depths of her handbag and removes a laminated ID on a chain. She grudgingly passes me the ID with her photo and name, some numbers, and "United States Secret Service" printed at the top.

"I understand from your phone message that Sandra Wilcox has passed away," Mrs. Kirkland tells me when I return her ID.

"We found the body of a woman early this morning," I tell her. "We believe it may be Sandra Wilcox."

"In the Reflecting Pool."

How the hell does she know she was found in the Reflecting Pool? "Did Miss Wilcox work for you?"

"She worked for the Secret Service," Mrs. Kirkland replies.

This comes as a surprise. I'd assumed the dead woman was a middle management bureaucrat at the Treasury Department. This information puts this death into a completely new perspective. A complicating one.

"Did you know Miss Wilcox well?"

"I knew her."

"Did you know she had a peanut allergy?"

Mrs. Kirkland looks disconcerted. Confused. "A peanut allergy?"

"That's right."

"No, I didn't. What has this got to . . . ?"

Mrs. Kirkland never looks me directly in the eye. Instead she seems to focus on my pocket square.

"Would you be able to identify Miss Wilcox?" I ask.

"You mean . . . identify the body? Of course. That's why I'm here."

"I'll make the arrangements," I say.

"What can you tell me about Sandra's death?" she asks.

"As you seem to have already been informed, she was found in the Reflecting Pool."

"Was she drowned?"

"What makes you think she was drowned?" I ask.

"She was in the Pool. Did she fall in?"

"We don't know. Our investigation has just begun."

"You're a homicide detective. What makes you think this is a homicide?"

"We don't think anything yet. It's an open case."

"I'll need all the information you have. I must report to my superiors. You understand." Her eyes shift to the tourist map spread out on my desk.

"What kind of job did Sandra Wilcox have in the Secret Service?"

"I'm afraid I can't give you that information. It's classified."

"I'm afraid I'm going to insist you give me that information."

She presses her lips together. She's obviously not the chatty type.

"And," I go on, "I will need the names of her friends and associates in the Secret Service."

She shakes her head. "That kind of request must be made through channels," she says defiantly.

"At least you can give me her home address."

"I'm not sure . . ." she hesitates.

"You have her home address," I insist. "Or you can get it on your little gizmo there."

She regards me with distaste, and nevertheless retrieves her phone, punches in numbers, and gives me an address near Calvert Street in Washington, DC.

"I understand you located an identification bracelet Miss Wilcox was wearing," Jessica Kirkland says.

How in hell does she know about the bracelet? "That's right," I answer.

"Please return it," she demands.

"Sorry. No."

Her face flushes. "It's the property of the Secret Service. It belongs to us."

"It's evidence in a possible criminal investigation. The bracelet belongs to me."

"I am also informed that you removed a device Sandra Wilcox was wearing on her wrist. Give it back."

"No," I say. "I'm keeping it."

"Why on earth are you keeping it? It just a device you can buy anywhere."

"Because it's evidence in a possible criminal investigation."

"What possible use is it in your investigation, Detective?"

"It will lead us to Sandra Wilcox's murderer," I say. "Now, unless you have any further questions, Mrs. Kirkland, let's go take a look at the body."

We go to the medical examiner's viewing room and stand behind a glass partition. Laura, the young assistant, is handling identifications this morning. She rolls out the gurney and gently removes the plastic sheet from the victim's face.

"That's her," Mrs. Kirkland says. "That's Sandra Wilcox." There is no emotion in her voice. No change of expression on her face that I can read. "Can I go now?"

"Of course." I gesture for Laura to return the victim's body and I escort Mrs. Kirkland to the waiting room where I have her sign the proper forms. I offer to have a police officer drive her to her office. She rejects the offer and hurries away. She doesn't look back. She doesn't say goodbye.

CHAPTER SIX

"I'm Kenneth."

A young man in his mid-twenties—tall, rail thin, with straw-colored hair—looks down at me, his eyebrows and eyelashes so pale as to be almost invisible. He wears a suit and tie and white shirt that look brand new and probably all came from Costco. He carries a bag with "Metropolitan Police Washington D.C. Police Academy" stenciled on it in bright white letters against a blue background. The young man smiles at me anxiously.

Kenneth—the name rings a bell, but I can't think why. I'm sometimes bad with names. "Hello, Kenneth. What can I do for you?"

The smile fades from Kenneth's face. The hopefulness in his eyes gives way to anxiety.

"I'm Kenneth, sir. Kenneth Blake." He swallows. "Your new partner? Sir?"

It comes back to me with a shock—Frank Townsend told me I've been assigned a new partner. After half a dozen qualified candidates have sensibly rejected the job, I thought I was in the clear.

The young man standing in front of me shifts his weight from his right leg to his left leg. "Kenneth," I say. "Why don't you take a seat?"

"Thank you, sir." He sits in the chair Mrs. Kirkland just vacated, carefully pulling his trouser legs up to maintain the crease. "Captain Townsend did talk to you about me?" he asks. "Didn't he?"

"Of course. He told me all about you."

"So there's no problem?"

"Problem? What problem?"

"About my being your partner? He told me you are very picky about your partners."

"Why don't you tell me something about yourself?"

Kenneth perks up at that. "I was born and raised in Freemont, New Jersey. It's just south of—"

"I know where it is."

"I went to Grover Cleveland High School. I was on the varsity baseball team."

"Which position?"

He looks anxious for a moment. "Outfielder. I took lots of civics classes."

"Why?"

"I wanted to be a policeman."

"Why did you want to be a cop?"

"My dad was chief of police in Somerville, New Jersey. My two uncles are firemen."

"Your dad told you not to go into police work. Is that right?"

Kenneth stares at me, mouth slightly open. "How did you know?"

"He said you wouldn't make it as a cop. Didn't have the chops. Something like that?"

"Has my dad been talking to you?" Kenneth's face is flushed.

"No. Tell me more about yourself."

"I went to Montclair State. I took pre-law. I can do shorthand."

"Then you came to Washington to get away from your family?"

"What makes you think that?"

"And you applied for a job with the Metropolitan Police."

"That's right. Went to the Academy. I just finished my eighteen-month probation period. And here I am."

"And here you are. What kind of police work have you been doing since you graduated?"

"I was in public affairs. I was assistant public spokesman. Maybe you saw me on TV."

"Can't say I have."

We sit in uncomfortable silence for a moment.

"At the Academy, did they teach you about searching trash containers?"

"Trash containers?"

"Never mind."

"Okay, Detective Zorn, I know my record doesn't sound like much. But I'm a quick learner. And I'm very enthusiastic."

"So I've been told."

"I just want to learn. I want to learn from you."

"What do you want to learn from me?"

"I want to learn how to be a great detective. Like you. Captain Townsend tells me you have the best record for solving homicide cases in the Washington police force."

"Do you have your personnel file with you?" I ask.

"Yes, sir." Kenneth rummages eagerly in his blue bag, removes a standard police administrative file folder, and passes it to me. I glance through it. It's thin. My cell phone rings, and I search for it among the pile of papers and file folders on my desk and find it under the map. There is no caller ID, but I recognize the area code: 207.

"Hello," I say, cautiously.

"Marko, come home."

"I am home."

"I mean your real home. There's trouble here."

"Damn it, I'm in the middle of a murder investigation. I can't just drop everything."

"You may be involved in a murder investigation here."

"Stop talking riddles."

"The police are snooping around. They've been to the house twice now."

"Who have you spoken to?"

"A man named Carpenter. Stuart Carpenter. You may remember him. He remembers you."

"I remember Stuart. We went to high school together."

"Well, he's sheriff here now. And he wants to talk to you."

"I don't want to talk to him."

"This is family. That's more important than work."

"I can't get away just now."

"They've found something."

"What have they found?"

"They say they've found a Timex watch."

"What kind of wristband does it have?"

"Stuart said it has an expansion bracelet."

"I'll catch a flight to Portland first thing in the morning," I say. "I should be at your place by two." I hang up the phone and study the young man sitting across from me.

"Here's the deal," I say. "Something's just come up and I've got to go out of town for a day. It's a family emergency. You stay here and man the fort—take any reports on the case I'm working on while I'm away such as anything from the medical examiner's office or from the crime scene investigators. If a man named Malcolm Wu calls, tell him I'll get back to him as soon as possible."

"If this Malcolm person sends a report, should I hold it for you?"

"He won't send a report. But he may want to talk to me privately. I'll call you while I'm away and you tell me what's happening. Think you can handle all that?"

"Absolutely. Sir."

"We'll try and see if this arrangement—this partnership—works. For a few weeks. On one condition."

"Anything, sir. Anything you say."

"Stop calling me 'sir.' Once we finish here, find Sergeant Borath. He's the old guy who needs a haircut. He'll assign you a desk and a telephone number and locker. He'll show you where the coffee maker is and the location of the men's room. That should complete your training to become a homicide detective."

"That's it?" Kenneth asks. "That's all?"

"That's all there is to becoming a great detective."

"When do I begin?"

"You already have. Did they teach you anything about murder investigations at the Academy?"

"Not much."

"That's good. Everything they teach you at the Academy is wrong."

Kenneth looks momentarily stricken, then recovers.

I remove the photo of the dead woman from the investigation file and push it across the desk to Kenneth. He takes it gingerly in both hands. "Holy cow! Is she dead, sir?"

"Her body was found this morning floating in the Reflecting Pool."

"You mean that pool in the middle of the National Mall?"

I push away some loose papers from the map lying on my desk. I stab my finger onto the map. "Here's the Reflecting Pool. She was found near the east end of the Pool. We found one of her shoes, about here." I point to a place south of the Pool. "And a bracelet the victim was wearing about here." I point to a place not far from the stand of elm trees.

"Just one shoe?" Kenneth asks.

"Just one shoe. Interesting, don't you think? We're still looking for the other."

"Was she . . . ?" Kenneth struggles for words. "Was she murdered?"

"I'm treating her death as murder."

"Awesome," Kenneth murmurs.

"Another condition if you want to work with me," I say. "Never say 'awesome' in my presence."

Kenneth nods vigorously. "What are you doing with the map?"

"I'm trying to reconstruct the victim's route. I want to know where she came from. As you may know, the Mall is surrounded by museums and government offices. It's unlikely she came from a museum in the middle of the night. Most likely she came from a government office." I point to locations on the map. "The Mint, the Department of Agriculture, the Department of Energy, Commerce, the Internal Revenue Service, the EPA, Justice, the FBI. And others."

"What makes you think she came from an office? She could have come from home."

"She was wearing working clothes. Not the kind of clothes a woman wears to a party or social event or to sit around at home."

"I don't see a pattern," Kenneth says, studying the map.

"Neither do I. There was no identification," I go on. "But we know her name. We also know she worked for the United States Secret Service."

"Wow. Is the Secret Service office on your map?" he asks.

"No. It's nowhere near the Mall. That's interesting, don't you think?"

"What do we do now?" Kenneth asks.

"We search for the killer. Go get yourself a desk and a locker, Detective."

"Actually, I'm not a detective, sir. I'm technically an investigator. It will be another year before I'm Detective Second Class."

"As long as you're working with me, you're a detective."

"Thank you, sir."

"We have the victim's home address," I say. "She has a roommate. Let's go visit the roommate. With any luck, we can look around her home and ask some questions."

"Should I bring my service weapon?" He pats the bag lying at his feet proudly.

"Have you ever fired that weapon?" I ask.

"No, sir. They issue our weapons on our last day at the Academy. I've had no occasion to use it in public affairs."

"We're going to talk to the roommate of our victim. Not a hardened criminal. I don't see any need to be armed. Do you?"

"I guess not."

"We need evidence gloves in case we're able to carry out a search of the victim's apartment. Sergeant Borath will show you where they're stored. Bring two pairs."

"Yes, sir."

"Is your service weapon in that bag?"

"Yes, sir."

"You take that bag and put it in your locker and secure it. Understand? I don't want you carrying your weapon."

"Do you ever carry your weapon, sir?"

"Not unless I plan to shoot someone."

CHAPTER SEVEN

A ROUND, PLUMP face stares up at us through the crack in the door. "Yes?" she whispers.

"Marko Zorn," I say, holding out my police shield and ID close to the gap. "Metropolitan Police." She barely looks at my ID. People rarely do. "This is my associate, Detective Blake." Her eyes glance briefly at Kenneth, then back to me. "May we come in, ma'am?"

She looks at us blankly through the gap.

"We have some questions."

The door shuts and we hear the metal sounds as the woman releases the door chain. She opens the door and steps back. "I'm keeping the door locked," she whispers. "You know—with Sandy and all—what happened—you know."

"You can't be too careful," I say. "Right, Kenneth?"

"Right, sir."

The young woman is short, a little overweight with straight brown hair parted in the middle. She looks at us with anxious brown eyes. She wears glasses, much too large for her face. She looks a bit like an insect.

We enter the living room of a small apartment furnished simply, with a two-seater couch and a couple of cheap side chairs from Ikea. The apartment was clearly rented furnished and decorated by some long-ago building manager in what was probably thought to be a trendy Scandinavian style but now looks dreary and a bit shabby and lacks any individuality. There is no hint who might actually live here.

Kenneth and I sit on the couch while the young woman sits on the edge of one of the chairs. I gesture to Kenneth to take notes and he removes his police-issue notebook from his pocket. It cracks slightly when he opens it and he sets it on his knee.

"I can't believe this." The young woman chokes, takes a deep breath. "How could such a terrible thing happen?"

"Please, your name," I say.

"Sure. Trisha. Trisha Connelly."

"Short for Patricia?"

She nods.

"You were Sandra Wilcox's friend?"

She shrugs. "I was her roommate. We knew each other but weren't really friends. You know. We didn't hang out."

The young woman has a nervous habit of twisting her hair in her fingers.

"Did you know Sandra had a peanut allergy?" I ask.

"Sure. When I moved in, she told me. You know: Be careful what I put in the pantry when I go shopping." Trisha makes a small, nervous laugh.

"Did you see Sandra last night?"

She shakes her head. "I watched the news at ten. She wasn't here when I went to bed."

"Could she have come in later?"

"I don't think so. I'm a light sleeper. I usually hear when she gets in. I worry about intruders. You know. All this crime going on. Did you read about the terrible shootings at the school this morning?"

"It's smart to be careful."

"She always puts the chain on when she gets in," Trisha says.

"Was the chain secured when you got up this morning?" I ask.

"No, it was off the hook."

"How long have you known Sandra?"

She twists her hair. "Eight months. Maybe nine now. Her former roommate got married and moved to Florida. She—that's Sandra—she put an ad up on Craigslist. I checked it out and moved in. I never thought it would end like this."

"Where do you work, Miss Connelly?"

She looks anxious. "I'm an economist. I mean, like I work for a congressional committee, you know."

"When was the last time you saw Sandra?"

She chews her lower lip. "Friday, maybe. No, last Thursday."

"You mean she didn't spend much time here?"

"It's not that. She had odd hours. She comes and goes. You know, she works for the Secret Service." Miss Connelly stops abruptly, confused. "Is that all right to say? Is it a secret?"

I sense Kenneth eager to intervene. Probably to say something helpful. Something encouraging. I need to put a stop to that. "It's not a secret," I say, quickly.

"Sometimes she'd be gone for days at a time," Trisha says. "You know, traveling with the President or the First Lady and all. Then back home. Like a few weeks ago she was in Thailand and she brought me back a pretty bowl. She told me she had a wonderful time there."

"You weren't close?" I ask.

"Sometimes we'd pass each other going to—you know. Maybe we'd have a breakfast coffee."

"Was she dating anyone?" I ask.

Trisha does the thing with her hair. "She mentioned—at one time she was seeing someone. One of the Secret Service guys, I think. That stopped before I moved in."

"Do you know why it stopped?"

She shrugs. "No. Sorry. She never talked about it. I mean, I didn't want to pry. You know."

"Do you know the name of the man she was dating?" I ask.

She shakes her head. "Lewis, maybe. Or Lorne? Something."

"Did you ever meet him?"

"Once. He came here to pick Sandra up. It was some kind of job-related thing."

"What was he like?" I ask.

"Seemed nice. He was African American, you know. Very polite. Good-looking."

"Would you be able to describe him?" I ask.

She looks embarrassed. "Just that he was black . . . Sorry."

"Did Sandra have any relatives?"

"Her parents died some time ago, I believe."

"That's it?" I ask.

She rubs her hands together nervously. "There's a brother, I think."

"Does the brother live here in the area?"

"I'm sorry. I don't think so. I certainly never met him. She didn't talk about him. There were problems, I think."

"What kind of problems?"

"You know. Problems."

"Did she have friends?"

"Just people at work. There was somebody, a friend maybe, in North Carolina. Or maybe in South Carolina. I can never remember which is which. Sandy visited her a couple of times."

"You have a name of this friend?"

"Sorry. Sandy'd talk on the phone with this friend a couple of times a month."

"That's it?"

"She did have a friend on the clerical staff at the White House, I think. Every once in a while, they went shopping together. And they had dinner together sometimes. I think."

"A name?" I ask.

"Sorry."

Kenneth, looking up from his notepad, says: "Do you know of any reason anybody might want to harm Sandra?"

Kenneth is anxious to be part of the questioning. He feels it's time for him to contribute something. He wants to prove to me he's a professional detective, not just a note taker.

She shakes her head. "No problems."

"Any issues with people in the neighborhood?" Kenneth asks. "You know, barking dogs?"

"Nothing like that. Sandy was very sweet. No one would want to harm Sandra."

"You've been a great help, Miss Connelly," Kenneth says in a soothing voice. "I know this must be difficult for you." He's seen too many cop shows on TV.

Miss Connelly shifts to the edge of her seat. She's getting ready to stand up, to show us out. She thinks our questioning is done.

The atmosphere up to now has been positive and friendly. Kenneth naturally assumes that means we got what we came for. And he thinks the interrogation has ended. It hasn't started. Tricia is at ease, no longer on her guard.

"Thank you, Miss Connelly," Kenneth says.

"No problem," she says.

"Actually, there is a problem," I say.

She opens her eyes wide and looks at Kenneth, as if for support. Kenneth stares at me, not understanding what's happening.

"When we came to the door," I say, "you indicated you were aware that something had happened to Sandra Wilcox."

"I guess."

"How did you know we were here about Sandra?" I'm not being friendly and Tricia tenses.

"I . . . I . . ." She does the hair thing.

"Tell us, Miss Connelly, who came here before us?"

"What makes you think someone was here?" Her voice is small, and she stares at the floor unhappily.

"Who told you about Sandra?" I ask.

She winces.

"Did they search the apartment?"

"I'm not supposed to tell."

"Who was here, Trisha?" I demand sharply.

"The people who came," she answers quietly.

"And you forgot to mention this to us?" I say.

Trisha hunches her shoulders.

"What people?" I ask.

She is silent.

"How many people came?"

"Three?"

"What did they say happened to Sandra?"

"They said she'd been killed during a robbery attempt."

"That's it?"

"That's all they told me. Sandra had gone for a walk, they said, and been attacked by muggers."

"And you believed them?"

She looks stricken. "Why wouldn't I?"

"Did these people who came here say who they were?"

"They said they were from the Department of Homeland Security."

"And you didn't think to ask for identification?"

She winces again. "They said like if I told anybody about them, I'd be in trouble. It was a question of national security, they said. I mean, I might lose my job. I can't lose my job!" She's close to tears. "They were very scary. Am I going to lose my job?"

"Who did the talking?"

"There were two men and a woman," she says. "One of the men talked to me. The others searched the apartment."

"What were they looking for?"

"You know, things."

"What did they take?"

"They took everything."

"Tell me, what did they take?"

"You know."

"I don't know. What did they take?"

"Papers. Bills. Receipts she kept in a box. Her laptop. Everything they could find."

"Now, Miss Connelly, I don't think you've been entirely honest with us."

"I . . . I . . ."

"In fact, I think you're lying to us."

She presses her hand to her mouth.

"Do you know what the penalty is for lying to a police officer? That's a serious offense. Right, Detective Blake?" I turn to Kenneth who pulls back, fearing I will demand he recite the code violations she has presumably committed. His face is ashen. He has no idea what the code says. Neither do I.

"What were these people looking for?"

"They were looking for the letter."

"Did they find *the letter*?"

"They couldn't find it."

"You're sure?"

"I'm pretty sure."

"Did Sandra get mail?" I ask.

"You mean like letters?"

"I mean like any mail. Any messages?"

"Sandra stayed connected with her friends and her office by cell phone," Trisha answers. "I mean, like texting. We all do."

"So no regular mail?"

"Mostly the mail was just, you know, bills—telephone, utilities, bank statements."

"And these people, the people who claimed they were from Homeland Security, they took all the mail addressed to Sandra?"

"That's right. They took everything they could find."

"So there's no trace of who corresponded with her? No bank statements? No phone bills that would tell us who she talked to somewhere in one of the Carolinas?"

"No, sir." The young woman is trembling.

"You said 'mostly,'" I say. "*Mostly* the mail was bills."

"I guess."

"There was some mail that wasn't a bill, wasn't there, Trisha?"

"Once," she stammers. "A real letter did come for her once. I remember because it was unusual."

"In what way was it unusual?"

"It was in a large white envelope. It had additional postage; you know. It came while Sandra was away on a trip with the President."

"When did the letter arrive?"

"Just about a week ago. While she was away."

"What did you do with the letter?"

"I put the envelope on the kitchen counter. That's where I put anything that comes for Sandy when she's away."

"Go on," I say.

"When she returned last week, Sandy found the envelope on the counter and seemed upset. I mean, that's why I remember so clearly. She took the envelope and went to her room and shut the door."

"Show me the kitchen. I want to see where you put the letter."

Trisha Connelly leads us along a short hall into a small kitchen that looks like every other kitchen young singles have: a white refrigerator, a microwave oven, a Nespresso coffee maker, a sink, and, next to the window, a small table with two chairs.

"I left the letter on the table there."

"Did the people from Homeland Security know about the letter?"

"I think so. Yeah. They asked if I'd seen a letter."

"And you said?"

She looks hopefully at Kenneth. Kenneth is trying to look sympathetic but has sense enough to keep quiet.

"I guess I forgot," she says.

I don't believe for a moment she forgot but I decide to let that go. She'd probably start to cry.

"Was the envelope hand-addressed? Or was it typed?"

"Hand-addressed."

"Was there a return address?"

She frowns. "I don't think so. No return address. I'm not sure I remember rightly."

"Did Sandra ever show you what was in the envelope?"

"No. I had the impression it was private. A love letter, maybe."

I'll have to get back to that. "Do you know where the letter is now?"

"Sorry. I never saw it again."

"How about the envelope?"

"Sandy threw the envelope away the next day."

"You said the people from Homeland Security never found the letter?"

"I told you, they were searching for that letter. They seemed disappointed they couldn't find it."

"When was the last time you saw the envelope?"

"It was in the trash the day after Sandy returned from her trip."

"And you looked inside?"

She nods, abashed. "I was curious. But there was nothing there. I mean, an empty envelope. That's all."

"You think she might have kept the letter?"

"That's what I think."

"And you think Sandra might have hidden the letter somewhere and the people who were here this morning weren't able to find it."

"I guess."

"What makes you think Sandra hid the letter?"

"She mentioned there was no good place to hide anything in our apartment. It's so small." She gestures vaguely around. "I took that to refer to the letter."

"Why would Sandra want to hide a letter?" I ask.

"I wondered about that."

"What made you think it was a love letter?"

"I don't know. I guess I just . . . I don't know." She twists her hair in her fingers.

"There must have been something about it. Something that made you think it was a love letter."

She looks anxious.

"Come, Miss Connelly. Did you open the letter while Sandra wasn't here?"

"No, sir. I never did anything like that!"

"Where did you say you left the letter while Sandra was away?"

"I told you. On the kitchen table." She points to the small table.

"Was it lying flat? Or upright?"

"I leaned it against the sugar bowl."

"And you passed it every time you went into the kitchen?"

"I guess."

"I'll bet you stopped and looked at it once in a while."

"Maybe."

"And you picked it up? Looked at it carefully?"

Her eyes are red. She's on the edge of tears again. I hope Kenneth's not tempted to give her a warm hug.

"Why did you think it was a love letter, Trisha?" I ask. "What was there about it that made you think that?"

She takes a deep, ragged breath. "It was the scent."

"Tell me about the scent."

"A very nice scent. Like perfume. I didn't notice at first. When the letter first came. But later, when I picked it up, I could smell a very faint scent."

"I expect you stopped at the kitchen table sometimes and held the envelope to your face and smelled the perfume."

The girl's face flushes. "I didn't do anything wrong. It was such a nice smell."

"That's okay, Trisha," I say, trying to sound non-threatening. "Can you describe the scent?"

"I don't know how to describe smells."

"Was it strong? Citrusy? Sweet? Spicy? Flowery?"

"That's it. Flowery. It smelled of flowers." She stops. Takes another deep breath.

"And when Sandra threw the envelope away, you picked it out of the trash and smelled the inside. Is that what you did?"

She looks pleadingly at Kenneth as if for help. He smiles at her in a friendly way but says nothing. "I guess," she whispers. "I've never gotten a letter that smelled of perfume. I've read about that sort of thing in books, of course, but no one has ever sent me one. Not a real one. Just in my imagination. You know what I mean?"

"I'm afraid I don't read books about scented letters. You said Sandra told you she'd found a place for the letter. Are those the exact words she used? 'Place'? She said she'd 'found a place for the letter'?"

"Yeah. Those were her exact words. She sort of laughed. Like it was a kind of private joke. I remember thinking it was an odd way of describing where she hid the letter."

"Detective Blake and I would like to look around the apartment now."

She looks panicky. "You want to look in my room? It's a horror."

"Not unless you have some dead bodies there."

"Nothing like that," she stutters. "Just dirty laundry. You know."

"I don't think it will be necessary for us to examine your laundry. I imagine the people from Homeland Security searched your room."

"Yes, sir."

"And they took everything related to Sandra."

"I guess."

"We just need to see Sandra's room."

Trisha Connelly leads us to a door at the end of the hall, and we step into a small bedroom. It's bright and sunny with a single bed, neatly made up, with a bright yellow duvet cover and a white pillow-case. The room is plain, almost austere. There's a chest of drawers, now empty; a closet, also empty; a wooden desk, painted white, probably that once held a laptop computer, now gone. Next to the bed is a small table containing a tissue box, the tissues all removed, and a blue ceramic reading lamp that looks like it might have come from Korea, with a white parchment shade. There are no books; there is nothing to read.

On the wall opposite the window is a framed print of several men in an open sailboat. I think it's by Winslow Homer and called something like "Prouts Neck." On the wall opposite is a photograph of a group of soldiers. They are in two rows: In the first row the men kneel on one knee. In the back row, the men are at parade rest. I can just make out patches on the left sleeves but not well enough to identify the unit. To one side stand two men: one with chevrons on his sleeve indicating he's a sergeant. The second man, also in a service uniform, has insignia and a name patch sown on. All are smiling broadly. It looks like some military unit on the occasion of a graduation or receiving a unit citation.

I've seen this room before. Rooms people in the military live in. Or former military. Rooms that are squared away.

"Okay, Detective Blake, find that letter."

"What makes you think the letter's here?"

"Sandra Wilcox did not throw it away, I'm sure of that. She hid it somewhere and she wouldn't have hidden it somewhere else in the apartment; where someone might find it. It has to be here in her own bedroom."

"Those people from Homeland Security searched here," Tricia says. "They were looking for that letter. They couldn't find it."

"Let's see if we can do a better job."

I study the Winslow Homer. "That picture seems out of place."

"Sandy was born and raised somewhere in Massachusetts," Trisha says. "She told me the picture reminded her of home. That was one of the few things she had that were personal. And that bedside lamp."

"What about the picture of these men in uniform?"

"Sorry. Sandy never talked about that photograph. She was in the Army, she told me. Maybe it was from then."

Kenneth puts on a pair of vinyl gloves and systematically goes through the room, opening closet doors, searching through the small chest of drawers and the bedside table. It doesn't take long.

"I can't find anything, sir," he says. "Sorry."

"There's nothing to find. They took it all. Where would you put something you want to hide in a small room like this?"

"Under the mattress, maybe?" Kenneth suggests uncertainly.

"They looked under the mattress," Trisha tells us. "They even cut it open and searched inside. They didn't find anything."

"Take that print down from the wall," I say. "Let's take a look."

Kenneth lifts the Homer print gently from the hook on the wall. It's an ordinary, inexpensive print, the kind they sell at the gift shop at the National Gallery of Art. There is nothing on the front. No alterations, no markings.

"Look at the back," I say.

Kenneth flips the picture over and lays it facedown on the bed. The back is covered with brown paper, which has been torn from the wooden picture frame. Nothing is hidden inside. The same for the photograph of the soldiers—just shredded backing paper.

"Turn on the light by the bed," I instruct.

Kenneth turns the switch, but no light goes on.

"Sandy said she always read in bed before she went to sleep." Trisha stands by the door, watching us. "That's why she needed the lamp."

"What did Sandy read?"

"I don't know. Books."

"And the people who came this morning took all the books with them?"

"I guess."

"What kind of books did Sandy read?"

"You know—books. She told me she liked novels."

"What's wrong with the lamp?" I ask.

"Maybe it's broken," Kenneth suggests.

"The person who lived in this room would not have a broken lamp by her bed. Certainly not if she was a reader. See if there's a bulb."

Kenneth picks up the lamp. "There's a bulb but it's not screwed in." He tightens the bulb and the light flares on.

"Now that's strange, don't you think?" I say. "Why would she leave the bulb unscrewed?" I take the lamp from Kenneth and re-move the lampshade using a small, brass screw at the top of the shade. I tear the parchment shade from its wire armature. There are two layers of parchment paper forming the shade. Folded between the two layers is a piece of stiff paper stock. I gently flatten the paper on the top of the bed. It's a cream-colored paper that smells faintly of roses and jasmine. One side is blank. On the other side is a hand-written message in purple ink, in neat, rather elegant, old-fashioned, cursive script. It reads:

THE MOON HAS SET, AND THE PLEIADES;
   IT IS MIDNIGHT,
AND TIME PASSES, AND I SLEEP ALONE.

There is no signature.

"Do you think it's important?" Kenneth asks, looking over my shoulder.

"I think it was important to Sandra Wilcox," I say.

"Am I going to get in trouble because I didn't mention the letter to those people from Homeland Security?" Trisha asks.

"You won't get into any trouble, Trisha. Isn't that right, Kenneth?"

Kenneth nods. "That's right, Miss Connelly. You're not in any trouble."

"Detective Blake and I are going to take this note with us. And we'll take the picture of the soldiers as well."

Trisha shrugs. "You can have anything you want. If the people from Homeland Security come back and ask for the letter," Trisha asks, "can I tell them you took it?"

"Absolutely. You should definitely mention my name."

I give my business card to Trisha. "Be sure to show this to anyone who asks you about the letter. Will you do that?" She nods. "And let me know."

I look at Kenneth.

"I don't have any cards made up yet, sir," Kenneth says. "This is my first day on the job, remember?"

"I'll call you if any mail comes for Sandy," Trisha says.

"There won't be any mail," I tell her. "Effective today, your friends from Homeland Security will have instructed the US Postal Service to divert Sandra's mail to them."

"They can do that?"

When Kenneth and I leave, we stop on the sidewalk in front of the building. "What was that letter about, sir?" Kenneth asks. "It seemed like you recognized the words."

"Maybe."

"What is it?"

"It's a fragment of a poem."

"What does it mean?"

"I have no idea."

Kenneth starts to move away. "Just a moment," I say. "We need to talk."

Kenneth stops, pivots to look back at me. "Sir?"

"You screwed up."

"I don't understand." His eyes are wide.

"During the interview you tried to be friendly with Miss Connelly."

"What's wrong with that? If we're friendly, won't people want to cooperate?"

"Witnesses are not your friends. Never forget that. Witnesses are the enemy. Always. Witnesses lie. Even innocent witnesses lie. Everyone lies. Even people who have no reason to lie. Trisha Connelly lied about that letter. Don't ever intervene during an interview again. Not until you've had a lot more experience. You confuse friendliness with truth. Like most normal people, you want to be liked. Homicide detectives are not normal people. You must learn that."

"I only meant to be helpful."

"I know what you meant. Don't be helpful. As long as she felt safe, she'd never have told us about that letter. She was embarrassed and didn't want to talk about it. That's probably why she didn't tell the people from Homeland Security about the letter. She was afraid it would make her look like a snooping roommate. Which she, of course, was."

"You were kind of mean to her. Sir."

"That's often necessary. I suppose there are times when one should be nice. Although I can't think of an occasion."

"You almost made her cry."

"That was the idea."

"You don't like her."

"I don't trust her."

"Don't you trust anybody?"

"Not really."

"Sometimes you have to trust people," Kenneth tells me.

"I don't see why."

CHAPTER EIGHT

LE ZINK IS a pretentious French restaurant run by two brothers from Serbia who, I'm pretty sure, are engaged in something illegal, probably involving large shipments of cigarettes. The restaurant has been decorated in a faux French brasserie style with fading pictures of long-dead French singers and actors on the walls and Edith Piaf singing softly in the background. Tonight, there are a few regulars at the bar including a middle-aged man—a bit louche and going to weight—always accompanied by a different woman. Tonight's conquest is about twenty and she wears a shiny miniskirt that does her no favors.

"Bad day?" The bartender's name is Roberta.

"You could say that."

Roberta is an attractive black woman, dressed this evening in a fashionable, pale-blue frock and wearing large hoop earrings. Roberta could have been a model, I think. Except that, for one, she speaks in a deep baritone and, two, for most of Roberta's life, Roberta was a DC cop. The day Robert told me his secret, we were in an unmarked police car on a stakeout of a crack house on North Capitol Street.

"I'm a woman," he told me. That certainly got my attention. "I've been living a lie for years."

I can sympathize.

"Now I'm going to come out," Robert told me. "You have no idea how that sets me free. Now I can be my true self." Robert explained the medical procedures he was undergoing. Like most men, I did not want to hear the details.

Roberta had to quit her job in the police department but found an undiscovered talent for making cocktails. She's a good listener and very discreet.

Roberta places my usual Van Winkle 23-year-old bourbon on the bar before me, and I absently stare at my reflection in the large glass mirror behind the bar—the glass mottled and stained with age—as the events of the day surge helter-skelter through my head.

There's the problem of Sister Grace and her feral family. My instinct is to walk away from her, but it's not that simple. It's dangerous to cross her and there's the money. The Soutine about wiped me out.

And there's the call from Maine, bringing back painful memories—my sister's violent death and the incident at Clarkson Creek I thought had been forgotten almost twenty years ago. That problem will have to be dealt with but must wait until tomorrow.

Throughout these random, half-formed thoughts the memory of those blue eyes haunts me.

I know I should focus on the murder of Sandra Wilcox—I do have a day job—and I try to concentrate on what I learned from the visit to her apartment and I think about that note and what it might possibly mean. That gets me nowhere.

"You have a visitor," Roberta says, looking over my right shoulder.

I become aware of a figure standing behind me. A woman in her mid-thirties.

"I'm Agent Lovelace," the woman announces. "May I join you, Detective Zorn?"

She slides onto the barstool next to me. Her hair is reddish brown—probably was bright red when she was a kid. She's about five-foot-seven and wears her hair in a pixie haircut—badly cut— and her skirt and jacket don't go together. Her eyeglasses are electric blue and are not the right shape for her face. She wears no wedding or engagement rings—in fact, no jewelry of any kind. She is without makeup and she has freckles on her nose.

She reaches into her purse and withdraws a black leather billfold, flips it open, and passes it to me. Inside are a gold badge and a laminated picture ID with a seal on a blue background. At the top an inscription reads "Department of Justice." At the bottom: "Federal Bureau of Investigation." The card identifies the lady as FBI Special Agent Arora Lovelace. I don't believe I've ever met an FBI detective lady with freckles. I pass the billfold back.

"You've misspelled your first name," I say.

"Tell that to my mother." She smiles a wide, generous smile and returns her billfold to her purse. Her nose crinkles when she smiles.

"You want to see my badge and ID?" I ask.

"Not necessary," she answers. "I know who you are."

"Can I buy you a drink then, Agent Lovelace?" I ask.

"I'd love one."

I gesture to Roberta who comes to take our order. Roberta is much too courteous to register any reaction to my companion's appearance. "Miss Lovelace, meet Roberta."

"A pleasure to meet you, Roberta."

"Roberta is an outstanding bartender," I explain.

"Can you make a decent whiskey sour?" Agent Lovelace asks. She pushes her eyeglasses up onto the bridge of her nose.

"Of course."

"Straight up," the FBI agent says. "No egg white, please. And no maraschino cherry."

"Of course not." Roberta moves away.

"To what do I owe the pleasure of your company?" I ask.

"Sandra Wilcox," the FBI lady says, then stops, apparently expecting me to say something. When I'm silent, she goes on: "You're the lead investigator in the Wilcox murder case. Right?"

"Before I answer that, I'd like to know where I stand with the Bureau. Is the FBI investigating the Wilcox murder? Or investigating me?"

"The FBI is interested in Sandra Wilcox. Not you."

The woman I'm sitting next to is not beautiful. Not in a conventional sense. Not the star of the movie. More like the attractive, wisecracking, funny sidekick, best friend. The face you remember when you forget the star.

"Does Carla Lowry know you're here?" I ask.

"Of course she does. She knows everything. She's the head of the FBI Criminal Division."

"I'm not a criminal."

"If you say so."

"Do you work for Carla?"

Agent Lovelace shakes her head. "Not technically. I work out of the FBI Washington headquarters with a task force dealing with domestic terrorist groups."

"But Carla knows you're seeing me."

"She sent me. She told me you can often be found here drinking by yourself."

"Did she tell you anything else?"

"She told me not to trust you. Not for one moment."

Roberta arrives with a chilled old-fashioned glass she places on a white linen napkin in front of Arora Lovelace, fills the glass from a silver shaker beaded with condensation. There is a tinkling sound from the shaved ice. Roberta reverently places a lemon slice in the drink.

Roberta tops off my drink.

"Okay," I say. "I confess. I'm investigating the death of Sandra Wilcox. Why does the FBI care?"

Special Agent Lovelace sips her whiskey sour. "Because Sandra Wilcox is on our radar," she tells me, putting her drink carefully back on its napkin. "And her violent death has raised red flags all over town."

"And you want to share information?"

"Something like that."

"Why didn't this request come through channels?"

"I'm a channel."

"Why didn't you just come to my office? Why meet me surreptitiously?"

"It's not surreptitious. It's a goddamn restaurant." She sips her drink. "I would have tried to meet up with you tomorrow but I understand you'll be out of town."

"And you know this how?"

Agent Lovelace shrugs off my question.

"I don't get it. For some reason, the FBI, or Carla Lowry, doesn't want anybody to know you're working with the police—with me—on this case. Why is that?"

She smiles at me enigmatically. "Can I have some olives, please?" she asks Roberta who nods and goes off.

"Tell me what you know, Detective Zorn."

"I don't know anything. My investigation just started this morning."

"All right, you don't know anything. Carla Lowry says you're a smart fella. You're supposed to have good instincts. What do you think you know? Strictly off the record."

"And in return," I say, "you'll tell me why the Bureau's interested in Sandra Wilcox."

"Deal," she says. "Strictly off the record."

Roberta brings a dish of olives. Some are dark green. Some are light green. They glisten in their oily bath reflected in the lights from behind the bar. Agent Lovelace selects one.

"Sandra Wilcox was found murdered this morning in the Reflecting Pool," I say.

"Why do you think she was murdered?"

I know I'll regret this but I take the plunge. "Because Sandra Wilcox told me."

Agent Lovelace looks at me sharply, an olive suspended a few inches from her lips. "You're kidding. Right? The dead victim told you she'd been murdered?"

"I know that sounds weird."

"*Weird?* It sounds worse than weird. It sounds seriously creepy. Do you often talk to dead people?"

"No. This is the first time."

"I hate it when police investigators go all mystical on me."

"It's more complicated than that."

"How can anything be more complicated than you talking to the dead?"

"Finding the victim this morning was a bad shock to me."

"You're a homicide detective. You must have been involved with many violent deaths."

"More than you might think."

"What was special about this victim?"

Why am I telling this woman this? I ask myself. A woman who's a stranger. A woman who probably does not have my best interests at heart. Maybe it's the Van Winkle. Maybe because I need somebody to talk to and Roberta is closely watching the man at the other end of the bar trying to get his date drunk. Maybe because I have a weakness for attractive women.

"When I found Sandra Wilcox, I thought I recognized her. I was wrong about that but I experienced a synaptic short circuit. In that first moment I thought she was someone I was once very close to a long time ago. I thought she was asking for help. Later, when I saw Sandra Wilcox in the medical examiner's office, I knew she wasn't the woman I once knew. But the eyes. They were Rose's eyes."

"Rose?"

"My oldest sister—her name was Rose—died almost twenty years ago. She was raped and murdered."

"How awful."

"Rose was found in a lake. In a pine forest in northern Maine. When I first saw Sandra Wilcox, I thought . . . I don't know what I thought."

"If you'd rather not talk about it, that's okay. I understand. It's none of my business."

"This morning, standing in the Pool, looking at her, it all came back. The rush of feelings. The horror. As if it had all happened yesterday. Trust me, I've not gone crazy. And I'd appreciate it if you didn't include what I've told you in your report to Carla Lowry. She might take it the wrong way."

Miss Lovelace pops one olive into her mouth and waits for me to go on. When I say nothing more, she looks disappointed. "Do you have anything more substantial than a conversation with a dead woman as proof Sandra Wilcox's death was murder?"

"Okay, here's what I think happened. Sometime last night Sandra Wilcox was taken or escorted, probably by force, to the Reflecting Pool. There she was drowned, then dumped into the Pool, presumably to make it look like it was some kind of accident."

"What makes you think the victim was taken or escorted? Maybe she was alone."

"There's the shoe."

"Explain the shoe."

"We found one of her shoes not far from the Pool. I'm assuming it fell off or the victim kicked it off on her way to the Pool."

"And?"

"What happened to the other shoe?" I ask. "We've searched the area. The other shoe's missing. Somebody collected that second shoe and removed it. That tells me there was probably at least one other person involved. Maybe several. What woman walks alone across the Mall in the middle of the night wearing one shoe? Her outfit indicates she came directly from work. She had no ID. No cell phone. No coil Secret Service agents wear in their ears."

Lovelace selects another olive. "Go on."

"She pulled off her medical identification bracelet."

"Tell me about the identification bracelet."

"Sandra Wilcox was allergic to peanuts and wore an ID alerting medics to her condition. She pulled the bracelet off her wrist as she got near the Reflecting Pool."

"What makes you think she pulled off her ID bracelet? Maybe it fell off."

"She had a small wound on her wrist. There are small spots of blood on the bracelet. I think she pulled her bracelet off violently and cut herself."

"Why do you think she would do that?"

"I believe she realized she was in great danger and wanted to leave a message."

Arora Lovelace stares at her glass. "That's awful," she whispers, more to herself than to me, and adjusts her glasses. "You think she knew she was going to die?"

"I'm certain of it."

"Why are you so sure Sandra was forced into the Pool?"

"She had abrasions on her knees," I say.

"Maybe she stumbled crossing the Mall."

"There were abrasions only on her knees. When someone stumbles or falls forward, they'll break the fall with their hands. She had no abrasions on her hands or arms. Her killer or killers must have been holding her arms when they forced her to her knees on the stone edge of the Reflecting Pool. Then pushed her head under water."

Lovelace looks at me intently.

"That's it. Now, your turn," I say. "Tell me about Sandra Wilcox."

She takes a deep breath and does the nervous gesture with her eyeglasses. "As you already know, Sandra was a Secret Service agent. She was in the military before that. Had an outstanding record. Then she left the Army."

"Why?"

"She told her commanding officer she didn't want to be assigned outside the continental US. For family reasons, she said. She joined the Secret Service six months after she left the Army. She seems to have done well in the Secret Service. She was assigned to the Presidential Protective Division only a few years after she became an agent."

"What's the Bureau's interest?"

Arora takes a deep breath. "Ten days ago, a man walked into the FBI field office in Denver and told the duty officer he was a member of an organization called the Brotherhood of the Aryan Dawn and he wanted to give the FBI information about the organization in return for protection. I flew to Denver that afternoon."

"Why you?" I ask.

"The Brotherhood is part of my portfolio."

"What's the Brotherhood?"

She studies my face cautiously. "You should understand that information about the Brotherhood and about our sources and methods are highly sensitive and are of no business of the DC police department."

"But you think this organization has something to do with Sandra Wilcox's murder. That makes it my business."

"What I tell you must remain confidential. The FBI and the Secret Service are engaged in a major investigation into this group. We don't want any more screwups."

I decide not to ask her just yet what she means by "any more screwups." "Tell me about the Brotherhood of the Aryan Dawn."

"It's a domestic terrorist group with a core membership of around a thousand but it has contacts with like-minded groups—every lunatic racist mountain man and urban guerilla in the country. Whites only, as you can imagine. The Brotherhood assassinated a federal judge in Austin because he was Jewish. They blew up a church in Pennsylvania."

"What do they have against churches?"

"Mostly their activities are to gain attention and recruits. But some are meant to raise serious money. They've carried out two major bank robberies, an armored car holdup and a warehouse robbery at LAX. We believe they now have a huge war chest. Until my trip to Denver, we had no idea what this money was for. I think we now have a pretty good idea."

"Tell me about the man who turned himself in."

"His name was Solly Nelson. I met with him in our Denver office. For almost three days—ten, twelve hours a day—we talked. The man was crazy scared. I'm afraid it did not end well for him."

"It often happens that way."

"He was born and raised in West Virginia and joined the Marine Corps when he was eighteen but washed out and was dishonorably discharged. He was a big man. Very muscular and strong and had tattoos on his arms with intertwined red and blue snakes. And a swastika tattooed on his left wrist."

"How did he get involved with the Brotherhood of the Aryan Dawn?"

"Nelson did time for armed robbery in Lewisburg. It turns out the federal prison system is the beating heart of the Brotherhood's recruitment efforts. While in Lewisburg, some prisoners told Solly about an organization which plans to overthrow the government after which a new order will be ushered in and its members would become 'Princes of the Earth.'"

"Your informant swallowed this crap?"

"Probably not. I think he was in it for a regular paycheck and a place to sleep. One of the prisoners at Lewisburg gave Solly a telephone number of a contact. On his release, Solly was broke and unemployed, with no prospects and he called the number. A few days later a man contacted him and they met one night in a bar in Durango. The man called himself *Sweet Daddy*."

"What's Sweet Daddy's real name?"

"Solly would never give me a name. All he said was that this Sweet Daddy had once been an officer in Special Forces with the rank of light colonel. He gave me the impression that this Sweet Daddy had been court-marshaled and dishonorably discharged."

"What was this Sweet Daddy court-marshaled for?"

"Nelson didn't know. Understand, my interviews with Solly were chaotic—a few fragments of information interrupted by harangues about the unfairness of life, pleas for protection, demands for money, self-justification for a wasted life, tearful expressions of regret."

"Did you get a description of Sweet Daddy?"

"Nothing helpful. He's maybe fifty. Sixty. He has thick, curly white hair and always wears a white suit and a bow tie."

"So your guy joins this lunatic group. Then what happened?"

"For a while it went fine. Solly even worked on a project with Sweet Daddy."

"What was the project?"

"Sweet Daddy was in the market for military-grade weapons. That was the point of the war chest. Because of Solly's military background, Sweet Daddy thought Solly could help. They found an arms broker here in the Washington area who arranged a major sale. This was part of the strategy: buy weapons, distribute them to like-minded zealots, start a war."

"You say 'part of the strategy.' What's the other part?"

"There was supposed to be an event that would initiate the revolution."

"What sort of event?"

"The Brotherhood plans to assassinate the President and, according to Solly, Sweet Daddy had found the man to do it. When Solly heard that, it all became too real for him. Until then all the talk of revolution and insurrection had been a fantasy game, but when he heard the killer had actually been recruited, Solly lost his nerve. Solly wasn't a complete idiot and he knew what would happen if there was an attempt on the President's life—a lot of people were going to be killed and he wanted no part of it. But there was a hitch. The assassin the Brotherhood had recruited suddenly disappeared. It seems the man wanted to see his son one last time. Sweet Daddy located the assassin and brought him back and Solly knew his time was up. The assassination was imminent so he decided he'd ask the FBI for protection."

"I take it he decided wrong."

"Solly slipped away from the Brotherhood's compound and hitched a ride to the local bus station and from there took a bus as far as Denver. That was as far as his money would take him. He arrived in Denver late at night and found a small café near the bus station. He waited in the café until nine the next morning, then walked into the FBI field office and turned himself in."

"Did you get anything of substance from your interrogations?"

"One critical piece of information. On our last day, Solly became panicky. He was desperate to get the Bureau to agree to bring him into the witness protection plan and he offered me a name in return: the name of the assassin. That was Solly's death warrant."

"What is the assassin's name?"

"Wilcox."

"You mean? . . . Just like . . . ?"

"The same name."

"Any first name? Any identification?

"None. Just Wilcox. That's all Solly knew. The Bureau immediately turned over everything we had to the Secret Service."

"You take this Brotherhood organization seriously?"

"We have to take it seriously. The US Government considers the Brotherhood of the Aryan Dawn one of the most dangerous domestic terrorist group in the country."

"And the FBI believes Sandra Wilcox is somehow connected?"

"Her murder can't be a compete coincidence."

"What did you mean by Solly's 'death warrant'?"

"My last interview ended at three forty on Tuesday afternoon. Solly was becoming hysterical and incoherent, and I terminated the interview, instructing him, as I did at the end of each session, to stay in his room. We'd put him up at a motel across the street from the FBI offices where he was under twenty-four-hour armed guard with an agent posted outside his door.

"I wrote up my notes for the day and transmitted them to headquarters. An hour and a half later one of the agents reported that Solly and his guard were both missing. They found our agent in the motel storage room with his throat cut. The chief of the FBI field office initiated a search, calling in the Denver police for help. We spent the night looking for Solly and our agent's killer. At four in the morning, the Colorado Highway Patrol reported finding an unidentified body in a ditch on the side of the road about two miles outside of Denver and thought it might belong to us. The director of the field office and I went to the scene where we examined what was left of the body. It was clear the victim's legs had been chained to the rear bumper of a car or truck and he'd been dragged, facedown, along country roads for hours. By the time we found him the victim had no face. But I recognized the tattoos—the intertwined red and blue snakes. And the swastika on his left wrist."

Roberta places a fresh whiskey sour in front of Arora and she takes a gulp.

"Okay," I say. "But what's this got to do with Sandra Wilcox?"

"When Wilcox—the assassin—disappeared, the Brotherhood went crazy searching for him and was in almost constant contact with its people around the country—by phone, texts, emails. They became sloppy in their security and we were able to intercept some of their communications. That was when we got a break. During the chatter we intercepted, there was a brief mention of another name. Someone named Sandra. No last name."

"You didn't make the connection between the name 'Sandra' and the name 'Wilcox'?"

"We didn't until this morning when the name Sandra Wilcox showed up on our system. As a murder victim. And as a member of the Secret Service."

"It looks as though when you sent in your report to FBI headquarters, someone realized Solly had given away the family jewels— the actual name of the assassin. The Brotherhood sent a killer to the motel to remove Solly and stop him from giving the FBI any more information. Was that the 'screw up' you mentioned?"

She slips off the barstool. "I've got to brief Carla Lowry on our meeting this evening."

"I have a message for Carla," I say. "The Bureau has a problem. Somebody tipped off the Brotherhood about Solly Nelson. And probably sidetracked the search for the name 'Sandra' when her name was picked up on your intercept."

She nods. "We're investigating both possibilities."

"I'd say there was a leak from within the FBI."

"We don't know that. Not for sure."

"No, but that's what you're thinking. That's why Carla is keeping my involvement secret."

"I'll pass along your thoughts."

"Another thought: the murder of Sandra Wilcox may have nothing to do with this Brotherhood organization."

"It must. What else could it be?"

I can think of at least one other thing it could be but decide not to mention just yet the handwritten message from an ancient poem I found hidden in Sandra Wilcox's bedroom. That would have to wait.

CHAPTER NINE

MY FLIGHT TO Portland goes smoothly and I even get a window seat and I try to sleep. That turns out to be hopeless. The specter that brought me to Maine won't leave me alone: A very old murder or should that be two very old murders?

I pick up a rental car at Portland airport and make good time on 95 going north. Just past Waterville I switch over to 201. Here I run into highway construction and some serious congestion that slows me down. Eventually the traffic stops completely. I take advantage of this delay by lighting a cigarette. I roll down the car window so as not to leave traces of my vice that will annoy the next person to rent the car. I arrive at my sister's house a little before three.

The house is set far back from the road and is surrounded by a neatly trimmed lawn and some flowerbeds my sister has been cultivating for years.

The place hasn't changed much since I left many years ago. Some fresh paint has been applied from time to time, a new room was added when Cassie had the twins. Otherwise it's pretty much the same as when my father bought the place half a century ago. The house holds many lifetimes of memories—some joyful. Some unspeakable.

By the time I'm out of the car, Cassie is hurrying down the front steps dressed in cargo pants and a vivid purple blouse. She wraps me in her strong arms, tight. "It's good to see you. It's been too long." She steps away and studies me. "Where's your luggage?"

"I'm not staying long. I've got to get back to Washington."

"You just got here." She tries to hide her frustration and anger.

"I'm catching a late flight back tonight."

"Honestly! You're impossible, Marko. Come inside. I've got some fresh coffee on the stove."

I follow her into the house and through a living room, rarely used for anything except Christmas parties and, sometimes, for a memorial service, and we go into the kitchen, spotless as usual and painted crisp white. In this rural area they haven't got the message yet that gray is in style. I sit at a long wooden table while Cassie pours black coffee into two heavy mugs. I take out my cell phone and my pack of cigarettes and place them in front of me.

"For God's sake, Marko, are you still smoking?"

"I'm giving up cigarettes. I swear."

She rolls her eyes while I check for any messages from my office. There's nothing.

"How are you doing?" I ask when I put away my phone.

"Doing just fine, thanks. As you'd know if you ever wrote. Or called."

"Sorry. I'm not much of a correspondent."

"Are you seeing anybody?" my sister asks. As she always does.

"Do you mean, am I going to get married any time soon?"

"Well, are you?"

"No plans along those lines."

"It's time you settled down."

"I don't have time to settle down."

"It's just that you're a very good-looking guy. In high school the girls couldn't keep their hands off you. Is there something wrong?"

"There's nothing wrong. It's just that, at the moment, a serious relationship wouldn't work."

"I'll stop prying, then."

"How is Doug doing?" I ask. "And the boys?"

"Doug still has his job at the mill. They're laying off people so it's a worry. So far, so good. Jess and Carly are fine. They're at school right now. They've grown a lot since you were last here."

We drink our coffee in silence. "Why have the police been snooping around?" I ask.

"They've reopened the Clyde Fenton case."

I feel a knot in my stomach. "I thought that investigation was closed."

"So did we all."

"How did this happen?"

"About two weeks ago some hunters were up around Crawford's Creek and found a half-buried skeleton. They thought at first maybe it was a deer except it didn't look like a deer. It looked like a man and they reported it to the sheriff. You know, Stuart Carpenter, he's sheriff around here now. He went up there to take a look and determined the remains were human. They'd been buried many years ago. Somehow the grave must have been exposed, maybe by the heavy rains we had a month or so back. The medical examiner in Bristol collected the remains."

"What did they find?"

"The remains are definitely human. Male. Not much left except the skull and some teeth. You know, after all these years—animals and insects, scavengers and all. Unfortunately, it doesn't look like the victim ever went to a dentist. So no positive identification from the dental records. But they're pretty sure it was Clyde Fenton and they think Clyde was murdered."

"I don't suppose anyone in Grand Forks is mourning Clyde."

"Of course not. But this opens up all those memories of Rose's murder. All those old wounds."

"You say Stuart Carpenter is sheriff now."

"Joined the force as soon as he got out of the service. Was deputy for umpteen years. Made sheriff three years ago. Or thereabouts."

"He any good?"

"He has a good reputation around here. Until now we haven't had cause to have any official dealings. Just the usual social things. He says he remembers you."

There's the sound of laughter outside and running feet and two teenage boys appear—skinny and disheveled. That would be Jess and Carly, Cassie's twin boys. They stand awkwardly at the kitchen door, mute. I can't remember which one is Jess and which one is Carly.

"Say hello to your uncle Marko, boys."

The boys mumble something I assume is "How do you do, sir?"

"You two run along now," Cassie says. "Get yourselves cleaned up. You look a holy mess."

The two boys slip away and Cassie pours more coffee. "Is there going to be trouble, Marko?"

"Kind of depends on Stuart, doesn't it?"

Cassie buries her face in her hands. "This business with Clyde Fenton brings back so much grief. I thought I'd forgotten it. Of course, I can never forget."

"None of us will forget," I say. "And yesterday it hit me again. I was investigating a murder and the victim reminded me of Rose. She had the same blue eyes and it all came back to me—how she disappeared, the search parties, how we found her in the forest. It seemed like I lived through every moment over the last twenty-four hours."

"Remember how she was laid out?" Cassie asks. "Right there in the living room. All those people came to pay their respects."

"I remember you and Mom serving the mourners bologna sandwiches."

"Mom and me here in the kitchen, making those damn sandwiches. Taking them out to the living room. I'd never seen such a bunch of hungry men. Eating the sandwiches. Talking. Even laughing. And Rose, in the middle of the room. In that box. I can still see that closed box. They couldn't fix what Clyde did to our Rose. Are we going to have to live through all that again?"

I hear the sound of tires on gravel.

"That'll be Stuart," Cassie says. "I'll bring him in."

They speak softly to one another on the front porch then come into the kitchen where I'm waiting. Stuart Carpenter is dressed in a light-gray police uniform and black leather boots. His pants and shirt are stiff with starch and pressed into sharp creases. Did Stuart change into a fresh uniform before coming here? He holds a Stetson in his left hand. At his waist he carries a revolver in a shiny black holster that matches his boots. He's put on some weight since high school and he's a little paunchy now, a little jowly. But basically, he's still in good shape.

"Hello, old buddy!" Stuart strides across the kitchen, smiling, and we shake hands. "I'm glad you could come. Really glad."

"Coffee, Stuart?" Cassie asks.

"I'll never say no to one of your brews." The policeman sits at the table, elbows on the table top, carefully placing his hat on the seat next to him. "How long's it been, Marko? Must be ten years at least."

"I'd say closer to fifteen."

"How long you staying? More'n a few days I hope."

"I'm tied up with some business in Washington. I have to be back in the office tomorrow morning."

Cassie puts a mug in front of Carpenter.

"They tell me you're a big shot in Washington," Stuart says.

"Mainly just an office drudge."

"Cassie says you're a police detective now."

"That's right. Homicide."

"I always thought you'd turn out to be a cop or a criminal. I'm glad you made the right choice."

"Cassie tells me you want to talk to me."

"I hate to open up a painful subject . . ."

"You mean Rose's murder?" I say. "Then don't." I don't know how I feel about Stuart Carpenter just now. Is he just an old friend from high school days? Or is he a policeman doing his job? Maybe both.

"I can't believe it's been almost twenty years." Stuart scoops several spoonfuls of sugar into his coffee. "Well, I guess there've been some developments."

"I understand you found Clyde Fenton," I say.

"That's right."

"You sure it's him? After all this time, there can't be much of him left."

"It's Clyde. We're pretty sure. We found the keys to his house under his body. Rusted and corroded all to hell. But they're his house keys. And the keys to his pickup. It's Clyde Fenton, all right."

"You think he was shot?"

"The way we figure it, Clyde got wind the police were on to him. Tried to hide out in the forest. Somebody tracked him down and shot him in the head."

"Maybe it was a hunting accident," I suggest, without much conviction.

"Doesn't seem like it. We found the round that killed Clyde. Lodged in a tree trunk where he was lying. A forty-five round. Not fired from a rifle. Definitely a handgun. Up close. That's the way we think it went down."

"What difference does it make?" Cassie asks. "It was twenty years ago. Why bring up these terrible memories? Rose's death almost destroyed this town. Do we have to go through it all again?"

"We have to close the case."

"What's the point?" I say. "Everyone involved is dead. Clyde Fenton's dead. Rose is dead."

"Not everyone. Not quite."

"Who, Stuart?" Cassie demands. "Who's left?"

"The person who killed Clyde Fenton. That's who's left."

"How about witnesses?" I ask. "Fingerprints? Any physical evidence?"

He shakes his head, not looking at either of us.

"Then you've got zip. You can't reopen the case. There is no case to reopen."

"It's murder, Marko."

"You'll get no medal for opening an investigation into the death of Clyde Fenton."

"Damn it." Cassie can barely restrain herself. "The man who shot Clyde Fenton should get a medal. They should put up a statue to him in the middle of town."

"I know how you two feel about bringing up memories of Rose's murder. Probably most of the people here in Grand Forks feel the same way. I don't want to see that happen any more'n you do."

"Then don't do it, Stuart." Cassie is angry now. "Drop it."

"There's no statute of limitations on murder, Cassie. The state officials in Augusta are going to have to review my investigation. To be certain I haven't overlooked anything. I can't just walk away from this."

There are tears in Cassie's eyes. "I don't think I can bear to go through it again."

"I need to show Marko something," Stuart says. "Down at the station house."

"What do you need to show Marko?" Cassie demands.

"It's okay," Stuart says. "It'll only take a few minutes. There's something Marko must see so I can close the case."

I stand up. "Let's go. Show me what you've got."

"Thanks for the coffee." Stuart stands, puts on his Stetson, adjusting it properly, using the tips of his fingers on the brim. He stops at the kitchen door. "It'll be all right. I'll have Marko home by dinner." Stuart nods and leaves.

"Is there going to be trouble?" Cassie asks me, her face strained with worry. She reaches out and grasps my arm. "Are you going to be in trouble? Is this going to be the end for us?"

What can I say?

Stuart is already in his police cruiser, the motor running when I get in. It's a white Ford with the words "Franklin County Sheriff" painted on the sides in large black letters. I slip into the passenger seat and Stuart says nothing until we're on the main road.

"I'm real sorry this business with Clyde reopened memories of your sister. I never meant that to happen."

He drives in silence for a few minutes. "You think about Rose?"

"All the time. I remember going out with the search party to look for her. I remember the yell from one of the men who first found the body."

"That was Lonnie White," Stuart says. "I don't think Lonnie's ever gotten over the sight. He still has nightmares after all these years." We drive in silence for a while. "You know I used to date Rose," Stuart says.

"Were you in love?" I ask.

"*Love?* Hell, I was sixteen years old. What's a sixteen-year-old boy know about love? We used to go out to the movies. Then she went away to college. Then she was dead. Somebody went out and found Clyde Fenton and shot him. Probably shot him where he was sitting, leaning against that tree trunk. If I'd found Fenton, I'd've shot him myself. I just thought you ought to know that." Stuart drives on.

The police station is located in a strip mall, sharing a building with the firehouse. Stuart parks the car in a spot marked "Sheriff Only." I follow Stuart through a small reception area. A deputy sitting behind a counter starts to get to his feet, but Stuart waves him down. The walls are covered with helpful signs and posters warning about preventing forest fires and instructions about performing the Heimlich maneuver and the FBI's most wanted. It's hot and stuffy in the room. No air-conditioning. This is northern Maine. No call for air-conditioning here.

Stuart walks through a door behind the counter and we're in what appears to be a combination squad room and office. Stuart and I are alone.

In the far corner is a small table on which lies an evidence bag.

"That's what we collected at the murder site," Stuart says. "Everything except the human remains. Those're at the medical examiner's office. I'd like you to take a look. You being an experienced homicide detective and all. I thought you might see something we might have missed."

I go to the table and go through the small pile. A few shreds of leather and fabric. Part of what was probably once a boot. A rusted key ring.

And a Bulova watch. With an expansion bracelet. Fused and almost totally rusted away.

"You said Clyde was buried," I say.

"That's right. That's the only reason there's anything left."

"Did you find the murder weapon?"

"Not a trace. I expect the killer tossed it in one of the lakes. Along with whatever tool the killer used to dig the grave."

I'd been on the trail since sunrise, wearing a heavy wool coat my mother insisted I take. I picked up the trail at the southeast edge of Travers' field—well-defined boot prints in a patch of dried mud, the left heel badly worn. The same boot prints the police found near Rose's body and had positively identified as Clyde Fenton's. I followed the trail into the forest for several miles then almost lost him at Clarkson Creek where he must have crossed the creek, then doubled back, and it took me almost an hour to pick up the trail again.

Around noon it was getting hot and I laid out my wool coat on the ground in the shade of a large elm, sat down and had an egg salad sandwich my mother had packed for me, wrapped in wax paper, an apple and a chocolate chip cookie.

I never doubted I'd find Fenton. I'd been hunting since I was a small kid—been born to it they used to say—and I've always had a feel for tracking. And Clyde Fenton was a stranger in the woods. He knew towns with paved streets. I knew it was only a matter of time before I'd find him.

It was almost three in the afternoon when I finally reached Clyde lying with his back against the trunk of a large tree, hidden in the deep shadows of the forest. A satchel lay on the ground next to him and in his right hand he held a Colt Python pistol.

"This ain't no game, son." He licks his lips. He has several days' growth of beard. He looks at the revolver I hold in my hand and laughs softly. It was my dad's and been in our home for years. I don't think I'd ever fired it before. I drop the entrenching tool I hold in my left hand.

"You killed my sister, Mr. Fenton."

"What are you gonna do about it, boy? Call the sheriff?" He stares at me through hooded eyes the color of rainwater. "You come to hear me say I'm sorry?"

"No, Mr. Fenton, I've come to kill you."

* * *

I search through the pile of evidence on the small table while Stuart stands at the door talking to the deputy in the outer office, his back to me.

The watch must have slipped off my wrist when I buried Fenton. I didn't miss it till I got home that night. Maybe I was nervous. Except I didn't feel nervous. Before it happened, I thought I might be scared when the time came. Panicky. Maybe sick to my stomach. None of that. I just felt empty. I always feel empty.

I pick up the watch from the table and hold it in my hand, feeling its weight, its heft. I remember Dad giving it to me on my fifteenth birthday. He'd made a big deal of it. He'd put it in a small box stuffed with white tissue paper. The watch I hold in my hand is fused together, and I can't see the backside, but I know there's an inscription that reads "Marko" with a date. This was my first watch. Although Dad never said anything, we all knew in his eyes I was now a man. He must also have known he didn't have long to live. I slip the watch into my right pants pocket. "Nothing here, Stuart," I say as I join the sheriff at the door. "I don't see anything that would help your investigation."

"I didn't think you would. But had to ask."

CHAPTER TEN

MALCOLM WU WAITS for me in his electronic lair. "I've accessed the victim's health monitor." There is no one nearby to hear what Malcolm has to tell me. "She got up on the morning of her death at seven. She had six hours of sound sleep."

"Interesting," I say. "But not helpful."

"From eight to nine there are indications of strenuous activity. I'd guess she worked out, maybe in a gym. Maybe she was running on a track. Then for the next few hours normal activity for an adult her age."

"That's all you have?"

"At one fourteen that night all hell breaks loose."

"Tell me about hell."

"Her blood pressure and heart rate suddenly spike. Way above normal. It looks like she was under major stress. This lasted until one forty-six. At that point all life signs stopped."

"What would cause that?"

"I don't know. In the minutes before that, she engaged in intense physical activity."

"What kind of activity?"

"Maybe rapid walking. And going up or down steps."

"How many steps?" I ask.

"Maybe ten steps."

"What happened during those thirty-six minutes, Malcolm?"

"No way to tell."

"How far can you walk in thirty minutes?" I ask. "If you're walking fast."

"I have no idea. I never walk. You owe me two beers and you didn't hear any of this from me. I never saw this device."

When I return to my desk, I call Frank Townsend's intercom number.

"Yes!" he growls.

"Good morning, Frank. Marko here."

"I know who you are. What do you want?"

"I want to drain the Reflecting Pool."

"Stop right there!"

"Call your friends at the United States Park Service. Tell them I'm on my way to the Reflecting Pool right now to do a site survey so we can begin the draining operation. Maybe you can call the same fellow you talked to when he complained about my behavior."

"They'll arrest you! The Park Service is very sensitive about their national monuments."

"Just call and tell them I'm coming." I hang up before Townsend can argue further. I cross the squad room to Kenneth's desk.

"Grab your coat. Let's play detective."

"Sir?" Kenneth looks worried.

I make a mental note not to tease Kenneth. I feel bad enough about being mean to him after our interview with Trisha Connelly. "Let's go. It's time you visited the crime scene."

"Cool."

It's midmorning and already the Mall is filling with tourists dragging bored children from one museum and monument to another. There are runners and joggers from nearby offices out for their exercise. We stop near the base of the Washington Monument. "Kenneth, you said you played baseball in school."

"Yes, sir."

"So you're in good shape. Good enough to walk fast."

"Yes, sir."

"Do you see where the Reflecting Pool is?"

He nods.

"I want you to walk there. Briskly. Don't stop. Try not to knock over any old people but maintain a steady, fast pace."

"You want me to walk fast from here to the Reflecting Pool?"

"That's the idea. Then stop and wait for me at the edge of the Pool. Got that?"

"Now?"

"Now."

Kenneth walks briskly off toward the Reflecting Pool. I check my watch and follow him at a leisurely pace. I figure if I walk slow enough, I can finish a cigarette before I catch up with him. I take out the pack of cigarettes and light one with my silver lighter. Even though we are out doors, I get dirty looks from passersby.

I walk through the World War II Memorial and stop to let pass an elderly man in a wheelchair, pushed by a pretty young woman no more than twenty. A World War II vet being shown the sights by his granddaughter or great-granddaughter. It pleases me to think so.

Kenneth has arrived at the Pool. He stops and waves at me. Tourists are clustered near the end of the Reflecting Pool outside the yellow police tape. Two bored, uniformed cops keep curiosity seekers away. I crush the cigarette butt into the pavement.

When I catch up with Kenneth, I check my watch. Six minutes, fourteen seconds.

I show Kenneth where Sandra Wilcox's body was first observed in the Pool and where we placed her on the ledge. We walk to where the single shoe was found, an evidence marker still planted, and to where I found the identification bracelet. The red marker with the number "8" is still in the ground.

There's nothing else to see. But it doesn't matter because we're about to have company. In the distance a battalion of bureaucrats is headed our way, led by a short, stout man in a double-breasted, gray suit, followed by a phalanx of assistants and aides and lawyers and uniformed Park Police, including Captain Fletcher who leans down and whispers into his leader's ear and points to me accusingly. The leader and his band head right toward me and stop a few feet away. The stout man glares at me.

"My name is Jeremy Torrance," he announces. "You're Marko Zorn."

"Guilty, sir," I say in a cheerful voice.

"I'm the director of the National Park Service. I'm told you want to drain the Reflecting Pool." He gestures dramatically at the Pool. "I won't have it!" He's has a large, ruddy head. His scalp shows through his comb-over.

"Is this your Pool, sir?" I ask.

"Of course not!" He's angry. I guess he doesn't appreciate sarcasm. "It belongs to the American people," he announces.

"I'm sure the American people won't mind if I drain the Pool so we can expose the killer of a young woman."

"How do you expect to find the killer by draining the Reflecting Pool?"

"We may find the victim's ID. A cell phone. Maybe one of those gizmos Secret Service agents wear in their ears. A shoe. Anything. The killer may have thrown the evidence into the Pool."

"Who's going to pay for this draining operation? It's not in the budget. Let the Park Police investigate this crime. Leave it to us."

"That's it!" I exclaim, figuratively smacking my palm to my forehead. "Why didn't I think of that? That's our solution right there.

Staring us right in the face. Yesterday Captain Fletcher here suggested much the same thing, didn't you, Captain?" The captain gives me a fishy look. "Maybe I was too hasty in rejecting his offer to have his people carry out the investigation."

"What are you getting at?" Torrance asks, suspiciously.

"If you have a problem with my draining the Reflecting Pool," I say, "why not have Captain Fletcher and his men go into the Pool themselves and search for the missing evidence?"

Captain's Fletcher's face contorts with consternation, but Torrance is beginning to like the idea. He's not the one who will have to spend hours wading through the dirty waters of the Reflecting Pool. Torrance turns to Fletcher. "Daryl, I think we may have a solution here. Get your men into that Pool."

"But, sir . . ."

"If you start now you should be finished before nightfall."

Torrance turns back to me, essentially dismissing Captain Fletcher and his troops. "The Department of the Interior wants to cooperate with local law enforcement," Torrance says to me.

"I'm sure you do," I say. "If Captain Fletcher finds anything, please inform my partner here, Detective Blake." I point to Kenneth. "Your chaps can keep any loose change they find."

"Got that, Daryl?" Captain Fletcher nods gloomily and goes off to organize his troops.

"I do have one question," I say.

"What's that?"

"Yesterday morning Captain Fletcher and several troopers arrived at the crime scene not long after I did."

"So?" Torrance asks.

"I don't imagine the captain routinely patrols the Mall at seven in the morning," I say.

"I don't suppose he does."

"So how did he get here so soon?"

"Is it important?"

"Maybe not, but I'd sure like to know."

Torrance stares at his shoes for a moment, apparently thinking about my request. "Our Operations Center received a call," Torrance says at last. "The caller said there was activity—some kind of police activity—on the Mall and said we should send in our own team to take over the investigation. The request was relayed to Captain Fletcher."

"Who called?" I ask.

"Someone from Homeland Security."

"Who was it that called?"

"They didn't identify themselves. They never do."

"You've been a great help." I nod to Torrance and walk away.

Kenneth stands at the edge of the Reflecting Pool watching the Park Police officers, seven abreast, take off their shiny shoes, roll up their trouser cuffs, and wade into the water. "Do you think they'll find anything?" Kenneth asks me.

"Not a chance," I say. "There's nothing to find. The killer would not have been careless and left any evidence where we could find it. Whatever evidence there was has been well hidden far from the crime scene or destroyed."

"Then why did you make them search the Pool then?"

"I wanted to find out how in hell the Park Service learned about the murder so fast."

"Did you find out?"

"Sort of. You stay here and keep an eye on our mermaids."

"Where will you be?"

"I'm going to see a man about a murder."

* * *

The Secret Service's headquarters is located in an undistinguished office building in downtown Washington. I step into the front lobby and approach the reception desk. "I want to see Mr. Decker," I announce to the receptionist.

"What is your business?" the man behind the desk demands. He's heavyset in civilian clothes.

"My name is Zorn." I show the receptionist my shield and police ID. "Marko Zorn. I need to speak with Mr. Decker about a homicide investigation."

The receptionist studies my credentials carefully, noting down pertinent information in a log. "The Director's not available," the receptionist says handing me back my ID and shield.

"You didn't check," I say. "You didn't call anybody."

"That isn't necessary, sir. We've been expecting you." The receptionist looks unperturbed. "The Director is not available."

"When will he make himself available?"

"I can't say, sir."

"That's a pity," I tell him. "I'm investigating the murder of a member of the Secret Service." I speak in a loud, annoying voice. "One Sandra Wilcox. Do you mean to tell me the Director of the Secret Service is too busy to help in the investigation of the murder of one of his own agents? Should I report to my superiors that the Secret Service does not care enough about its employees to cooperate with an official police murder investigation?"

I sense men and woman gathering behind me, waiting to get to their appointments. They're already late and glance at their watches and glare at the back of my head. I'm the asshole causing everyone to be inconvenienced. I imagine they are all also straining to hear every word I say.

The receptionist glances at the gathering crowd. "I'll make a call," he says. "Please take a seat." He points to a couch along one wall, above which hang photographs of the President and the Director of the Secret Service.

"I'm comfortable where I am," I tell him. "I'll wait right here."

The receptionist grimaces, then makes a quick call, his voice lowered and, in a short time, a man approaches me, smiling a phony smile.

"I'm Francis Roth. Can I help you, Detective?" He wears a picture ID on a chain around his neck.

"I'm here to see Mr. Decker."

"The Director is unavailable," Roth says. There is a silence while each of us waits for the other to continue. Roth gives up first. "He's out of the office. Can I help you?"

"Are you the Deputy Director?" I ask.

Roth looks uncomfortable. "No, that's Andy Wood."

"Are you the Assistant Deputy Director?"

"I'm the Deputy Assistant Director."

"Is that better than Assistant Deputy Director?" I can never remember—is an Assistant better than a Deputy? Or is it the other way round?"

"What can we do for you?" Roth's face flushes, his smile long gone. The people waiting in line for their appointments stare at us in fascination.

"I'm investigating the murder of Sandra Wilcox," I announce.

"I understood that Jessica Kirkland filled you in," Roth tells me.

"You understand wrong. Mrs. Kirkland didn't seem to know anything. I have many questions."

"I'm not sure how we can help."

"Why don't we find out?" I suggest. "Do you have an office in this building where we can sit and help one another? Or do assistants or deputies share their office with other assistants and deputies?"

"Of course, I have an office." He's getting seriously huffy now. Maybe he'll want to prove how important he is by talking to me. "Follow me." Roth leads me past the reception desk and through a metal detector. Roth seems surprised when I set off no alarms. "You don't carry a weapon?" he asks as we head toward a bank of elevators.

"I don't like guns."

"Kind of odd for a homicide detective, isn't it?"

"Maybe I'm an odd detective."

We enter the elevator and rise silently three floors. The elevator doors slide open, and I follow Roth down a corridor, and we enter an office furnished with institutional, government-issue gray metal-frame chairs, and a metal desk heaped with file folders. Institutional pictures decorate the wall.

We sit opposite one another in the metal-frame chairs. "Did you know Sandra Wilcox?" I ask.

"A bit," Roth replies.

"Did you know she had a peanut allergy?"

"A what?"

"Never mind," I say.

"We have over 30,000 special agents, you understand," Roth explains, defensively.

"When was the last time you spoke with Sandra Wilcox?"

"I don't know. Not recently."

"Where do Special Agents spend their time?"

"That depends on their assignments."

"Like the Presidential Security Detail?"

"That is one. The Secret Service has many responsibilities. We have offices in several locations around the city and around the country."

"Where was Sandra Wilcox on the night she was murdered?" I ask.

Roth rubs his hands together. "I can't really say."

"You can't *really* say because you don't know or you can't *really* say because you don't want to tell me."

He smirks. I swear to God, Roth actually smirks. "Both."

"Okay, who does know where Sandra Wilcox was on the night she was murdered?" Long silence. "Mr. Roth?" I urge. "Her schedule?"

"I suppose the shift supervisor would know."

"And who is that?"

"I can't tell you. That's classified information."

"Would it surprise you to know that Agent Wilcox was assigned to the White House the night she was killed?"

Roth flinches. His hands grasp the arms of his chair. His knuckles are white. "I can't comment. I really know nothing about her whereabouts that night."

"Of course you don't."

"I have nothing more to say, Detective."

"I have reason to believe she was at the White House until about one fifteen at which time she left and went to the Mall. Does any of this sound familiar to you?"

Roth's face is drained of color. "I can't be of any help."

"How long was Sandra on the Presidential Protection Detail?"

"I never said she was on the Presidential Protection Detail."

"You didn't have to."

I get to my feet and Roth rises, too, obviously relieved to see me go. "I'll escort you to the front entrance," he announces.

"That's not necessary. I can find my own way."

Roth opens the door to his office and gestures for me to go through. "I'm afraid outsiders must be accompanied at all times." He smiles. Not friendly. "You know . . . rules."

CHAPTER ELEVEN

"MR. ZORN?" A voice calls out urgently. A tall, athletic black man, in his mid-thirties, wearing a business suit, white shirt, an understated tie, and the five-pointed star, the badge of the Secret Service, on his left lapel, grasps my left arm. "You and I have got to talk."

"You are?"

He looks around nervously. Crowds of men and women surge in and out of the entrance of the Secret Service headquarters. "Not here. Somewhere private. It's urgent."

Am I being set up? I wonder. Is this some con Roth has cooked up to entrap me into something? But the man standing before me looks sincerely distraught. I don't think he's faking it.

"There's a bar on 7th Street. O'Toole's Irish Sports Pub," I say. "Meet me there in ten minutes. I'll be in the booth at the back."

The man nods and disappears quickly into the scrum of pedestrians. I walk slowly away, careful not to look back. I stop at a small store with a sign that advertises "Food & Gifts" and pick up this morning's *Washington Post*. Then, on impulse, I buy a pack of cigarettes. I promise myself I won't open it until late this afternoon. I walk two blocks and, in less than ten minutes, I'm in O'Toole's, sitting in a booth where I can watch who comes and goes.

As usual, it's cool and dark in O'Toole's. At this early hour the lunch crowd hasn't yet arrived. What makes O'Toole's a sports pub are several large TV screens above the bar, all but one turned off this morning. Half a dozen employees are watching the one operating TV that's showing a soccer game. The commentary is in Spanish. What makes O'Toole's Irish are some sad-looking shamrock decals glued to the beer-stained bar.

Two guys sit at the bar, one looks vaguely Hispanic, the other, a broad-shouldered man, could be anything. I can't see his face. He wears what looks like a knock-off Rolex watch on his left wrist. The band and the bezel are bright gold and sparkle with fake diamonds. He has a thick roll of fat at the back of his collar.

The Metro section of the *Washington Post* contains a two-column story about the discovery of a woman's body in the Reflecting Pool the day before. No identification is given and no cause of death announced. There is an official statement from the Park Service saying nothing but no statement at all from the DC police. The rest of the article is taken up with irrelevant and trivial historical factoids about the Reflecting Pool, mostly involving sexual shenanigans. At the end, the writer adds a paragraph about the recent crime wave in Washington and the influx of illegal drugs and suggests a connection with the death of the woman in the Pool. I quickly lose interest and glance at the front page, which includes an article about the death of a general who, it seems, was a big deal and who is scheduled to be buried in Arlington Cemetery. The White House spokesman has announced that the President and the First Lady will attend the funeral. It's a slow news day.

Exactly ten minutes after I left him, the man I met on the street in front of the Secret Service headquarters enters. He glances quickly at the men watching the soccer match, a little more carefully at the two men at the bar, then slides into the booth opposite me.

"Thank you for seeing me like this, Detective Zorn."

"How do you know my name?"

"I was standing behind you at the reception desk at Headquarters. I couldn't help but overhear you. Sorry. Didn't mean to eavesdrop."

"Who are you?"

The man pulls a laminated plastic ID badge on a chain from his shirt pocket and shows it to me. It's just like the ones Roth and Mrs. Kirkland had except this dog tag tells me the man is named Larry Talbot and he's a Secret Service Special Agent.

"You're with the DC police?" Talbot leans forward across the table, his voice low. "You're investigating the death of Sandra Wilcox? Is that right?"

"Tell me what your interest is."

Talbot glances around and assures himself no one is close enough to hear. "First some ground rules. Are you going to make a record of what I tell you?"

"That's what I would normally do."

"And you would put your notes in a case file. That right?"

"That's right."

"I don't want you to write down what I say here today. Not for your case file. Not for anywhere. Is that understood? What I say is for you only."

"If I don't agree?"

"Then this conversation ends right now. I say goodbye and I walk out that door."

"You'd be trusting me to make no record. Somebody you've never met before."

"Sometimes you have to trust someone," Talbot says. "Even a stranger."

"So I've been told. You think the Secret Service has ways to access confidential DC police files?"

"Of course we do."

"Okay. No record. No file."

Talbot shifts his position in the booth, glances around to see no one is listening. The place is beginning to fill up with the early lunch crowd. Three young women take a table nearby but show no interest in us. Each places her cell phone on the table. Two more men take seats at the bar. One is tall and overweight with thinning hair. The second man is short and stocky. Neither looks at us.

"I'm not supposed to be talking to you," Talbot says. "I'm not supposed to talk to the police. I'm out on a limb here."

"Who told you not to talk to the police?"

"The top brass. They say Sandra was killed in a robbery attempt that went wrong. End of story."

"And you don't believe that."

"Of course not, that's why I had to speak with you."

"Why don't you believe it was a botched robbery?"

"Why would Sandy be out in the Mall in the middle of the night?" Talbot glances around the bar. "That makes no sense."

"Did she like to take walks by herself? You know—to get away from it all?"

"She'd never do that. She was on duty the night she died."

"Tell me about you and Sandra Wilcox."

"Sandy was a friend. A very close friend."

"Meaning?"

"Just what you think it means." He takes a deep breath.

"Do you know if she had any allergies?"

"Of course. She was allergic to peanuts. What has that got to do with anything?"

"When did you two meet?"

"About two years ago we were both assigned to the Secret Service's Atlanta Field Office. We started going out. It went on from there."

"Were you two thinking of getting married?"

"Nothing formal. No engagement. No ring. But yes, we talked about it."

"And then you two were no longer thinking about getting married."

"Maybe."

"What changed?"

"Maybe I changed. Maybe she changed. Who knows?"

"When did this change happen?"

"Our relationship was fine until she was transferred here to DC."

At this point, one of the waiters decides to acknowledge the existence of paying customers and wanders over to take our orders. He glances over his shoulder, anxious not to miss a goal.

"One *cerveza negra*," I say and look at Talbot who shakes his head. "Nothing for me. I'm on duty."

The waiter disappears.

"When Sandy was transferred to DC," Talbot goes on, "it was kind of sudden. I was transferred here three months later—to a Counter Assault Team. I tried to pick up the relationship where we'd left off. But it didn't work out. I'd invite her to dinner. She'd have an excuse. It was very polite and cordial. No harsh words. Nothing like that."

"You think Sandra might have fallen in love with someone?"

Talbot actually grimaces. "I think she was seeing someone."

"Who was it?" I ask.

"I don't know. She would never tell me."

The girls at the nearby table order a round of margaritas.

"You think it was somebody in the Secret Service?" I ask.

"Sandy didn't really know anybody except the people she worked with. She wasn't a party girl. It had to be somebody in the Service."

At this point our waiter places a bottle of beer in front of me.

"Where were you the night before last?"

"You can't suggest . . ."

"I'm not suggesting anything. I just want to know where you were the night Sandra was murdered."

"Are you saying I killed her? I loved her."

"Sorry, that doesn't wash," I say. "In my experience, love is the prime motive for murder."

"I was on duty at our office in the Old Executive Office building until about ten that evening. Then I was out drinking with friends."

"Witnesses?"

"Many."

"About a month ago Sandra took a trip."

Talbot nods. "She went to Greensboro, South Carolina."

"Did she tell you about that?"

"She visited her sister-in-law."

"What's her sister-in-law's name?"

"Anne Lovell."

"Sandra had a brother?" I ask.

"Tony, I think his name is. I never met him."

"You ever meet Anne Lovell?"

"Never."

"Do you know why Sandra visited Anne Lovell?"

"Family business, I think. Sandy never said. She was very private about family matters."

"Who's handling the investigation of the Wilcox murder within the Secret Service?"

"A man named Patrick Grier," Talbot says. "He's the Director of the Office of Protective Operations."

"I need to talk to Grier. How do I reach him?"

Talbot takes a small book from his inside jacket pocket and scribbles a note, tears the page off and hands it to me. "That's his private cell number. Whatever you do, don't tell him I gave it to you. He'll kill me."

At this point, Talbot's cell phone rings and he takes it from his pocket. "Yes," he says in a low voice. He listens intently then returns the phone to his pocket. "I've got to go. That was Headquarters. They want me back on the double."

He places his business card on the table and stands up. "Will you find the son-of-a-bitch who killed my Sandy, Detective?"

"I will."

"I know you can't bring Sandy back, but I'll never rest until I know her killer is burning in hell."

"I'll try to arrange for that," I assure him.

CHAPTER TWELVE

THE PUB HAS filled up. Customers, young people mostly, from nearby offices, take their seats at their tables and study the food-stained menus. The staff disperses from watching the game on TV and returns to their stations. The girls at the next table are beginning to show the effects of the margaritas. They laugh loudly and their voices rise in pitch. My waiter shows up to ask whether I need anything else.

The beer the waiter brought earlier is now almost drinkable. Like most sports bars, the beer is served ice cold to the point it has no taste. I order another beer and some onion rings. I figure I'll be at O'Toole's for a while.

My cell phone rings. It's FBI agent Lovelace. "I have something for you," she says. "Something's going on, something I don't understand. And don't like. I keep running into a stone wall. My investigation is being blocked."

"I'm having the same experience," I tell her.

"What's happening?"

"We should compare notes. Can you meet me for dinner this evening?"

"You buying?"

"Depends."

"Le Zink? At eight o'clock. I like Roberta." She hangs up.

Kenneth Blake is next on my call list. "Kenneth," I say. "How are the Park cops doing?"

"They're still wading through the Pool. They're not happy."

"They find anything?"

"Lots of really disgusting stuff."

"Then you might as well go back to the office. I'll be away the rest of the afternoon."

My onion rings and frozen beer arrive. I drink some of my old beer, and eat two greasy onion rings. Then make what will be the first of two more calls.

Howard Walsh is so high up in the federal government that my nose bleeds when I visit his office. It takes most people a week just to get an appointment to speak to his assistant. My name usually serves to cut through this. The fact that I can get through doesn't mean my calls are welcome.

"Zorn? What do you want?" The voice is a deep, rumbling baritone familiar to millions of TV viewers from his appearances before congressional committees and Sunday talk shows.

"How is Billy?" I ask. This is mean, but I'm in a hurry and I need to get to the point.

"Leave Billy out of this," Walsh says, impatiently. "What do you want?"

"I need your help." Silence at the other end. "Have you ever heard of a woman named Sandra Wilcox?"

"No. Should I?"

"She was murdered. Her body was found in the Reflecting Pool on the Mall. I'm the investigating officer."

"I saw something in the paper about that. What's it got to do with me?"

"She was a Secret Service agent."

"What of it?"

"The Secret Service is part of the Department of Homeland Security. That's your department."

"It's not *my* department. I just work here. And the Secret Service is not part of my portfolio."

"Somebody has issued a gag order on my investigation into the murder of this Secret Service agent. People have been told to shut me down. No one is supposed to cooperate with me. Or with the FBI."

"Why is the FBI involved?"

I ignore his question. "Here's what I want, Howard. I want to know why this gag order was issued. What are people worried about?"

Long silence. Then: "You just want to know why someone has issued a directive not to cooperate with your investigation?" Walsh asks. "Is that all?"

"That's all." Another silence.

"What was the name of the victim again?"

"Sandra Wilcox."

"Okay. I'll make a few calls. No promises. That's all I'm prepared to do."

"Just a phone call or two. And say hello to Billy for me."

"You make me sick." Walsh slams down the phone at his end.

I really hate to bring up Billy. A few years ago Howard Walsh's son got himself into some trouble that could have resulted in serious prison time and, incidentally, end Howard's political career. I was the investigating officer on that case and I overlooked a few issues and cut some corners. Walsh owes me. I don't like to call in my debts so callously, but I need to bring home the urgency of my situation.

I dial the number Talbot gave me.

"Hello! Pat Grier here," the voice on the other end of the line announces.

"My name is Marko Zorn. I'm with the—"

"I know who the fuck you are, Zorn. How the fuck did you get my telephone number?"

"I'm investigating the murder of Sandra Wilcox."

"I know that. Don't bother me!"

"You're in serious violation of the District of Columbia Penal Code, sir," I say.

"What are you talking about? What violation?"

"Obstruction of justice. Illegal seizure of property. The details will be explained at the hearing."

"What property are you talking about? What hearing?"

"Your people entered the apartment of the late Sandra Wilcox and seized her computer, private papers, and correspondence. All without a warrant."

"Fuck off, Officer. This is none of your business."

"I must insist that you turn over to me all items seized from Sandra Wilcox's apartment. Forthwith!" I like the word "forthwith."

"We did not seize anything. Some items were given to certain authorized agents willingly by Sandra Wilcox's roommate."

"Trisha Connelly had no authority to give you squat. Least of all items pertaining to a criminal investigation." I also like the word "pertaining."

"This is a Secret Service investigation," Grier yells at me. "The DC police have no business interfering. Understand? We are within our rights to take whatever materials we think necessary."

"You'd better have your lawyers review the DC Penal Code on that point. If you do not comply, forthwith, I'll come to your office with a van and a couple of large cops. They'll load the van with the evidence you stole. If you make trouble, I will charge you with resisting arrest."

"If you or your flatfoots come anywhere near my office, I'll have you and your men fired."

"You might want to reconsider that, Grier."

"Fuck off!" The phone goes dead. The exchange with Grier went rather well, I think.

There's no point in hurrying. I wait patiently for the call I know is coming at any moment as I drink my beer and eat two more onion rings.

CHAPTER THIRTEEN

My phone rings. "Damn it, Zorn, what are you up to?" Frank Townsend demands.

"I'm investigating a murder."

"I know that. I'm getting more calls complaining about you. Yesterday it was the Department of the Interior. I'm told you made half the members of the Park Police wade through the Reflecting Pool. So far they've found nothing."

"Do you care?"

"Not really. But now it's the Department of Homeland Security. How many government departments are you going to piss off today?"

"How many are there?"

"Try to stay out of trouble." He cuts off the call.

Almost immediately my phone rings again. The caller ID reads "unknown."

"Hello," I answer. I'm instinctively suspicious of phone calls when the caller hides his identity, but this is probably the call I'm expecting.

"Is this Detective Zorn?"

"Could be."

"My name is Matt Decker. Do you know who I am?"

"You're the Director of the Secret Service."

"I understand you want to meet with me."

"That's right, Mr. Decker."

"Pat Grier says he just spoke on the phone with someone from DC Homicide. He said the man acted like a jerk and a major asshole. Could that have been you?"

"Certainly sounds like me."

"I think we should talk."

"Good idea," I say. "How about now? I can be at your office in ten minutes."

"Good," Decker says. "I'm looking forward to meeting you, Detective Zorn. I've heard so much about you."

I take a final swig of my beer, abandon my dreary onion rings, drop a twenty-dollar bill on the table, and leave O'Toole's. Seven minutes later, I'm back in the reception area of the Secret Service headquarters. There's a different receptionist on duty. He has the same attitude. Before we can get into a pointless exchange about what I want, two men detach themselves from the crowd. "Detective Zorn?" one asks. "Come with us, please." They lead me to the bank of elevators, and we take one that has a sign that reads: "Reserved for The Director." We ride silently to the ninth floor. My escorts take me to an office with an impressive door and a nice waiting room.

"This way, sir." One of my escorts gestures for me to enter. We're in a standard government-issue office but with more pictures on the wall, all with pretty frames. What distinguishes this office from a hundred others I've visited is that it's filled with guns—machine guns, machine pistols, rifles, shotguns, antique flintlocks. They hang on the walls, decorate the tops of bookcases, end tables, and a large desk. Next to a couch there is a coffee table on which sits a semiautomatic Stoner SR 16 rifle. And, of all things, a hand grenade that looks like a flash-bang type. I don't like hand grenades, not even flash-bang ones. My experiences with them have not been happy.

Standing behind the desk is a man in his sixties, well built, trim and athletic. He has a thick, distinguished, black mustache. "Detective Zorn," he says, coming from around his desk. "Come right on in. I'm Matt Decker. Glad to meet you." He gestures at the couch. "Let's talk."

I sit on the couch, a few inches from the grenade and the Stoner. Decker sits in an armchair opposite, legs crossed. I must look anxious because Decker says: "They're all harmless, Detective. They're real enough but none are loaded."

"I don't like your toys, sir."

Decker ignores my comment. "What can we do for you?"

"I have questions about the murder of one of your agents."

Decker leans back in his chair and opens his hands in a gesture of welcome. "I'm sorry things got off on the wrong foot. We want to cooperate with the police. Really we do."

"Then give me back the items your people seized from the apartment of Sandra Wilcox."

Decker smiles patiently. "I'm afraid our eagerness to cooperate with the police has its limits."

"What limits, Mr. Decker?"

"Look, we're in the middle of an investigation into the death of one of our most valued agents. This investigation is going to be exhaustive."

"Glad to hear that. I want the computer and documents your people took."

"I have personally directed the Service to spare no effort in uncovering the truth about what happened to Agent Wilcox. I assure you, when we have completed our investigation, we will share the results with the DC police."

"And when will that be?"

He makes another vague gesture with his hands. "Hard to say. You know how these things are."

"No, how are *these things*?"

Decker shrugs.

"What was Sandra Wilcox doing in the White House on the night she died?"

"I never said she was in the White House."

"I know you didn't but she was."

"Maybe she was at home. Or out with friends."

"She wasn't at home. Should I spell out what happened?"

"You can try."

"At one fourteen Sandra Wilcox was on duty somewhere in the White House. Somebody forced her to leave the building and took her beyond the perimeter security fence, then led her, by force, to the Reflecting Pool in the Mall where, at one forty-six, she was murdered."

Decker stares at me. "You're just guessing. How can you know any of that? I have no comment on your speculations."

"Trust me, I know what happened. I've calculated the time between when she was accosted until she reached the Reflecting Pool. I know how long she walked. She had to have come from the White House. What I don't know is who was with her. I need to see the White House logs showing who came and left the building that night. Who was in the White House between one and two on the night she was killed?"

Decker shakes his head. "The logs are not available to the public."

"I'm not the public!"

"Sorry."

"You're not going to tell me what you know about Sandra Wilcox's private life. Who she was seeing? Who her friends were? What her outside activities were? You're not going to give me squat?"

"Sorry. Afraid not. Maybe later." He leans forward in his chair. "We all follow orders, Detective. You follow orders . . ."

"Sometimes."

"Well, I follow my orders."

"And you've been ordered to shut me down."

Decker smiles. "No comment."

"How long was Sandra Wilcox in the Secret Service?"

Decker struggles for a moment to decide whether that's part of the information he's not supposed to share, then, remembering it's in the public record, comes clean.

"Five years, I think. I'd have to look up the exact dates."

"And she was assigned to the Presidential Security Detail. That's pretty fast, isn't it?"

"I never said Agent Wilcox was on the Presidential Security Detail."

"You don't have to. Let's say hypothetically that Agent Wilcox was on the Presidential Security Detail. Five years would be pretty fast—hypothetically speaking."

"I suppose—hypothetically."

"I understand your agents usually spend six or seven years in various field offices before being assigned to the Presidential Protective Division."

"That's normal."

"The Presidential Security Detail is the most prestigious unit in the Secret Service. How did Miss Wilcox make that assignment so fast?"

"She was talented and disciplined." Decker has obviously given up the charade. "We reward people like that."

"I'm sure there are many men and women in the Secret Service who are talented and disciplined."

"Of course."

"What was special about Sandra Wilcox?"

"I admit her case was a bit unusual."

"A bit?"

"Off the record—there was some influence brought to bear."

"Who by?" I ask.

"Sandra worked out of the Atlanta field office for a while. President Reynolds and his wife made a trip there to attend some political event. The First Lady was given the usual FLOTUS treatment. You know, visiting orphanages and homeless shelters. That kind of do-gooder bullshit. We ran into a personnel problem with the President's detail. The detail was short two agents, and we moved two from the First Lady's shift. Then Mrs. Reynolds decides she wants to visit some goddamn juvenile detention center. An unscheduled change in one of the principal's schedule. That's what we call a pop-up. She's interested in prison reform. You know, 'hug the hardened criminal and he'll become a perfect citizen.' That's her thing.

"Mrs. Reynolds likes to mix with people," Decker goes on. "A real headache for us. This afternoon she's going to some damn book signing to promote her new book. Can you believe? Right now, we're facing a major threat to the President and First Lady, and she decides to go to a goddamn bookstore."

"Which bookstore?"

"I don't know. Somewhere on Connecticut Avenue. Next week she's attending a Broadway show. These are major headaches for us."

"Tell me about what happened in Atlanta."

"We assigned some of the agents from the Atlanta field office to the First Lady's detail."

"And one of them was Sandra Wilcox, I'll bet."

"Nothing particularly unusual there," Decker says. "As it happens Sandra was on the shift that accompanied Mrs. Reynolds to the juvenile detention center. The two got into a conversation. That's strictly against the rules, you understand. It distracts the agent from their job. But if a principal engages one of our agents in conversation, it's hard not to respond without being rude. As soon as she decently could, Agent Wilcox disengaged. But it seems she made a good impression on the First Lady."

"What happened?"

"Two weeks after the Atlanta event, Mrs. Reynolds calls me to her private office in the White House. She wants Sandra Wilcox assigned to her protective detail. I said no, of course. We don't approve of the principals interfering in assignments. It totally fucks up our personnel system. But the First Lady was adamant. She insisted we make the assignment. You ever met the lady?"

"Never."

"She can be very persuasive. Mrs. Reynolds insisted Agent Wilcox be assigned to her security detail and, in the end, she got what she wanted. As usual. We assigned Agent Wilcox to Presidential Security training at our facility in Beltsville. I have to say, Sandra did very well there. Six months after Atlanta, she was relocated to Washington and attached to the First Lady's security team."

"Did the President's wife explain why she wanted to transfer Agent Wilcox?"

"The security detail is a very peculiar human dynamic and principals react differently. When they're in a security situation, particularly when mixing with the public, the principals are surrounded by four to six agents. Often very close. The detail leader is within inches of the principal at all times, standing just behind or to one side of the principal. They are there to pull the principal out of the way or may even throw them to the ground in case there's an incident. So they are almost touching the principal at all times. Mrs. Reynolds was uncomfortable with a man doing that. She felt it was more appropriate if the detail leader were a woman. That's where we assigned Sandra Wilcox whenever we could."

"So Agent Wilcox is on the First Lady's security detail?"

"No longer. Two months ago, the President directed that Agent Wilcox be transferred to the President's security detail. In the end, the President, of course, got his way."

"On the night Sandra was murdered, she was on the President's security detail?"

Decker shakes his head. "Sorry, I can't go there. Information regarding specific security assignments is off limits."

"I think that Sandra might have been having an affair with one of your agents. Maybe even an agent on the President's security detail."

"I can't comment on that."

"Who would know where Agent Wilcox was on the night she was killed?"

"Sorry, that's classified. I can't share that information. Look, you may be focused on a single incident, but we have a lot to deal with just now. We have a credible threat to assassinate the President. The President, accompanied by Mrs. Reynolds, is scheduled to attend a funeral service at Arlington National Cemetery. We tried to persuade the President not to go, but he's insistent. He says he's not going to let some lowlife thug bully him out of attending the funeral and honoring an American hero. See what we have to contend with?"

"I don't think I'm going to get any help here," I say.

"To you this is a simple case of murder. Very tragic, of course. But there is much more at stake here than you realize. Between us—and this is strictly confidential and must not leave this room—your case involves matters of national security. Of the most sensitive level. Take my advice, leave the Wilcox case alone."

CHAPTER FOURTEEN

A SECRET SERVICE agent stands at the bookstore entrance watching arriving customers suspiciously. Several more agents are posted inside. One stands next to a collection of books on gardening and another next to the latest cookbooks. I join a long line waiting to buy a book.

At the far end of the room is a table covered by a thick green felt cloth. A few feet away stands a small table stacked with books with bright yellow covers. I wait in line at this table where two clerks are selling the yellow books. I'm disheartened to see the woman in front of me buy five copies. When my turn comes, I buy one lone book. The title reads: *The Future Is You America*. I think, shouldn't there be a comma after "*You*"?

After about ten minutes, there is a stir at the back of the room and several more Secret Service types materialize. Then the famous author herself appears and there is a ripple of polite applause.

Mrs. Marsha Reynolds, the First Lady of the United States, smiles brightly at the crowd, waves in a decorous, ladylike fashion, and takes her seat at the felt-covered table. She has auburn hair, touched with white, cut short and severe. She is dressed in a conservative business suit.

Behind her stand two women and a man. The man and one of the women are young—hardly more than twenty. These are aides or interns or whatever they call them in the White House, there to attend to any needs of the First Lady. Otherwise, they stand back, careful not to take the limelight away from Mrs. Reynolds.

The third woman is different. A little older, perhaps in her thirties, she is striking—tall and slender and graceful, with perfect, pale skin—what old novels used to describe as alabaster—large hazel eyes and platinum blonde hair tied up in a coil at the back of her head. She wears a simple but elegantly cut pants suit and a gray, shimmery silk blouse. She places a plastic water bottle and a glass along with several fountain pens on the table just within reach of the First Lady but not too close. She leans down and speaks softly to the First Lady, and they both look out over the line of people waiting to get their books inscribed, doubtlessly gauging how long the book signing is going to take. The platinum blonde woman's hands are slender; her lacquered nails a brilliant scarlet.

I notice a man slip in behind the group at the green table. I think for a minute he must be Secret Service. He studies the crowd carefully, watching faces and hands. He's short and muscular and almost bald on top, dark brown hair on each side. A security type but not Secret Service I decide. He isn't the neat, buttoned-up package the Secret Service favors. Hired muscle, I suppose, here to protect the First Lady from the middle-aged ladies waiting to get an autograph.

A woman with tortoiseshell glasses and wearing a gray cardigan sweater stands and asks for silence. "Ladies and gentlemen," she announces in a soft, cultivated voice. "We are honored to have with us here today Mrs. Marsha Reynolds, the First Lady of the United States." There is warm but civilized applause. No whooping or hollering here. "In addition to her many other accomplishments, Mrs.

Reynolds, a lawyer by training, has taken an active interest in reforming the criminal justice system, particularly for juveniles who are victims of drug abuse. She is the author of a new book on this subject. The book has been hailed as an important contribution to the field." There is more decorous applause. Several among the audience take pictures with their cell phones.

"Mrs. Reynolds will be happy to sign copies of her new book, *The Future Is You America*."

With that, the line begins to inch forward toward the table covered by the green cloth. I'm eighth in line, behind the woman with five copies of the book.

When the woman with five copies reaches her destination there is a lot of animated conversation between her and Mrs. Reynolds. I note that Mrs. Reynolds has adopted a kind of fixed smile. I amuse myself by admiring the platinum-blonde lady. Our eyes meet and I think she smiles at me. That could be my imagination.

When it's my turn, I place my lone copy of the yellow book on the table. Mrs. Reynolds looks at me with the kind of vacant smile that means nothing. I notice from the corner of my eye the muscular security guy watching me.

"Would it be okay to inscribe your book to my sister?" I ask.

"Of course." Mrs. Reynolds picks up a pen. It's a Mont Blanc.

"My sister is a schoolteacher. Once a week she visits the local state prison and teaches basic reading. She is a great admirer of your work, Mrs. Reynolds. She thinks what you're doing to help America's children is phenomenal."

"What's your sister's name?"

"Mona," I answer, "Mona Nightly."

Mrs. Reynolds writes on the inside page of the book, passes it back to me. The inscription reads: "With Very Best Wishes for Mona Nightly, Marsha Reynolds." This is followed by the date and

"Washington DC." "Please give your sister my best wishes. She's do-ing important work."

I observe the platinum blonde watching me with curiosity. "Thank you," I say and hurry away, carrying my precious package under my arm. I work my way past the line waiting to have their books signed, through the crowd, past the bored Secret Service agents, out the door, and onto the street.

I feel bad about making Mrs. Reynolds inscribe a book to some phantom named Mona, but it had to be done.

CHAPTER FIFTEEN

"IT'S A FUCKING war zone out there," Hal Marshal declares. "A fucking war zone."

"You mean the fentanyl epidemic?" I ask.

"That's bad but there's worse to come. I'm telling you, Armageddon is scheduled to begin next week at six in the morning."

"I missed that memo."

"Actually, the end of the world already started this morning. Fort Sumter was fired upon. Didn't anyone inform you?"

"You've lost me."

"That's because you don't pay attention. You don't listen to the streets. You ought to get out more." Hal Marshal pushes his massive form back from his scarred desk, his ancient swivel chair creaking under him, and heaves himself to a standing position, walks around his desk, and stands before a large map of Washington, D.C., his feet apart, his fists on his hips. He reminds me of General George S. Patton at the Battle of El Guettar. All that's missing are the pearl-handled revolvers. And some tanks.

"What are you talking about?" I ask.

"You homicide dicks are clueless. You, for example, are dealing with the murder in the Reflecting Pool. Am I right?" He doesn't wait for me to answer. "A single murder. You miss the big picture. What's really going on. The true life and death of our city."

Marshal vastly exceeds the police department's weight limits, but management prefers to ignore that. Hal is indispensable. He's been running the gang division for years and he knows every pimp, dealer, whore, killer, thief, thug, and would-be thug in the area. He also knows the name of every bent cop in the city. His job is secure.

"See that?" Marshal points to the map. "That's the real world, my friend. Not your penny-ante crime scene. For me, the entire city is a crime scene."

I see an ordinary map of Washington with lots of pins and colored flags and markings and icons written in pencil on Post-it notes. Over the years I've come to recognize some of the symbols. Bright red stars mean street homicides, blue for domestic violence, green squares for drug markets. Hal's even been generous enough to include a black cross showing where my Secret Service agent was killed. The map is thick with multicolored pins showing gang activity. Where I see streets and parks and monuments, he sees the tides of crime. He sees armed men—squads of thieves, battalions of burglars, armies of criminals—moving through the streets of Washington. He studies his map as if it were a large canvas, reading the ebb and flow of violence.

"The black pins, that's Sister Grace's territory," he says, pointing to a black swath covering most of the city. "The red pins represent M30 gangs. There's a truce between them and Sister Grace. In the last few days, she's lost almost a block and a half in Southeast Washington to a bunch of Cubans. Meanwhile, in Anacostia, Sister Grace's people have been pushing out the Guatemalans."

"And the blue pins?" I ask.

"Some El Salvador gangs trying to cut into her drug business."

"So what's the problem?"

"All of this is going to change completely in six days."

"What happens in six days?" I've brought a Styrofoam container of Lipton tea, Hal's preferred beverage. He stirs in some artificial sweetener. He's been using artificial sweetener for years in hopes it will help him lose weight.

"The guns."

"Tell me about the guns."

"Word on the street is there's a shitload of weapons—automatic weapons, military grade—coming on the market. A huge buy."

"How reliable is this 'word'?"

"Very. The weapons are on their way now and due for delivery in Washington next Thursday at six in the morning."

"Where do they come from?"

"The immediate source is a major dealer in El Salvador. The weapons originated in North Korea. Where else?"

"Who's buying?"

"We don't know. That's what worries me. Somebody from out of town has contracted for delivery here. But there's more than one interested party. Sister Grace wants them. Cloud wants them. They've both let the word out they'll pay top dollar to get those weapons. And there are other potential buyers."

"What happens if Cloud gets them . . . ?"

"There will be hell to pay."

"Won't Sister Grace keep things under control?"

I've worked with Hal ever since I made detective and we have a complicated, sometimes fraught, relationship. We both know more about the other than is altogether healthy and we don't really trust one another. I don't think we even like one another much. So we get along fine. He knows every bad cop on the force. The ones who take bribes, who are on the payroll of criminal syndicates. He knows I ignore the rules and cut corners. I suspect he even knows something about Billy Walsh and the others. But he knows on important things, I'm clean. I have strict standards. He doesn't know what these standards are exactly but he senses they exist. He knows when it comes to the important things, I'm reliable. We help one another when necessary and we don't ask awkward questions. He gives me a heads-up about dangerous people I need to watch out for and I feed him information about certain criminal activities I have no business knowing about.

Hal shakes his head mournfully. "For years, Sister Grace kept things under control. If there were territorial problems, she'd intervene. She might have some troublemaker whacked from time to time but things would soon settle down."

"And now?"

"Maybe she's getting old. What is she, a hundred and fifty? She doesn't seem to be able to keep her people in line anymore."

"You think she's not running the show?"

"Looks to me like no one's running the show. I'm not sure she can do that anymore. Her organization's falling apart."

"You talk about war," I say. "What kind of war?"

"A war for the control of the city. Cloud's boy Lamont is challenging Cloud. You heard about the shooting at the schoolyard? That was Fort Sumter. Lamont's already been operating independently, cutting into Cloud's drug operations. He's cut out Cloud completely in certain parts of the city. Lamont operates out of a warehouse in Southwest where he stores his drugs and runs whatever illegal activities he's doing. Until today, Cloud tolerated Lamont's independent activities."

"Until today?" I ask

"This morning Lamont crossed the line and challenged Cloud directly. Lamont tried to eliminate one of Cloud's lieutenants—

tried to shoot him down in that schoolyard. Cloud's guy got away. You heard what happened to the bystanders. Now it's open war between Cloud and Lamont. There's no going back."

"Tell me about Lamont."

Marshal returns to his desk, sinks into his creaking chair, and drinks some tea.

"Lamont likes killing people. His father disappeared when Lamont was like five or six or something. His mother was a crack addict. When Lamont was about ten, a dude named Tyshan moved in. Tyshan was a real piece of shit. One day Lamont goes out and gets himself a gun. Tyshan comes home, drunk as usual, and Lamont shoots him dead. Right there in the living room. Ten rounds. Pow! Pow! Pow!"

"Was Lamont arrested?"

"The kid was ten years old, for Christ sake. Nobody wanted to send the boy to prison. He was given probation and counseling."

"I take it that didn't help."

"He murdered his counselor. By that time, he was thirteen and he already had a reputation for extreme violence. There were witnesses to his murders, but when it came time to testify, everybody remembered to forget. One time we even had Lamont on tape for another killing. He walks into a liquor store in Northeast, holds up the place, and then, for no reason except because he feels like it, he shoots the owner dead. Maybe he don't like Koreans. At the trial, fifteen people swear he was playing craps someplace across town at the time of the shooting. Understand, people are scared to death of Lamont. Want to know what I think?"

"What do you think?"

"What I think is, Lamont's a fucking psychopath. Why are you asking about Lamont? He involved in one of your cases?"

"Not that I know of."

"Don't expect to get a conviction if he is. Nobody's going to testify against either Cloud or Lamont. There's one rule on the streets: Snitch and you're dead. Snitch on Cloud or Lamont and your family's dead, too."

"I have no plans to arrest either Cloud or his buddy."

"Now it's your turn. What have you got for me?"

I'm silent for a moment, thinking carefully about how to answer. "Sister Grace and Cloud are on the verge of open war."

"Elaborate."

"Sister Grace knows Cloud wants to take over her organization. And she knows she's in danger from him. Sister Grace thinks Cloud plans to kill her. So she plans to kill him first."

"And you know this how?"

I don't bother to answer. This naturally aggravates Hal. He's been running the gang division for years, but he has never laid eyes on Sister Grace—never seen a picture of her—isn't even sure where she lives. Yet here I am with what seems to be inside information.

"Do you know how Sister Grace intends to do a this?" Hal asks.

Tricky question. I have no good answer. So I stay quiet.

"This is bad," Hal continues. "With Cloud and Lamont at war with one another and now the old lady going to war with Cloud and his people and now these guns coming on the market, I tell you, six days from now at six thirty in the morning, that's when the shit hits the fan. That's the end of the world."

CHAPTER SIXTEEN

"You have company, Marko." Roberta places a glass with Van Winkle in front of me.

Arora Lovelace is standing next to me. She's made an effort to comb her hair. It has not done much good.

"Good evening, Miss Lovelace," Roberta says. "Delighted to see you back."

"Good evening, Roberta. May I have one of your lovely whiskey sours?"

"Of course." Roberta glides away.

"And a good evening to you, Detective." Arora settles herself on the barstool next to me.

I smile at her. "You said you're getting interference in your investigation. Tell me about that."

"I'm running into major obstruction. As soon as I begin to get into Sandra Wilcox's background—her family and friends, people she knew—what her life was like—I get shut down. That includes by the Secret Service, the Department of Homeland Security, even the Army has stopped cooperating on anything to do with Sandra Wilcox. Phone calls and emails are not returned."

"Can you tell where this is coming from?" I ask.

"No idea at all. Or why."

"Have you learned anything in your investigation?"

"We're checking US Army records and getting a fix on Tony Wilcox, Sandra's brother. He was in the Army assigned to Delta Force. He was trained as a sniper and apparently was very proficient. He served in Iraq and later in Afghanistan. He's married and has one child. He had medical issues during his Afghan tour and was sent home and medically discharged. He spent some time in a VA hospital. There may have been some suicide incidents, but the Army is being coy about that."

Roberta places a chilled old-fashioned glass in front of Miss Lovelace and fills it from a frosted shaker.

"You know where Tony Wilcox's wife lives?" I ask.

"North Carolina, I believe."

"What's the FBI's theory about Sandra Wilcox's murder?"

"We think Tony Wilcox or somebody within the Brotherhood murdered Sandra Wilcox."

"That's ridiculous," I say.

"Why ridiculous? It makes perfect sense to me."

"It makes no sense to me." I remove from my pocket the note I found in Sandra Wilcox's bedroom and place it on the bar. "I want to show you something. Somebody sent this to Sandra Wilcox at her home. Very recently."

Arora Lovelace studies the note carefully, front and back, reading the handwritten inscription several times.

"You didn't think to tell me about this?"

"I didn't know whether I could trust you."

"Of course, you can trust me," she says hotly. "I'm with the FBI. We're on the same team."

"Are you so certain?"

She studies the note again. "Expensive stock. Expensive perfume."

"Does the inscription mean anything to you?"

"It's a quote," Arora says. "I seem to remember it from some college seminar I took years ago. The course was called something like 'Love in the Western World,' would you believe? What's that got to do with Sandra Wilcox's murder?"

"I have no idea but I'm certain there's a connection."

"I don't see it." She's upset because I didn't share a piece of evidence and because I'm trying to derail the FBI's theory. "Leave the investigation into the Brotherhood to us. That's what we do. And we're good at it."

"Then why did Carla Lowry want you and me to collaborate? Why did you want to talk with me if I'm supposed to stay out of your investigation?"

"Our main focus must be on this Brotherhood and their plans," she answers. "But there are still questions about the murder of Sandra Wilcox. We thought you could help us with loose ends."

"Sandra Wilcox is not a loose end." I try to hide my irritation. "She's a victim."

"Don't lecture me!" She drinks her whiskey sour. "And don't patronize me! If we're going to cooperate, we need to be honest with one another."

"I'm being honest." I try to keep my voice calm and reasonable, but it's not working. This is getting out of hand. We're both becoming angry.

"How about dinner?" I ask, trying to break the tension. She pushes her glasses onto the bridge of her nose and looks thoughtful. I can almost see the gears spinning in her head. Is he hitting on me? Would it be appropriate to accept? Rude to refuse? Unprofessional to have dinner with a police detective working on the same case?

She shrugs. "Okay. But no shop talk."

* * *

We are seated in the dining room by one of the Serbian brothers who claims his name is Dumont. Like many criminals in their dealings with the police, he is both cautious and overly solicitous. He is clearly consumed with curiosity about Miss Lovelace, uncertain whether she is in law enforcement or, like him, a thief. The brothers have not made up their minds about me.

The lights are dim, the menu is handwritten in purple ink. Charles Aznavour sings plaintively in the background.

The man claiming to be Dumont bows himself away, disappearing into the kitchen where he is doubtless conspiring with his brother. We order an overpriced dinner and an adequate California Chardonnay then talk generalities, each probing the other to get a fix on who we really are. She asks about my past, about my experiences in the police, what I did before I joined the force. I tell her a little, some of it true.

"Did you always want to become a policeman?" Arora asks me. An innocent question. But maybe not entirely innocent.

"Not at all. When I was young, I wanted to join the circus. I wanted to be a trapeze artist."

"Why didn't you?"

"I'm afraid of heights. How about you, Agent Lovelace?"

"Call me Arora."

"Then it's Marko for me."

"I'm an Army brat," she says. "I lived all over. Germany. Korea. New Jersey."

She tells me anecdotes about her experiences in the FBI. She makes no reference to a husband, present or past, or to any love life, present or past. I decide to let that go until a better time. Instead, I tell her an amusing anecdote about my recent trip to Hamburg.

Although I normally avoid having sex with FBI Special Agents on a first date, I consider making an exception with Arora and think about asking her back to my place for a drink. We're having coffee.

Then she goes and spoils the mood. "You're wrong about the Sandra Wilcox murder. From what we've learned, Sandra had no enemies. She hardly knew anyone in Washington."

"It only takes one."

"There had to be some connection to this terrorist militia."

"I don't believe it. This was a carefully planned murder. Not the actions of some middle-aged loonies with fantasies of revolution."

"Have it your own way." She takes her purse and leaves.

CHAPTER SEVENTEEN

I'M TWO BLOCKS from the restaurant and I'm in serious trouble.

Ahead, a black SUV pulls directly toward me at high speed, headlights dark. Going the wrong way down a one-way street. In my rearview mirror, I glimpse a white van bearing down on me. In seconds, they'll box me in.

It's a residential section of Georgetown—mostly old brick buildings, in Federal Style, narrow streets lit faintly by tasteful lamps. There is no traffic here this time of night. The Jag is fast. But not that fast. I have no way to outrun them.

I jam hard on the accelerator and the Jag surges ahead. I turn, tires squealing, at the next corner. I take another left, switch off my headlights, and pray I don't run into some good citizen out walking her dog. I turn a sharp left, where I fishtail on a patch of cobblestones then speed ahead. Directly in front of me is a twelve-foot-high iron gate and a seven-foot-high brick wall. I jam the breaks hard, skidding to one side of the street, stopping half on the sidewalk.

And I'm out. The wall encloses Potomac Gardens, an oasis of trees and shrubs, flowers and sparkling fountains during the day, a sanctuary of peace and tranquility in the heart of a busy and frenetic city, populated normally by bird watchers and young mothers pushing strollers. And people like me looking for peace.

I know the gate is locked after dark. The lock is an old iron affair and not hard to open with time and the right tools. None of which I have. Behind me there is the sound of racing cars, and I make a wild run for the wall and at the last second leap. And just make it. I grasp the top of the wall and jerk myself up on the top.

I hear a crack. The unmistakable sound of a high-powered rifle at close distance. And then another. I feel no impact. No pain. It's sloppy shooting. Before I disappear over the edge, I catch an instant glimpse of the shooter. A man stands next to the SUV in dark shadows aiming a long gun. The shooter is within easy range. Either an amateur or he's firing fast and doesn't take the time to set up the shot. The next shot will be well placed.

I'm over the top and, falling to the ground, land heavily on my hands and knees. I bruise my left knee. My hands sting. I must have landed on pine needles.

There are muffled shouts from the other side of the wall and somebody is at the iron gate trying to force the lock. It's old but it holds. My attackers will follow me in seconds over the top of the wall. I make out the faint light from the homes in the neighborhood. No light where I crouch.

I plunge through the darkness. What I hope are leaves and vines brush against my face. I zigzag left, counting my steps—ten—then pivot right—fifteen more strides—then drop to my knees and wait.

Judging by the voices, there are two of them. I hope neither has a flashlight.

I struggle for my cell phone, keeping it close to my chest to cover the light from the screen, and dial 911. When I get the standard response, I whisper: "There's a murder in progress in Potomac Gardens. Officer down." The voice at the other end calmly asks who I am and asks me to repeat the location. I say again, "Murder in progress in Potomac Gardens in Georgetown. Officer down." I hear voices near me and cut the connection.

One of my pursuers is no more than ten feet away to my left and moves cautiously through the trees. There's another behind me. No one has thought to bring a flashlight. We're all lost in the dark.

I'm on my feet and running as fast as I can—returning the way I came—counting the steps so as not to get completely lost.

And suddenly, I'm hit in the face and thrown to the ground. I lie on my back, half dazed, on a bed of pine needles and dead leaves. I touch my face and feel blood. There's a gash above my right eye and I brace myself for a second attack from my unseen opponent until I realize my opponent is probably a tree. I've run into some goddamn tree trunk or tree branch.

From behind, I hear a shot. Then another. I roll over on my stomach and see a muzzle flash maybe twenty feet away.

They must have heard me hit the tree. Or maybe I grunted. Now they're firing in what they think is my direction. Firing blind in the dark. I count one, two, guns.

There's a curse. "Stop shooting," somebody shouts. They realize they're shooting at one another now.

A man's voice calls out from a distance and somewhere a light is turned on. I figure the caretaker has been woken and switched on a floodlight. I can even make out the silhouette of one of the shooters, crouched down. No details. A dark shadow among dark shadows.

Suddenly, there's a light among the trees. Somebody with a flashlight is moving toward us. I curse to myself. It must be the caretaker. There is a shot from what seems a few feet to my left and the flashlight flies into the air. I hear the anguished cry as somebody feels the impact of a round and falls.

In the distance there are sirens—I count at least two patrol cars. There will be more. People all over the neighborhood will be calling 911 now, reporting the sound of gunfire. The police cars pull up to the main gate of the garden: Police officers will be piling out, guns drawn. The streets in the neighborhood and gardens will be swarming with cops in minutes. This is an upscale neighborhood populated by rich and powerful people, and the police response will be overwhelming.

My attackers know this. There are shouts, and I sense they're escaping, groping their way among the trees and bushes, back toward the wall, trying to get the hell away before the police crowd through the trees. There are more approaching sirens and some cop on a bullhorn is yelling warnings. Time to make myself scarce. I don't want to try to explain what is going on.

I get painfully to my feet, making as little sound as I can in case one of my attackers has decided to stay behind. I hobble among the trees until I see faint streetlights over the top of the wall. That gives me something to aim at. I take a deep breath and run for the wall, at the last minute jumping for the top. I'm able to just grasp the top and pull myself over.

The street below is empty. There is no sign of the SUV or the white van. I swing over the top and drop to the street below. There I crouch for a moment, keeping a low profile, head down, then dash for the Jag. It's just as I left it. The key still in the ignition, the car half on, half off the sidewalk. Lights in the homes along the street are turning on. Curtains are cautiously shifting. A few heads peer out. At the end of the street there are flashing lights of a patrol car and a fire engine. Time to get out.

*   *   *

I pull the Jag into my garage and secure the door, check security around and inside the house and find no signs of intrusion. No van is in sight. No unidentified cars are on my street. After locking up, I brush the dead leaves and twigs from my hair, go to the bathroom, and check my face. I have a nasty cut on my right forehead. I wipe the blood away with a damp towel. In the kitchen, I pour myself a glass of Wild Turkey to help settle my nerves.

I'm too keyed up to sleep so I carry the Wild Turkey with me. As an afterthought, I go to my bedroom and remove my .45 from its place secured behind the bedside stand and I go out to my deck. I settle into my lounge chair in total darkness. In the distance I hear the faint sounds of traffic and the rustle of leaves in the trees in the park below my house. Somewhere in the distance, a dog is barking. There are other soft noises I can't identify.

I rub my knee that still hurts from my fall and feel my bumps and bruises—the palms of my hands, my right forearm. My scalp is sticky with drying blood. I'm too old for this kind of thing. It's not as much fun as it once was.

I switch on my phone and listen briefly to police radio calls. As expected, in addition to my own 911 call, many neighborhood residents reported the sound of gunfire. There's a report of one casualty, still alive, being taken to a hospital. No reports about any of my attackers. There is no mention of me.

I switch off the police band and listen to "Lonely Woman." Ornette can always soothe my nerves and, for a while, I let my mind go blank and just listen. It's cool, there's a slight breeze, and I almost doze off.

Eventually, I rouse myself and turn my mind to my immediate problems. There's the men who tried to kill me tonight. Are they connected to Sister Grace and her feral family? Or maybe the Brotherhood of the Aryan Dawn? Or maybe something from out of my past? Some individual or organization I've pissed off along the way? There's a long list.

There's a whooping sound I think may be an owl somewhere. I know there are bats in the trees around my house, but I'm pretty sure humans can't hear bats.

I turn my mind to the girl in the Reflecting Pool and her blue eyes I can't forget. Frank Townsend could be right. Maybe it's a routine crime best left to junior officers. But I know better. Someone with power is trying to shut me down. That seriously annoys me.

Then there's Arora Lovelace. Does she have an agenda she's not telling me about? Everybody has an agenda. I get that. Sometimes agendas are innocent. She's a mystery to me, and I don't like mysteries.

This gets me nowhere. Too much wine at dinner is not helping. Maybe it's Arora's smile. I pour myself a second glass of Wild Turkey and come back to Sister Grace and her demented orders for me to take care of Cloud.

The sky in the east is getting bright when I finish my drink, and I'm beginning to see the outlines of a plan to get out of this mess. It will be dangerous but it's the only way.

CHAPTER EIGHTEEN

TWO MEN WHO might be related to the receptionist at the Secret Service building are waiting for me at FBI headquarters. One of them makes me sign in; the other examines my police ID carefully then announces: "You're expected, Detective. Your escort will be with you shortly."

A few minutes later a pert young woman, her bosom bedecked with laminated plastic IDs, takes me to an office high in the building and deposits me in an austere waiting room. I introduce myself to the young man sitting at a desk who examines my police credentials then asks me politely to take a seat until I'm called.

I look through the magazines to keep visitors entertained while they wait. I've often wondered what kind of reading matter the head of the FBI's Criminal Division keeps in her waiting room. I'm hoping for something like *True Detective* or at least *Guns and Ammo*. Instead, I find back issues of *Time* and *The Wall Street Journal*.

I'm reduced to studying the pictures on the walls: The President, the Attorney General, the Director of the FBI. I lose interest in them and return to *"Time"* when the door to the waiting room opens and Arora Lovelace enters. She looks surprised. I imagine I do, too.

"What are you doing here?" she asks.

"I don't know," I answer. "What are you doing here?"

"I've been summoned," she tells me. "You?"

"Same thing."

We sit on the couch, side by side, and wait in silence. The phone on the reception desk chirps constantly, but discreetly. The receptionist, a young man with neat, close-cut hair, parted in the middle, handles the calls efficiently and smoothly. Try as I might, I can't hear what he says on the phone.

Arora looks at the gash on my head that I tried to hide by combing my hair over the wound. "Rough night?" she asks.

"Slipped on my bathroom floor."

The receptionist speaks to us: "Agent Lovelace. Detective Zorn. The Director will see you now."

The receptionist is on his feet and opens the inner door for us. Arora Lovelace goes in first. I follow, still limping.

Carla Lowry, the Director of the FBI's Criminal Division, sits behind her desk that is littered with papers and files. "That will be all, Ben," she says to the receptionist who leaves the room, shutting the door silently behind him.

"You two, sit down," Carla commands.

Arora Lovelace and I sit in chairs facing the desk. Carla Lowry pulls off her reading glasses, placing them carefully among the documents on her desk, then comes around from behind her desk and stands in front of us, half leaning, half sitting on the edge of her desk.

She studies us, looking first at Arora, and then at me. Her eyes seem to focus on the bruises on my face and the gash on my head. "Okay," she says. "Let's keep this short. You two are investigating the murder of Sandra Wilcox. Right?"

We both nod.

"You are running separate investigations. But coordinating." Arora glances at me. Carla doesn't wait for an answer. Which is just as well.

"It looks like one or both of you have put your foot in it."

"It?" I try to sound innocent. As usual, Carla ignores me.

"I've been getting pushback about your inquiries," Carla tells us. "You've made some people unhappy."

"Who have we made unhappy?" I ask.

"None of your business. Suffice it to say there have been suggestions—not so subtle suggestions—that the investigation into the murder of Sandra Wilcox be put on the back burner."

"That's outrageous!" Arora Lovelace blurts out. Then calmer. "The murder of a federal agent should never be put on the back burner. The murder of anyone!"

Carla Lowry holds up her hand, a gesture for silence. "The way it has been put to me is to leave the investigation to the Secret Service. Leave it to the national security teams."

"That's the same thing as putting the case on the back burner," I suggest.

Carla Lowry gives me a skeptical look.

"Have you been ordered to stop the investigation?" Arora asks.

"Not in so many words. And I'm not stopping the investigation. Nothing pisses me off more than to have some politician tell me how to do my job."

"So, what are we doing here?" I ask.

"I think I owe you a warning," Carla tells us. "There's a lot of high-level interest in this case. I can take the heat, but you   " she's looking at Arora Lovelace. "You might get in trouble."

"Are you telling me I should stop the investigation?"

"I don't want you to stop the investigation. I want you to be worried." Carla Lowry turns to me. "Now Marko here, he can take care of himself. And if he gets in trouble, okay. If he gets chewed up by the system, who cares? But you, Agent Lovelace—" she turns back to Arora— "you're one of us. You work for me, in a manner of speaking. I don't want to see you hurt. If you decide to stop your part of the investigation, I'll understand. It will not be held against you."

"I'm determined to find out who murdered Sandra Wilcox," Arora announces.

"Good," Carla says. "That's what I thought you'd say." Carla seems to relax a bit—to the extent she ever relaxes. "What have you two got so far?"

"The Secret Service believes a domestic terrorist group called the Brotherhood of the Aryan Dawn had Sandra Wilcox killed."

"Why would the Secret Service believe that?" Carla asks.

"They think the Brotherhood recruited Sandra to work with them—to plan the assassination of the President. Then killed her to keep her quiet or maybe because they no longer trusted her or no longer needed her."

"What was her connection to this Brotherhood?"

"The Service suspects the assassin the Brotherhood recruited may be Tony Wilcox, Sandra Wilcox's brother."

"Do you buy their theory, Agent Lovelace?"

"It makes sense to me."

"Marko, you look skeptical."

"It sounds plausible spelled out like that but I don't buy it. It doesn't feel like a job by the Arian Brotherhood."

"If it wasn't this militia group, who did kill Sandra Wilcox?"

"I don't know."

"You better find out. See what you two can uncover on any line of inquiry."

"Have you found your mole yet?" I ask.

"Mole?" Carla's face is frozen.

"You know, the person who intercepted Agent Lovelace's report to Headquarters containing the name of the assassin. Who then promptly told the Brotherhood about Solly Nelson, who then arranged to have your agent and the defector killed. That mole."

Carla is furious with me. "That's none of your business. That is strictly a Bureau internal matter. Stay out of it!"

I give her a moment to calm down. "There's one more thing."

Carla covers her face with her hands for a moment. "I know I'm going to regret this. I know I shouldn't ask you what 'one more thing' is."

"I want an airplane."

"I want a vacation. What are you talking about?"

"There's one line of inquiry we need to explore further."

"And that is?"

"Anne Lovell."

"Who is Anne Lovell?" Carla demands.

"Sandra Wilcox's sister-in-law," Arora explains. "Tony Wilcox's ex-wife."

"Tell me why I should care."

"She and Sandra kept in touch," I say. "She's the only one outside the Secret Service that Sandra Wilcox seems to have talked to recently. Somebody must talk to Anne Lovell and find out what she knows."

"Two Secret Service agents talked to her yesterday," Carla says. "They didn't learn anything useful."

"That's because they didn't know the right questions to ask."

"And you do, I suppose."

"Yes, I do. I need to talk to her."

"And how do you propose to do that?"

"She's living just outside of Greensboro."

"Greensboro, you said? As in Greensboro, North Carolina?"

"I know the Bureau has aircraft at Andrews Air Base. Arrange to have me flown to Greensboro. Today. There's a small airport there. All I need is an hour with Anne Lovell. Then bring me back to DC."

"That's all you want? Would you like me to have you canonized as well?"

"I believe I'd have to be dead for that."

"That can be arranged. Do you have any idea how much this trip would cost the American taxpayer?"

"I have no idea. But think of the potential payoff. If I could learn something—anything—that could stop this domestic terrorist group, it could prevent the assassination of the President of the United States and the FBI would get the credit. Not the Secret Service."

"You seem to forget that we're all on the same team here," Carla pronounces. "Federal agencies do not compete for credit."

All of us in the room know better than to believe that.

Carla turns to Arora. "Agent Lovelace, do you have an opinion on Zorn's proposed trip to North Carolina?"

Arora makes her nervous gesture, pushing her glasses onto the bridge of her nose. "Yes," she tells Carla. "I think we should talk to Anne Lovell."

"*We?*" Carla is genuinely shocked.

"We're at a dead end in the investigation," Arora says. "In tracking down this militia group and in solving the Sandra Wilcox murder. We need a break. I don't know what the sister-in-law can tell us. Maybe nothing. But it's worth a trip to talk to her."

Carla Lowry settles back in her desk chair and scans her cluttered desktop. I wonder whether she's searching for something sharp to throw at me. Then she says something I don't expect.

"Maybe you might learn something. But if the Bureau is to provide transportation and support, then this is a Bureau operation."

"Meaning?" I ask.

"Meaning that Special Agent Lovelace will go and she will have the lead. If you go with her, Marko, it is only to carry her luggage. Is that perfectly clear? This is an FBI operation from beginning to end."

I feel Arora watching me closely. I shrug. "Okay," I say. "Fine. Deal. Special Agent Lovelace has the lead."

"I'll call Andrews and make the arrangements," Carla says. "But there is one more thing before you go." She picks up a paper and puts on her reading glasses. "My incident report this morning tells me there was a shooting in Potomac Gardens in Georgetown last night. Witnesses report hearing what sounded like gunshots. There was even an anonymous 911 call reporting an attack on a police officer. When the police arrived, they found the caretaker wounded. Everyone else involved had disappeared including the so-called police officer. This was not some minor dispute between two drunks. This was no robbery gone bad. This was an armed attack. Strange, don't you think, Marko?"

It's a rhetorical question and I don't feel a need to answer. "Did they identify the shooters?"

"Nothing."

"I'm not sure where this is going."

"One of the neighbors reported seeing a convertible parked on a side street near the gardens about the time of the shootings. It was described as a foreign roadster. Green. You drive a green Jaguar convertible. Isn't that right?"

"It's not really green. It's more lime colored."

"The phone used to call 911 was one of those cell phones that are untraceable," Carla Lowry says, looking at me intensely. Her eyes flick to the gash on my head. "I've asked the NSA to identify the caller. I'm not optimistic."

"Fascinating."

"I think so. Do you know anything about this incident?" Carla demands.

"Not a thing."

"I didn't think you would. Now get out of here, both of you. Go find the son-of-a-bitch that killed that woman."

CHAPTER NINETEEN

"DO YOU AND Carla Lowry have a history," Arora demands, placing her coffee mug into its saucer. Arora watches me, her expression unreadable, as we sit in the FBI cafeteria, waiting for the call. There's a coolness between us. "Because, if you do have a history," she says, "I need to know."

"You could say we have a history," I say.

"Good history? Bad History?"

"You know. History."

"You mean like *The Decline and Fall of the Roman Empire?*"

"Not quite that long but more complicated."

The cafeteria is one you find in most government buildings, an operation outsourced to a large corporation that won the contract with the General Services Administration by making the lowest bid. Which accounts for the quality of the coffee.

Arora picks up her mug and drinks. "It's none of my business," she says. "But if we're going to work together, I need to understand the conditions. Is there anything in your past relationship with Director Lowry I should know about?"

"Nothing that affects this case."

She looks at me skeptically. "What about last night?—after we parted company at the restaurant. What happened?"

"Nothing happened."

"You have bruises on your face. You have a cut on your head.
You're limping. You didn't have any of that last night when we had
dinner. Was there anything to the incident Director Lowry mentioned you want to tell me about?"

"Nothing. I was at home, on my deck overlooking Rock Creek
Park, when this incident took place."

"How do you know when the incident took place? Director
Lowry didn't mention a time."

"Just guessing."

Arora's cell phone rings. She looks at me enigmatically, then answers the call. Arora nods and murmurs a few "yeses" then the conversation is terminated and Arora gives me a thumbs-up. "We're
on!" she says. "There's a plane waiting for us at Andrews."

We take my Jag, figuring we'll get to Andrews faster than by either of us requisitioning an official car. Arora is silent on the hour's
drive. There's clearly a lot on her mind that she doesn't want to talk
about. When we reach the main gate of Joint Base Andrews, we're
stopped by a heavily armed Air Force sergeant wearing a Kevlar vest
and combat helmet. He's not impressed by Arora's FBI credentials.
Even less by my Metropolitan Police ID. He is impressed by my Jag
convertible. Arora makes a quick call to the FBI base-liaison office
and, on speaking with someone there, the guard grudgingly opens
the gates, lets us through, and gives us directions on how to find our
destination.

The FBI office is housed in one of the many undistinguished
buildings scattered around the base. An FBI clerk meets us as we
drive up, shows me where to park the Jag, and escorts us through the
building directly out onto the tarmac. A few hundred feet away a
Learjet 70, with FBI markings on its tail, awaits us. We hurry across
the tarmac. The front steps have already been lowered and we

clamber up quickly. At the top, we're met by a man in some kind of uniform who gives us a half-assed salute.

"Terry Snowden," he tells us. "Second officer. We're all fueled and serviced and ready to roll. Buckle yourselves in. We leave in a few minutes."

With that, he pulls up the steps behind us, secures the hatch, and disappears onto the flight deck while Arora and I find our places on the empty 8-seat aircraft that's obviously been operating for some time. The seats are comfortable but worn. There is no cute flight attendant offering free drinks or instructions about flotation devices. Instead we hear the disembodied voice of what I suppose is the First Officer.

"We're cleared for takeoff and will be leaving momentarily. It looks like clear weather to Greensboro and it should be a smooth flight. Hang on."

We're in motion, rolling along taxiways, and then turning onto the takeoff runway. We pause briefly, and then we're moving again. Fast. Out my window I catch a glimpse of a monster Boeing 747 aircraft half a mile away—Air Force One. Surrounding it are uniformed service personnel and armed guards. Almost before I know it, we're airborne, rising into thin clouds.

Our FBI aircraft lands without incident at Piedmont Triad Airport in North Carolina. When the plane has come to a stop in front of what appears to be a service building, the Second Officer emerges from the flight deck, smiling.

"Good trip, folks?" he asks and, without waiting for an answer, opens the hatch and lowers the steps. A hurricane of hot air sweeps into the aircraft as if he'd opened a furnace door.

"We'll wait for you here," the officer tells us. "We must be airborne no later than three forty. If you're later than three thirty, you'll have to find your own transportation back to DC." He makes another half-assed salute, and Arora and I hurry down the steps and across the broiling tarmac.

An FBI sedan is waiting for us at the edge of the landing strip. A man climbs out as we approach and holds the passenger door open for us.

"Martin Tolls," he tells us. "Charlotte field office." Arora introduces herself. "Special Agent Lovelace." She shows Tolls her FBI ID. "That's Detective Zorn. DC police." She waves vaguely at me.

"Get in," the local FBI guy tells us. "Get out of the heat. I've got the AC going full blast."

We climb into the car and Tolls quickly closes the doors behind us. We gratefully breathe in the cool air. Tolls gets in the driver's seat, slides the shift into drive, and we're on our way, out of the airport and onto a four-lane highway, through a small town with some fast-food restaurants, a filling station, a small motel, a Waffle Shop, and two tanning salons. I wonder why there are two. Then we're in the country.

"How far are we going?" Arora wants to know.

"Fifteen miles. Give or take."

"Is Mrs. Wilcox expecting us?" I ask.

"It's Miss Lovell now. She uses her maiden name. I talked to her within the hour and told her you were on the way."

I think about how I'm going to approach this Miss Lovell. I imagine Arora is doing the same.

"There's a guy there with her," Tolls informs us. "His name is Ron."

"Permanent guest?" I ask.

"Pretty much."

Twenty minutes later we turn off the interstate highway onto a two-lane road, go through a small town, past an Exxon filling station, a motel, a garage, and a Dollar Store and, just outside of town, we pull into a driveway. In front of us is a small ranch-style house with a breezeway in which is parked a Ford pickup. On the front lawn a child's blue tricycle lies on its side.

"You want me to come in with you?" Tolls asks.

"You stay here and keep cool," Arora answers. "I don't want to overwhelm Miss Lovell by having a crowd question her." She glances at me but adds nothing.

Arora and I climb out of the car and, once more, into the heat. We walk briskly, or as briskly as the heat allows, to the front door. Arora rings the bell.

After a long delay, a big man with a bushy beard, wearing an earring in his left ear and tattoos on his arms, opens the door. He does not look happy to see us.

Arora holds out her FBI ID. "Hello," she announces amiably. "My name is Arora Lovelace. I'm with the FBI."

The man doesn't bother to examine the ID. Instead his eyes turn to me.

"Who's this guy?"

"That is Detective Zorn. Of the Washington DC Police Department."

"What's he doing here? We're not in Washington, in case you haven't noticed."

"May we come in?" Arora asks. "We've come to see Anne Lovell. And it's very hot out here."

"Too bad." The man stands in the doorway, ostentatiously blocking our entry. "Annie's tired. She's said all she has to say."

"Our office called a little while—"

"Why can't you just leave her alone?"

"We're investigating a murder, sir," Arora announces firmly.

"And you think Annie's involved?"

"I don't know. All I know is, I'm dying out here."

Grudgingly, the big man moves aside and Arora and I step into the foyer and the man shuts the door behind us. It's a bit cooler.

From somewhere in the interior of the house I hear a woman's voice. "Ron, who's at the door?"

"Nobody," the big man answers.

"I heard the doorbell ring."

"Some cops, honey. I'll take care of it."

It's clear we have a problem. A problem we must fix. Somewhere in the house, there's the sound of a child laughing.

As Arora steps ahead, I hold out my hand to the bearded guy. "I'm Marko," I say. "Thanks for letting us meet with you folks."

The big man allows himself to have his hand shaken. Reluctantly. I use a firm, manly grasp. Then I put my left hand on his right arm, just above the elbow, where it's a friendly, man-to-man kind of thing.

"I'm Ron," he says, cautiously.

I'm halfway there, I think, and I lean into him, speaking in a low, sympathetic voice. "How she doing, Ron? How she holding up?"

I can see the confusion in his eyes. I'm supposed to be the enemy. But I seem to be almost human. Arora stands a few feet away, watching. She understands what I'm doing and keeps her distance.

"What do you people want?" Ron asks.

"We're here to ask about Sandra Wilcox," I say. "Can I ask you a favor? Can you stay with us while we talk to Miss Lovell? I'd feel a lot more comfortable if Miss Lovell had a friend present. Know what I mean? Maybe, if it gets too stressful—" I glance at Arora standing a few feet away but too far to hear what I'm saying. "Sometimes the Feds can get a little pushy. Particularly women agents. Know what I mean? Maybe you could jump in and cut us off if it's getting too much for Miss Lovell. It would help me and I'd really appreciate that."

He looks at me, a bit baffled, then nods. We're allies now. Against the universe of uppity women. And against Washington.

"Let's talk to Annie," he says and gestures for us to proceed down a hallway.

Arora goes first. I follow. Ron presses a card into my hand. I take a quick glance. It's a standard business card and it tells me the man is Ronald Bannister MD Pediatric Surgeon. I'd had him chalked up as a car thief or chicken farmer. I'm once again reminded not to judge people by their tattoos.

We enter a small, sunny living room furnished with a couch and coffee table and a couple of old armchairs. The place is neat and clean.

A large, shaggy dog lies sleepily on the floor in a pool of sunlight. He or she raises its head and regards us without interest. In one corner, a young boy, wearing a Captain America T-shirt, is playing a video game. I can hear the faint sound effects from across the room.

A woman of about thirty sits on a couch. Her face is worn and prematurely lined, her eyes red-rimmed, her posture tense, her hands clenched.

Arora goes directly to her. "I'm Arora Lovelace. I'm with the FBI. Thank you for seeing me."

The woman on the couch starts to get to her feet.

"Please don't get up, Miss Lovell."

The woman settles back onto the couch and tries to smile.

"Somebody called," the woman on the couch says. "Said to expect visitors from Washington."

"This is my associate, Mr. Zorn." Arora makes a gesture to include me. The woman studies me carefully. She is clearly trying to sort us out, to figure out who is who.

"Won't you both sit down," the woman says. Habits of a lifetime, habits of being a good host, overcome her suspicion of two strangers in her home. She turns to her companion: "Ron, why don't you get us some iced tea. That's a dear." She turns to me. "Iced tea?"

"I'd love some," I say.

"Some cookies? You, Miss Lovelace?"

"No cookies for me, thanks," Arora says. "But the iced tea sounds great."

"Bring four glasses, Ron. And bring a plate of cookies just in case." Ron disappears into what I assume is the kitchen.

"You folks come all the way from Washington?"

"That's right, ma'am."

"You come by bus?"

"Actually, we flew into Piedmont Airport," Arora explains. "We were lucky to catch a ride."

The woman looks a bit mystified as she tries to parse that. "And you come all this way to talk to me?" She turns to me, as if expecting an explanation from me.

"That's right, ma'am," Arora says. "We have some questions, if you don't mind."

"I didn't know the FBI had lady agents."

Arora's mouth tightens.

"There are many women in the FBI," I explain quickly.

Anne Lovell looks dubious. Or maybe just confused. "You're not an FBI agent?" she says, looking at me. "Are you?"

"I'm with the Washington DC police. Would you like to see my identification?"

She shakes her head. At this moment Ron comes back into the living room carrying a plastic tray decorated with a picture of Santa Claus drinking a Coke. Ron gives Anne a glass of iced tea, ice cubes clinking, then passes one to Arora, then one to me, and finally, takes one himself. He places a heaping plate of cookies on the coffee table and settles onto the couch next to Anne Lovell.

Anne Lovell looks directly at me. "Is Tony in trouble?"

I can see Arora flush slightly. She's upset, or at least peeved, that Anne Lovell acts as if she's not there or doesn't count somehow. I don't know Arora well enough to know whether she will keep her cool.

"It's all right, Annie." Ron squeezes her hand.

"What happened to Sandy?" Anne Lovell asks.

"She died," Arora says, gently.

Anne's face crumples with grief.

"Mrs. Wilcox . . ." I say.

"It's Miss Lovell now." The woman takes a deep gulp of air. "Please call me Anne." She seems to relax a bit.

"Here's the situation, Anne," I say. "We're investigating the death of Sandra Wilcox. We think she may have been murdered."

Anne puts her hand to her mouth but says nothing.

"Did you know Sandy?" Arora asks Anne Lovell.

"Sure."

"Did you know she had a peanut allergy?"

"God, she never let us forget." Anne laughs gently. "We didn't see her as often as we'd have liked. She was at our wedding. Tony and mine. She was in the Service then, you know."

"I heard," Arora says.

"She was away a lot so we couldn't get together as a family very often."

"I understand," I say.

"But then, when Tony took sick," Anne continues, "you know, Sandy came and stayed with us. She tried to help with Tony. Toward the end, it was more than I could deal with." She glances briefly at the child in the corner who is absorbed with a computer game. "Sandy was a lifesaver. Really."

"Have you talked to Sandy recently?" Arora asks.

"She was here over Memorial Day weekend," Anne tells us. "Just a few weeks ago."

"She was here? In Greensboro?"

"Sure. She took little Tony to the water park."

"Little Tony?" Arora says. She looks at the child. "He's Tony Wilcox's child?"

"That's right. Tony!" Anne calls out. "Come over here and say hello to our visitors."

The boy switches off his Xbox and crosses the room to stand next to his mother. He clutches his device closely to his chest.

"Tony, these people have come all the way from Washington to talk to Mommy." She ruffles the boy's hair affectionately.

Little Tony, who seems to be about five years old, does not seem impressed with that information. "Say hello," his mother says.

The boy says "hello" silently.

Anne gestures toward me. "This is Mr. . . . . I'm sorry, I forgot your name."

"My name is Marko," I say.

"And this is FBI Agent Arora," Anne goes on.

The boy's hazel eyes open wide.

"You're a real FBI agent?"

"That's right, Tony," Arora replies. "I'm a real FBI agent."

"Do you have a gun?"

"Tony!" Anne says loudly. "You know what I've told you about asking too many questions."

"That's all right, Miss Lovell," Arora says. "I don't mind." To Tony: "Sometimes I carry a gun. Not today."

"Have you ever shot anybody?"

"Tony!" Anne exclaims.

"No, Tony, I haven't." Tony looks disappointed and loses interest in Arora.

"I apologize," Anne says. "He's usually very well behaved."

"It's all right, Miss Lovell. People always want to ask me that question, but they're usually just too shy to ask."

"I wish one of you would tell us what this is all about," Ron says. "What happened to Sandy? What's Tony got himself into?"

Arora looks at me, nodding slightly to indicate I should answer his questions.

"Here's what we know," I say. "Sandra was found drowned."

"Could it have been an accident?" Ron asks.

"It doesn't look that way."

"Who did it? Who would hurt Sandy?"

Arora says, "We think Tony might have gotten involved with some people who are very dangerous."

"You mean the Brotherhood of the Aryan Dawn?"

"You know about the Brotherhood?"

"Tony told us about them," Anne says.

"Tony told you?" I didn't expect this. "He talked to you about the Brotherhood?"

"Yeah. When he visited us here in Greensboro."

"He wouldn't shut up about it," Ron intervenes. "It was crazy talk. The enemy is taking our country away from us, he kept saying. That kind of thing. Over and over. I think he was trying to sign us up."

"Tell us about Tony." Arora's voice is low, encouraging.

Anne glances at Ron as if for approval. "Tony and me, we grew up together. Went to the same high school in Colorado Springs and all. He was the sweetest kid. He loved to hunt and fish. He was a crack shot with a rifle. Well, I guess you know all about that. He was planning on going to college but then he got it into his head to join the Army. Went through basic training, then shipped out to Iraq."

She looks at me. Then at Arora. I can see the confusion in her eyes. She doesn't know which one of us to talk to. She takes a drink of iced tea and goes on.

"Tony trained as a sniper. His tour in Iraq went well. He returned Stateside and was given a lot of medals. He was a kind of war hero for what he'd done there. That's when we got married."

She stops and seems lost in thought. "We had the baby and I thought everything was fine. Then Tony was sent to Afghanistan. He had problems there and they sent him back. Tony was sick for a while. In a VA hospital. Our marriage wasn't working out and we separated. I moved to North Carolina to be near my family. Then, a month ago, Tony called. Out of the blue. He wanted to see his boy."

"Tony came here to North Carolina?" Arora asks.

"It was okay at first," Anne says. "Tony seemed happy. Then Sweet Daddy showed up."

"Tell us about Sweet Daddy," Arora says.

"One morning—this would have been three or four weeks ago—I was in the kitchen getting breakfast ready and I saw this man standing in front of our house. I went to the kitchen door and asked him what he wanted. 'Tell Tony Sweet Daddy has come.'"

"That's all he said?"

"That's all he said. The man frightened me. I can't explain why. He made my skin crawl. Ron was at the hospital, and I didn't want the man in the house. I got Tony and he came down. He and the man talked, standing out front. Then the man left. I asked Tony who the man was and all he'd tell me was he's 'The Leader.'"

"Can you describe the man who came for Tony?" Arora asks.

"He was around sixty, I'd say. Not tall. His hair was white. Curly. And he wore a white suit. And a bow tie. That's all I can remember. Sorry."

"That's all right."

"I was very upset," she goes on. "There was something about the man that disturbed me. The next day the man returned and waited outside our house and Tony went off with him. They spent the day together. The same thing the next day. I could see Tony changing. He became agitated. Angry over little things.

"I called Sandy. Thought she should know about Tony's visitor. Understand, she and Tony were very close." Anne dabs at her eyes with a paper tissue. "They lost their parents when they were young. Basically, Tony raised Sandy and they looked after one another. Until Tony left for military service they were inseparable. On the day he left for his last oversees assignment, he said to me, 'If anything happens to me, please take care of Polly and little Tony.'"

"Who is Polly?" I ask.

"Polly was his name for Sandy. It's a baby name. When she was very little, he called her Pollywog. All their life he called her Pollywog or Polly for short. Until little Tony came along, Sandy was the most important thing in Tony's life. And he was the most important thing in hers."

Anne's shoulders shake with sobs while Ron holds her hand. We sit in silence until Anne recovers.

"I told Sandy about Sweet Daddy and how Tony seemed to be changing. She said she'd come to North Carolina and talk to Tony. She drove from Washington that night and she and Tony spent hours talking. Actually—arguing."

"About what?"

"About the Brotherhood. About Sweet Daddy. They sat here in the living room. I remember Sandy saying Sweet Daddy was dangerous. He was using Tony. Sweet Daddy was evil. Sandy pleaded with Tony to have nothing to do with him. 'For the love of God, get rid of this man or he'll destroy you, he'll destroy us all.'

"The next day Sweet Daddy arrived in the morning, as usual, and waited for Tony out front. It was raining and Sandy went out and confronted the man. They both stood in the rain."

"Do you know what they said?" I ask.

"I couldn't hear most of it. Not at first. At the end I could make out some. By that time, they were yelling at one another."

"Can you remember any of their words?"

"Sandy told the man to leave Tony alone. Sweet Daddy told Sandy she should not turn Tony away from his fate—from his destiny. He said he was Tony's savior and she would regret interfering until her dying day."

Arora leans forward. "He said '*dying day*'?"

"Those were his exact words. 'Anybody who interferes will be crushed,' the man said. 'Tony is mine,' he yelled. 'Stay out of my way, bitch, or I'll burn you.'

"At that, Sandy charged at Sweet Daddy, and he stepped back and hid in his car, locking the doors. He was intimidated by her, I could see, by her anger. By her strength. He lowered the car window a crack and called to Sandy, 'You're my enemy.'

"Sandy went back to Washington later that day. She was scheduled to travel somewhere with the President and First Lady. Two days after she left, Sweet Daddy showed up again. This time he didn't come near the house. He stayed in his car. Tony went to meet him and they spent the day together."

"That's when the business with the gun started," Ron interjected.

"What gun?"

"Tony left early one morning," Anne explains. "Tony said he and Sweet Daddy were going over to Clinton for the gun show."

"That's two hours' drive," Ron explains. "But Tony insisted he had to go to Clinton to find the kind of gun he needed. One that had been specially adapted."

"That evening Tony came back with his new gun." Anne is almost crying now. "I don't allow guns in the house. You know—because of the boy. But Tony insisted he had to keep it with him at all times. He kind of went crazy. Started yelling and screaming at me. Said I was plotting against him, was spying on him and reporting him to the CIA. He said I would perish on Doomsday. Along with all his enemies. Then the range shooting began."

"Tell us about the range shooting."

"Tony'd leave the home early in the morning," Ron says. "Take his rifle and go to a nearby shooting range. He'd practice shooting for hours."

"What was he practicing for?" Arora asks.

"I asked him," Ron said. "'Doomsday,' he told us. 'What's Doomsday?' I asked. 'Just *Doomsday*. When the enemy shall perish.'"

"Understand, I like Tony. He's a good kid. He's had some tough times but he has a good heart. When he first came here, we got along great. Even went out a few times for beers. But later . . . later he changed. He became angry very quick. That was after Sweet Daddy appeared. Tony said it was the enemy who made him that way."

"Did he say who the *enemy* was?"

"Tony was crazy by that time. There was no enemy. Except in his head."

"You said he used a specially adapted rifle," I say.

"That's right. A left-handed rifle. Tony was left-handed, you know. The day came when Tony totally lost it. Tony began ranting. Standing right here in the living room. He was holding his rifle in its carrying case then took the rifle out of its case. I was scared to death. He'd never done that in the house before. He was normally very careful with weapons. I took little Tony into the bedroom and locked the door. The next day Tony was gone. Sweet Daddy picked him up first thing in the morning, and that's the last I ever saw or heard from Tony."

"Do you know where they went?" Arora asks.

"He just said they were going to Washington, DC."

"Is Tony in trouble?" Ron asks.

"Tony's in big trouble," I answer.

*   *   *

"Did you guys learn anything useful?" FBI Agent Martin Tolls asks as he drives us back to the airport.

"Not much," Arora answers. "A few details is all. Doesn't move us forward in solving Sandra Wilcox's murder."

"Your trip was a waste of time, then?"

"Not a complete waste," I say. "We learned one very important thing."

Arora looks puzzled.

"Tony Wilcox is left-handed."

CHAPTER TWENTY

"I THINK I know a way you can help," I say to Kenneth

Part of my brain is telling me: Marko—stop this! Don't do it! It's that part of my brain I usually pay no attention to.

Kenneth's at his desk when I appear clutching my morning coffee, still limping slightly from the bruise to my leg. Kenneth is reading what appears to be a manual on the identification of tire treads.

"How can I help?" Kenneth asks with bubbly excitement.

"We're looking for a left-handed sniper." I know I'm making a mistake the minute the words are out of my mouth.

* * *

Arora and I had left Greensboro on the FBI jet on time and got back to Andrews Air Base in early evening. We didn't talk much on the trip back. She finds a seat in the back of the plane and is on her cell phone. When done talking, she works on her laptop computer, I suppose writing up a detailed report of our meeting. She's still angry with me. When we arrive at Andrews, I offer to drive Arora home, but she declines, saying she'll catch a ride into the city with one of the special agents at the FBI liaison office at the base.

*   *   *

"Good morning, sir," Kenneth says enthusiastically when I sit at my desk. "What's this about a left-handed sniper? How does that help with the case?"

The Office of Human Resources once required me to attend an all-day team-building exercise that stressed the importance of cultivating a positive atmosphere in the office. "A happy workplace is a productive workplace," I was instructed. Is it because I feel bad about how I treated Kenneth when we interviewed Sandra Wilcox's roommate? I try to create a sense of good spirits even though I'm never in good spirits until much later in the morning.

"Our murder victim, Sandra Wilcox," I tell Kenneth, "has a brother. His name is Tony Wilcox and he was a skilled sniper in the U.S. Army before being medically discharged. This Tony was married at one time. Yesterday I went to Greensboro, North Carolina, and met with Tony Wilcox's ex-wife. She told me her brother was left-handed. Do you feel ready to take on an assignment, Kenneth?" Part of my brain is screaming at me: don't do this!

"Absolutely, sir."

"It will be a kind of undercover assignment," I say. "And there might be some risk. You think you're ready to handle this?"

"Sure I am."

"I believe Tony Wilcox may be in the Washington area," I say. "Tony will try to practice shooting every day as if he's in training. Which, I suppose, he is."

"How do we find him?"

"He can't go around shooting a high-powered rifle in the city. Can't even do it in the country. He might shoot a cow or something."

"So he has to go to a firing range."

"That's exactly right. I want you to draw up a list of firing ranges and gun clubs in the area and contact them. Snoop around a little. Keep your eyes open for a highly skilled, left-handed sniper."

"Absolutely." Kenneth makes a note on a piece of paper. "A left-handed sniper."

"If you should find someone fitting that description, don't approach him. Don't go near him. Don't under any circumstances tip your hand you're on to him."

"Got it," Kenneth says eagerly.

"This Tony is a trained killer. He knows how to use weapons and he's mixed up with a very dangerous crowd. This group, maybe even Tony himself, may have killed Sandra Wilcox. If you observe anybody who looks suspicious, you are to contact me immediately. Under no circumstances approach Tony on your own. Is that clear?"

"Very clear, sir."

Kenneth goes to his desk and starts a computer search of local shooting ranges. I watch him at his desk from across the squad room. What could go wrong? I ask myself. Before I have time to think through what I've done, my phone rings. "Detective Zorn?" a voice demands.

"That's me."

"I'm Myron Clark." There is a pause. I can tell the man at the other end expects me to know who he is. "Myron Clark," he goes on, his voice irritated. "Special Assistant to the President."

"Oh, yes, Mr. Clark." The name rings a bell. I'm not much interested in politics but even I have heard of Myron Clark. He's quoted frequently in the New York Times and shows up on CNN. "Yes, Mr. Clark, what can I do for you?"

"We must talk."

"About what?" I ask, innocently. I know perfectly well where this is going.

"We need to talk about Sandra Wilcox."

"That could be difficult. This is an ongoing police investigation."

"Come to my office. Immediately."

"I suppose I can manage that. Where is your office?"

"The White House." Left unspoken was: *You idiot. Where else would my office be?*

"Okay," I say. "Can we set a time?"

"Now."

"You mean *now*?"

"I mean now. Come to the checkpoint on 15th street. Someone from the White House staff will meet you there. Be here in fifteen minutes."

I'm about to leave when Kenneth hurries over to my desk. "I've found something, sir." He's holding a map of Virginia in one hand. "There's a range near Springfield. I'm going to check it out."

I'm distracted by the White House phone call so I don't do what I know I should do. I should say no. I should say wait until I get back. Instead, I murmur, "Great, Kenneth."

I decide against using a police cruiser or my Jag. Parking is a bitch near the White House so I grab a cab and go to the 15th Street entrance only to find a traffic jam at the checkpoint. Half a dozen limousines and SUVs are stacked up at the entrance that is swarming with uniformed Secret Service agents—many more than normal.

I show my police ID and I'm moved through quickly when I give the name of the man I'm here to see. I'm processed through a security check where I have to deposit my police badge, my cell phone, and my watch and silver lighter into a little plastic box. I don't have to take my shoes off.

At the end of the security belt an attractive woman with platinum blonde hair is waiting for me. She's the same woman I saw at the book signing attending the First Lady. She observes me with amusement as I put my police badge and ID into my jacket pocket, slip my watch on my wrist, and retrieve my silver lighter from the plastic bin.

"Nice lighter," she says.

"I like nice things."

"Detective Zorn." She holds out her hand and we shake. Her nails are a bright scarlet and her grip is firm. "My name's Shaw. I'll take you to Mr. Clark's office. Please follow me. Sorry about the delay at the checkpoint." We walk along a path in front of the White House. Or is it the back? I can never remember which is which. We pass half a dozen Secret Service agents in black battle dress uniforms, armed with P10 submachine guns. They watch us carefully as we pass.

"Heavy security today," I say.

"We have a situation. Your first time in the White House?"

"I've been here a few times. I'm usually let in through the service entrance."

Miss Shaw leads me down a dozen steps and we approach one of the entrances to the West Wing. "I've seen you before." Miss Shaw studies my face carefully. "At the bookstore. When the First Lady signed copies of her new book. You bought one."

"You're very observant."

"I wouldn't take you for someone with a deep interest in prison reform."

"You'd be surprised what interests me," I tell her.

"This way to the service entrance," Miss Shaw says as she leads me to a side door. Two uniformed Secret Service guards meet us just inside the door and examine my credentials and I'm taken through metal detectors. Once again, I place my credentials, my watch and lighter, as well as my cell phone, into a plastic box.

The guards keep my cell phone.

"You'll get your phone back when you leave," Miss Shaw informs me. "It's the camera. They don't like cameras."

Miss Shaw is not required to go through security procedures. I notice a man standing in a side corridor, watching us. He's the same man I saw at the bookstore observing me. Miss Shaw leads me down a nondescript hallway and we stop outside a door. "Have you met Mr. Clark before?"

"I've never had that pleasure," I reply cautiously, sensing there's more to her question than a mere pleasantry.

"Then you're in for a treat." With that, Miss Shaw opens the door and steps inside. "Mr. Clark, your visitor is here."

She gestures for me to enter the office and shuts the door behind me. I'm in a small, well-appointed office with modern art on the walls, a Persian carpet on the floor, a teak desk, well-oiled, and a conference table, surrounded by six upholstered chairs.

Standing in the middle of the room is a short, compact man, not much over thirty. His hair is a dirty blond, cut in a pageboy style, with a fringe bang reaching almost to his eyebrows. He wears a Tattersall waistcoat, a bow tie, and no jacket. I'd seen Myron Clark on TV and realize once again how misleading TV can be. His face is pasty; not like he looks on TV. Does he use makeup? I wonder.

He's on the phone as I enter and he turns sharply and fixes me with a glare, raising his left hand, palm toward me, a gesture indicating I'm to stop where I am, well away, so I can't hear his phone conversation. I stand in the middle of the room while the man talks urgently to someone, his back toward me, then he slams the phone down and turns to face me.

"You're Zorn." It's not a question. It's an accusation. "No need to sit down. You won't be here long enough to sit."

He strides across the room until he's only a few paces from me. I have to look down at him. "Knock it off," he says, loudly.

"Knock off what?"

"Don't play dumb with me! The Sandra Wilcox investigation."

"You want me to stop my investigation of the murder of Sandra Wilcox?"

"I don't *want* you to! I'm *telling* you to."

"Why would I do that?"

"Leave the investigation to the Secret Service."

"No."

"Are you not hearing me? This is not a request. This is an order!"

"I don't take orders from you."

"Do you know who I am?"

"No. Who are you?"

Clark's pasty face reddens. "Are you trying to be a jackass, Detective?"

"I can't help it. It just comes naturally."

"Are you actually trying to make me mad?"

"Why do you care whether the DC police investigates a murder?"

"I ask the questions here. Not you."

"Then you're wasting my time."

"You've been snooping around where you shouldn't. Talking to the wrong people. Even harassing Sandra Wilcox's sister-in-law. Stop it!"

"I'll talk to anybody I like. Can I go now?"

"You'll go when I tell you to go! Your investigation is over. Drop it! You've irritated a lot of people—important, powerful people."

"And a lot of people have irritated me."

"Do you understand in what serious shit you are?" Clark demands.

"I'm beginning to get a sense of that."

"Do you realize I can have you broken so you spend the rest of your pathetic career running the police impoundment lot?"

"I'm not dropping the Wilcox case. Now if you'll excuse me, I have a murder to investigate."

I walk briskly to the door.

"I didn't tell you to go."

"I don't need your permission. I don't give a rat's ass who you think you are. Don't waste my time again."

I open the door and step out of the office, closing the door behind me. Loudly. I feel pleased with the effect of my exit.

Miss Shaw is waiting to escort me to the gate. "How did it go?"

Behind us I hear the man swearing and screaming obscenities. There is a loud crash. I think Myron Clark broke something.

"Memorable."

"This is one of Myron's better days. You should have seen him yesterday when he was in a bad mood."

We go to the security checkpoint where I retrieve my phone.

"It was a pleasure to meet you, Detective Zorn." She smiles an enigmatic smile. "Until next time."

Watching us from twenty feet away is a heavyset man standing among the trees. Arms crossed over his chest, he leans against a black Secret Service SUV. He looks vaguely familiar but his face is in shadow. All I can really make out is a glittery gold watchband on his left wrist.

CHAPTER TWENTY-ONE

I FEEL MY heart race when I see the messages waiting for me that came in to my cell phone while I was with Myron Clark: six calls from Kenneth that went immediately to voice mail. I have a bad feeling about this. There is also one text message from someone who does not wish to identify himself.

"I've got something, sir." Kenneth's voice is full of excitement, almost breathless, but low, as if he's making an effort not to be overheard. "Please call." "I think I've found him, sir. Call me." "I need to talk to you. It's kind of urgent." "Call me as soon as you get this message." And finally: "I'm at a shooting range near Springfield, Virginia. Geoff's Shooting Range and Gun Club. The man we're looking for—he's here right now. Please call me."

I call Kenneth's number, but there is no answer. There could be many reasons he doesn't answer my call, I tell myself. Perfectly reasonable reasons. I do not convince myself.

The text message reads: "Meet me in McPherson Square at the NE corner bench at eleven sharp." It's ten to eleven. Ten minutes to go five blocks. There are no cabs in sight so I go on foot—hard to do through Washington traffic without being hit by a bus or bicyclist. I dodge and weave through traffic, annoying several drivers, and arrive at McPherson Square, out of breath, with about a minute and a half to spare. I limp through the park until I spot my target sitting on a bench studying his cell phone.

Howard Walsh, my senior contact at the Department of Homeland Security, looks up. He's African American, in his sixties, tall, good-looking, wearing a tailored suit. His hair is short and gray at the temples, his trim mustache is white. There is no smile. No "glad to see you" expression on his face. Why should there be?

"Let's walk together," Walsh says. "I don't want to be seen sitting next to you."

I'm still breathing hard from my run and my leg hurts. We walk side by side along one of the park paths.

"I don't know what you've gotten yourself into this time," Walsh says, "but I want no part of it. I strongly recommend you stop whatever it is you're doing."

I breathe deeply to catch my breath. "Have you found out why I'm being shut down?"

"I've made some discreet calls and talked to some people. Some very important people. They were not happy to talk to me when I told them it was in connection with Sandra Wilcox. They wouldn't tell me why you're being closed down."

"Okay, if not *why*, then *who* is trying to shut me down?"

"You don't want to know."

"Yes, I do."

"I've been warned to stay out of it. And I'm giving you the same advice."

"Thank you for the advice. Now tell me, where is this coming from?"

Howard Walsh turns toward me. "This makes us even. I don't owe you anything. I don't want you to ask for any more favors. We're even."

"Okay. Deal. Who's behind this?"

"Don't say I didn't warn you, Zorn. It's coming from the White House."

"Who in the White House?"

"I don't know. And I'm not asking. I'm washing my hands of this whole business. I want nothing more to do with it. This goes way over my pay level. Or yours. Understand?"

Howard Walsh walks off briskly, leaving me in the middle of the park, alone.

I call Kenneth again. No answer.

When I return to police headquarters someone must have told Frank I'd returned because he's suddenly standing at my desk, looming over me. "Marko! What the fuck's going on?"

"I'm investigating a murder."

"I know that! What are you doing to piss off the entire federal government?"

"Just asking questions . . ."

"The Department of the Interior. The National Park Service. I can live with that. But the Secret Service? What did the Secret Service ever do to you? And now I'm getting calls from some yo-yo in the White House. And the mayor's getting calls. We can't have that! We can't have that. What the fuck am I supposed to tell the mayor?"

"Tell him the mystery of the Sandra Wilcox murder will be revealed soon."

Without a further word Frank Townsend walks quickly away. I decide not to tell Frank about Kenneth just yet. No need to get Frank worked up until I have more information.

I call Kenneth again. Again, no answer. I send him three increasingly urgent text messages. A low-level sense of dread is gripping me. I call the Virginia State Police to find out if there have been any car accidents reported in the Springfield area. There are none.

I entertain myself for a while by fantasizing how I'll wring Kenneth's neck when he waltzes in at the end of the day. But my euphoria doesn't last long.

I call Malcolm Wu and ask him to come as soon as possible. He shows up in three minutes. "What is it now, Marko? What felony do you want me to commit?"

"I've lost my partner."

"Your police partner?"

"That's the only partner I have. I've been trying to reach him on his cell phone, but he's not answering."

"Probably just turned it off. Or the battery is run down."

"Maybe. Can you find out where his phone is?"

"Sure. Do you have the access code for his phone?"

"Access code?"

"Guess not. I'll have to hack it. Give me his cell number."

Malcolm sits at Kenneth's desk and I watch him for a while, hunched over the keyboard of the desktop computer, then decide I could better use my time trying to track Kenneth down by more conventional methods. It's then I realize I know nothing about Kenneth's private life because I've never bothered to ask him. I don't know who his friends are. Who he talks to. I'm beginning to feel guilty about neglecting him.

He has parents in New Jersey somewhere and their names and numbers are in his personnel file. I consider for a moment calling them but reject that idea. A call from the DC police department asking where their son is would unleash a frenzy of anxiety. That call might have to be made but only as a last resort.

Malcolm sits at my desk. "Any luck?" I ask.

"I've located your partner's cell phone. And luck had nothing to do with it. It's on the side of a road in Northern Virginia—looks like about thirty feet from the main highway. I can show you on the screen."

Malcolm types something on my keyboard and a map appears on my computer screen.

"How did you do that?"

"You wouldn't understand."

"You're probably right." I study the screen and examine a map showing roads in the Northern Virginia area and a blinking cursor off to one side. "It looks like he threw the phone away. Or someone did." I'm feeling sick.

"I hope you find your partner," Malcolm Wu says as he hurries back to his den.

Kenneth's official photograph is in his personnel file. He looks at me, standing straight, shoulders back. Trying to look serious. Looking very young. I slip the photo into my pocket.

I call Arora Lovelace on her private cell phone number. "I've lost Kenneth," I say when she gets on the line.

"You lost who?"

"Kenneth Blake. My partner. I asked him to check out some local shooting clubs and firing ranges to see if maybe our shooter, Tony, might show up to get in some rifle practice."

There was silence on the phone. "You sent this kid to do that?"

"I didn't think there was a real chance he'd actually find anything."

"And now you think what?"

"Kenneth left a voice mail saying he saw the shooter at a range somewhere near Springfield."

"My God! You think he might have been made?"

"I don't know what to think. I told Kenneth on no account to approach or speak to anyone who fits Tony's description. I told him to stay away and let me make contact. He tried to call me but my phone had been temporarily impounded by the Secret Service so I missed his calls."

"And now?"

"Kenneth is enthusiastic. When he couldn't reach me, he may have tried to make an approach, despite what I told him."

"Why would he do that? When you instructed him specifically not to."

"It's complicated."

"You better tell me."

"When he and I were interviewing Sandra Wilcox's roommate, I criticized him for messing up the interrogation. I may have been a bit harsh. He may have been trying to prove himself to me."

"Can the Bureau help?"

"No, but you can. I'm going to go to the shooting range but I need a second pair of eyes. I can't ask one of my fellow officers. The word would get back to my boss, and he'd go ape shit. Can you go with me and help me look around?"

"Of course."

"You can pretend to be a gun nut. You'll be there to try out a new weapon. Are you familiar with a Dragunov?"

"What's that?"

"Then I suggest you unbutton the top button of your blouse."

"It's going to be that kind of operation?"

"I want you to gain the confidence of the shooters at the club. Whatever you have to do to make friends. Get them to trust you. To talk to you."

"I'll unbutton two buttons."

"Good girl. Go out Route 66. There's a parking area just west of the 495 intersection. Meet me there in one hour."

CHAPTER TWENTY-TWO

Arora is waiting for me in a beat-up Datsun when I pull my Jag into the pullover in the shade of some trees.

"What's the drill?" Arora asks when we meet between our two cars.

"We're going to a place called Geoff's Shooting Range and Gun Club. It's up the highway about a mile. You go ahead and register. Pay your fee and establish yourself as an avid shooter. I'll follow in a few minutes. I don't want us to be seen together."

"I got it."

"Maybe you could be a helpless girl who needs advice about her new gun."

"I don't do helpless."

"Okay. Meet some local enthusiasts. Tell them you want to get in some practice. See if anybody's seen a left-handed sniper. Then shoot the shit out of some targets. Have you fired sniper rifles?"

"I qualified on an M 21 and SR 25."

I open the trunk of the Jag and remove a leather rifle carrying case. We stand in the shade of the trees where we can't be easily seen by passing motorists and I open the case and hand her the weapon.

"I don't think I've seen a gun like this."

"It's a Dragunov SVD."

"A Russian sniper rifle? It's a little exotic for a Virginia shooting club. Isn't this going to draw a lot of attention?"

"That's the point. The gun guys will be curious. Most of them have probably never seen one. Certainly, never fired one. They'll swarm around you to get a look."

"You talking about my tits or your rifle?"

"Whichever works."

"How come you happen to have a Russian sniper rifle?"

"Never mind."

We return the Dragunov to its case and put it and three boxes of 7.62 ammunition into the back seat of Arora's car.

"I have something for you." She retrieves a manila envelope from the passenger seat of her Datsun and removes a glossy photograph. "This is a picture of Tony Wilcox," she says, passes me the photo. "Courtesy of the Department of the Army."

"You just got this? Just this one picture?" I ask.

"The Army is not being very cooperative."

The young man is maybe twenty, in military fatigues. Hair cut close to the scalp. He wears no unit insignia.

"This is an old photo," Arora tells me. "The Army claims they have nothing more recent."

"The Army is lying."

"Of course, they're lying. They're shutting me down."

I head for my Jag. "Let's go find my partner."

The parking lot of Geoff's Shooting Range and Gun Club is almost full when I arrive a few minutes later, Arora having gone ahead. I expected to find pickup trucks and RVs but mostly there are late-model luxury cars, including Mercedes and BMWs.

The reception area is clean and well maintained. Near the door is a bulletin board covered with scraps of paper and business cards offering a variety of services and activities in the area. To one side there is a long counter above which hangs a sign listing prices and hours: outdoor pistol, outdoor rifle, trap, skeet, etc. I hear the pop, pop, pop from the firing range beyond.

On the range a dozen men and a couple of women are shooting rifles and shotguns. Several are using small arms. In the center of the range I see Arora, lying prone, sighting the Dragunov through a scope. Three heavyset men kneel next to her, apparently giving her friendly advice on how to handle the weapon. A fourth man stands to one side, spotting Arora's targets through field glasses.

"Can I help you?" a baritone voice with a trace of a pleasant southern drawl asks.

"I'm looking for Geoff."

"Geoff retired a few years back. I'm the manager here. The name's Vernon."

"Hello, Vernon." I show him my DC police shield. "My name's Marko Zorn."

Vernon's lips tighten when he sees my police ID and his eyes narrow with suspicion. "My papers are in order," he announces.

"No sweat, Vernon. I'm not interested in you. Or your place of business."

He shifts his weight from one leg to the other, allowing himself to relax a bit.

"I'm looking for a friend of mine."

"You're free to look around."

"Young guy. Maybe around five foot eleven. Sandy hair." I show the man Kenneth's photograph. "Name of Kenneth Blake."

"You say he's a friend of yours?" Vernon studies the picture. I can tell he recognizes the face.

"That's right. He's my partner."

"You ATF?"

"DC Metropolitan Police."

Vernon nods. "You hurt your leg, friend?" he asks. He glances at my left leg. I must have been limping when I came into the office.

"It's nothing. Got busted up while I was playing touch football with some buddies."

"You gotta watch that kind of thing. Get to our age and the body don't heal up like it did when we were young. You say you're looking for your friend?"

"That's right. He doesn't answer his phone."

Vernon winces. Something I've said has struck a nerve, but I don't know what.

Vernon studies Kenneth's photo carefully. "He's a cop. Right?"

"Did he say that?"

"No. But he's a cop."

"So he was here?"

"Sure. A couple of hours ago. Snooping around."

"How was he snooping around?"

"You know. Asking questions."

"What kind of questions was he asking?"

Vernon is getting worried. "I don't know what questions."

"Did he ask you questions?"

"Maybe."

"What did he ask you?"

"About who comes here? What our membership is? He said he wanted to join a shooting club, but that was bullshit. We don't have terrorists here."

"Did my friend use the word 'terrorist'?"

"No. But might as well have."

Vernon is silent for a while. I think maybe he's going to shut me down. "I got nothing against cops, understand," he says at last. "My brother-in-law's a police sergeant in Alexandria. About a week ago,"

Vernon goes on, "two guys come here. One of them a young guy. Nervous type."

"They do any shooting?"

"The young guy did. And he was amazing. A professional, I could tell."

"What do you mean by *professional*?"

"Ex-military. SEALs maybe. Maybe Special Forces. You can tell. It's the way they handle their weapon. The way they prepare for the shooting. Very methodical and steady. They never hurry. They follow a set routine. Most of the guys here, hell they're paying by the hour. They want to get as many rounds off as they can. Most of the guys who come here, they're basically plinkers. Not this kid. He was a power shooter. Looks like he's in training for competition. Then, when he's ready, he blows away his targets."

"Was this shooter left-handed?"

"How'd you know?"

"How often did this guy come here?"

"Maybe six, seven times. Including this morning. There was another guy with him. An older fella."

"Did you get their names?" I ask.

"They signed the register. I never really talked to them. They weren't friendly types. In fact, none of our regulars spoke with them. These guys didn't mix. That's why I noticed them. They just come here and shoot. And go."

"I'd like to see the register."

"Follow me." Vernon leads me to the front counter, opens a heavy volume and flips through the pages, then swings the book around so I can read the entries. He points to one handwritten entry. "Annie Oakley," it reads.

"That's when they first came," he tells me. "Their first day here. They came again two days later. Then missed a couple of days. Then pretty regular after that." He flips through the pages, pointing out each relevant entry. I note the times and dates.

"I wouldn't normally do this. Show you the register and all. But . . ."

"But what?"

"There was something funny about these two guys. Usually when someone comes here when they're not shooting, they stand around and talk. You know—gun talk. About their weapons. About special weapons they'd seen for sale. New ammunition. Our regulars love to talk guns. It's one of the reasons they come here, to meet people like themselves, to gossip. You know."

"And these two men didn't gossip?"

"Not even to each other. It was strictly business from the moment they walked in the door."

I take the photo of Tony Wilcox from my pocket. "This the shooter?" I ask.

Vernon studies the photo closely. "This is an old photo."

"An old photo."

Vernon passes the picture back to me. "That's the shooter."

My heart is racing. The hunt is on and I've gotten the first real sight of my quarry. "Can you describe the man the shooter was with?" I ask.

"I'd say around fifty."

"White hair?"

"That's right. Curly white hair. Wears a bow tie. He had a swastika tattooed on his left arm. Just above the wrist."

"You see many tattoos like that?"

"Sometimes. We don't encourage that sort here. People like that aren't welcome here."

"What kind of weapon did the shooter use?"

"Military issue M-14. Modified for a lefty."

"Thanks, friend," I say. "I'll look around."

Arora is about halfway down the line, and I stand behind her for a few minutes, watching her shoot, until she's emptied her clip.

"What kind of weapon's that you're using, lady?" I demand.

Arora switches the safety on and places the rifle by her side onto the mat. She rolls over and studies me. The men who surround her stare at me, annoyed at being interrupted.

"It's a Dragunov."

"Why are you shooting a piece of communist shit?"

Arora looks offended. Or pretends to look offended. "It's not a piece of shit, sir. It's a precision sniper rifle."

The men around her nod their heads in vigorous agreement. I look up and down the range. "I understand there was a serious shooter here earlier today."

"We're all serious," one of the men tells me.

Arora gets to her feet. "My friends tell me there was a guy here," she says. "What, just an hour ago, you say?—this guy was shooting at a professional level. He was a lefty. That right, Marv?"

A skinny man with a thick beard answers, "That's right. Fired fifty rounds. All shots clustered. Every time. Dead center."

"What range?" I feel the adrenaline surge through my arteries.

There is a confused exchange among the men.

"Cal," Arora murmurs. "You were spotting the targets. You know the range?"

A young man in need of a haircut says, "There was another guy spotting..."

"Can you give me a range estimate?"

Call scratches his nose. "I'd say 1,000 meters. Easy. Maybe 1,200."

"That's some shooting."

"Didn't I tell you?" Arora says, packing the Dragunov in its carrying case.

I take the picture of Tony Wilcox from my pocket and show it to the men. "This the guy who did the shooting?"

They pass the picture one to another. Several nod. "That's him."

"What's this about?" one of them asks. "How come you have a picture?"

"I'm a freelance photographer. I'm planning a photo shoot of skilled snipers."

"You gonna include this guy we're telling you about?"

"If I can find him. If I can't, I might settle for some cute girl shooting at something. Like this pretty lady here," I say, staring hard at Arora.

She scowls at me.

I take out the photograph of Kenneth. "Have any of you guys seen this man?" I ask.

They glance at the photo. Most shake their heads.

"He a shooter, too?"

"An associate."

"Never saw him," another murmurs. "Me neither," a heavyset man says, loudly.

"I saw him," the man called Cal says. "He was with his friend."

"His friend?" I ask. "What friend?"

Arora studies the man carefully. The others turn their attention to him.

"You know. His friend. The sniper."

"You're saying my friend was friends with the shooter?"

"Sure."

"What makes you say that?"

"When the shooter left, your friend went with him."

I'm finding it hard to breathe. "They walked out together? Is that what you're saying?"

"I saw them get into a car together. Your friend and the shooter."

I nod to Arora and she moves away, waving to her new friends.

"Anybody else with them?"

"I guess. There was the guy he was with. And there were a couple of other guys waiting for them in the car."

"What kind of car?"

"Sorry. Didn't notice."

Arora is waiting for me in her Datsun. "My partner, Kenneth, left the range with the shooter. We have to assume it was not voluntary."

"That means we don't have much time," Arora says.

She gets out of her car, removes the Dragunov in its case from the back seat, and silently passes it to me. I store it in the trunk of the Jag.

"That means we have no time."

CHAPTER TWENTY-THREE

"You did what?!!" Frank Townsend bellows, jumping to his feet, his fists pile-driving onto the top of his desk. "You did fucking what?!!"

"I've lost Kenneth."

"How the hell did you manage that?"

"I'm investigating the murder of a Secret Service agent named Sandra Wilcox. Her murder may be connected to a domestic terrorist group and this group recruited a sniper—former Delta Force. This group has come to Washington to start the revolution."

"How?"

"By assassinating the President."

"Oh, shit! What have you gotten us into?"

"I believe the would-be assassin's name is Tony Wilcox."

"Wilcox? Like the victim in the Reflecting Pool?"

"Her brother. I figure Tony Wilcox would need some place to practice shooting a high-powered rifle."

"Why would he need to practice?"

"Sniping is like any other skill. If you don't practice every day you lose your edge. Tony has come to Washington to fire one shot. One shot to change his life. One shot to change the world. He plans to kill the President."

"Where does Kenneth fit in?"

"I sent him to check out local shooting ranges."

Frank's face is ashen. "On his own?"

"It looks like Kenneth found Tony Wilcox," I explain lamely. "Then Kenneth left the gun club with the shooter."

"You mean he's with the presidential assassin now?"

"That's the way it looks."

"How could you let that happen?"

"I didn't think Kenneth would find anything." That sounds pathetic, even to me.

"You should have kept an eye on the boy. Why the hell do you think I assigned Kenneth to you? To protect him. Not send an inexperienced, unseasoned officer off on some lunatic investigation involving people who plan to assassinate the President of the United States. You were supposed to keep him out of trouble. That was your job, Marko."

"I screwed up. Maybe he'll turn up. Maybe he'll be okay."

"He damn well better be. Or it's your ass."

"I think I know somebody who can help."

*   *   *

"I'm here to see Sister Grace," I tell the tall African American in dreadlocks standing in front of the liquor store.

"You're in the wrong place, mister. Ain't nobody by that name live 'round here."

"That's a shame. She's a good friend of mine."

"I don't think you got any friends in this neighborhood."

The door to the liquor store opens, and the kid with the hoodie comes out and grins at me. "What you doin' here, Mr. Detective?"

"I'm here to see Sister Grace."

"She send for you?"

"I'm here on my own account."

"Sister Grace don' normally talk to people she don' send for."

"Just tell her I'm here. Tell her we need to talk."

"What's in it for me?"

"Twenty bucks. Fifty if you get me inside in five minutes."

The kid looks at me quizzically, then pivots and disappears into the liquor store. Less than five minutes later the kid is back and gestures for me to follow. He leads me into the store and the same old white-haired man smiles at me. Then I'm in the back alley. This time there are at least ten armed guards patrolling the area. I follow the boy into the former show room and Cloud steps directly in front of me. Once again, he pats me down, and finds nothing but my cell phone. Four men stand immediately behind Cloud. I don't see Lamont anywhere.

"Know what I think?" Cloud mutters. "I think you overstayin' your welcome."

The kid opens the door from Sister Grace's parlor and gestures for me to enter. He holds out a hand and I give him a twenty.

"You said fifty." I press two more twenties into the kid's hand.

Sister Grace is seated on the same divan she'd been on last time. The obese cat lies sleeping in her lap. Sister Grace gestures for the boy to leave. "Get out! You hear!"

She points with her cigarette toward the armchair opposite the divan and I sit, facing her. She strokes the obese cat's fur. Is it my imagination or does Sister Grace look worried?

Sister Grace stabs out her Marlboro. "I ain't seen no action yet, Detective. Far as I can make out, Cloud still walkin' 'round."

"These things take time, Sister Grace."

"I don' got time. You don' got time." She studies my face. "Looks to me like you got in a fight. An' you lost."

"I ran into a tree."

"Looks to me like the tree won. My people tell me somebody tried to shoot you down t'other night. From what I hear, it was a near thing."

"Was it your people doing the shooting?"

"If it was my people they wouldn't 'a missed. I believe the people after you were a couple of white crackers. Why you here, Detective? I din't invite you."

"I need your help, Sister Grace."

"What kind a' help you lookin' for?"

"You said you have eyes and ears everywhere. You know everything that goes on in the town."

"What if I do?"

"My partner has been kidnapped. I want you to help me find him."

"You mean your police partner?"

"That's right."

"Missing policemen ain't none of my business."

"The kidnapping is connected to a big gun-buy in a few days' time."

Sister Grace studies the cigarette in her hand. Her hand is shaking. "I heard about that gun-buy. I have my people tryin' to find out what's goin' down."

"The man who snatched my partner is the buyer."

"You want me to be a police snitch. That don' sit well with me." She lights another cigarette. "I don' know who the buyer is. All I know, it's close to a million-dollar deal. The guns are supposed to arrive here in a day or two. The buyer's from out of town so I have no connections. This gun-buy a big concern to me. I can't afford to have a lot of heavy-duty weapons fall into the wrong hands."

"You mean Cloud?"

"I mean I don' want these weapons in anybody's hands but mine."

"If I find the buyer, I find my partner. Will you help me find the buyer?"

"I'll ask around. If I learn somethin', I'll let you know. But if I do, you gotta do somethin' for me in return."

"What's the deal?"

"I find I have a new problem." She stares silently for a long time at the burning end of her cigarette. "Where was I?"

"You said you have a new problem."

"'Course I do. I want you should hammer Lamont. I want him gone. Understand?"

"I told you, I won't do that."

"Things be gettin' way outa hand 'round here. They's a war 'bout to start 'tween Cloud and Lamont." She crushes out her cigarette. "I need 'em both out of the way."

"Get one of your boys to do the job."

"My boys are tough, but they ain't no match for Cloud or Lamont. You think Cloud be bad," she goes on. "Wait till you meet Lamont. Lamont a truly wicked man."

"Just leave Cloud and Lamont to work out their differences between them. You can stay out of it."

"Ain't that simple. The day the guns hit the streets, war begins, and I'm dead. That for damn sure. Lamont's got ambitions. Big ambitions. He plan to take over the city. And he startin' to make his moves now. My people tellin' me Lamont was after some of Cloud's crew when he shot up the schoolyard. They's real bad blood between Cloud and Lamont now. Real bad."

"How did that happen?"

"The same as always. A woman. Lamont want what Cloud got. That include his woman, Mariana." Sister Grace studies me carefully. "I think you know this Mariana girl. My people tell me Lamont's been lustin' after that girl for months but 'til now he had sense enough not to show his hand. Now he's makin a play for the girl."

"Tell me how to find the man who's buying the guns, and I can deal with both Cloud and Lamont."

She studies me skeptically. "You can really do that? You can fix this?"

"Absolutely, Sister Grace, don't I always?"

CHAPTER TWENTY-FOUR

A BLACK CHEVROLET Suburban swings around the corner at the end of the block and comes barreling toward me. I'm almost at police headquarters on my way back from meeting with Sister Grace when the Suburban comes to an abrupt stop and two men climb out.

The Suburban has tinted windows, and I can't see inside so I don't know how many more big men are waiting to pile out if called upon. Tinted windows like this are illegal in Washington, so I know this is no ordinary vehicle. It has US Government plates. I don't know whether this is reassuring or whether I should be worried.

"Detective Zorn, come with us." The man is muscular, with an almost bald head. It isn't a request.

"What if I say no?" I ask.

"I'll pretend I didn't hear you."

I'm hustled into the back seat of the Suburban where I sit between two burly men in identical blue suits. One wears a pink tie, the other a red tie. I suppose that helps tell which is which. The bald guy takes a seat in front. The Suburban pulls away and speeds down the street.

"Am I under arrest?"

"Depends on your definition of *arrest*," the man on my right says. He's the one with the pink tie. I figure these guys aren't into small talk, and we pass the rest of the trip in silence.

The Suburban slows briefly while driving through the West Gate of the White House, then swings around the semicircular drive and stops in front of the door to the West Wing. The same door I entered earlier.

One of the black-uniformed Secret Service armed guards pulls open the back door and I'm hustled out onto the pavement and through the entrance door. Once again, the security detail checks me for weapons and takes my cell phone. Standing on the far side of the security barrier, Miss Shaw waits for me.

She smiles. "Follow me," she says in a pleasant voice. I fall into step beside her. A small, heavyset man with a fat neck and wearing a Rolex watch follows us about ten feet behind.

"We can't seem to have enough of you here in the Executive Mansion, can we, Detective Zorn?" Miss Shaw asks cheerfully.

"Does Myron Clark have more things he wants to shout at me?"

"You're done with Myron."

She offers no suggestion as to why I'm here as we walk through the West Wing in silence. We stop at a door and she steps inside part way and says something I can't hear. She turns back to me.

"Go right in." I enter.

I'm standing in a dark, wood-paneled office furnished with comfortable furniture—a leather sofa, two wingback, dark brown, leather armchairs, and a polished coffee table. To the far side is a large, ornately carved mahogany desk with a green leather top. There is no phone or computer on the desk. Just a single pad of paper imprinted with the White House crest. There is a well-supplied bar on the far side of the room. The walls are covered with photographs of government officials and politicians—both US and foreign—including several presidents and a couple of archbishops and a pope. Many have been signed with warm wishes. No lethal weapon is in sight anywhere in the office.

Standing in the middle of the room is a tall man, about sixty. He's in his shirtsleeves and wears blue suspenders, his hair is gray. There is a faint aroma of expensive aftershave lotion in the room.

"Detective Zorn?" The man crosses to me and holds out his hand and we shake. His grasp is firm and assured. "I am Hollis Chambers. Delighted to meet you. I think." He smiles genially. "Can I get you a drink? I understand you're a bourbon man. Or do you not drink when you're on duty?"

"Am I on duty?" I ask. "My captors neglected to explain my status. I don't know why I'm here."

"Of course. How could you?" Hollis Chambers goes to the bar, pours bourbon into a glass. "Ice, Mr. Zorn?"

"No ice."

"Good man. I drink scotch myself. Dates back to my days at Harvard. I think I got most of my bad habits at Harvard."

Holding a glass in each hand, Chambers crosses the room, passes me one. "Let's make ourselves comfortable, shall we?"

Without waiting for an answer, he settles into one of the wingback armchairs. I sit in the chair facing him. "To the confusion of our enemies," Chambers says, raising his glass and looking at me over the top. He takes a substantial gulp and places the glass on a fancy coaster, embossed with the White House seal. I take a sip from my glass.

"First, let me introduce myself. My name is Hollis. My title around here is Special Adviser to the President. Some damn-fool thing like that. Second, I must apologize for the cowboy tactics used to get you here. You referred to 'your captors.' I assume you were shanghaied off the street with no explanation."

"Something like that."

"I deplore that kind of treatment. Miss Shaw urged a more civilized method to get you here. She was very insistent. I should listen to her." He takes another drink. "But I was in a hurry and I needed to talk to you. You're a hard man to find. You tend to disappear from time to time."

"That's part of my job." I don't say what job.

"It was urgent I speak with you. And I didn't want anybody to know you were coming to see me. And I didn't want to give you the chance to contact your associates, maybe someone in your police department, or perhaps the redoubtable Arora Lovelace."

"I haven't agreed to keep our meeting confidential."

Chambers sips his drink. "Your house is being watched, you know. And your phone tapped. You've been under surveillance for several days now." Chambers smiles genially.

"Who's watching me?"

"I don't know. If I were you, I'd find out."

"Why am I here? I've already been interviewed, if that's the word, by somebody in the White House. A Myron Clark . . ."

"Ah, Myron. I'm afraid Myron lacks polish. A rough diamond."

"You could say that."

"I gather your—what did you call it?—your interview did not go well."

"You could say that, as well."

"Once again, Miss Shaw warned me about that. She thought I should be the one to speak with you."

"She sounds like a smart lady."

"Smarter than you could possibly know." Chambers gets to his feet. "May I refresh your drink? I know I could use another." Without waiting for me to answer, he takes my glass and goes to the bar and refills the glasses.

"I'm going to share some information with you." He speaks from the bar, his back to me. "Information I'm going to ask you to keep in strictest confidence."

"I make no promises. I'm investigating a homicide. If what you tell me bears on my investigation, I will use it."

Chambers returns, carrying the two glasses, passes me one and takes a seat. "Of course. I would not dream of perverting the course of justice."

"You'd be surprised how many perverts there are in my business," I say.

Chambers laughs, almost spilling his scotch. "When Myron spoke with you—well, he wasn't fully in the picture."

"What is this picture you want me to know about but not talk about that Myron wasn't fully in?"

"I assume Myron asked you not to investigate the death of Sandra Wilcox."

"He ordered me to stop my investigation. Which I did not take well."

"Quite understandable. The fact is, we're dealing with a situation here. Keeping the information confidential will in no way compromise your investigation."

"I'm listening."

"On the night Agent Wilcox died, we were having a crisis here in the White House."

"I never heard of any crisis," I say. "There's been nothing in the news."

"And there never will be. In two days, the President and the First Lady are scheduled to go to Arlington National Cemetery to attend the funeral of General Harry Durkin. Durkin was a major figure in the US military and on the political scene. And also, one of the President's bitterest opponents."

"What has any of this to do with Sandra Wilcox? Or me?"

"In a sense, nothing. That's just the point. Despite their enmity, the President is determined to attend the funeral. For political reasons he feels he must be there to give the eulogy."

"I understand there's a plot to assassinate the President. That must complicate things," I say, trying to cut the explanation short.

"You are well informed. The existence of this plot is supposed to be secret. How did you come to know about the threat? Never mind. The Secret Service has imposed the highest-level security protocols for the next few days. All information about the President's activities is now secret and that includes all security arrangements."

"Is that why the White House logs have been closed?"

"Who came and went the night Agent Wilcox was killed is being treated as a state secret."

Chambers stares into his empty glass. "Would you care for another, Detective Zorn? I'm afraid I can't join you. I've reached my allowed limit. You know how doctors are." Hollis Chambers looks forlorn. "The Secret Service has discovered evidence of a serious breach of security within the White House itself. Somebody has been leaking information about the President's schedule. Enough to compromise his security. I needn't tell you how serious this is. I'm sorry to say, it looks as though Sandra may have been the source of the leak."

"You have evidence of this?"

"Nothing I can share. But suffice it to say, there's evidence she had contacts with a domestic terrorist group that is planning an insurrection."

"What happened on the night Sandra was killed?"

"We don't know for sure. Matt Decker, Chief of the Secret Service, believes she was warned she might be under suspicion and managed to escape from the White House to avoid arrest."

"Then what do they think happened?"

"Decker and his people are investigating that."

"So this group killed her. Is that what you think?"

"That's what Matt Decker thinks. I have no personal opinion."

"I need to know when Sandra Wilcox left the White House on the night she was murdered. And how did Sandra learn she was under suspicion? Is there another conspirator in the White House?"

Hollis Chambers shakes his head. "I'm sorry," he says softly. "I can't go any further. All the details about what happened that night are being treated as Top Secret. I must warn you, sir, you are in dangerous territory. This case touches on matters of national security."

"That makes no sense."

"We must not let this terrorist group learn what we know. It would put the President at risk and could lead to an insurrection with who knows what consequences."

"But you just told me this group already has sources—what do they call them? 'moles'—inside the White House."

"That's what the Secret Service suspects. We don't actually know anything. Until we can stop this group, everything to do with Sandra and her death is off limits."

"It looks like I'm at a dead end."

"It looks that way," Chambers murmurs. "I'm sure you understand."

"No, I don't understand. And, with respect, I don't think you are being entirely honest with me."

He shrugs.

"I have a question for you, Mr. Chambers."

"Go ahead."

"Did you know Sandra Wilcox?"

"Not really. The Secret Service agents, when they're on duty, have no time for socializing or idle talk. The White House is not a social club."

"You never talked to her?"

"From time to time," Chambers answers. "When the President and First Lady traveled, there were some down times on Air Force One. We might exchange a few words. Miss Wilcox was on the security detail for the First Lady for over a year, and on three or four occasions I accompanied Mrs. Reynolds on these trips. I spoke with some of the Secret Service agents on these occasions."

"Including Sandra Wilcox?"

"She was one of many."

"What is it you do here in the White House, Mr. Chambers?" I ask.

He laughs gently. "You're not the first one to wonder about that. I have known Eliot and Marsha Reynolds for many years. I was Eliot's law partner in Cleveland. I worked on his campaign when he first ran for office and I've been with him ever since—his run for governor, his first campaign for President. His reelection campaign."

"You're saying you're a kind of a family friend?"

"You could say that. I think of myself as a fixer. I bring no special expertise. I have no political ambitions of my own. No ambitions of any sort. Only to serve Eliot and Marsha Reynolds loyally."

"Just one more question."

Chambers nods graciously, spreading his hands—an invitation.

"Did you know Miss Wilcox had an allergy to peanuts?"

"She did? How would I possibly know that?"

I stand up. "Thank you for the drinks."

"I hope, in light of what I've told you," Chambers says quietly, "you might be less eager in your pursuit of justice."

"Not a chance."

"Why do you care? What's so important about Sandra Wilcox?"

"I'm a police officer. I'm responsible for a murder investigation."

"I don't mean to be rude," Chambers says, "but I don't believe you. You must have had many cases you could not close."

"Far too many."

"You do not strike me as a vigilante. According to your records you have—how should I phrase this?—you have shown flexibility in some of your more delicate investigations. I'm told you showed understanding in the case of Billy Walsh, Howard Walsh's boy. I ask for understanding in this case. What is it about this case that makes you so determined? You have no connection to the victim and yet you persist in pursuing the truth. Miss Shaw tells me you're a stubborn man. But there's more than that here. Why do you care what happened to Sandra Wilcox?"

What can I say? How do I explain why her death is important to me? She needs my help. She's beyond help—but I can't turn away. Whatever the cost.

"She looked me in the eye."

"I don't understand."

"I was one of those who pulled Sandra Wilcox's body from the Reflecting Pool. I looked into the water and she stared back up at me. I can't forget her blue eyes. And I won't stop until I discover her killer."

Hollis Chambers nods. "I see." He doesn't see. Not really. "Thank you for coming, Detective Zorn. I hope you will take my advice and drop the Wilcox case."

Miss Shaw waits for me just outside the door. "I trust your meeting was more satisfactory than the last one," Miss Shaw says, amiably.

"Pleasanter, certainly. Satisfactory? Not really."

"I'm sorry to hear that." She regards me thoughtfully. "You're going to persist in finding out what happened to Sandra Wilcox, aren't you?"

"Absolutely."

"I'm not surprised."

"What games are you people here playing?"

"Games?"

"I don't like playing games. Especially when I don't know the rules."

"We play by our own rules here in the Executive Mansion."

"Why don't you explain the rules to me?"

She looks intently into my eyes. "Why not?" She smiles. "Shall we say dinner tomorrow evening at the Anchorage Restaurant?"

"That sounds fine."

"Tomorrow at seven then. I look forward to it." She smiles. "You have much to learn."

CHAPTER TWENTY-FIVE

"I COULD BE fired for talking to you." Larry Talbot, Sandra's friend in the Secret Service and sometime lover, says, his voice hushed. He sits opposite me in a bar nowhere near the Secret Service headquarters building, a place where no one who knows Talbot is likely to be.

"Who told you not to talk to me?"

"Matt Decker, the head of the Secret Service."

"When was this?"

"He called me into his office this morning."

"What exactly did he say?"

"He told me Sandy was mixed up with some domestic terror group."

"What does he think she did?"

"He claims she was involved in a plot to assassinate the President. He thinks the terrorists decided Sandra was a high risk and feared if she was arrested, she could give away the game. But that's absurd. I know Sandy. She would never betray the Service. Would never betray her country."

"You're sure she'd never betray the Service, even to protect her brother?"

"Not even for that. I know they were close. When her brother washed out of the Army, she took it very hard. That doesn't mean she'd commit treason for him."

"Sometimes people surprise us. Sometimes we don't know people as well as we think we do."

"You sound just like Decker. Now they're beginning to suspect me. They're questioning anyone who knew Sandy well. Decker didn't say so, but it's clear they think there was another person involved. And I'm under suspicion."

"What makes you think that?"

"I've been suspended. I had to turn in my badge and weapon an hour ago. But it's not me I'm worried about. It's Sandy's honor. Her memory."

"Larry, I need to know about the night Sandra was murdered," I say. "Tell me what you know."

Talbot leans across the table, closer to me, speaking softly. "I don't know what happened. I didn't even know where Sandy was that evening."

"Sandra was in the White House," I say. "The Secret Service will not confirm that but that's the way it looks. Tell me how the protective detail is organized."

"The security details work eight-hour shifts. There's a day shift, an evening shift, and a night shift."

"If Sandra was on night shift that evening, what time would she have arrived?"

"Around eleven thirty."

"Where would the detail be located?"

"In W-16. That's the Secret Service holding room in the White House."

"Where were you that evening?"

"I'm assigned to the evening shift of the Counter Assault Team, and my group was in the Old Executive Office Building. The President and First Lady were in the White House that evening hosting a formal dinner. So the Counter Assault Team was standing down.

I was relieved by the night shift and I and a couple of the guys, we went to a bar on 15th Street—Ernie's. It's a hangout for Secret Service agents. We go there to unwind."

"What time did you leave the Old Executive Office Building?"

"It would have been around eleven thirty. Maybe a little after."

"Then what happened?"

"About midnight I got an urgent message on my cell ordering me to the White House."

"Who called you?"

"The shift supervisor, Alan Drake. I went immediately. Must have gotten there a few minutes after twelve."

"Why did they call you?"

"Sandra had disappeared."

"What do you mean?"

"They told me Sandy was in the holding room at the beginning of her shift. And then she wasn't there. The shift supervisor called her on her cell. There was no answer and they searched the immediate area but found nothing. That's when Drake called me and others in the area. This is serious shit. The Service is very strict about having security details at full complement at all times."

"What people are normally in the White House at that hour?"

"Depends on what might be going on. That night it was quiet. So you would have, in addition to the Secret Service detail, the communications teams and a skeleton stenographic and secretarial group. There are usually some military liaison types in their offices and often a few from the chief of staff's office. And because the President and First Lady were having a formal dinner, there were the usual crew in the mess and servers bringing and taking whatever."

"Quite a few people."

"Not compared to the daytime staff. Unless there is some crisis, the White House at night is kind of sleepy."

"And there was no crisis."

"None that I know of."

"When I've visited the White House," I say, "I'm always brought in through one of the entrances on the north side."

"That's standard procedure."

"Are there entrances, say, on the south side?"

"Several. They are normally reserved for formal events."

"There are steps on the south side?" I ask.

"That's right."

"Can someone within the White House leave the building and gain access to these steps?"

"Yes, if they have clearance."

"You said there are steps on the south side. How many steps?"

"I don't know. Ten. Twenty. Why?"

"Sandra could have left the building through the south entrance."

"I suppose she could have."

"Could anybody else have left that way without being challenged?"

"Not unless they had a White House pass."

"What happened after you got to the White House on the evening Sandra disappeared?"

"Drake had called headquarters and more search parties were organized. They searched the offices and public areas in the White House. The mess, the parking area. When they couldn't find her, they expanded the search area to include the Rose Garden and grounds, expanding the perimeter to the outer fences. Then, about an hour into the search, one of the agents reported Sandy had been seen outside of the White House at about one fifteen."

"I need to see the log showing who entered the White House and who left that evening."

"You can't. Nobody is allowed to see them now. I looked at them the night Sandy disappeared, but by next morning they were closed."

"Do you know if Sandy was logged in when she arrived that night?"

"Yes."

"You're sure?"

"Absolutely. I checked the logs myself."

"How about when she left?"

"No record of her leaving."

"So Sandy entered the White House but never left."

"That's the way it would appear. But we know she did leave."

"Who saw Sandra outside the White House?"

"One of the women on the evening clerical staff. She'd finished her shift and was on her way home. She was in a cab and had just left the 15th Street checkpoint when she saw someone she thought was Sandy."

"What then?"

"She'd heard Sandy was missing and that people were looking for her. She called White House communications and told them she'd seen Sandy."

"I need to talk to that secretary. I need to know exactly when and what she saw."

"The Secret Service has already interviewed her."

"I must talk to her myself. What's her name?"

Talbot is silent, struggling to remember. "Valerie. Valerie North," he says at last.

"How do I reach her?"

"I understand she's been put on administrative leave and told to stay home. I can't tell you anything more, except Valerie and Sandra were friends. I've never met Valerie. She's just a name Sandra mentioned. I don't even have an address or phone number."

"There must be a phone book listing White House staff. Get me a copy."

"I can't. The White House is now off limits to me."

"Do you know anyone on the White House secretarial staff? Somebody who might know this Valerie's home phone number?"

He stares at the tabletop. "Maybe," he says softly. "I know a couple of the girls."

"Give me a name."

"If I do this, I could be fired."

"I understand. It's your call."

Without a further word, he takes his notebook from his pocket and writes down a name and a telephone number.

"I'll take my chances," Talbot says. "If this helps you find Sandy's killer, it'll be worth it." He looks at his watch. "I better get back before they send a search party for me. But before I go, there's something I need to tell you about. A few of us have got together and organized a memorial service for Sandy. It's tomorrow at Saint Luke's on Massachusetts Avenue. At three in the afternoon. I'm not religious, but Sandy was, and it troubles me that Sandy should leave this world without any observance."

"I'll be there."

He leaves without looking back. I'm about to follow when my phone signals I have a text message. Someone wants to meet me at the entrance to the Metro Subway station on 7th Street. The message says the caller has something for me from Sister Grace.

When I arrive at the Metro entrance, I pass through groups of teenagers, mostly Black and Hispanic. A couple of men stand nearby trying to look innocent, several plainclothes cops among them. After a few a minutes, a voice calls out: "Detective!"

It's the kid I'd seen at Sister Grace's headquarters. He's short and skinny and wears a hoodie. "You have something for me?"

He studies me suspiciously. "You a cop?" he asks. "They say you a cop."

"Did Sister Grace send you?"

The boy looks around. "Yeah. She has a message for you."

"What's the message?"

"You gon' give me some money for the message?"

"I'm gonna take you direct to Sister Grace and she gonna whup your ass."

The kid does not look impressed by my threat.

"What's the message?"

"Sister Grace say she losin' patience with you."

"What's that mean?"

The kid shrugs. "I don' know. Just she losin' patience is all. She say you know what that mean."

"That's all she said?"

"They's more. She say you should look for a man called Black. He can tell you what you need to know."

"Who's *Black*?"

The kid shrugs. "How do I know?"

"Did Sister Grace tell you how to find this man named Black?"

"Maybe."

"Maybe? What's 'maybe' supposed to mean?"

"You got another of them twenties, mister?"

I take a wad of twenties from my pocket, pull off one and give it to the kid. The kid eyes the bankroll. "Forget it," I say. "How do I find this man Black?"

"Ask Fast Freddie. He can tell you where to find Black."

"Who's Fast Freddie?"

"I don' know. Just Fast Freddie. She say he'll lead you to the man you want."

"How do I find this Fast Freddie?"

The boy shrugs. "He sells used cars or somethin'. Jus' tellin' you what Sister Grace say. Can I have one of those twenties?"

"If you do something for me. Easy money."

"Sure, Mister Policeman."

"Do you know where to find Lamont?"

"Lamont stayin' away from the club these days, you know."

"Do you know where he is?"

"I know where he hangin' out. What you want with Lamont?"

"None of your business. Tell him I have a business proposition for him. Something that will make him a very rich man. You got that?"

I take out another twenty. "Get that message to him. Just him. Don't tell anyone else."

"Sure. No problem."

I write my cell number on the twenty and give it to the kid. "You tell him I have a deal for him that will make him a big man. Tell him to call this number."

The boy snatches the twenty. "Just that?"

"What's your name?"

"I tell you if you give me money." I peel off another twenty.

"Okay. Your name."

I can see the kid considering holding out for another twenty. "My name's Otis," he says at last.

"How old are you, Otis?"

The boy stands up straight, to his full height. "I'm seventeen."

"If you're a day older than fourteen, then I'm the man in the moon."

"Okay, Moon Man." The boy snatches the bill and disappears into the crowd.

CHAPTER TWENTY-SIX

BY THE TIME I get back to headquarters it's dark outside and the squad room is empty. Most of the lights are dimmed and the telephones have stopped ringing.

For the hundredth time I check for emails, for texts, for phone messages. Nothing from Kenneth.

I pick up my phone. To my surprise Hal Marshal's in his office. "Hal, why aren't you home with your loved ones?"

"We're on the edge of a volcano is why."

"I've got a question you can help me with."

"I'll see what I can do. Come right on up."

I get to his office in five minutes, bearing my customary container of tea. Hal is, as usual, sitting at his desk staring at his wall map. There are more pins clustered around the city. A lot more than last time and they seem to me much more disorganized.

"What's going on in the streets?" I ask.

"I'm not certain. My snitches are going silent. That means either nothing's happening or something really bad is about to go down. My usual sources are scared and have gone into hiding. They're not hanging around their usual places. They're not returning my calls. That's bad."

"You told me Lamont Jones is going to challenge Cloud for control of the drug market and Sister Grace's entire organization. Is that what's going down?"

"It don't make sense for Lamont to challenge Cloud. Neither Cloud nor Lamont got the firepower to take the other down."

"What about the gun-buy people are talking about?"

"That would definitely tip the balance in favor of whoever gets those guns." Hal makes notes on a yellow pad. "You said you had a question."

"Have you ever heard of someone named Freddie?" I ask.

"There are hundreds of people named Freddie."

"Maybe someone known as Fast Freddie. Someone who's sleazy, criminal, and probably dangerous."

"That's about everyone I know."

"How about a Freddie maybe connected to used cars?"

"Now that does ring a bell. I've heard of a Fast Freddie who pretends to sell cars but I don't remember where. I'll check."

What I think is going to take a few minutes turns out to take over an hour. Hal begins by going through a couple of Rolodex files, then some loose cards he keeps in his desk drawer. Then he checks his computer. Finally, on the verge of giving up, he pulls open a file drawer from an ancient, dented steel cabinet. This is another reason Hal will never be let go from the police force—nobody would ever be able to find anything.

"I'm getting there," Hal says. "I'm getting warm." Hal tugs a yellowing scrap of paper from his files and sits at his desk, a look of triumph on his face. "I knew it. I knew it."

"What is it?" I ask.

"Frederico. Frederico Hernandez."

"Otherwise known as Freddie?" I ask.

"Otherwise known Fast Freddie, Marcel, Roger the Badger, and a dozen other names. Otherwise known as a low-level hood with a long, undistinguished rap sheet, mostly involving fraud, check kiting, dealing in stolen cars and fencing stolen property."

"Is there any way I can locate this distinguished citizen?"

Hal studies the paper he's holding. "The last address I have is a car dealership called Ultimate Used Cars in Anacostia." Hal scribbles an address on a scrap of paper and hands it to me. "If you meet this Frederico, give him my regards."

CHAPTER TWENTY-SEVEN

ARORA LOVELACE STANDS in front of my house, looking angry. "Going somewhere?" she demands as I step out my front door. It's seven in the morning.

"What are you doing here?"

"I thought I'd get up-to-date on your investigation into the Sandra Wilcox murder."

"I have nothing new to report."

"Really?"

"I'm exploring various avenues of investigation."

"Such as?"

"I got a tip."

"What tip?"

I can see she's having a hard time keeping her temper. "If we're going to work together, we can't keep little secrets from one another."

"The leader of the Brotherhood may or may not have contacted a man in Anacostia about a sale of weapons. I'm going to check him out."

"I'm coming with you." Arora stands firmly in my way.

"This is personal."

"This is not personal!" she almost yells. "It's not just about you. It's not even about your partner, Kenneth. Let's go check out your tip."

Just a coincidence, Arora showing up just as I'm leaving? I wonder. Awfully convenient. Has the Bureau bugged my phone? It comes back to me what Hollis Chambers said about my house being watched and my phone tapped. It would be just like the FBI to do that while at the same time working with me on the Wilcox case. But this is not the time to find out. When that time comes, I'll have it out with Carla Lowry. Today I need to see Fast Freddie. I can make an issue of it with Arora and tell her to get lost. But this would take time. And there's no good reason to refuse her help.

"Let's go for a ride," I say.

"We'll take my car. Your car's far too conspicuous."

As we cross the Anacostia River, I ask: "What's this really about? You didn't just happen to stop by."

"I told you, I want to know what you've learned."

"You could have phoned. Carla sent you, didn't she? She told you to track me down so you can keep an eye on me."

"I'm supposed to keep you out of trouble."

"Good luck with that."

"Give me the address where we're going. I'll navigate. Tell me about your tip."

"Some friends of mine have heard that somebody with a garage in Anacostia is involved in gun sales."

"Friends of yours?"

"That's right."

"What kind of friends?"

"Old friends."

We find Ultimate Used Cars on an out-of-the-way back street in an otherwise deserted strip mall—dirty and windblown. The few other businesses along the street are vacant—long-since shuttered and abandoned. We identify the lot from the dreary red and yellow balloons that bob listlessly in the breeze. Once-bright pennants hang from sagging ropes. In front, a dozen car wrecks are parked posing as secondhands.

The street is deserted except for a light-colored van a hundred or so feet up the block. Arora parks her Datsun across from the lot, and we walk among the rusting wrecks. In the back of the lot there is a wooden structure with a sign reading "Garage" and "Body Work." It has overhead, corrugated rolling-metal doors, closed and secured by a heavy padlock at the bottom. Above the doors is a tattered, weather-beaten sign that reads: "Lube" and another that reads: "Alignment."

To one side of the garage is a small building with a sign that reads: "Office." At that moment two men emerge, watching us as we cross the lot. One is tall, maybe six feet, a little thick around the waist. With a bristle mustache. The second man is short and skinny.

"Good morning, folks," the short man says. "Can we help you?"

"We're looking for Fast Freddie. Either one of you named Freddie?" I ask.

"Freddie? I don't know any Freddie." The short man turns to his companion. "You know anybody by that name, Floyd?"

"No, sir. Don't know nobody by that name."

"You two work here?"

The shorter man turns to his friend, then back to me. "We're just looking at cars. Right, Floyd?"

"That's right. No one name of Fast Freddie around here."

"Why don't we check the office? Maybe Freddie's in the back. Darling!" I call to Arora who is a few yards away looking at a dented Buick. "I'm going into the office. See if I can find the manager."

Arora waves at me cheerfully. "I'll come with you, dear." She strides across the lot and we head for the office door.

"Freddie's gone for the day," the short man says. "The office is closed."

"We'll wait."

Arora and I walk briskly into the office, leaving the two men in the lot watching us.

It's a small room dominated by a large, battered, wooden desk, its surface scarred with decades of coffee stains and cigarette burns along the edges. There's a calendar on one wall, a year out of date, and flyers advertising car-towing services scattered on a small table near the door. An empty water cooler stands in one corner, littered with dead insects. There's no one in sight.

As Arora begins a search of the office, I go through the drawers in the desk and find a few old invoices and a metal letter opener. One drawer has a cheap lock used on cheap office furniture, and it takes me less than a minute to jimmy it open, using the letter opener. Inside there is a small, battered notebook, bound with a rubber band. I slip the book unobtrusively into my inside jacket pocket.

"Nothing here," Arora announces from across the office.

"Nothing here either," I say. "Let's check out the garage."

I follow Arora through a metal door into the garage area. A couple of cars sit on the oily floor. Along the walls are wooden workbenches with a few greasy tools. Torn newspapers litter the floor. More flyers interspersed with calendars and advertisements for motor oil are stapled to the walls. High above the floor are dirty windows covered with wire mesh screens.

"Marko," Arora calls to me. "You better come see this." She stands at the edge of the grease pit.

A man lies at the bottom of the pit, facedown. He is dressed in a cheap business suit and looks quite normal except the back of his head has been crushed.

"I guess Freddie wasn't fast enough."

My rage surges through my body. "I'm going after those two guys."

Arora holds up her hand. "I smell something."

I smell something, too. A fire with the distinct smell of gasoline.

The door to the office we'd just come through slams shut, and I hear the sound of a dead bolt pushed into place from the other side.

"Check the back door!" I yell at Arora while I run to the door to the office. It's locked tight.

"We're fucked!" Arora calls to me from across the garage, struggling with the back door. "Can't budge it."

I rush to the large roll-up doors. The padlock on the outside has secured it shut. My mouth and nose are filling with the smell of burning gasoline.

"How long have we got?" Arora calls to me.

"Ten minutes tops," I yell back. "Before this whole place goes up in flames and the roof collapses on our heads." My heart is beating fast. Heat from the outer walls burns my skin. The roar of the flames deafens me. Smoke seeps through cracks in the wooden walls, stinging my eyes.

"In that car!" I yell, pointing to a battered Chevy. I pull open the door and climb into the driver's seat. Arora jumps in beside me. There are no keys in the ignition, and I fumble as I try to hot-wire the starter.

"Do you want me to do that for you?" Arora says through clenched teeth.

"I got it! I know what I'm doing! I got it!" The engine turns over. I put the car in gear, release the clutch, and press the accelerator to the floor and we're moving just as the back wall begins to collapse in flames.

The car lurches foreword and we blow through the roll-up steel doors, flinging us forward, and we're speeding through the lot. The big man stands in front of us, holding a gun, his mouth open as we speed toward him. At the last second, he leaps to one side.

I bring the car to a skidding stop. Arora and I jump out. The garage and office building are engulfed in red and blue flames. Smoke twists into the sky. Over the sound of the roaring flame I hear the pop—the sound of a shot from a small-bore handgun. Followed instantly by the clang as the round strikes the roof of the car a few inches from my head.

Arora's drawn her service Glock and is crouched behind the dented Buick. The big man stands twenty feet away, shooting wildly at us, not taking time to aim. A round hits the passenger door where Arora is crouched. I jump behind the cab of a Ford truck and catch a glimpse of the short man running toward the white van parked up the street. The big man fires twice more. Arora, a couple of cars to my left, returns fire, but her target darts behind a pickup and she misses.

The big man races toward the van, dodging among the parked wrecks, his gun in his right hand. He stops when he reaches the van, takes one more wild shot at us, jumps into the van and the van speeds up the street, disappearing around the corner.

We slowly stand up, coughing and gasping, trying to clear our lungs of smoke and gasoline fumes. Arora's face and clothes are smudged with soot and fly ash, her hair a tangled mess. Her hands and arms smeared with grease. Somehow, she's not lost her glasses, which she pushes firmly back on the bridge of her nose.

We check the area, Arora holding her weapon in both hands, slightly crouched. Once satisfied we won't be visited by any more shooters, she replaces her Glock in her shoulder holster.

"Who the hell are those guys?" Arora asks.

It's a rhetorical question and doesn't call for an answer. I figure we'll be seeing them again.

CHAPTER TWENTY-EIGHT

"LET'S SEE IF I've got this straight." Carla Lowry sits at her desk, arms crossed, looking at us over her half glasses. "You went on an unauthorized investigation. You blew up a garage. You left a murder victim at the scene of the crime. You engaged in a firefight with some unidentified persons. But you neglected to report any of this to the local law enforcement authorities." She looks intently at me. "Marko here doesn't count."

I notice Carla's not making notes.

We'd managed to wash ourselves up a bit before coming to see Lowry at FBI headquarters and we'd removed most of the ash from our faces and the grease and oil from our hands and arms. I'd tried to brush off smoke stains from my clothes, but there are still splotches. Arora's hair is a catastrophe.

"Are you two okay?"

"I'm missing no body parts," Arora answers.

"Your orders, Agent Lovelace, were to keep an eye on Marko here, not take part in a felony break-in."

"There was no break-in, ma'am," Arora says. "The doors to the office and garage were unlocked and open. More or less."

Carla looks skeptical. "Don't you two know better than to get yourselves locked inside a burning building?"

"Lesson learned," I say.

"Okay. Did you find out anything from this debacle?"

"The leader of the Brotherhood," I say, "made contact with a man named Fast Freddie in connection with an illegal purchase of a large amount of military-grade weapons."

"And you know this how?"

"From a confidential source."

She gives me a sour look. "We have every agent on the East Coast looking for this terrorist group and for your partner and, so far, have come up empty. Same with the Secret Service. And you, Marko, manage to locate a contact before lunch. I won't waste my time asking you how you managed that. You'll only lie. So you got a tip that someone involved in a weapons deal was located at this location. Then what?"

"We decided to investigate."

"Without going through channels? Without backup?"

"Those things take time. We don't have time. My partner's in danger."

"I thought the Bureau rewarded initiative," Arora observes.

"It does not reward idiocy, Agent Lovelace. During this event, you drew your service weapon? Is that correct?"

"Yes, ma'am."

"And you discharged your service weapon?"

"Yes, ma'am."

"Why did you do that, Agent Lovelace?"

"We were under attack from two hostiles."

"Are you convinced the use of your weapon was justified?"

"Absolutely."

"You know there are procedures in situations like these."

"There was no time for procedures," I interrupt. "Procedures kill you. If Agent Lovelace had not taken defensive action, we would have both been killed."

"Maybe. You say you fired your service weapon at one of the hostiles, Agent Lovelace."

"Yes, ma'am."

"You missed. I'm recommending you take a small arms refresher course. Understood?"

"Yes, ma'am."

"Who was the victim in the grease pit?" Carla asks.

"I expect it was a man named Fast Freddie," I tell her. "We didn't have time to chat."

"Did either of you discover anything of use during this escapade?"

"No, ma'am," Arora replies, adjusting her glasses. "We searched the office but found nothing."

"Marko?" Carla asks.

I'm acutely conscious of the weight of the notebook resting in my inside jacket pocket and wonder whether its shape and weight is obvious. "I'm afraid not. We found nothing of use."

"It looks like the whole operation was just a royal screw-up," Carla Lowry observes.

"It wasn't a total loss. We have a visual ID of the men leaving the garage. The killers who are probably members of the Brotherhood."

"I suppose that's better than nothing," Carla says, morosely.

"There's one more thing," I add. "When we arrived at the used car lot, there was a car parked about a hundred feet north of the lot."

Arora nods in agreement.

Carla Lowry picks up her pen. "Make? Model?"

"Chrysler Town and Country minivan," I say.

"Silver or light gray," Arora adds.

"2004 model."

"2005," Arora corrects me.

"I'll inform the Secret Service immediately," Carla says. "And the DC police. And ATF. They'll track down that vehicle."

"One more thing." I study Carla intently. "Is the FBI tapping my phone?"

"Next question."

We both get quickly to our feet. "And, Agent Lovelace," Carla says. "Go home, take a shower, and get into some decent clothes. You look like a circus clown. You're a disgrace to the Bureau."

When we leave the FBI headquarters, I offer to take Arora to my place so she can take a shower there. She expresses gratitude for my generosity and says it's the worst idea she's ever heard. She hails a passing cab. Just before she climbs in, she whispers, "We made a good team, Marko."

My cell phone rings. It's Frank Townsend. "Where are you?" he yells. Without waiting for an answer, he goes on, "Get back to the office. Now! There's someone here who must talk to you."

I conclude from Frank's tone there's no point in arguing and I head back to police headquarters. I go to the men's room and examine myself in the mirror. I have smudges of smoke on my face, my hair's a mess, and my jacket—a nice Brioni—is torn at the right shoulder. I wash up as best I can and comb my hair. I go to my personal locker where I keep my service weapon and spare shirts and jackets. I hang up my torn Brioni jacket and put on a Stephano Ricci jacket I keep here for emergencies. I'm almost presentable now.

When I get to Frank's office, he's talking to a man—short, a bit stout, probably athletic in his youth, but now gravity and age have taken their toll.

The man is in intense conversation with Frank as I enter. He leans in close to Frank, poking his index finger into Frank's chest. They stop and turn to face me when I arrive. Their expressions are not friendly.

"Marko," Frank almost shouts, "this is Nat Blake."

I try to remember who Nat Blake is.

"Nat is Kenneth's dad."

The man approaches me, his fists clenched, his face red, and I think for a moment he's going to take a swing at me. But he stops a few feet away and glares. "What the hell did you do to my boy?"

"I've told Nat," Frank says, "police from every jurisdiction in the area are looking for Kenneth at this very moment. So is the FBI. So is the Secret Service."

Kenneth's dad does not seem impressed. He's interested in one thing: me. "What the hell have you done with Kenneth?" I feel the spittle on my face. "Who the hell do you think you are? You put him in harm's way. You put an inexperienced young officer in danger."

I think about explaining that was not my plan but decide an attempt to justify myself would only make matters worse.

"Frank told me," the older man continues. "He assigned Kenneth to you because you were the most experienced police officer on the Metropolitan police force. He said you were used to handling dangerous people. He said you would look after my boy."

The man takes a deep, ragged breath. I look at Townsend. He studies a pile of papers on his desk.

"This behavior is inexcusable! Unprofessional!" Nat Blake goes on. "I was a police officer for twenty-eight years. Do you hear me? I'm a law-enforcement professional. I ran a tight ship. Nothing like this ever happened on my watch! I'm calling my congressman. Understand? I'm going to demand a congressional investigation. There will be consequences."

He turns to Townsend. "Sorry, Frank. We're old friends, I know. I got to do what I got to do."

I can see Frank cringe. Kenneth's dad stops to take another gulp of air.

"Mr. Blake," I say, "we have every resource of the state and federal governments out searching for Kenneth right now. I have several solid leads. We will find your boy. I promise you." I don't say whether Kenneth will be dead or alive when we find him. "Within twenty-four hours, we will find Kenneth."

This is, of course, total bullshit. Frank Townsend knows that and looks at me sharply. But Kenneth's dad doesn't know me and is so desperate for any glimmer of hope he decides to believe me.

"You find my son." The man almost chokes. "You bring Kenneth back. Safe. You hear? Otherwise you and the DC police department here will experience no end of hurt."

CHAPTER TWENTY-NINE

"THE LADY HAS already arrived, sir," a young man at the reception desk tells me. "She's waiting for you in the Montpelier Lounge. Lena will show you to your table." Lena, it turns out, is a pretty, young woman from somewhere in South Asia. She takes two leather-bound menus in hand, and I follow her through the large dining room. The Anchorage Restaurant is located on the Potomac River and its large picture windows look out over the water. Tonight, the river sparkles with the running lights of pleasure craft and tour boats.

The light in the dining room is tastefully low, the tablecloths and napkins pristine white. At the Anchorage, the waiters speak in subdued voices and the busboys do not speak at all. The loudest sound in the room is that of butter knives touching butter plates.

One of Miss Shaw's minders sits at a long bar watching me closely.

Miss Shaw has selected an out-of-the-way table in an alcove. A Fendi black leather purse hangs from a little hook on the side of her seat. She is dressed in a leather miniskirt that shows off her shapely legs. She smiles and waves away Lena and her menus and gestures for me to take a seat.

I sit across from her. "I spotted a member of your protective detail at the bar. Are you never alone?"

"There's another one near the front door, in case you were wondering." Her voice is low.

"Secret Service?"

She shakes her head. "I don't rate Secret Service protection. That's limited to the President and his family. People like me have to depend on hired guns. I assured my guys you are harmless. I hope you aren't going to make a liar of me."

"You're safe with me."

"I doubt that."

Why does Miss Shaw need protection? I wonder. And from whom? I ask myself, again, why I'm here and what does this woman want? She's not here because she's bored or needs some man to buy her dinner. She wants something from me and that worries me. Of course, I want something from Miss Shaw. I'm not sure just yet what it is.

A pretty young black girl clutching a pad stops at our table. "What can I get you from the bar?" she asks.

"A gin martini, please," Miss Shaw says. "Bombay Sapphire. Straight up. A splash of dry vermouth. Forget the olives. They just take up room."

"And you, sir?" our server asks.

"Wild Turkey. Ice and branch water on the side."

The server nods and glides away.

"I hope you're not in a rush this evening," Miss Shaw says. "I was hoping we would have time to get to know one another."

"There's a lot going on just now. I may be interrupted at any moment. My partner is missing and every cop in the metropolitan area is out looking for him. The city is on the verge of a gang war. The streets are being flooded by the deadly drug fentanyl. And I am deeply engaged in the investigation of the murder of Sandra Wilcox. Apart from that, you have my full attention."

"I know all about your murder investigation."

"Did you know Sandra Wilcox?" I ask.

"I knew her—professionally. As women, we dealt with many of the same challenges in our professional lives."

"What kind of person was she?"

"Very serious."

"Did she have enemies?"

"Among the White House staff? I doubt it. She was friendly and agreeable. I can't speak to her private life. I would know nothing about that."

"Did you know Sandra had an allergy to peanuts?"

"Did she? I had no idea. But how would I possibly know a thing like that?"

"What about Sandra's love life?"

Miss Shaw shakes her head. "Fraternization is strictly against White House rules. Sandy, I think, was the kind of person who observed rules. I heard she was once seeing a Secret Service agent but that was before being assigned to the Protective Detail. For the last year or so, I doubt she had time for love."

"Do these White House rules apply to you? Do you have time for love?"

Before she can answer our server brings our drinks and we make a silent toast to one another. Miss Shaw's hands are slender and pale with fine bones. Her nails are a bright scarlet.

I lean in closer. "What's really going on here?"

"We're having drinks and engaged in a civilized conversation. Like normal people."

"I don't think either of us is a *normal* person. I mean, what's going on with the Sandra Wilcox investigation? I'm being shut down. On orders from the White House."

"Whatever gave you that idea?"

"Are you the one shutting me down, Miss Shaw?"

She places her right hand gently over her breast. Her scarlet nails glitter. "Who, me?"

"Yes, you."

"I'm just a working girl."

"I don't mean to be rude but I don't believe you. You have your own security detail. These gorillas, I assume, are from a private security firm but are paid out of White House funds. Working girls in the White House don't rate their own security team. You're something special. I believe you have a more important role than you let on."

"I like to think I can sometimes be of help to the President and the First Lady."

"How long have you known Mrs. Reynolds?"

She shrugs. "A few years. We go back a ways."

"What's your relationship with her?"

"That's personal. Not really any of your business."

"I'm making it my business. You're more than an employee. You are a trusted and loyal aid. How did that come about?"

She shakes her head. "You're out of bounds, Mr. Zorn."

"Save us both a lot of time and trouble. I will find out, with or without your help. You're hiding something. I'm quite capable of learning what it is you're hiding."

She looks deep into her martini glass and seems to be making up her mind. "You know, that can work both ways."

"How do you mean, *both ways*?"

"I've done research on you."

"You've looked me up on Google?"

"I have access to more powerful search engines and resources than that."

"Then you must know all about me."

"I find I know almost nothing about you, really. I know the superficial stuff, sure. I also know that, from time to time, you engage in activities that are, to say the least, questionable, if not strictly illegal. You cut corners. You are sometimes involved with some very dubious people and some very dangerous organizations. If you insist on looking into my past, I might be obliged to dig further into yours and reveal some of what I learn."

"I'll take my chances."

She regards me steadily with her hazel eyes. "If I should share something with you—something about my history with Marsha Reynolds—will you promise to go no further with your investigation into my past?"

"If what you tell me does not bear on the murder investigation of Sandra Wilcox, I promise to go no further."

"I guarantee it has nothing to do with Sandra. It's something that happened many years ago. And for my part I will reveal nothing of what I learn about your past. That seems only fair."

"So we have an arrangement? A kind of mutually assured destruction pact. That sounds like a deal I can live with."

She takes a deep breath. "Marsha Reynolds saved my life. Many years ago. I once lived in a small town with my mother, my stepfather and my two brothers. Never mind where that was and what the family name was. Bad things happened there. Very bad things. When I was thirteen, I ran away from home and ended up in Cleveland, Ohio. For over a year I lived on the streets there. I became crazy addicted on drugs. That was before fentanyl came on the market, but the stuff I took was bad enough. If something hadn't happened, I would certainly have died in the gutter. Or worse."

"What happened that changed things?"

"I murdered my pimp."

That's not quite what I expected Miss Shaw to say. My brain reels as I try to reconcile that image with this cool, poised sophisticate sitting across from me wearing designer clothes.

"Surprised, Detective Zorn? I guess I'm not exactly your idea of a strung-out street whore killer."

"Not quite what I expected. But you have certainly got my attention. What happened to you? Because something obviously did happen."

"The police arrested me soon after the killing and I was assigned a court-appointed lawyer who spent almost five minutes with me and told me to plead guilty to all charges. I was facing life in prison and I knew I'd never come out alive."

"Where does Mrs. Reynolds enter your story?"

"Eliot Reynolds was at the time governor of Ohio, and Marsha was personally active in juvenile criminal reform. She was particularly concerned about wayward girls living on the streets. Somehow, she heard about my case, and we met briefly in prison and talked. She talked. I doubt I said much. Marsha hired some high-powered defense lawyer who persuaded a judge that what I did was an act of self-defense. Completely bogus, of course. I gutted the fucker because he wouldn't pay the money he owed me."

"Who knows about your past?"

"Nobody. Except Marsha. And Hollis Chambers, of course. And now, you. Not even the President knows for sure."

"What happened when you were released?"

"Marsha Reynolds got me into a drug rehab program. And, would you believe? I got clean. I've been clean for over twenty years now. Marsha found me a foster home. A lovely, loving, elderly couple from Oklahoma named Shaw who straightened me out and later adopted me as their own. My entire past was erased, and I found a new life for myself. And I took to that new life—peanut butter and jelly sandwiches, church socials, proms. I became captain of the high school girls' soccer team. The whole bit. I did well in high school. My grades were good enough to get scholarships for my choice of colleges. After graduating from Yale, I got a break and was hired by a New York investment firm. I'm pretty sure Marsha had something to do with that. After two years I was hired by a hotshot New York hedge fund and I made heaps of money."

"Did you keep in touch with Mrs. Reynolds?"

"Not much. She sent Christmas cards and occasionally a birth-day note. I think she wanted me to forget my past, forget what I once was. Forget what I might have become. Then Eliot ran for president and was elected and everything changed. Two days after his inauguration, Marsha called and offered me a position on the White House staff."

"You accepted?"

"Of course, I accepted. Although I had to take a major cut in pay. But I didn't hesitate. I said yes."

"Why did you say yes?"

"Loyalty, Detective. It's that simple. I owe a fierce loyalty to Mar-sha Reynolds. I owe my life to her. I would do anything for her." She sips her martini and looks at me over the rim of her glass. "Are you satisfied now that you've discovered my dirty little secret?"

"I suppose I must be satisfied."

"And my sordid history will stay between us? You won't poke around any further into my past? And, for my part, I will be discreet about yours."

"Agreed."

"I was sure you would agree. We're very much alike."

"Should I take that as a compliment?"

"It wasn't meant as a compliment."

Our server appears at the table ready to take our next order. Miss Shaw waves her away, impatiently.

"Are you always on duty like this?" Miss Shaw asks. "Do you never think of anything except murder and crime?"

"Sometimes I think about other things."

"Like what?"

"You know—marching bands, kittens, a leisurely day at the beach. The smell of suntan oil and the taste of mimosas. That kind of thing."

"Just you alone? That doesn't sound right. You don't seem like the kind of man who has to put on his own suntan oil."

"Certainly not. I need help with my back."

"I don't imagine you have a problem finding help."

"Call me Marko."

She bites her lower lip. "I don't think I'm there just yet. I'd need to know you better."

"We share one another's secrets. We are kind of coconspirators. Isn't that enough?"

"I don't really know you. Except for a few illegal bits."

"Ask me anything you want."

"Are there any significant others I should know about?"

"Not for the time being."

"Have you ever been in love? I mean seriously in love."

"I'm not sure where this is going."

"Where do you want it to go?"

"I don't even know your first name, Miss Shaw."

"I think it's more interesting to keep some mystery in our relationship."

"I didn't know we had a relationship."

"Why not wait and see?"

"I don't like mysteries."

"Is that why you became a detective? To solve mysteries?"

"Would you like another martini?"

She studies her glass. "I would, thank you. But perhaps not here. There are people watching us, have you noticed? I am not unknown around town and am an object of much curiosity. I have a better idea." She drinks down the rest of her martini. "Why not come home with me and I'll make you a proper drink. Maybe we can share some more secrets."

"I never say no to an invitation like that."

"Did you use your own car to come here?"

I nod.

"Good. Then you can drive me home. I came by official car but I told the driver not to wait. I told him I expected to be engaged for the rest of the evening."

I drop some bills on the table and we leave. On the way to the front door, she stops and speaks briefly to her security man. He glances at me and nods. She takes my arm, and we go to pick up my car. The valet parking attendant looks admiringly at Miss Shaw, then runs to retrieve my Jag.

Miss Shaw lives in a small, elegant home in the Palisades area of Washington, a quiet, upscale neighborhood. Her house is on an out-of-the-way, tree-lined street where all the cars are parked in their own driveways or garages. Her house is of red brick, partially covered by ivy. I park in her drive, lined with small, carefully trimmed yew trees, and follow her inside her house. We stand, for a moment, awkwardly facing one another in the vestibule.

"Do you still want a drink?" Her voice is husky.

"Maybe later."

She grasps me by the back of my neck and pulls me toward her, her pelvis tight against me. "Hope you have plenty of time." She kisses me, mouth open. I can't answer. Not when somebody's tongue is down my throat.

CHAPTER THIRTY

THE TASTE OF her, the scent of her, the feel of her under me—she's in my blood. Maybe if I pace around the empty squad room, I'll get her out of my system. It doesn't work. I stand by the window and observe a dozen police cruisers and police vans and two police buses lined up in front of headquarters, uniformed officers in riot gear, piling in, ready to be transported to trouble spots. Hal Marshal's large form moves slowly among them.

I examine Kenneth's desk as if I might find some clue to his whereabouts. The desktop is empty, except for a photograph of a middle-aged couple. The man I recognize as Nat Blake, Kenneth's father. I assume the woman is Kenneth's mother. It has a cheap, faux-leather frame, the kind you buy in any drugstore. I'm pretty sure Kenneth's is the only desk in the police department with a photograph of the detective's mom and dad.

My phone rings and the caller ID indicates "unknown."

"Detective Marko Zorn?" the voice at the other end announces.

"Who wants to know?"

"We have your boy."

"If you harm him—" I start to say but am cut off.

"Let's keep this short. And don't bother to trace this call. You can't. Kenneth is breathing and is in one piece. I can't say for how long."

It's a man's voice. Not young. I detect no identifiable regional accent.

"Keep your hands off Kenneth."

"You are in no position to make demands, Detective. If you don't do as I say, your boy's in serious shit."

"Who is this?"

"You'll find out. Soon you'll know my name. If you survive that long. Knock off your investigation," the voice orders. "Same goes for your girlfriend from the FBI. Tell her she'll make a lovely corpse. Got that?"

I'm silent.

"Are you hearing me? If you don't stop nosing around, we cut off your boy's thumb. Are you listening? Would you prefer the left thumb or the right thumb? Your call. We will have it delivered to your office. By special courier. I don't trust the Post Office on these important things, do you? Then comes a hand. A foot. Every six hours. Well, you get my drift. If my people see you doing any further investigation like the fun and games at the garage this morning it will be all over for your boy. I kid you not."

"Do you not know who I am?"

"I care not at all who you are."

"You should. I don't like threats. People who threaten me end up badly. If you touch Kenneth or Agent Lovelace, I will destroy you. You must have heard by now what I'm capable of. Let Kenneth go and we can talk."

There's a short laugh. "You are droll, Detective Zorn. There's nothing to talk about."

The connection is cut.

I call our IT unit and tell them to trace the incoming call. I don't expect them to find anything, but it has to be tried. I sit back in my chair and feel a pain in my left shoulder and think about the voice on the phone. "Stop the investigation," the man said. Strange, he doesn't say which investigation.

I'd got as far as Fast Freddy, but that led to the bottom of a grease pit. Fast Freddy is never going to tell me how to find a man named Black. I call forensics and tell them to bring me the photograph of the soldiers Kenneth and I found on Sandra's bedroom wall. While I wait, I open the Wilcox murder file and go through dozens of photographs of the crime scene, witness statements and detailed forensics reports. They tell me nothing I don't already know.

Stapled to the murder file are three photographs of the victim. One is obviously a picture taken at the Department of Motor Vehicles for a driver's permit. Another shows Sandra Wilcox in a group at some kind of party. A notation states this picture was originally taken with Sandra Wilcox's own cell phone camera. She's sitting on a couch holding a can of Coors beer. The notation indicates the photo was sent to the DC police anonymously. The third photo shows Sandra dressed in a casual summer dress sitting on a broken column. Behind her are what seem to be ancient ruins. A typical tourist photo—a trip to some exotic location. It must have been summertime. Or at least somewhere tropical. Sandra Wilcox is smiling happily at the photographer. The notation states this was also sent to the police department anonymously. Who took that picture? And who is sending these pictures secretly?

A messenger from the forensics lab delivers the photograph of the soldiers. It's wrapped in a thick envelope with official police forms taped to the outside showing who had possession of the photo, dates and times, what tests were done and what was found. Nothing useful was discovered. Only Sandra Wilcox's fingerprints. No surprise there.

I remove the picture from its envelope and lay it flat on my desk and study the men in the photo. Fourteen men, young and eager. I compare the faces with that of Tony that Arora gave me. He's there—standing in the back row. There's nothing to discover in his face. He looks like a thousand other young recruits. Looks like a nice kid. They all do.

I switch on the desk lamp to give me more light and turn my attention to the men standing to one side. One is a sergeant. I can make out a lot of stripes on his sleeve—an old-timer. The second is an officer wearing a sleeve patch with an emblem. It's hard to read in the poor quality of the photo, but I recognize the lettering: "AIR-BORNE," and below that, the outline of an arrowhead crossed by three diagonal lightning bolts. I am looking at a Special Operations detachment. Almost certainly Delta Force.

I can just make out the outlines of the officer's name stitched above his left pocket. But I can't read it. I realize I need a magnifying glass; I have none. I'm supposed to be a detective and I don't even have a magnifying glass. It occurs to me there is one place I might find what I need so I cross the squad room again to Kenneth's desk and pull open the middle drawer. There I find a magnifying glass. We have at least one serious detective in the police department.

I take the glass with me—I'm sure Kenneth won't mind—sit at my desk, and look for name patches in the photograph. The enlisted men have no name patches—which would be standard in a Special Operations unit. But the officer does. I shift the photo around in the light until I can't make out a name. Crowley. A lieutenant colonel in Delta Force.

I call Arora immediately. Her voice is sleepy.

"You remember what you told me about your informant in Denver?"

"Of course I remember," she tells me impatiently. "It's the middle of the night."

"He told you he thought Sweet Daddy had been a light colonel in Special Forces."

"That's right."

"I have a name for you. Crowley. No first name. Just check military records for a man named Crowley dishonorably discharged. Maybe we can nail this guy."

I sit at my desk feeling mildly pleased with myself for identifying Crowley until my shoulder begins to hurt again. I figure I'd better find out what's wrong and go to the men's room for an inspection. I twist around in front of the mirror and see small smears of blood seeping through my shirt. Miss Shaw, I think, doesn't have fingers. She has claws. I must remember that.

As I put my jacket back on, I remember the jacket I left in my locker with the torn seam and the book in its inside pocket. I retrieve the jacket and return to my desk where I remove the book from the pocket. It's small, bound in fake leather, old and tattered, held together by a thick rubber band. At some point, coffee or soda must have spilled on it. Many pages are warped and stained a brownish color and some stick together. The book is filled with notations—names and addresses—written mostly in pencil in an almost unreadable scrawl. Many entries have blurred to the point they are barely legible and many have been scratched out.

I recognize some of the names. Many are deceased or in prison. Some I remember as murder victims, their bodies found in some landfill or floating in the Potomac. I don't know quite why but I'm beginning to feel optimistic—or am I just desperate?

One name jumps out at me. Black. First name Artemis. Next to the name is a notation that reads: "Other Worlds Action Comics," followed by an address on Capitol Hill. Black. That's the name Sister Grace gave me. "Look for a man named Black. He'll lead you to the man you're looking for."

The name Artemis Black comes up frequently on our online police records system, but there is no home address listed—only his so-called business address. I need to pay Mr. Black a personal call, but that will have to wait until first thing in the morning.

I go home and dispose of my bloody shirt and ruined jacket. The shirt is a lost cause, which is a shame as it came with the last special order from my purveyor in Jermyn Street. I take a cold shower to wash away the blood from the scratches on my back. And maybe to wash away Miss Shaw. That doesn't work.

* * *

Early in the morning I go to visit Artemis Black. Other Worlds Action Comics bookstore is closed tight. A sign on the door informs me the store opens at ten. Across the street is a coffee shop where I take a table near a window where I can observe the store and I order a cup of what passes for coffee. While I settle in to wait, I make a call to someone named Susan Watkins from the White House stenographic pool. After several rings, the phone is answered. "Hello?" A female voice is cautious. Or maybe just sleepy.

"I'd like to speak with a Susan Watkins."

"Who are you?"

"My name is Marko Zorn . . ."

"If this is about Sandra Wilcox, I don't want to talk to you."

"I'm with the DC Police Department."

"I'm hanging up. Don't call me again!"

"Would you prefer that I come to your home? We can arrange to do that if you'd prefer."

"I wouldn't prefer that. Don't come here."

"Very well, we can just speak on the phone."

"No."

"Then we'll have to pay you a visit."

"What do you want?"

"I want to speak with Valerie North and I don't have her phone number. I believe you can help me contact her."

"Valerie? On the White House secretarial staff?"

"That's right."

"Who gave you my name?" The woman is angry.

"That's not important. What's important is that I speak with Valerie."

"What's this all about? Why do you want to speak with Valerie?"

"This is a murder investigation. Can you help me?"

There is a long silence at the other end, and I hear another voice engaged in a heated, whispered exchange. Suddenly a man's voice is on the line. "Who the hell are you?"

"Metropolitan Police."

"Susan told you she doesn't want to talk to you."

"Then I'll have to come visit in person. Which is a waste of everyone's time."

"What do you want?"

"A telephone number."

"This is police harassment."

"If you want to experience police harassment, just refuse to give me the number I need in a criminal investigation."

"If we give it to you, will you leave us alone?"

"You'll never see me or hear from me again. Guaranteed."

Another long silence at the other end. Then the man's voice comes on the line again. He gives me a local telephone number. "Don't tell anyone you got this number from here," he barks. "Understand! And don't call again." He hangs up.

I immediately dial the number he gave me. After two rings, the phone is answered. "Hello?" a woman's voice says.

"My name is Marko Zorn. I'm with the Metropolitan Police. We need to talk."

"I've been expecting to hear from you," the woman answers.

"Are you Valerie North?"

"I'm Valerie North. You're calling about Sandra? Is that right?"

"Correct. I need to talk to you."

"We can talk. Although I don't think I have anything useful to tell you. I've already been interrogated endlessly by the Secret Service."

"Are you free to meet me today?"

"I'm on administrative leave. I can meet with you any time. But not here. Not in my home."

"How about four this afternoon in the lounge of the Four Seasons hotel."

"Fine."

"How will I know you?"

"I'll be the one looking scared."

"Lots of people in this town look scared. Any other identification?"

"I'll wear a red beret."

CHAPTER THIRTY-ONE

OTHER WORLDS ACTION Comics opens promptly an hour late. It's located on a nice street on Capitol Hill. It is not a nice store. The front window is dusty and filled with old action figures from early Star Wars movies. The store itself is small and crowded with racks of comic books and sci-fi paperbacks and, mostly, porn magazines. There are several life-size mannequins; one is Spider-Man and another Batman. There's an old movie poster tacked to one wall, its edges torn and curled. The text reads "In Space No One Can Hear You Scream."

At the back of the room is a door with a sign reading: "Staff Only." A short, muscle-bound man in his early twenties, who looks like he works out in a gym every day, lounges next to the door, seated on a folding metal chair, tipped on its back legs. His arms and thighs bulge with muscle.

Several men paw through the stacks of porn magazines. They look up at me anxiously when I come in, then turn quickly away.

The man behind the counter is maybe fifty, his long gray hair tied in a ponytail that dangles halfway down his back. He has a bushy, tobacco-stained mustache and has small, piggy eyes. His belly hangs over his belt. He looks mean.

The man does not take his eyes off me as I approach the counter. "Good afternoon, Mr. Black," I say affably.

"Who's Black?"

"I'd say chances are you're Artemis Black."

"You're a cop. I don't talk to cops."

"I want to buy some guns," I explain.

"We sell comic books here."

"Who reads comic books?"

"Lots of people. Kids read comic books."

I look around at his customers. "They don't look like kids. They look like perverts to me. Is that what they are? Perverts? You cater to perverts here."

"Time you left, mister."

"We haven't finished our business."

"Our business is finished."

"Normally when I want to make a business deal, I start off nice. Maybe exchange a few pleasantries. Maybe talk about the weather. I might ask how the Redskins are doing? You know, establish a trusting relationship between us. But I'm in kind of a hurry today, Artemis. So I'll skip the garbage part. I'm told you know where I can get guns."

"I don't know anything about guns."

"Oh, you disappoint me. Didn't I just explain I'm in a hurry?"

"I don't give a fuck if you're in a hurry. Get out of here!"

"Or what? You gonna call the cops? That what you're gonna do, Artemis?"

"Cops don't scare me none."

"Cops don't scare you? That's plain stupid. You ought to be scared."

"And I'm not afraid of you."

"That's even stupider. You should be very scared of me."

The man's eyes shift to the lug sitting by the door marked "Staff Only."

"What's behind the door over there? That the way to a back room? Or is it a basement? You got more comic books down there? Some I might like to see?"

"None of your business what I got down there."

"I think I'll make it my business."

"Luke!" Black yells out. "Get rid of this prick."

The muscle-bound young man near the door lets his metal chair legs drop to the floor, stands up, and lumbers toward me.

"Luke, escort this man onto the street. Feel free to use unnecessary roughness."

The man called Luke reaches out to grab my arm. I swing around and slam my fist deep into his gut. Luke is strong but he's slow. My punch catches him by surprise and pumps all the air out of his lungs. Unless you're trained for this kind of thing, this will essentially disable you for several minutes.

Luke staggers back, clutching his stomach, and falls onto a table covered with magazines. The table collapses under him, spreading him and the magazines over the floor. He lies motionless, his face in pain, gasping for air.

The customers in the store run for the exit, crowding each other in their panic to get out. Black stares at me, mouth open in rage.

"You were saying about unnecessary roughness," I observe.

Black moves along the counter. He's after something. Maybe a baseball bat. Maybe something like a shotgun. So I reach across the counter and grab hold of his ponytail. And slam his face onto the countertop. Very hard. He squeals in pain.

"No games, Artemis,"

"What do you want?" Black gasps, trying to twist away. It's hard for him to speak with his mouth smashed onto the countertop.

"I want to talk to you about guns."

Black is mute. His eyes flick hopefully to Luke who's beginning to stir, desperately sucking in air. I jerk Black around the edge of the counter where he is far from whatever weapon he was hoping to reach.

"Luke, you had enough?" I ask.

Luke nods, his eyes flicking back and forth in fear.

"That's very good. Very good. Now you go to the front door. You leave the store. You lock the door on your way out. Understand?"

He nods vigorously, obviously relieved I'm not going to hurt him anymore. "Yes, sir," he gasps.

"Good boy. Now leave."

Luke scrambles to his feet, still gasping for breath, and stumbles among the scattered magazines to the front door. He stops and looks back at us blankly.

"Lock the door on your way out. And don't come back today. We're closed for business. Mr. Black and I have private matters to discuss."

Luke flees, pulling the door shut behind him. I turn to Black. "Why don't we take a peek at what's in the room marked 'staff only'?"

The man tries to shake his head but can't really move. I lead him through the store until we're standing in front of the door Luke had been guarding.

"Open it."

"It's locked," Black stutters. "Luke has the key."

"That's okay." I step back and kick the door open. The doorframe is made of thin, dry wood and the bolt tears easily through the frame. Beyond is a dark staircase.

I pull Black around so he's standing at the top of the stairs, facing me. I grab him by his shirt collar. "Now let's get back to business."

He nods unhappily.

"I'm told that you broker gun deals."

He stares at me, frightened. "Who told you that?"

"Guns. That right? You deal in guns?"

"I don't know what you're talking about."

"Right now you're involved in the sale of a large shipment of weapons."

"You got the wrong guy."

"You've been contacted by someone. Right? A man who wants to buy guns."

Black is silent, his mouth twisting with fear.

"I expect by now you've heard about what happened to Fast Freddie. I suspect there was a falling-out between Fast Freddie and the man who wants to buy guns. What do you think, Artemis?"

"I don't know."

"Now, here's the situation. I want the name of the people who're selling these guns. And I want to know how to reach this man who's buying them. How do I make those contacts? Telephone number? Email? Text? That's not hard now, is it?"

"You—you can't do that. I'm a businessman."

"I'm sorry you said that. I'm real sorry." I give Artemis Black a hard shove, and he stumbles backwards and falls, shrieking, rolling, arms and legs flailing, down the stairs.

There's a light switch at the top of the stairs and I turn it on. At the bottom of the stairs Artemis Black lies on the floor in a contorted huddle. I walk down the stairs and kneel over his twitching body. "Did you hurt yourself?"

The man is obviously in serious distress. Judging by the odd angle of his lower left leg, he has a compound fracture. There are tears in his eyes.

"You could have killed me."

"I could have. But I didn't. "

"Don't hurt me again."

"Who contacted you about those guns?"

Black's mouth opens and shuts wordlessly.

"Okay," I say, "I'm sorry to be so rude but I'm in a particular hurry today. Here's the way it's going to be. I'm going to drag you to the top of these stairs and push you down again. And then again. Until you tell me what I want."

I think Black groans.

"Have I made myself clear?"

"Okay," he gasps. "Just don't hurt me." Black takes a deep, painful breath. "A guy contacted me. Said he wanted a major gun-buy."

"Who contacted you?"

"A guy."

"What guy?"

"Just a guy."

"This guy have a name?"

"I don't remember."

I kick Black in the leg and he makes a muffled scream. "I'll bet you remember now."

"Okay. He called himself Sweet Daddy."

"You normally do business with people with funny names?"

"I do business with anyone who pays me. He's the one with the money. He's the one who'll take possession of the product."

"What did Sweet Daddy look like?"

"No idea. I never saw him."

I make as if to kick him again. "We never met. I swear. Everything was done by phone or text."

"What is Sweet Daddy looking for?"

"A thousand automatic weapons."

"Did you say a thousand?"

"This is a major buy," Black chokes. "Took me weeks to find a supplier who could handle an order that size."

"Where do these weapons come from?"

"North Korea. You can't get this shit from anybody else."

"What kind of weapons the North Koreans selling?"

"Skorpion machine pistols."

"What's their price?"

"Nine hundred for each weapon. With a twenty-round banana magazine and ammunition. Total of $900,000. Cash."

"How do you pay?"

"I don't. Sweet Daddy does."

"Do you receive the shipment?"

"I never get close to the merchandise. Some guys I know handle the actual transfer. They meet the truck bringing in the guns, hand them off to Sweet Daddy. I don't want to be anywhere near that stuff."

"Where are the weapons right now?" I ask.

"Nashville. Loaded on a truck ready for shipment to Washington."

"Who are the guys who will handle the actual transfer?"

"The main one is a guy named Cal Skinner. I don't know the others."

"Where's this Skinner right now?

"He's on his way to DC."

"How do I reach this Skinner?"

"I don't remember."

I kick Black's broken leg, and he makes a very loud gasp.

"Do you not hear me? How do I reach Skinner?"

"There's a cell phone number you call," Black gasps. There are tears in his eyes.

"Give me the number."

"It's in my wallet."

"Get it."

"I can't. I think you broke my goddam arm. The wallet's in my back pocket."

I reach over Black's fat belly and find a thick wallet in his pocket.

"It's on the back of a Starbucks receipt," Black says. "It's a 301 area code."

I search through the debris in Black's wallet. Among several one-hundred-dollar bills, some crumpled blank checks, and what looks like an old condom, I find the Starbucks receipt.

"This it?" I ask.

Black nods.

"How do I find Sweet Daddy?"

"I have no idea. All contacts from now on are between Skinner and Sweet Daddy. I'm out of the picture. Which is where I want to be."

"What was Fast Freddie's role in all this?"

"I don't know."

"Sure you do, Artemis. Put on your thinking cap."

"Freddie is a moron."

"I'll bet. What was his part of the plan?"

"He has a garage where certain people like to keep stuff. Stuff they don't want certain other people to find. He was supposed to take delivery of the weapons. Hold them for the buyer."

"What went wrong?"

"Freddie went wrong. Freddie demanded more money and that didn't sit well with Sweet Daddy. This morning he put Freddie out of business."

"Where is the delivery set for now?"

"I don't know. Skinner will have to find a new location."

"I'm leaving you now." I get to my feet and toss the wallet far away.

"You aren't going to tell anyone where you got the information about Sweet Daddy, are you? I don't want to end up like Fast Freddie."

"The lesson is: don't do business with people like Sweet Daddy."

Black gasps in pain, holding onto his broken leg. "What do I get out of this?"

"You get to live."

CHAPTER THIRTY-TWO

WHEN I LEAVE Other Worlds Action Comics I return to the restaurant I'd been to before and sit at the same table where I can watch to see if Action Comics gets any action. I see no evidence of any visitors, anybody who might come to check on Artemis Black's welfare. I order something the menu describes as an omelet. Just before I can make my first call, I get two text messages: one from Arora that says: "Bingo! Call me." The second from Miss Shaw informing me a car will pick me up at my home at five this evening. There is nothing about last night's violent romp ending, if memory serves, on her kitchen countertop. The White House switchboard informs me Miss Shaw's not available when I call her back.

"We hit pay dirt," Arora exclaims, enthusiastically, when I reach her. "The name you gave me last night—Crowley. He's our guy."

"How did you learn that?"

"We've gone to the Department of Defense. This is Delta Force material and it's all treated as Top Secret. So Defense is not being cooperative. But I got something."

"First name?"

"Dexter. Full name Dexter Crowley. But wait! There's more. Crowley and our boy, Tony Wilcox, served in the same unit at Fort Brag for almost nine months. Crowley was Wilcox's commanding officer until Crowley was court-martialed."

"What was the charge?"

"Selling military weapons on the black market. The Army wanted Crowley tried and sent to prison, but because anything to do with Delta Force is highly classified, they didn't want a public trial so they just cut Crowley loose."

"Does the Bureau have any record of what became of Crowley?"

"That's what I'm working on. So far we have nothing. I'll let you know."

As soon as Arora hangs up, I call the number Artemis Black wrote on the back of the Starbucks receipt. My call is picked up on the first ring.

"Who's this?" a man's voice demands.

"I want to speak to Skinner."

"Who are you?"

"George Washington."

"You some kind of joker?"

There's a long silence. I sense rapid, muffled consultations at the other end of the line, hand cupped over the receiver. Finally, a new voice comes on the phone.

"Who are you?"

"I told your friend. I'm George Washington."

"Clown!" the voice tells me.

"I want to negotiate the delivery of one thousand Skorpion machine pistols."

"Not on an open line, asshole!"

"I understand you're expecting a delivery of such items."

"I already have a buyer."

"You don't have a place to deliver the shipment. I do. If you want the deal, you're going to have to go through me."

"I'm owed a fee. Ten thousand dollars."

"If you behave, you'll get your fee."

Another long silence. "I'm supposed to take delivery the day after tomorrow. So if you're legit, we have to close soon."

"When can we meet?" I ask.

"I'm coming to Washington tomorrow. We can meet when I arrive. At midnight."

"Where?"

The man gives me the address of a motel on New York Avenue. "You better be on the level, George. If you're not kosher you end up in a culvert somewhere. I kid you not." Skinner has obviously been watching too many bad gangster movies.

I dial a new number. The phone rings seven times then a voice answers.

"Leave me alone!" I'm instructed.

"Guess who, Leonard?"

"I never guess. And I know who you are. Go away. I'm trying to sleep."

"No time for sleep, Leonard. Wakey-wakey. There's work to be done."

"Not interested."

"I have $15,000 dollars for you. Does that pique your interest?"

"How illegal is this?"

"Not very," I explain.

"Not very?" the man at the other end of the line exclaims. "What's that supposed to mean?"

"The part I want you to do isn't especially illegal. I think."

"Can you come now? With the money in cash?"

"I'm on my way," I tell him and cut the connection.

There is just enough time to go home and retrieve the tote bag Sister Grace gave me that still holds $25,000 in cash.

Leonard works out of an apartment in the Adams-Morgan district of Washington. It's an old, low-rent building occupied mostly by out-of-work actors and artists. It's on a street cluttered with bars and Ethiopian restaurants.

I trudge up five flights of stairs. The place smells of weed and South Asian cooking. A man lies crumpled on the second landing. I feel for a pulse, but there is none. Almost certainly he's a victim of an overdose of some street drug. I'll call the medics but there's no hurry. The man is not going anywhere.

I knock on Leonard's door and, after a delay, I hear the sound of chains removed and locks unlocked. Leonard opens the door a crack, peeps out.

"You alone?"

"I'm alone." I push my way through the door. Leonard shuts, locks, bolts, and chains the door behind me.

As usual the breath is knocked out of me by the essence of cat that overwhelms Leonard's apartment. I have no idea how many cats Leonard has. I asked him once and he claimed not to know. I'm not allergic to cats but I always have a hard time breathing the first few minutes I visit Leonard.

"You been in a fight?" he asks.

I still have the bruises from my encounter with the tree. "Something like that."

Leonard is tall and stooped and frail. He looks emaciated, his face creased with deep, vertical lines. His head is crowned with thick brown hair, obviously dyed, that appears to grow straight up from his scalp. He must be over seventy but could be much older.

I've never asked him what it is he actually does, holed up in this crowded apartment. He never asks what I do, which suits us both. As far as I can tell, Leonard hasn't left his apartment in a decade. I suppose someone from time to time must deliver cat food and whatever it is he eats. What I do know is that, when it comes to electronics and cell phones, he is a magician.

Leonard's home is a one-bedroom apartment with a small kitchen. Not that the kitchen looks much like a kitchen or is ever used as a kitchen. Every square foot of the apartment is crowded with cardboard boxes overflowing with electronic tools and devices and coiling wires and heaps of circuit boards. Today there are several disassembled telephones on the stove and a partially disassembled old cathode ray TV set in the kitchen sink. Every chair and table is heaped with boxes, spilling tools, wires, USB jacks. What space is not taken up with boxes is covered with sleeping cats.

I asked Leonard once where he ate his meals. He said he ate, when he found the time, while sitting on his bed. He told me he lived on a diet of cold breakfast cereal he eats directly from the box.

"You know your phone is being tapped," Leonard tells me.

"I'll look into it."

"That's why I prefer that you not call me in the future."

"How am I supposed to contact you?"

"You're supposed to not contact me. What is it you want me to do for you that isn't especially illegal?"

"Do you have two burner phones you can modify for me?"

"Of course."

"Let me see them."

Leonard opens the refrigerator and removes two cell phones from the crisper drawer and places them on the kitchen counter. "What do you want done to these?"

"Two things. I want you to rewire these two phones so they will only connect with one another. If you punch in a number on phone A." I hold up one phone. "It must connect only with that phone." I pick up the second phone. "Phone B. No matter what number you dial."

"Why do you come to me for that? Any ten-year-old kid can do that for you."

"I don't know any ten-year-old kids."

"Get to the point. What else do you want me to do? That's not especially illegal?"

I lift the second phone. "I want you to wire this phone so it becomes an electric detonator."

"I told you last time I don't like to work with detonators."

"You've done this for me before. Besides, there's nothing illegal involved. Maybe I'm just setting off fireworks."

"I'll bet. You planning a Fourth of July party for your friends?"

"It's a kind of party."

"Fifteen thousand dollars?" he asks.

"Fifteen thousand," I answer.

"Let's see the money," Leonard demands.

"You don't trust me?"

"Not for a second."

I open my tote bag and pull out fifteen thousand dollars in small bills, still bundled together with rubber bands. He counts it out quickly, but carefully, and drops the money into a kitchen drawer.

Leonard pushes away a laptop computer and several coils of heavy wire to make room on the kitchen table. He rummages around for tools, pulls up a wobbly barstool, hunches over the two phones, his back to me, and gets to work, snatching up tiny screwdrivers and needle-nose pliers from time to time.

"There you are!" he announces after twenty minutes, swinging around on his barstool to face me. "All done. Ready for your fireworks display. You'll need a nine-volt battery to give it juice. Otherwise, you are good to go." He pushes the two cell phones into my hands. "Mind the polarity when you do the final assembly. You notice, I'm not asking what you plan to use this detonator for."

"You notice I'm not telling you."

CHAPTER THIRTY-THREE

THE DEAD MAN is where I left him on the landing. Once on the street, I call 911 and report there's a man who looks like he's OD'd. I give them the address, cut the connection, hail a cab, and tell the cabbie to take me to the Four Seasons Hotel in Georgetown.

When I arrive, I find a comfortable lounge chair in the reception area where I observe who comes and goes through the front entrance. Almost exactly on time, a woman enters the hotel lobby. She's in her early forties, conservatively dressed, wearing a bright red beret. She looks definitely anxious and stands uncertainly, studying the crowd. I get to my feet and approach.

"Mrs. North?" I ask.

She looks me up and down. Cautious and suspicious. "I'm Valerie North. You are?"

"Marko Zorn. Let's find somewhere we can talk."

"Sure," she says. "Somewhere private."

I lead her away from the reception area and into a quiet corridor that, for the moment, is deserted. We sit on a small couch not far from the elevator banks.

"Thank you, Mrs. North, for agreeing to meet with me."

"It's Miss North." She examines me strangely. I realize I still look like I've been in a brawl. Probably not what she imagined a DC homicide detective is supposed to look like.

"You should know," Valerie North says to me, "I almost didn't come. After our phone call, I decided not to meet with you. Then, at the last minute, I changed my mind."

"What made you change your mind?"

"I want to see justice for Sandy." She bites her lower lip

"What do you mean by *justice*?"

"I've been told not to talk to you, you know."

"Who told you that?"

"Someone named Jessica Kirkland. She's in the Secret Service. She says it's a question of national security. I'll lose my job if I speak with anybody but her."

"You don't work for Jessica Kirkland."

"No, but if I cross the Secret Service, I could lose my security clearance."

"Yet you're prepared to talk to me anyway."

"You know what they're saying about Sandy. They're saying she's a traitor. That can't be true. And Mrs. Kirkland said you're dangerous and not to be trusted. She said you were making trouble, even hinted you might be involved in some kind of conspiracy with domestic terrorists."

"You believe that?"

"I don't know what to believe anymore."

"Did you know Sandy well?"

"We met when she was assigned to the Presidential Security Detail. She being new to the city, I was able to give her some advice. We kind of hit it off."

"Did you know she had a peanut allergy?"

"Of course."

"How did you two meet?"

"In the White House Health Room. We were both into serious workouts."

"Did you know she had a brother?"

"Tony? The one in the Army? She mentioned him. They were very close. I never met him."

"What can you tell me about Tony?"

"Sandy didn't talk about him much. It was kind of a private, family thing. I just know she was worried sick about him."

"What was Sandra worried about?"

"Her brother got involved with some really bad people. Sandy said they were crazies. At one point she was so worried she tried to persuade him to break off his connection to these people. He refused."

"Do you know if Sandy had any close friends here in Washington?"

"She was very private about her personal life. I think at one time she was seeing a fellow Secret Service agent."

"Do you think there was anybody new in her life?"

"I think there was. Sandy was very much in love with someone. I don't know who he was."

I take the photographs of Sandra Wilcox from the police file from my pocket and I show Valerie North the photo of Sandra Wilcox sitting on a couch holding a can of beer. "Do you recognize this picture?"

"Sure. I took it."

"Tell me about when it was taken."

"There was a party. White House staff mostly. About a year ago. Somebody was retiring. You know. I persuaded Sandy to come."

"Did she have a good time?"

"I guess. Although she didn't stay late."

"And you took her picture?"

"I borrowed her camera and took it. Then emailed it to myself."

I show Valerie the other picture—the one with Sandra Wilcox sitting on a broken column. "You know this picture?"

"Sandy sent it to me. She was on one of those official Presidential tours. She had a day off."

"Did she send you lots of pictures? Like when she was on her official travels?"

"This was the only one. I don't think she ever used her camera."

"So who took the picture?"

"She never said."

"Do you have other pictures of Sandra Wilcox?"

"No. Those are the only ones."

"It was you who sent them to the police?"

She nods.

"Why did you do that?"

"The day Sandy died, Jessica Kirkland came to my office. She told me to clear out my things and go home and to wait for further orders."

"Did Mrs. Kirkland ask about photographs?"

"She asked whether I had anything from Sandy. Letters. Emails. Pictures. Anything."

"You didn't tell her about these two pictures."

Valerie bites her lip again. "I didn't much care for Mrs. Kirkland. Or her attitude. When I got home, I searched around and found those two pictures. I didn't know what to do with them. I thought of burning them, but that made no sense so I put them into an envelope and mailed them to the police. Anonymously."

"Tell me about the night Sandy was killed."

"I work on the secretarial staff at the White House and my shift ends at one in the morning. On that night, as usual, I caught a cab to go home. As I was leaving the security entrance on 15th street, I caught a glimpse of some people about a block away and I thought I recognized one of them as Sandy."

"What time would that have been?"

"I can't be positive. About one fifteen. Maybe one twenty."

"Where did you see her?"

"Just outside of the perimeter fence."

"You said 'one of them.' There was someone with Sandra?"

"There were three of them. At first I thought she might be out walking with her lover. She was walking very close to one of them."

"Who was she with?"

"I'm sorry. I don't know. It was dark."

"Tall? Short?"

She shakes her head. "Sorry."

"This person—was he walking in front? Side by side?"

"He was walking behind Sandy. Now that I think about it that was a little strange. Not like a normal couple would walk, you know."

"What was he wearing?"

Valerie closes her eyes. "I'm trying to remember." Long pause. "A poncho. The hood pulled up around his head."

"But it wasn't raining. Hadn't rained in days."

She nods.

"Color?"

"I couldn't tell in the dark."

"What made you call the White House Operations Center?"

"I knew Sandy was on duty that night. She'd never be outside when she's on duty. And I heard the Secret Service detail was looking for her. It was then I realized something was wrong. That's when I called."

A man enters the far end of the corridor. He's dressed in a business suit and wears a blue shirt and a blue tie. He takes a seat on a divan some distance from us and opens a newspaper. He doesn't look at us at all. Which is worrisome.

"It's time we finish here," I say to Valerie. "I want you to walk away. Go to your right. Not the left. That will take you to the main reception area. Don't stop. Just go out the front door. There are usually taxis waiting. Take the second one in the queue. Tell the driver to take you to the Mayflower Hotel. When the cab drops you off at the Mayflower, take another cab and go home. When you get home, please lock your doors."

"Am I in danger?"

"No, Miss North. But I don't want to take any chances. Now go. And don't look back."

She grabs her purse, gets to her feet, and walks away. As soon as Valerie North has disappeared around the corner, I stand up and go to the man at the end of the corridor ostensibly reading a newspaper. Except he isn't reading anything. He's staring at me.

"Hi, Norm," I say, holding out my hand. "What brings you to DC?"

The man is clearly disconcerted and gets awkwardly to his feet, clutching the newspaper to his chest.

"Norm? You remember me. Alan," I say. "Alan from Des Moines."

"I'm sorry," the man says, trying to look over my shoulder, looking for Valerie North. "I don't think we've met," he says, anxiously.

"Sure we have. I'm Alan. Term insurance. Sarasota. You remember."

The man tries to slide away from me, nervously looking to his right and left. "We've never met. If you'll excuse me . . ."

"You're telling me you've forgotten that cute honey blonde? What was her name? Dora something?"

"We never met, mister." He steps away. "I'm busy."

"How about drinks later? Meet in the bar at six?"

His face is red with anxiety and he walks quickly away.

"Six at the bar," I shout. "Don't forget."

CHAPTER THIRTY-FOUR

THIS TIME I ride by myself in a comfortable seat in the back of a government limousine. The two men who pick me up at my home are courteous and solicitous, but they don't say why they've been sent to take me to the White House or who I'm supposed to meet.

When we stop at the West Wing, one of the men leaps from the car and opens the back-passenger door for me. Miss Shaw waits for me on the steps of the main entrance. She skips down the stairs to meet me. The weather is warm and she wears a summer frock in a pastel print.

"Hello, once again, Detective Zorn," she says. "I hope you got home safely last night."

"I found blood on my shirt."

"Sorry about that. I sometimes get carried away. Or so I've been told. I'll try to restrain myself in the future."

"Is there a future?"

"That's up to you. I couldn't help but notice, you seem to have old wounds on your body."

"Football at Princeton," I say.

"They looked more like bullet wounds to me. And one seemed to be a knife wound. In your groin area. I doubt that happened during Princeton football practice. Am I correct in surmising a lady was somehow involved with that one?"

"That's personal."

"I'm happy to say it did not affect your performance."

I follow Miss Shaw through the doors into the West Wing, through the usual security check, where I once again give up my cell phone. She leads me along a nicely carpeted corridor, through several other doors, each guarded by Secret Service agents. The two members of her security detail watch us from one of the side hallways.

Miss Shaw and I stop in front of an elevator door.

"Where are we?" I ask.

"We're in the Executive Mansion of the White House itself."

"Are you going to tell me who I'm seeing this time?"

"Why don't we let that be a surprise?"

"You're full of surprises."

"I try."

The elevator door slides silently open and we step in. It's a short trip—only one floor—and the door opens again almost immediately. Miss Shaw takes me down a corridor painted some soft shade of blue and with thick wool carpeting, also blue. Miss Shaw stops at a door and knocks softly, then opens the door and waves me in.

"I'll see you when you're finished," says Miss Shaw enigmatically. I step into the room and she closes the door behind me.

A woman sitting on a couch rises and crosses the room. "Good evening, Mr. Zorn. I'm Marsha Reynolds." She holds out her hand and we shake. Her grip is firm, assured. "Please, won't you have a seat?"

The First Lady wears a pants suit with a loose-fitting gray blouse and flats. She takes a seat on the couch, folds her hands in her lap. She wears a simple wedding band. I sit in an armchair opposite her.

"Or is it Officer Zorn? I'm afraid I don't know the proper protocol. I've never met a homicide detective before."

"Congratulations. You can call me Marko, if you like."

"I think not," she says, firmly. "Thank you for coming to see me. I know you must have a busy schedule."

I do not answer.

She smiles briefly. She's trying to be friendly, but it's obviously an effort. "Have we met before?"

"I don't think so," I reply. There is no point in my telling the truth at this point. There will be time for that later.

"You look somehow familiar." She shrugs. "Of course, I meet so many people. It's hard to keep track. But we must talk. It's very important that we talk."

"Fine. Let's talk. About what?"

"You know about what." Her friendly mask slips a bit. There is tension showing through her genial façade. "Hollis told me about his meeting with you." She stops, expecting me to say something. When I'm silent, she goes on: "It's about Sandra Wilcox." Another awkward silence. "Hollis suggested you back off your investigation."

"It's not *my* investigation, ma'am. It's an official investigation into the murder of Sandra Wilcox."

"However you wish to put it, the fact remains, there are sensitive issues involved."

"There often are in a murder investigation. Murder tends to bring out the worst in people."

"I'm talking about serious repercussions. Repercussions that could harm this country. This is not an idle request. This involves national security."

"Did you know Agent Wilcox?"

"She was on my protective detail for over a year."

"Then she was transferred to the President's detail. Why was that?"

There is anger in her eyes. "I did not ask you here so you could interrogate me. I am the First Lady of the United States of America. People do not cross-examine me. Even the attorney general of the United States would not dare do that. Certainly not a rank policeman."

"I guess that's why I'm a rank policeman and not the attorney general of the United States."

Her face flushes. "How dare you! How dare you treat me like a common criminal!"

"That's my job."

"Your job is to act in the best interests of your country. And the best interests of your country will be served by leaving the investigation of the death of Sandra Wilcox in the hands of the Secret Service."

She stops, her hands trembling, and makes an effort to control her emotions. "Let's start over. We want to cooperate."

"*We?*"

She doesn't explain. "Leave the investigation to the Secret Service." She's calm once again.

"I can't do that."

"Of course you can. You're just being stubborn. I have complete confidence in Matt Decker, the head of the Secret Service."

"Mr. Decker seems like a competent guy. But he's got more immediate problems to deal with. I'm told there's a plot by some crazy group to assassinate the President."

"I'm aware of that. Matt keeps us informed and the Secret Service is taking appropriate steps to neutralize the threat. That's not your concern." She sits back on the couch and contemplates me. "Leave it alone, Detective Zorn. Drop it."

"I'm afraid I can't leave it alone. I have a question for you, Mrs. Reynolds."

"Am I to be interrogated again?"

"Did you know that Sandra Wilcox had an allergy to peanuts?"

She stares at me, a little stunned, for a moment at a loss for words. "You want to know whether Sandra had an allergy to peanuts?"

"No," I say. "I want to know whether you knew she had an allergy to peanuts."

She studies me carefully as if to determine whether I'm being rude or just obtuse. She decides to humor me. "Yes. I was aware Sandra had an allergy. She told me about it many times. Is it important?"

"Yes, ma'am. It's important. Did you know her well?"

"She served on my security detail for a year."

"That doesn't really answer my question, does it?"

"Sandra was with me virtually all that time."

"I understand these security arrangements can be close, almost intimate."

"That's correct. Why are you asking me this?"

"Did that make you feel uncomfortable?"

"You've been talking to Matt Decker. I suppose I was uncomfortable. Uncomfortable with men, I mean."

"That close contact was easier for you with women agents?"

"It was easier with Sandy. She was very supportive. Very understanding."

"I have another question."

Mrs. Reynolds makes an impatient, angry gesture. "Very well."

"What is it that Hollis Chambers does here in the White House?"

She looks perplexed. "What has this got to do with Sandra's death?"

"I don't know. Probably nothing. I'd still like to know."

"He's an old family friend. He's our chief adviser."

"He told me he brings no expertise."

"What he brings is honesty and integrity. He brings unquestioned loyalty. These are rare qualities in Washington." She pauses. "Satisfied?"

I get to my feet. "I suppose I'll have to be."

"I didn't say for you to leave, Detective. I have a question for you."

"I suppose that's only fair."

"Why do you care so much about Sandra Wilcox? Why do you persist in investigating this one particular murder case? You must have many open cases. What is it about this particular case that makes you so stubborn?"

"The murder of Sandra Wilcox is personal."

CHAPTER THIRTY-FIVE

LAMONT SITS IN the bleacher seats watching a pickup basketball game. The few people here to observe the game sit as far from him as they can. Lamont wears expensive sneakers, orange laces left untied, a soft leather coat, and expensive, stylish Bulgari sunglasses. And a smart fedora—pale blue made of straw—that nearly hides his orange hair.

Sitting a few rows behind him are two big men in dreads, wearing Jordans, laces untied, leather jackets and sunglasses, but cheaper brands. Lamont's bodyguards watch me sullenly as I take a seat a few feet from him.

We watch the game in silence for a couple of minutes. Lamont leans in toward me and looks at my left wrist. "What that watch you wearin'?"

I pull up my jacket sleeve an inch or so to show him. "A Vacheron Constantin."

"Old?"

"1964."

"How much you askin'?"

"Not for sale."

Lamont pulls up the left sleeve of his leather jacket revealing a heavy man's watch. "Rolex Oyster."

"I can see that," I say.

"I'll trade you for that Vacheron."

"No deal."

"I paid $12,000 for this baby," Lamont tells me proudly.

"You got ripped. It's worth maybe half that."

"You don't know shit, Detective." He turns away and watches the game. "Otis tol' me you wanna' talk a business proposition. I don't normally talk to policemen. Especially not to you."

"You scared to talk to a cop? If I scare you, I'll go away."

"Not scared of no cop. Not scared of nobody. Especially not scared of you."

"That's a big mistake." We sit in silence for a while, watching the game. "I'll bet you're scared of Cloud, though."

Lamont tenses. "Who tol' you that? That a flat-out lie. Like I tol' you, Lamont Jones ain't scared of nobody."

"Okay. Just saying. Maybe you aren't scared of Cloud, but I'll bet you do what he tells you to."

"We be partners, unnerstand? Used to."

"Just saying. Cloud's top dog in this town. He's got the crew. He's got the city. He's got Mariana."

"What Mariana got to do with it?" Lamont demands, angry. "You come here to talk shit or you come here make me a business proposition?"

"I've got a shipment of guns I'm looking to sell."

"What kind of guns?"

"Skorpions."

"Never heard of no Skorpions."

"Skorpion is a submachine pistol. With the magazines I'm supplying, it fires twenty rounds full automatic."

"How many you lookin' to sell?"

"I have 1,000 coming the day after tomorrow."

"They any good, these Skorpions?"

"Perfect for close-up work. Anybody who has these, they're going to outgun any organization in town. Hell, anybody who has these machines, they're going to own this town."

"How much you askin'?"

"$900 each. Cash deal."

Lamont whistles. "That almost a million dollars. It might take me a day or two to put that kind of money together."

Lamont turns in his seat to face me directly. "You tell Cloud about these Skorpions? I know he in the market."

"I thought I'd offer you first refusal. If you can't handle the deal, Cloud gets the Skorpions."

"You tryin' to cut Cloud out of the deal?"

"If you can't make a deal without Cloud saying okay . . ."

"I don't need Cloud's okay. I can make my own business decisions."

"I thought you were Cloud's boy."

"You thought wrong."

"Downtown, that's not the way we see it. Downtown we say you're just his driver. If Cloud says 'jump' you jump."

Lamont's body twitches in anger. "You got a big mouth, mother-fucker. Maybe too big for your own good. You keep talkin' shit, and I gonna stomp yo punk ass."

Lamont reaches inside his leather jacket, smoothly takes out a Ruger automatic from his shoulder holster, and presses the muzzle hard against my left temple. Lamont's two goons are on their feet and draw their own guns in case Lamont needs help. He doesn't. The basketball players disappear from the court, and the few remaining people on the grandstand are on their feet and rushing to the exits as fast as they can.

"Put that damn thing away. Somebody might get hurt."

"Only person gonna get hurt is you." Lamont jams his gun harder into the side of my head. "Who's scared now? Do I look scared to you? What's to stop me from blowin' your head off right now?"

"You shoot a police officer in public like this, it's the end for you. Besides, if you do, Cloud gets the Skorpions. He gets to keep everything, including his crews. And he gets Mariana. He'll own this city."

Slowly, Lamont takes his gun from my head and replaces it in his holster. "Why you want to burn Cloud, mister?"

"Cloud and I don't get along."

"You think you an' me gonna get along? We gonna be best friends?"

"If Cloud gets these guns, you better watch your back. What I hear, Cloud don't like competition. For the streets. For his woman."

"I can take care of myself."

"From what I hear, he's saying Lamont's not man enough to run this city. Not man enough to handle Mariana."

"You have these guns?" Lamont demands. "Or you talkin' trash?"

"There's a truckload of Skorpions on the way to DC right now. I take possession as soon as they arrive."

"You throw in that watch you wearin' and we got ourselves a deal."

"Okay. We have a deal. Cash. But there's something else."

Lamont studies me.

"I hear you have a warehouse in Southwest you use to store stuff," I say.

"What if I do?"

"I need that space."

"What for?"

"To store the Skorpions when they get here. Out of sight. Where ATF can't find them. Where Cloud can't find them."

"I can handle the handoff."

"That would be a mistake. You don't know the people who are bringing the guns. They might plan to steal your money. They might even be Feds. You're better off having no contact with the sellers until the shipment is safe in your own warehouse. Leave that to me."

"Okay. You can use the warehouse." He gives me a street address in Southwest Washington. Then gives me an eight-digit series of numbers. "It's a cyber lock," Lamont explains.

"I'll call you when the Skorpions arrive. I'll tell you when to come to the warehouse to pick them up. It's time I left, Lamont. I've got to go to a funeral, and I never want to be late for a funeral."

CHAPTER THIRTY-SIX

THE CHAPEL IS modern with abstract stained-glass windows and pews and floors of bleached hardwood. What is probably a baptismal font looks something like a fish.

My visit is pointless, I know. I've attended too many memorial services, too many funerals and wakes, for people who've been murdered. I've never known the killer to have a sudden attack of conscience and stand up in the middle of the service and confess his guilt. It never seems to work out that way. I suppose I may have a vague hope maybe brother Tony might show up.

I sit in a pew at the back where I can observe who comes to the service for Sandra Wilcox. Around a quarter to three a few people begin to trickle in. They find their seats after looking quickly around to see who else is attending and then reading the program, not speaking to one another, heads bowed. No eye contact. I can't tell whether they're here to pay their respects or, like me, to observe who's there.

Mrs. Kirkland from the Secret Service arrives and takes a seat two pews in front of me. I suppose attending church services for murdered Secret Service agents is part of her administrative duties. She doesn't acknowledge my existence. A few minutes later, Larry Talbot walks down the center aisle looking to his right and his left. He catches my eye but does not stop. He takes a seat in the front pew, here to say goodbye to his onetime lover.

A few minutes before three, Trisha Connelly, Sandra Wilcox's roommate, shows up. I'm a bit surprised. She told Kenneth and me she and Sandra Wilcox were roommates but not close. Maybe she's here to add to her gossip store. She moves quickly, head bowed, and takes a seat at the far end of a pew, pretending to be invisible.

A young man in a black outfit with a white clerical collar steps up to the pulpit at the front of the chapel. He shuffles through some notes, then looks out at the people gathered before him. He begins to intone something then stops as a late arrival enters the chapel. It's Valerie North. I'm sorry to see her here. She should have taken my advice and stayed home, out of sight. I'm pretty sure senior members of the Secret Service present are taking notice. She looks around anxiously, then slips into a back pew. She's dressed in a dark dress and wears a small, black velvet hat and white gloves.

At that moment I sense movement at the end of my pew, and Arora Lovelace takes a seat but not close to me. She says nothing and pretends to read her program. Her face is grim, jaw clenched. The knuckles of her hand holding her program are white.

"We have come together to say farewell to—" here the minister consults his notes—"to our sister, Sandra. We offer prayer and trust . . ."

I sense a new arrival. Carla Lowry strides down the center aisle. Maybe she's here to represent the FBI, a sister agency. Probably she's here for the same reason I am. To see who's come and who hasn't come. She makes eye contact with no one and takes a seat in the front pew.

The young minister resumes: "Almighty God, look on your servant, Sandra . . ."

Arora takes a deep breath and leans in toward me. "Marko, who the fuck *are* you?" she whispers—so loud everyone in the chapel can hear.

The minister stops abruptly, for a moment disconcerted. He looks out over those seated before him, looking for the source of disturbance. Several people turn to stare at us. Mrs. Kirkland glares at us, then turns away.

Miss Shaw, in a dark-purple, silk dress, arrives. This comes as a shock to me. I would have thought the White House staff would want nothing to do with Sandra's memorial service. Miss Shaw stops and surveys the scene, smiles at me, strolls halfway down the aisle and takes a seat in an empty pew.

"Excuse me?" I say to Arora in what I hope is a low, civilized voice. The minister is droning on about something, but I'm not really paying attention. "What's this all about?" I ask.

"Let us pray, then, for our sister, Sandra," the pastor or minister or whatever he is intones solemnly. It's a desultory business. He's obviously never heard of Sandra Wilcox, knows nothing about her, and knows no one he is facing in the chapel. And he doesn't have a clue about what he's gotten himself into. "May angels surround her . . ." he goes on.

"You told me you were in Hamburg," Arora whispers in my ear, a little softer this time.

"What of it?"

"The State Department has never issued a passport for anyone named Marko Zorn."

Several people turn and hush us. The minister glares at us, annoyed and unhappy, and then begins to read the Twenty-Third Psalm.

"Must have been a clerical error."

"Bullshit, Marko!" Arora whispers through clenched teeth. "What's going on?"

More disapproving looks in our direction.

"Nothing's going on."

"Homeland Security has no record of you leaving or returning to the US in the last five years." Arora's voice rises and several more people turn to look at us again. "You fucking don't exist."

A middle-aged man in a blue suit and a trim beard, sitting across the aisle, turns in his seat and gives us the death stare. Arora settles back in her pew. Finished with me—for the moment.

The young minister is saying something about "I know that my Redeemer lives." Somebody plays "Nearer My God to Thee" on an organ somewhere.

When the music stops, the minister asks: "Does anyone here today wish to say a few words in memory of our sister, Sandra?" He looks anxiously at those in the chapel, gazing suspiciously at Arora and me, praying, I suppose, that we don't ruin the ceremony any more than we already have.

There is an embarrassed silence during which people study their programs intently and try not be noticed. I'm saved from having Arora launch into me again when Larry Talbot rises to his feet, turns, and faces those attending.

"Sandra was a beautiful soul," Talbot begins. His voice is low. A bit uncertain. "She was my friend." He stops and takes a deep breath. "We met during a Secret Service training exercise in Laurel, Maryland. At a shooting range. How romantic is that?" He stops again and tries to contort his face into a smile. It comes out a grimace. Talbot looks around at the small crowd as if searching for comfort from those watching him. I doubt he finds any. "We got to know each other well when we were both assigned to the Atlanta field office. We'd meet at a small coffeehouse called Sammy's. I'm sure many of you know it."

Talbot stops and studies those sitting in the pews. Suddenly his anger and bitterness boil up. "Sandra was a loyal and loving friend. Unlike those who are afraid to come here today. Friends who today deny her." Talbot stops, at a loss for words. "Sorry. I don't know what to say." He swallows. "Sandy devoted her life to her country. She gave her life for her country. I only wish there was something I could do. Something to honor her memory; to honor her life and her name. Something that might make things better for somebody else." He stops searching for words. "I can't. Except to honor her here today." He bows his head. "Thank you," he murmurs and abruptly sits down.

"Why should I trust you if you lie to me?" Arora hisses at me, unable to contain herself any longer.

I decide not to answer. There is no good answer to that question. I feel bad about Arora. I was beginning to like her and was beginning to think we had a good relationship. That, after all this was over, we might see one another. Then everything falls apart.

There is an awkward silence in the chapel. I think, this is it. No one else is going to say anything. I even wonder whether I should stand up and say something. But what could I say? I know nothing about Sandra. I never met her; she's a total stranger. And always will be. But I feel some notice of her passing must be made.

The people in the chapel stir as someone else stands up to speak. It is Valerie North. She clears her throat nervously. She holds a prayer book in her hands, not looking at the rest of us.

"I've never spoken in public before," she says. "I don't know what one is supposed to say. Except Sandy was my friend. She was loved by everyone who ever met her."

Not everyone. At least one person who met her did not love her. Maybe the one in the poncho and hood on a day when there was no rain. Maybe someone who is here in the church today? Watching? As I am.

"That's all I have to say." Abruptly Valerie sits down and bows her head.

There is embarrassed silence. Then, of all people, Carla Lowry stands up, turns to the congregation and faces us. Her face is grim.

"My name is Carla Lowry. I didn't know Sandra Wilcox. I never met her. She was not my friend. Until recently, I'd never even heard her name. I don't know what she was doing in the last days and weeks of her life and I make no judgments but I do know she served her country with honor. I am here to pay my respects and to honor her for that service."

With that Carla Lowry looks over the gathering defiantly, daring anyone to contradict her, then sits down.

There is another prolonged silence while the young minister waits anxiously for someone else to say something. Obviously, there was nothing in his seminary training to prepare him for a memorial service quite like this. When no one volunteers, he announces hurriedly: "Let us pray," and recites the Lord's Prayer, too fast, I think.

"Amen." Collecting his notes, he leaves quickly by a door in the back of the chapel so he doesn't have to speak to any of us attending the service.

Almost immediately Carla Lowry stands up and strides down the center aisle. She stops at the end of our pew. "Come with me, Agent Lovelace," she says and makes her way out the chapel door.

Arora gets quickly to her feet. "We're not finished, Marko." With that she turns away, furious, and follows Carla. She leaves her program, crumpled, on the pew.

As quickly as they can, the remaining participants leave the chapel. They are silent and don't look at one another while someone plays some dirgeful music on the organ I think is supposed to be "Amazing Grace, how sweet the sound".

I'm the last one to leave. At the back of the chapel there is a sign-in register. The only name is Larry Talbot's. I add mine. I hesitate, trying to think of something appropriate, then write, "I will not forget you." It's not much, but I have to leave something for Rose's sake. I go out through the front chapel doors. For a moment I stand on the outer steps in the sun and light a cigarette. I hear a voice behind me.

"An interesting service, don't you think?" Miss Shaw stands a few paces from me. Obviously, she's been waiting for me to leave the chapel.

"I thought it was the pits."

"Memorial services are supposed to be the pits. That's what they're for."

"I don't see your security detail today, Miss Shaw."

She nods toward a black SUV parked a few yards away. "It was a church service. I didn't think their presence was called for." She smiles enigmatically. "The young woman you were seated next to," Miss Shaw asks. "Was that Agent Lovelace by any chance?"

"That was Agent Lovelace."

"She seemed agitated."

"Very."

"Do you own a tuxedo?"

At first, I think I must have misheard her. "Excuse me?"

"You know. A tuxedo. Those outfits with cummerbunds and bow ties men wear. Do you own a tuxedo or are you one of those who must rent one for each occasion?"

"I own several."

"Come to the White House this evening. The President wants to speak to you. Privately."

"I'm busy."

She pretends she doesn't hear me. "There's a reception. It's black tie. The President will slip away from his guests to speak to you. I will send a car to pick you up at your home at 7:20. Remember: black tie. Don't forget to shine your shoes."

She smiles pleasantly and walks to her waiting SUV.

CHAPTER THIRTY-SEVEN

MISS SHAW AND her SUV have disappeared, but I can't shake her memory. The way she looks at me with her hazel eyes. Her confession—if that is what it was—what was that really all about? Was it all a lie or was she trying to make us coconspirators? But what kind of conspiracy?

There seem to be no cabs cruising Wisconsin Avenue at the moment so I start to walk toward Massachusetts Avenue when a black Lexus sedan comes to a stop in front of me and the back-passenger door is flung open. Inside is the most beautiful woman I've ever seen.

"Get in, Marko," she says. "I'm in trouble."

Her name is Mariana. The woman I'd first met while she stood in line waiting to get into a concert. The woman I lost my heart to. Briefly. The woman who I almost lost my life because of. I climb in and pull the door closed behind me. The Lexus is already in motion before the door is fully shut.

"I am in fearful danger, Marko. Help me."

The man at the wheel is one of Mariana's many cousins. Mariana squeezes my hand gently and a sweet erotic tremor surges through my arm. She is dressed in a stylish short skirt and designer jacket and she holds a beaded clutch purse in her hands. As always, her hair and makeup are perfect.

"What kind of danger?" The part of my brain I usually ignore is telling me I should stop now; I must not get involved with this woman. But my brain is outmatched by Mariana's magic. Mariana is my narcotic of choice.

"It's Cloud. He's gone crazy. He's going to kill me."

"I told you to leave Cloud."

"I know. I know. I should have listened. He's going to kill me."

"Can you hold out for another day?" I ask. I can't tell Mariana what is about to happen and that her problems with Cloud may soon be permanently over. After last time, I can't trust her. I haven't completely lost my mind.

"I don't have another day. Cloud believes Lamont wants me to become his woman."

"Why would he think that?"

She looks away suddenly, staring out the car window.

"Why, Mariana? Why does he think that?"

"I may have said some things. Maybe I hinted I found Lamont attractive."

"You shouldn't have done that."

"I know. I wasn't serious. I just wanted Cloud to be jealous. And now . . ."

"And now what?"

"Cloud says he's going to kill me."

"Then get out of town."

"I would have left, but Cloud has my passport. My green card. Even my driver's license. I have no money. I have nothing. This car. My clothes. My jewelry. My apartment. They all belong to Cloud."

"I can get you money. I can get you a fake passport. Even a green card. But that would take almost a week."

"I'll be dead in a week."

"Do you have someplace safe you can go? Some friends you can stay with?"

"Cloud knows my friends. He would find me and kill me and kill my friends."

"What about your family and relatives?" I nod toward the driver.

She shakes her head. "I can't put my family in danger. Help me, Marko. Are you going to let me die?"

"I'll try and arrange protection for one night."

"Will you stay with me? Will you protect me?"

"I can't."

Mariana looks stricken. "You must stay with me. Cloud will come after me. I know. He has ways of finding me. You're the only one I know who can protect me from Cloud." She squeezes my hand fiercely.

"There are things I have to do."

"What things?" Her large, dark eyes glisten with tears. She leans close to me, so close I can feel the heat of her body. "Things more important than me?"

There's no point in telling her I'm supposed to meet the President of the United States. That would cut no ice with Mariana.

"You must protect me," she says. "You're the only one."

That's what she'd said last time. I want to believe her. She must read my mind. Maybe she sees the doubt in my eyes. "I'm so sorry about the other time," she whispers softly. "I know I made a terrible mistake. I can't tell you how sorry I am. I never meant for it to turn out that way. I'll make it up to you. I promise. Help me. Please."

"I know a man who's an expert in protecting people. He can take care of you."

She looks doubtful. "This man, is he as nice and sweet as you are?"

"Much nicer. Much sweeter. You'll like him. It will only be one day. He'll protect you."

I make the call. I have grave doubts about what I'm about to do but I don't see I have much choice. I'm already too far in.

Larry Talbot is cautious when he answers his phone. I can tell from the background noise he's in his car, presumably driving home from the memorial service.

"Thanks for coming to the service for Sandy. I needed a friendly face."

"I'm going to ask you for a favor. A very big favor. Probably the biggest favor anyone has ever asked of you."

"Go on," he says, cautiously.

"I'm with a woman who's in great danger. There is a very dangerous man who wants to kill her."

"What's this got to do with me?"

"She needs protection. For twenty-four hours."

"Why are you asking me?"

"Protection is your profession. You know how to use weapons. You know how to protect people. I'm asking you to stay with this woman for one night."

"You're asking me to protect a woman I don't know."

"That's right."

"I'm not a security guard."

"I'd do this myself but, as you know, I'm deep into the investigation of Sandra's murder. There are people I must see tonight who will lead me to her killer. It would just be for one night."

"Who's threatening this lady?"

"Her boyfriend. A local gangster. I have to warn you, he's very dangerous."

"That sounds like a standard police problem."

"Not with this guy. I need someone with very special skills. You're no longer on duty with the Secret Service. Take your free time and help this woman. I assure you the threat to her is very real."

"In the Secret Service, protection is a team job. Four or five agents are always involved in a protection detail. What you want is something completely different from what I'm trained to do."

"You're a professional."

"I'm not a professional bodyguard. You can hire those easily. There are people who do this kind of thing. I'm a government employee. What you're asking me to do is probably illegal."

"You have training no professional security guard has."

"And why should I do this?"

"For Sandra."

"What does that mean?"

"You said in your eulogy you wished there was something you could do to honor Sandra's memory. I'm giving you the chance to save another woman's life. I know it won't bring Sandra back. I know it won't take the pain away. But think of it as a gift for Sandy."

There is silence at the other end of the phone line. I don't push him. I feel Mariana watching me intently.

"How do I do this?"

"Do you have a weapon?"

"I turned in my official service weapon. But I have my personal Beretta."

"The name of the lady is Mariana. She lives in an apartment on Upper 16th Street. I'm taking her there." I give him the address. "Can you meet us there now?"

Larry Talbot is waiting for us at the entrance to Mariana's apartment building. The driver lets us off and drives quickly away. I hustle Mariana across the sidewalk and through the front doors.

"This is my friend Larry," I say to Mariana as we stand for a moment in the impressive front lobby of her building. "Larry will look after you tonight, Mariana. You'll be in good hands."

Mariana smiles her incandescent smile. "Marko didn't tell me you were so good-looking. He said you were nice. Promise to be nice to me."

"I'll try," Talbot says, clearly starstruck by Mariana.

"Marko is sometimes mean," Mariana says. "He sometimes yells at me."

"I'm sure he has good reasons."

Mariana opens her eyes wide with feigned consternation.

"Let's get the hell out of here," I say.

"See what I mean, Larry?" Mariana whispers confidentially.

I take Mariana firmly by her arm and guide her to the elevator bank. The front desk guy, who is probably called a concierge in a fancy place like this, watches us as we disappear into the elevator.

Mariana's duplex is on the top two floors. When we enter, I direct Mariana to sit on a white, fur-covered sofa in the living room. Which she does, pretending to sulk. She places her purse on the floor at her feet. Her hands are clasped tightly together.

"Give me your keys."

"I need them," she tells me petulantly.

"Not tonight, you don't. Give me the keys." I hold out my hand. Mariana picks up her purse, removes a set of keys, and flings them at me.

"Give me your phone."

She looks anxious. "I need my phone."

"No phone. We don't want you to call anybody. Or anybody to call you. Not your friends. Not your family. Do you understand? Nobody. Give me your phone."

Reluctantly, she takes her cell phone from her purse and places it in my hand.

"Give me the other one."

"That's my only phone."

"Give me your purse, Mariana."

Her face flushes with anger. "No."

"Your purse!"

"You have no right." She looks beseechingly at Talbot.

I snatch the purse from her hand.

"You can't do that! That's personal."

I rummage through the purse and remove a second cell phone that I hand to Talbot.

"Are there any other entrances to your apartment besides the front door?" I ask Mariana. "A kitchen entrance? An old servant entrance?"

"I don't think so."

"We'd better check ourselves," Talbot says.

"Don't move, Mariana," I tell her. She watches, her eyes wide with innocence, as Talbot and I go through her apartment, searching every room, every closet, every possible hiding place.

We go through a large kitchen, a dining room, and what I suppose is some kind of sitting room. Upstairs are the living quarters. We ascend a spiral staircase and check out the master bedroom and two guest rooms. Wherever I see a landline phone, I pull the wires from their jacks and give the phone to Talbot.

We stop at the top of the spiral staircase.

"I need to warn you. Mariana's in real danger. The man after her is a dangerous criminal who's killed people. Cloud Walker almost killed me. I'm sure you can handle him. But be careful with Mariana. She has a very sick relationship with Cloud. She can change her mind and decide to contact him. Whatever you do, don't let her make any calls. And don't open the door to anybody but me."

"I get the idea."

"Secure the dead bolts on the front door when I leave and don't let Mariana out of your sight. Not for one minute. No matter how much she pleads with you. She can be very persuasive."

"You don't trust her?"

"Absolutely not."

"It sounds like you speak from experience."

"A few years ago, during one of her breakups with Cloud, I took her out. Well, more than took her out. She spent several nights with me. When she decided to return to Cloud, she swore to me she would never tell Cloud what she'd done."

"I take it she did."

"I don't know why. And she didn't let me know she'd told Cloud. So, I wasn't prepared when Cloud came after me. By this time tomorrow, the danger will be over. But until then, Mariana is a mortal threat to you—the most dangerous woman you will ever meet."

CHAPTER THIRTY-EIGHT

A LINCOLN TOWN car stops in front of my house at seven fifteen sharp. The chauffeur, no security type this evening, properly opens the rear door for me, respectfully touching his visor cap. The car has been recently washed and polished and gleams in the streetlights.

"Good evening, sir." The chauffeur bows me into the back seat of the limousine where I make myself comfortable. While the driver takes me down Connecticut Avenue, I examine the well-stocked bar and the not-so-well-stocked collection of reading material. Apart from today's edition of the *Wall Street Journal*, all I find is an outdated *Guide to Our Nation's Capital* and some flyers from local hotels.

The limousine glides through the main Pennsylvania Avenue White House gates and pulls up to the front entrance to the East Wing where Miss Shaw is waiting for me. This time she's wearing a black cocktail dress that might be a Diane von Furstenberg with Christian Louboutin pumps. Her platinum blonde hair is done up in an elegant chignon.

A dozen limousines are lined up in the circular driveway and a multitude of uniformed drivers are mixed in with Secret Service agents and security types. Back in the darkness, Secret Service agents in their black uniforms, armed with P90 submachine guns, stand among the trees.

Miss Shaw inspects my tuxedo. "You have an excellent tailor, Detective."

"Why am I wearing this outfit?"

"You are not unknown to the powerful in this town and are not always welcome. We thought, in a tuxedo, you'd be less conspicuous."

"Rather than wearing my usual trench coat and gum shoes?"

She ignores me and I follow her through the parking area.

"Why am I here?"

"You are meeting with the President. It is strictly off the record. No one knows you're entering or leaving the White House this evening."

She takes my arm and leads me through the east entrance used for security screening, guarded by armed Secret Service agents, and a tall young woman who, Miss Shaw informs me, is the White House Social Secretary. The tall lady checks off visitors' names as they pass through. Neither she nor the Secret Service agents bother with me when they see I'm accompanied by Miss Shaw.

We enter the East Wing. A Marine captain, in full dress uniform, is waiting at the entrance to the White House proper to greet the guests, and he directs us to a flight of marble stairs. Miss Shaw's brilliant red-sole shoes click on the white marble steps. At the top we are on the state floor of the mansion where a large social gathering is underway.

The reception area is filled with men and women in formal clothes, many of the men wearing medals and service decorations. Scattered among the guests are men, and a few women, in military uniforms—the aides and escorts, I assume, and various generals and admirals. The women guests wear ropes of pearls and diamond brooches, their hair recently washed and coifed and teased to perfection. A young Marine nods to us as we pass. "Good evening, Miss Shaw."

At one end of the room is a long open bar, the table covered by a heavy, white damask tablecloth, tended by bartenders in starched white jackets. A string orchestra, its members in splendid, red Marine Corps uniforms, plays dance music. A few of the more adventurous, or possibly just younger, guests dance to some show tune.

A dozen servers glide among the guests, holding trays with flutes of champagne and seltzer water—the latter, I suppose, for the alcoholics in the crowd. Some servers carry trays laden with expensive-looking canapés: little things on wooden skewers and others impaled on red, white, and blue toothpicks. Dainty white napkins with the White House crest in blue are proffered.

Hollis Chambers stands at the far side of the room in deep conversation with a man wearing a turban accompanied by a middle-aged woman in a beautiful sari. Chambers moves his head slightly and our eyes meet. He looks deeply disturbed, then turns away. Across the room, Mrs. Reynolds is talking animatedly with a group of women. She wears an elegant, black Alexander McQueen satin and lace evening dress. When she catches sight of me, her laughter stops. She disengages from the other women and strides across the floor determinedly to me.

"I understand you're here to talk with Eliot," Mrs. Reynolds says. "You know you're becoming an intolerable nuisance."

"That's my job."

"Please listen carefully to what Eliot says." She fixes me with an angry glare. "This is serious business." She turns on her heels and returns to her guests.

I feel a gentle tug on my arm. Miss Shaw whispers, "Come with me."

We pass a long table heaped with bowls of shrimp on crushed ice, thinly sliced ham, sausages with sauces on the side.

I follow her down a corridor, through what I think is the Blue Room, and stop at a door that she opens and then ushers me inside.

"Wait here," she says. "I'll get the President."

"You seem to be in charge of this place."

"Pretty much." She smiles. "This will take only a few minutes."

She shuts the door quietly, leaving me in a small room furnished with a few antique chairs. On one side is an unused fireplace with a vase holding artificial flowers. I amuse myself while I wait by looking at the pictures on the wall—a mixture of oil paintings of men in wigs and engravings of landscapes. I try to identify the men in the wigs but mostly fail.

The door opens and Miss Shaw escorts President Eliot Reynolds into the room. The President studies me while Miss Shaw says something to him in a low, urgent voice I cannot hear, presumably explaining who the hell I am and why the President must talk to me.

He smiles brightly, a smile I've seen a thousand times on TV and on magazine covers while Miss Shaw fades out the door.

"Good to meet you, Mr. Zorn," the President says heartily, shaking my hand. "I've heard a great deal about you."

"I'll bet you have," I reply. "Sorry to take you away from your guests."

"I'm delighted to slip away. These things are terrible bores."

There is an awkward silence. I have the impression the President has been given talking points to bring up with me but, for a moment, can't remember what they are.

"You wished to speak with me, Mr. President?"

"Yes. Yes, of course. It's about this terrible business with the death of Agent Wilcox."

"A terrible business."

"Marsha told me about your conversation. And Hollis. You've talked to him as well, I believe."

"That's right."

A long pause. "It seems we're at something of an impasse."

"If you mean that I'm determined to investigate the death of Sandra Wilcox and expose her murderer and you want me to drop the case, then yes, we're at an impasse."

Reynolds studies me quizzically and seems almost at a loss for words. I suppose, as leader of the Free World, he's not accustomed to being contradicted by some low-level public servant. His talking points don't seem to have covered this contingency.

"You seem to forget I have influence in this town," the President says.

"I don't take bribes, Mr. President."

Reynolds' face flushes. Now I've pissed the President off, majorly. Reynolds shakes his head in disbelief. "If not as a favor to me, then as an act of loyalty to your country. I don't believe I'm overstating the case when I say this matter could affect the future of the nation. Please consider this."

"When I spoke with Hollis Chambers, he alluded to a major crisis on the night Agent Wilcox was murdered . . ."

"That's right. A crisis."

"A crisis which prevents me from getting the information I need to find Sandra Wilcox's killer."

"That's right."

"With respect, Mr. President, I don't believe any of that. There was never any crisis."

President Reynolds stares at me in shock.

"I'm being lied to."

"I beg your pardon," the President sputters.

"I don't like being lied to."

"You're out of line."

"I suppose I am."

"Drop the Wilcox case."

"Sorry, Mr. President, but I won't stop until I've found Sandra Wilcox's killer."

"Why do you care about this particular case? What difference does it make to you if this one criminal among many escapes justice?"

"That's what I'm paid to do, Mr. President."

"It's more than that."

"All right," I reply. "Because I promised Sandra Wilcox justice."

There is a long silence while he tries to process this. "Then that's the way it will have to be." All the phony geniality has gone. The President's face is stone cold, his manly jaw clenched. "Let us hope for the best."

He opens the door. Miss Shaw steps in. "We're finished," he growls to Miss Shaw and strides from the room.

"Did the President ask you for something?"

"He asked me to do him a favor."

"And you said no."

"That's right, I said no."

She sighs, takes my arm, and leads me toward the White House entrance. "I think you're done here, Detective."

"That's it?"

"You have disappointed us, Detective."

"Sorry about that."

"It's not a good idea to disappoint people like us. Never forget, life is not a zero-sum game."

"Did you really think I'd forget my promise to Sandra Wilcox and, after our little frolic, do whatever you wanted?"

"That's the way it usually works."

"I didn't think sex was so transactional."

"Sex is always transactional."

CHAPTER THIRTY-NINE

THE WHITE HOUSE limousine drops me off at my house thirty minutes later. I'm alone and about to go inside when a stretch Lincoln, not all that different from the one that just dropped me off, comes speeding down my street and stops in front of my house. Two large men swing open the car doors. They are not from the White House. These men are Cloud's people.

The two men are on me, one in front, one in back. I can see they carry shoulder holsters with heavy automatic weapons.

"Come with us, Zorn."

"What if I don't want to?"

"Then we break your legs."

"Okay," I say. Cloud is the man I must see.

The Kotton Klub is located on a stretch of U Street in Northwest Washington. The interior is a bit run-down, but the clientele is loyal and enthusiastic. Although guns are strictly forbidden, people have a way of getting shot here. Its liquor license is always on the verge of being pulled and the police have been trying to shut it down for years. The owners of the Kotton Klub have influence downtown.

My escorts double park the Lincoln in front of the Klub and hustle me out of the car, past a velvet rope and a long line waiting to get in, the majority attractive young women—a mixture of black, white, and Latina—and through the front doors.

We step into the dark, noisy club where music blasts top amp from loudspeakers scattered around the ceiling and strobe lights flash on and off, blinding me, then leaving the Klub in darkness for seconds at a time. I'm disoriented and have no idea how to work my way through the dense crowd of gyrating bodies or even where I'm going.

"This way, Detective Zorn," one of my escorts tells me. We move through the dancing, laughing crowd, go past the crowded bar and through a door in the back, marked "Private," into a sitting room with its own bar and bartender, and with comfortable chairs. It's quiet here, the music muffled.

Cloud waits for me at the small bar wearing a beautifully tailored silk suit. I feel the phantom twinge in my chest.

"How come you all dressed up, Detective Zorn?" Cloud demands. "You goin' to a party? Or maybe a funeral? Maybe goin' to your own funeral?"

"I like to look sharp when I come to your club."

"Where's Mariana?" Cloud demands.

"How should I know? She's your lady, last I heard."

"I tol' her to be here at the club. She never showed up." Cloud studies me with deep suspicion.

"I have no idea where she could be."

"She's not answering her phone. I been trying all evening."

"Maybe she has a headache."

"I sent some of my boys to her apartment. There was no answer when they knocked on the door. When they tried to open the door, it was locked from the inside. How you figure that?"

I shrug. "Sorry. Have you asked Lamont? Maybe he can help."

Cloud's body tenses, and I think for a moment, he's going to slug me. Then he controls himself. "Why you think Lamont might know about Mariana?"

"I don't know. Just trying to be helpful."

"What you know about Mariana and Lamont?"

"Nothing."

"What's this I hear about you selling machine pistols these days?"

"Where'd you hear that?"

"How come you go to Lamont with this deal? How come you don' go to Cloud?"

"Who told you about the guns?"

"You got genuine Skorpions? Not some Chinese knockoff shit?"

"They're genuine."

"I ask how come you didn't come to Cloud with this deal? I'm the main man in this town. Lamont's nobody. You understand? He may talk big but he nobody."

I say nothing.

"You lookin' to make me angry? Right now, you under the protection of Sister Grace. But you never know how long that gonna last. Sister Grace be an old lady. No tellin' when she might pop off. Could be next week. Could be tonight. You never know."

"She looks healthy to me."

"Accidents happen. Know what I mean? Accidents sometimes happen to old people."

"That's none of my business."

"You better make it your business. How many of these Skorpions you lookin' to sell?"

"One thousand."

"What's your price?"

"Total $900,000."

Cloud whistles. "That a big order. What Lamont want with all them guns?"

"I forgot to ask. The Skorpions would make his crew the most powerful organization in town. Maybe anywhere on the East Coast. He'd have more firepower than the DC police. Hell, more firepower than the U.S. Army. He'd have more power than the President of the United States over there in the White House. He'd own this town. And he could have anything or anybody he wants."

"I own this town. Lamont jus' talk."

"Maybe he thinks different."

Cloud looks me directly in the eye. "Maybe Lamont thinkin' too much. Maybe you talkin' to the wrong people."

"You interested in the deal?"

"Sure," Cloud answers. "How do I get these Skorpions?"

"Nine hundred thousand dollars," I say. "Cash on delivery."

"Okay. Cash. Where these Skorpions now?"

"They're on a truck ready to be shipped to Washington. As soon as they arrive, I'll store them in a safe place. I'll call you as soon as they arrive and tell you where you can pick them up."

"I want those guns. An' don' let Lamont get his hands on them. Understand?"

"They're all yours, tomorrow. At six in the morning. You bring $900,000. That clear? You bring the money; you get your guns."

"An' Lamont's out of the picture."

"Like you say, you own this town."

"If you see Mariana, you tell her to get her ass here. Now!" He turns away, stops. "Don' fuck with me, Detective. You do, Sister Grace won't be able to help."

As soon as I'm well away from the Klub, I call Talbot. "She's asleep," he tells me.

"Any problems?"

"A couple of times some people banged on the door. They tried to unlock the door, but the dead bolt is secure. Mariana's cell phone's been ringing constantly. Other than that, it's quiet."

"Has Mariana given you any trouble?"

"Not a thing. She hasn't tried to leave. Or to make a phone call. We've had a very nice conversation."

I'm not reassured.

CHAPTER FORTY

FROM OUTSIDE THE Friendship Motel, it looks dingy and run-down. Inside, it looks worse. In the lobby the chairs are worn, the carpet threadbare and stained, the front desk ratty and smelling of disinfectant. Two cats lying on one of the couches raise their heads to study me as I enter. They dare me to make them move.

"We're full," a man behind the desk announces in a bored voice without looking up. He's about seventy, bald, his nose aflame with broken veins.

"Just delivering flowers to your guests," I announce and head for the elevator. I'm not carrying flowers, but the deskman doesn't care. There is a very old elevator. The cab lurches and bumps slowly to the third floor.

There is one ceiling light bulb in the hallway that I remove, leaving the hall in darkness. That's the way I prefer it when making house calls. I knock on door 3B and inside I hear muffled voices. The door opens a crack, and an eye peers out at me from a dark room.

"Yeah?" a voice demands.

"I'm here to see Skinner."

"Who wants to see him?"

"A guy with ten thousand dollars in small bills."

There is more silence broken by urgent whispers.

"You want the money or not?" I ask. "Or should I leave it here in the hall for the cleaning crew?"

The door opens and a large man with a swarthy complexion and a fierce mustache looks me up and down. "What's with the monkey suit?" he demands. He looks over my shoulder into the dark corridor to confirm I'm alone, then steps away from the entrance. "Get in here. Quick!"

As soon as I'm inside, he slams the door behind me and I'm in the dark.

"Turn on the lights," I say.

"Why should I do that?" someone asks.

"Because I like to see the people I do business with."

After a brief pause, someone switches on a table lamp next to a bed. I'm in a small, cramped room with one unmade bed with dirty sheets. There is a door leading, I imagine, to a bathroom. Three men watch me. One is the swarthy guy, wearing a leather sheath at his belt, with fancy stitching, containing what looks like a serious, six-inch Bowie knife. The second is a short man wearing bib overalls carrying a 12-gauge over-and-under shotgun aimed vaguely at my head. The third is older. He's in his shirtsleeves and wears a ratty, food-stained tie. He has a holster at his belt holding what looks like a Colt revolver.

There are greasy pizza carryout cartons on the bed and floor. The place smells of pepperoni and cheese and beer. There are a dozen Bud and Coors cans on a side table and as many more empty cans stuffed into a wastebasket.

"Search him," the man with the tie orders. The guy with a knife pats me down. He's clumsy and unsteady, and I smell beer on his breath.

"Clean."

"Which one of you is Skinner?"

"None of your business," the tie man says. "Let's see the money."

"I like to know who I'm talking to." The three men look at one another.

"I'm Skinner," the man with the dirty tie and Colt revolver says.

"Okay," I say. "Tell me how I collect the Skorpions and how I contact the buyer. Then you get your fee."

"Not so fast, pal. We get our fee. Then we give you the contact info."

I drop the tote bag onto the bed. "Open it," Skinner orders.

I open the tote bag to reveal bricks of dollars, in small bills, bound together with rubber bands. I spill the money out on the dirty sheet.

"Count it, Earl," Skinner orders the short man.

The man with the shotgun steps to the bed, slings the shotgun under his left arm, and starts counting. I'm somewhat reassured to note these bozos are amateurs, drunk and without a clue what they're doing.

The two others watch as Earl counts the money. Skinner stands next to the bed, switching his gaze from the money, then to me, then back to the money. Immediately behind me stands the big guy with the six-inch knife.

It takes a long time for Earl to go through the money. He fumbles often, his hands shake. Earl has been drinking a lot of beer, I think. And he's scared shitless.

"There's $10,000 here," Earl mumbles at last.

"What's to prevent me from just taking your money and collecting our fee direct from the buyer?" Skinner asks me.

"That would be dishonest."

"Do I look like a Boy Scout to you, mister? You're just a middleman. We don't need a middleman. We have a buyer. We double our profit."

"I wouldn't do that if I were you."

"What you gonna do about it? There are three of us. Just one of you. We got guns. You got shit. That don't look like good odds for you."

"The odds look fine to me."

"Earl," Skinner orders. "You can shoot this man now. But don't get any blood on the money."

Earl staggers a bit, moving the shotgun from his left to his right hand, so it's inches from my chest. He doesn't stand a chance.

I grab the shotgun barrel and jam it back into Earl's face. He yells in pain and tries to grab the gun back, but he's slow and clumsy. I swing the gun around so my finger is on the trigger. The big man with the mustache draws his knife and lunges at me.

I squeeze the trigger, the shotgun muzzle barely six inches from the man with the knife, striking him in the upper right chest. He staggers back, slamming against the wall, his knife spinning from his dead hand. He leaves a long smear of blood on the wall when he slides to the floor. A 12-gauge shotgun blast at very close range will do that to you.

My ears are ringing from the blast. I turn so the remaining two men are in my sights and point the shotgun at Skinner who stares, one hand on the gun at his belt, at the man on the floor who twitches a couple of times and then lies still, eyes and mouth open.

"You killed Trevor," Skinner says, his voice shaking.

"It looks that way."

"Why'd you go and kill Trevor for?"

I point the shotgun at Skinner's face. "Should I improve the odds in my favor again, you think? There's one round left. Who should I use it on?"

Skinner shakes his head.

"Move over there." I point the shotgun at the corner of the room where dead Trevor is stretched out on the floor. The man I'd just taken the shotgun from stumbles across the room. "On the floor! Next to your buddy."

He gets down on his knees.

"All the way," I order. "Lie on the floor. On your stomach."

He does what I tell him.

"You," I say to Skinner, "very slowly unbuckle your belt."

"My belt? What you want my belt for?"

"Your belt. Let your pants fall to the floor. With your gun and holster. Don't do anything funny or you end up like Trevor."

Skinner starts to undo his belt and tugs nervously at his buckle but has a hard time. Finally, the buckle comes loose and his pants sag, then drop to the floor around his ankles.

"Okay," I announce, "let's get back to business. What's the arrangement to pick up the Skorpions?"

"They're on a truck."

"Where's the truck?"

"Can I put my pants back on?" Skinner asks.

"No. Where's the truck?"

Skinner glances at his watch. "Should be parked at a truck stop somewhere on I-95 South 'bout now."

"What's the plan?"

"The driver's waiting for me to call and tell him where to deliver the goods. The original destination had to be changed. It got blown up, I hear. Once the driver has the new address, he'll meet us at the agreed location."

"Where is the buyer in all this?"

"I call him and give him the address where he is to pick up his merchandise. That's it as far as I'm concerned. Can I put my pants on now?"

"No. I'm going to give you an address. You call the driver. Give him this address." I write out the address on a pad of paper next to the phone. "Just the address. No small talk. No chitchat. Tell him to be at this address at five thirty in the morning. Got that?"

"I need my cell. The driver's number's on speed dial. And the driver won't answer the phone unless he recognizes my caller ID."

"Where's your phone?"

"In my pants pocket."

"Very slowly take the phone from your pocket."

Skinner reaches down to his pants bunched around his ankles and gropes for the phone.

"Very carefully now," I say. "If you so much as touch that gun it's over for you. Your friend over there can bury you with Trevor."

"I'm being very careful."

Skinner pulls his cell phone from his pants pocket.

"Make the call."

Skinner stabs at his phone several times and, after a minute, says: "Hello. You arrived?" Silence. "Okay. Here's the address." Trevor reads the address I gave him. Then reads it again. "Be there at five thirty." He switches off his phone.

"Very good, Skinner," I say. "Go across the room. But leave your pants where they are."

Reluctantly, Skinner steps out of his pants, crosses the room, and stands, in his underwear, near where Trevor lies crumpled on the floor. I retrieve the Colt revolver from his belt holster, collect the note with the address, put the revolver and note along with the cash in the tote bag, and put it under my arm.

"Here's the way it's going down," I explain. "I'm going to leave now."

"What are you doing with my money?" Skinner demands.

"I'm taking it with me."

"You can't do that! It's mine."

I point the shotgun at Skinner's face. "This says otherwise."

I collect the shotgun, Skinner's pants and his cell phone, grab hold of the tote bag, and go to the door.

"Can I have my pants back?" Skinner whines.

"No."

"What am I supposed to do with Trevor?"

"You'll figure something out."

CHAPTER FORTY-ONE

I LEAVE THE motel to make my call on the phone I took from Skinner.

"Yes!" a voice demands.

"Sweet Daddy? Or should I call you Colonel Crowley?"

"Who the hell are you?"

"I'm the guy your boys tried to kill at Fast Freddie's."

"How did you get this number?" Crowley demands.

"Skinner suggested I call you."

"Skinner's a dead man."

"Let's discuss the arrangements for delivery."

"I don't know what you're talking about."

"Thanks to you, we have to change the location for the delivery."

"I don't want to talk to you. I want to talk to Skinner."

"Skinner's occupied burying one of his associates. You have to talk to me or you don't get your shipment, Crowley."

"Stop using my name, asshole!"

"Whatever you say, Crowley."

"Where's the shipment?"

"Approaching Washington this very moment. I take possession of the goods in a few hours."

"When can I pick up my stuff?"

"When I see Kenneth."

There is a long silence at the other end. "This has nothing to do with your boy."

"Then we have nothing to talk about. Bye-bye."

"Don't hang up."

"I need to see Kenneth."

"He's okay."

"I see Kenneth, then you take the shipment. That's the deal. I'll call you when the shipment arrives and tell you where you can pick it up. You bring Kenneth."

"I tell you, your boy's okay."

"I decide that. Bring Kenneth or there's no deal."

"If you screw me, you're finished."

"I decide who's screwed, Sweet Daddy."

The connection is cut. Next I call Larry Talbot. No answer. I call again, thinking maybe I punched in the wrong number. Again, no answer. I'm getting a bad feeling about this. Is Mariana okay? Has Cloud or his people got to her? Why is Larry Talbot not answering?

I'm a block away from Mariana's apartment building when I know things have gone very bad. A dozen police cars, their lights flashing, are stopped in front of her building on 16th Street. Two ambulances are pulled up onto the sidewalk. Uniformed police have blocked off 16th Street, directing traffic to detour around the site.

I abandon the Jag in the middle of the street and race toward Mariana's building, swerving around cars, flashing my badge at the policeman blocking the street, diving under the yellow police tape and running to the front entrance.

I know the cop guarding the entrance. "A shooting," he tells me.

I charge through the entrance and head for the elevators. The doors are just about to close but one of the homicide detectives I know holds the door open for me.

"One dead," he announces.

"Man or woman?"

"I don't know. I just got here."

"Who's in charge?"

"Frank Townsend."

"Why's Frank here?"

"We're running out of investigators. You know, with the street violence. And we just received a call about a murder at a motel on New York Avenue. Some men were seen putting a body into a dumpster."

The corridor is filled with cops. Residents of the other apartments on this floor peer out their doors, dressed in pajamas and night-gowns—curious and frightened.

The door to Mariana's apartment stands open. Two cops block the way. I know them both and they wave me through.

There is a crowd of crime scene technicians, medical examiner personnel, photographers, and detectives.

Larry Talbot lies sprawled on the couch. Blood soaks into the white fur. His Beretta lies on the floor at his feet. Carl Nash, one of the crime scene investigators, kneels next to the body.

"Shot twice," Nash tells me. "In the head. Once from a distance, looks like. Once up close."

I'm sick to my stomach and have to take several deep breaths before I can speak. "Have you identified the victim?"

"Not yet. Will go through his pockets when the medical examin-er's done."

"Can you tell me what happened?"

"It looks like the victim was standing here by the couch. Someone must have come through the front door and shot point blank. The poor son-of-a-bitch didn't have a chance."

"Any other victims?" I'm almost afraid to ask.

"None so far."

I walk quickly into the dining room, then the kitchen. There's no sign of Mariana. I race up the spiral staircase to the living quarters. She's not in the master bedroom. The bed looks unslept-in. Mariana's clothes in her closets look undisturbed. I check the two guest bedrooms. There's nothing to see. I don't know whether to feel relief or rage.

I go down the spiral staircase for one last look at Larry Talbot.

"Marko!" someone yells. It's Frank Townsend, charging through the crowd toward me.

"Get the hell out of here!"

"I can help."

Frank stands directly in front of me, his face flushed, breathing heavily. "This is a crime scene. It's closed to everybody but authorized official investigators . . ."

"I'm a senior detective."

"Not anymore you're not. You're relieved of duty as of this minute."

"I'm in the middle of a case . . ."

"You hear me? You're out! Done! Turn in your weapon and your badge first thing in the morning."

"This is crazy . . ."

"You're off the force. If I have my way, you will face criminal charges! Now get out of here. This is a crime scene. Out! Before I have you arrested."

CHAPTER FORTY-TWO

FUCK FUCK FUCK fuck. My voice is hoarse so I must be yelling. I slam my fists on the Jag's wooden steering wheel. I see the image of Larry Talbot's bloody head against the white couch. My hands shake and a uniformed cop manning the police line farther up the street watches me anxiously through the Jag's windshield. He must hear me screaming and probably thinks I've lost it. He's not wrong. Fuck fuck shit shit shit fuck fuck.

I take a deep breath and grip the steering wheel until my hands ache and I force my nerves to settle. Slowly I release the steering wheel. My hands have stopped trembling. It is safe for me to drive now. It is safe to get to work and do what I have to do.

By the time I get home, my pulse is steady. It's dark outside, and when I look out the windows, I see my reflection. And the bloody face of Larry Talbot. My anger and guilt will have to wait until another day. I'm ready now and it's time to make my move.

I reset the security checks, including motion sensors for the entire house. I change into street clothes, then return to the kitchen and search the shelves next to the oven and pull out a large roasting pan. I'm not sure why I have a roasting pan. I rarely prepare my own meals, certainly nothing as elaborate as to need roasting.

In the basement I pull up a tall chair to a wooden workbench. Here I drill four small holes in each corner of the roasting pan. I open a false wall panel above what was once a bar, open the door of a heavy commercial safe, and remove a box covered in red plastic.

After putting on my glasses, I carefully remove the box's red plastic covering, open the box, and take out several pounds of Semtex. I prefer Semtex to C-4. Call me old school. I form the Semtex into six shaped charges and secure them carefully into the roasting pan. I attach the blasting caps into the shaped charges, then wire one of the cell phones Leonard prepared for me into the blasting caps. Semtex is stable and easy to work with but I like to show high explosives proper respect and I take my time and work cautiously. With this charge, if something should go wrong, I'd blow the house to pieces, not to mention me.

I pack my explosive roasting pan, along with a power drill, a small tool kit, a pair of vinyl gloves, a small flashlight, and a handful of metal screws into a tote bag, then secure the safe door and clean up leftover debris.

The preparation takes me less than an hour. I pick up a 9-volt battery from a kitchen drawer, lock up, and I'm ready to go.

A half hour later I'm cruising in the neighborhood near Lamont's warehouse. There is nothing suspicious—no cars parked on a dark street that shouldn't be there, no one lurking in a doorway. I find a small, derelict office building not far from the warehouse. To one side is a parking area partially hidden from the street by a dilapidated wooden fence where I park the Jag.

Five minutes later I'm on an empty street in front of Lamont's warehouse. There's a cool breeze and I step into a doorway to keep warm. After ten minutes, headlights appear several blocks away moving cautiously down the street toward me. It looks like an old International 4300-series medium truck, painted white, the name and logo of some former owner painted over. There are dents in the fenders and scratches along the sides. The license plates are from Alabama. The truck is followed by a dark gray SUV. It is 5:38 a.m. They are on time.

I step into the street, leaving the tote bag in the doorway, and stand with my hands at my sides where they can be easily seen. The truck comes to a slow stop twenty feet away. The driver watches me through the dirty windshield. We stand like that for several minutes, each gauging the other. Then four men get out of the follow-SUV and circle around me. Two hold rifles, one a shotgun. They stand about ten feet away from me.

Finally, the truck door opens and the driver climbs out of the cab and walks toward me. He can't be much over twenty. "Where's Skinner?" The man has a slight Hispanic accent.

"He's tied up."

"We don't deal with strangers."

"Too bad. I guess you'll just have to turn around and go back to Nashville."

"I don't want to hang around here."

"I'll bet you don't. We can settle this in a hurry. I represent the principal. I take the truck and what's in it."

"I thought we were supposed to keep the truck."

"Okay. If you want to wait. You can work out the details with Skinner. That may be a while."

The man looks at his watch. "It's gonna be light soon. Give me an additional $20,000 and you get the truck."

"Wait for Skinner to work that out."

The man looks anxiously at the other men, then looks at his watch. "Fuck it! Let's go."

The driver tosses me the truck's ignition keys. As I catch them, the men rush to the SUV, pile in, and, in seconds, are gone. Leaving me alone on an empty street with the truck and 1,000 Skorpion machine pistols and ammunition.

The warehouse is made of concrete blocks. There's an old, fading sign on the front that says: "Holden Kitchen Supplies." In front there is a large, corrugated metal roll-up door for use for delivery trucks. To one side is a normal door next to which is a sign reading "Employees Only."

I lock the truck and walk around the building and inspect the immediate area. I see no signs of surveillance. No cars or small trucks with tinted windows. No man hanging around pretending to smoke a cigarette. At this hour, the area is deserted. I look especially closely for CCTV cameras on surrounding buildings. There are none. In a few hours, trucks and vans will be arriving, picking up and delivering goods. But, for now, I have the area to myself.

I return to the front of the building and locate the cyber lock on the small front door. In the dim light, it's hard to read the numbers on the lock, and I have to use my small flashlight—something I don't like doing. It draws unnecessary attention. I fumble the first time and have to punch in the numbers a second time. The lock clicks and I push open the door. The warehouse is empty. There is no sign of activity inside except for a couple of dried-up pigeon feathers lying on the concrete floor.

From inside, I unlock the roll-up door, open it, and drive the truck inside then pull the door shut. At the back of the building there is another door, which I unlock, and I step into a narrow alley. The wind blows empty paper coffee containers and scraps of newspapers around my feet.

Inside the warehouse a little early-morning daylight filters through dirty windows. I don't want to turn on a light that would alert anybody passing along the street the warehouse is in use. I put on the vinyl gloves and insert the 9-volt battery into the detonator.

I slide under the truck on my back, balancing the roasting pan on my chest. Here it's completely dark and I switch on my flashlight to survey the underside of the truck. Above me is ancient mud and dirt and what appears to be decades of grease. And God knows what else. Perfect, I think. I secure the pan to the underside of the truck bed with the small screws. Meanwhile bits and pieces of crap cover my hair and face.

I'd prefer to place the pan on the truck bed among the crates of Skorpions and ammunition. That way it would be less likely to be torn loose by some obstacle in the road. But I can't take that chance. I'd have to remove half the crates from the truck to do that and the pan would have been immediately obvious if anybody unloaded the truck. So I place it beneath the truck bed, out of sight.

CHAPTER FORTY-THREE

MY FIRST CALL is to Crowley.

"Yes," he says cautiously, his voice barely audible at the other end of the line.

"Your shipment has arrived, Sweet Daddy."

"I told you, no names."

"Right you are, Sweet Daddy."

"Fuck you! Where do I pick up my merchandise?"

"I see Kenneth first."

"I collect my shipment. Then you see your boy."

"Simultaneous. You come to me with Kenneth. I talk to Kenneth. You get your guns."

There is silence at the other end. Then, "Where do I go?"

I give Crowley the address of the warehouse. "How long will it take you to get here?" I ask.

"Thirty minutes. If I see anybody there but you, you're all dead."

Crowley and I cut off the call simultaneously.

My next call is even shorter.

"If you want to close our deal, come to this address." I give Cloud the warehouse address. "Be here in forty-five minutes. And don't forget your payment."

"I'm bringing it with me. And I'm bringing backup. My stuff better be there," Cloud replies. "As advertised."

During my final call, Lamont confirms he'll buy the Skorpions and will be at his warehouse in forty-five minutes with the money.

"Don't forget the watch," he adds.

I hide my cell phone, along with my tools, in a crevice in the wall and put the remaining rewired phone Leonard prepared for me in the back pocket of my pants. I walk around the truck to be sure I've left no signs of my activities. I check that the keys are in the ignition and the cab doors and rear doors are unlocked. I survey the interior of the warehouse. Everything is as it should be. My work here is almost done.

I step out onto the street in front of the warehouse to wait, leaving the roll-up doors wide open. I know it's early in the day but I need a cigarette. It's been an awful twenty-four hours and I'm deeply shaken by what happened to Larry Talbot. I worry about Mariana. I tell myself I deserve a smoke.

It's still cold in the street and the breeze has picked up but the sun feels good on my face. The neighborhood is deserted. No delivery trucks are in sight, no sign of anybody headed for an early shift.

Twenty minutes later, a Jeep Grand Cherokee followed by a vintage Oldsmobile sedan, painted green, pull up to the warehouse doors. The driver of the Jeep studies me carefully through the windshield, turns and speaks to somebody I can't make out in the passenger seat next to him. The two vehicles pull slowly into the warehouse, stopping just in front of the truck. I follow by foot. The Jeep doors are thrown open, and a man steps out of the passenger side. He carries a Browning automatic pointed at me. He nods and four men, each armed with a shotgun, pile out of the Grand Cherokee behind him and quickly close the warehouse doors.

The driver-side door of the Olds opens slowly and a tall man I remember from Fast Freddy's emerges. I seem to recall his name is Floyd. He has a swastika tattooed on his left wrist. He approaches me cautiously, and I hold my arms out on both sides and try to look innocuous and non-threatening. Floyd pats me down, finding nothing but the cell phone, which he takes and walks to the Olds, leans down and speaks quietly to the passenger in the front seat. There's a long exchange I can't hear, then the passenger door opens and a second man steps out.

This should have been my big moment. I am finally face-to-face with the man I've been hunting for what seems like weeks although it's been only a few days. The man I've been obsessed with. There should have been trumpets. *Oh Clouds Unfold!* Instead he's a short, dumpy, middle-aged man in a rumpled, dirty white suit and a bow tie, with pale, rheumy eyes who looks no more threatening than your average beagle.

"He's clean, sir," Floyd says. "Except for a phone." Floyd tosses the phone to the man in the white suit who examines it carefully, then puts it into his jacket pocket.

"I guess you must be Sweet Daddy," I say. "Or do you prefer Crawley?"

"None of your business."

"Where's Kenneth?" I demand.

Crowley gestures toward the Oldsmobile. "He's fine. Show me the guns."

"Kenneth first," I say.

Crowley sighs. "Cass!" he yells at the man holding the Browning. "Bring him out."

The man he calls Cass pulls open a back door of the Olds. There is movement within and a figure appears, hands bound. The figure stands beside the car, head down, and staggers slightly. I walk to him.

"That's far enough," Crowley yells at me.

I continue walking. "I'm going to speak with Kenneth," I yell back. "I'm going to see for myself he's okay."

Kenneth has several days' growth of pale beard. His hair is uncombed. His face is drawn. But there are no signs he's been injured.

"You all right? Did they hurt you?"

"I'm fine, sir." His voice is raspy. "They pushed me around some, but I'm fine." He's trying to sound brave but he's clearly deeply shaken. "Thanks for coming to save me."

"I haven't saved you. Not yet, I haven't. The worst is yet to come." I don't tell Kenneth the only reason he's alive is because Crowley had to keep him as a hostage. Once Crowley has taken over the gun shipment, Kenneth is no longer of any use. Me neither.

I face Crowley. "I've brought you the Skorpions. I'm taking Kenneth with me."

"Not so fast. I examine the guns first." Crowley turns to Floyd. "Open the truck."

"Yes, Mr. Crowley." Floyd disappears and a moment later I hear the sound of metal squealing and the tailgate falling open. "All clear, Mr. Crowley," Floyd calls.

Crowley walks to the rear of the truck and studies the piles of wooden crates filling the truck.

"Open one," Crowley says.

I should have anticipated this. Should have given myself more time.

Floyd pulls out one of the crates and places it gently on the ground. He pries open the wooden cover, tossing it to one side. Inside lies a Skorpion machine pistol nestled in straw and covered in thick black packing grease. Floyd lifts a Skorpion from its crate and hands it cautiously to Crowley who takes it in both hands, lifting the weapon gently up and down as if it were a newborn baby.

"Isn't she a beauty?" Crowley crows to no one in particular. He unfolds the wire stock and holds it against his shoulder. He swivels around, pointing the Skorpion first up at the roof, then at me, then at Floyd, who cringes. Finally, back to me. He pulls the trigger and the hammer clicks.

"It's not loaded. You have to load the magazines and then rack the magazine into the gun first."

"Bring some ammunition, Floyd."

"You better remove the packing grease before you fire it," I say. "Or it'll jam."

Crowley's shoulders sag a little. He looks forlornly at the Skorpion then passes it back to Floyd. "We'll test-fire them at the compound," he says. His hands are smeared with black grease he tries to clean with a dirty handkerchief. "Pack it up, Floyd. Button up the truck. We're ready to roll."

Floyd reattaches the lid and replaces the crate securely in the back of the truck then swings the tailgate closed.

"Larry, you and Finney take the truck and go to the compound."

"You coming, Mr. Crowley?" the man called Larry asks.

"I'll follow in the Olds. I've got some personal business to care of. Call me when you reach the compound. I'll send a message to our people then and let them know."

Larry and a second man climb into the truck cab and look at Crowley as if for further instructions. Crowley nods and Larry starts the truck engine. Floyd and one of the other armed men pull open the warehouse doors and, with a roar and a cloud of blue exhaust, Larry, the truck, and the Skorpions are gone. Floyd immediately pulls the doors shut.

"Post guards at the entrance," Crowley orders. "No one comes in here 'less I say so."

Floyd directs two men with shotguns to take positions in the street just outside the warehouse front doors.

"What happens now?" I ask.

"We wait."

"Wait for what?"

"Wait until I tell you to stop waiting. I want to be sure the goods arrive without interference."

So much for my escape plan.

Five minutes later the silence is broken by the sound of cars approaching. A car door slams and voices yell angrily.

"What the hell's going on?" Crowley demands. "You expecting visitors?" Before I can answer there's a fusillade of gunfire. A dozen rounds. One of Crowley's men rushes back into the warehouse. He's trembling. Breathing hard. He's lost his shotgun.

"There's a bunch of men out there," he yells. "They're shooting at each other. I think they killed Norm."

"Go out there and find out what's going on," Crowley orders me.

There's another round of gunfire. Maybe thirty or forty shots. Small arms mixed with some automatic weapons. There are curses and screams.

"Get out there!" Crowley yells.

"I'll go out back and circle around and see what's happening."

"Your boy stays here in case you got a mind to run for it."

I slip out the back door of the warehouse. Floyd follows me and crouches just outside in the empty alley. The only movement is from newspapers drifting in the breeze, the only sound, small-arms fire from around the corner.

"We're in the middle of a fucking war," Floyd gasps, gripping an AK-47. "They're a lot of men shooting at each other."

"Go back inside the warehouse and wait for me." I keep my voice low. "You'll be safe there. Stand just inside the door. If somebody tries to get in, shoot 'em. Anybody. Except me, of course." Floyd disappears back into the warehouse.

I work my way cautiously toward the corner of the building, keeping close to the wall. I look around the corner and see an SUV stopped near the front of the warehouse, its windshield shot out. A man lies on the ground near the driver's door. He is one of Cloud's bodyguards who took me to the club last night. Crouched behind the SUV, Cloud and one of his enforcers are firing handguns at something or somebody I can't see.

I move quickly away, heading for the back door to the warehouse. I've gone maybe ten feet when I feel a gun muzzle pressed into the back of my head.

"Last time I missed," a familiar voice says to me. "No way that gonna happen again."

I turn and Cloud steps back so he's well out of my reach in case I should make a grab for the Walther automatic he's pointing at my right eye. I feel the bullet fragment twisting in my gut.

"I'm going to put you down, Zorn."

Cloud is alone, his crew nowhere in sight.

"Don't do that."

"Why the fuck not?"

"Without me you're a dead man."

"Who's gonna stop me?" Cloud is breathing heavily.

"There's some dudes around the corner think they will. They're coming after you."

"That's Lamont. My people will take care of him." Cloud doesn't sound confident. A new volley of gunfire erupts—closer this time. Cloud looks scared. Something I never thought I'd see.

"Your boys are all dead or out of the fight," I say. "You've got no one left. I can fix it for you so you can get out of here alive."

"How you gonna do that?" Cloud's voice shakes, but the hand holding the Walther is steady.

"I get you into the warehouse by the back door. You wait there for Lamont. He'll come in the front looking for you. Bam! Bam! Bam! You take out Lamont. And you take your guns. Just follow me."

"Let's go," Cloud orders. "Don' forget, I'm right behind you."

We crouch down and slip along the side of the building. There's rapid gunfire around the corner sounding like they're getting close. We reach the back door of the warehouse. Cloud gestures silently with his gun for me to go in first. I snatch open the door and dive inside. Cloud is right behind me.

I land flat on the floor. Floyd and Cass stand on either side of the door we just burst through, Floyd holding his AK-47, Cass a shotgun.

"What the fuck's going on here?" Cloud yells. "Where's my truck? Where's my stuff?"

"Drop your weapon!" Cass yells.

That's probably the wrong thing to say. Cloud spins and fires three rounds from his Walther into Cass's face, which disintegrates.

Floyd fires a burst from his AK-47 toward Cloud, but he's too slow. Too clumsy. Cloud has bolted through the open door back into the alley. Facing him is Lamont, holding a gun in each hand, firing round after round into Cloud. Cloud fires twice and Lamont goes down.

"Shut the door!" I yell at Floyd, scrambling to my feet.

Floyd slams and locks the door to the ally. Outside, the shooting comes to a stop and there's only silence. Somewhere a cell phone rings. Crowley stands at the far end in the warehouse. He takes a phone from his pocket and listens for less than fifteen seconds, then switches off.

"They've arrived," Crowley says to Floyd as we approach. "Time to call in the troops." Crowley starts to punch in a text message on his phone.

I stop close to him. "I wouldn't do that, Crowley."

"You gonna stop me?"

"Not me. The FBI."

"What you talking about?"

"The FBI's been tapping your phones. You use that phone, the FBI will triangulate your location and be here in minutes."

"How do you know that?"

"The lady your boys tried to kill at Fast Eddie's was FBI and she told me."

Crowley tosses his phone to the floor as if it were a poisonous snake.

"You can use my phone," I tell Crowley. "It's a burner. It won't be in the FBI system."

"How come you're being helpful?"

"I want to get out of here. Same as you. And I don't want to have to explain those dead bodies."

Crowley takes the phone he took from me and punches in a number. He holds the phone to his ear and listens intently. "Hello. Hello. Can you hear me?"

He jerks the phone away from his head and stares at it in shock. I can hear a loud buzzing sound. "What just happened?" Crowley yells. "What did you do?"

Crowley's face is red with rage, the artery in his neck pulsing. "That was a bomb. You fucking put a bomb in my truck!" Crowley screams to Floyd. "Get Tony here! Get him now! Tell him to bring his weapon."

Floyd speaks to someone in the back of the Olds. The passenger door opens and a figure emerges—tall, slender, muscular, dressed in a U.S. Army enlisted man's dress uniform—blue trousers, dark blue tunic with shoulder cords, heavy black spit-shined combat boots, white belt. He carries an M14 rifle.

"Tony," Crowley shouts. "Come here."

Tony Wilcox crosses the concrete warehouse floor toward us, his boots making sharp clicks from the metal inserts in his heels. He wears service ribbons on his chest. One of them is a Silver Star.

Crowley points to me. "That's the enemy. Detective Zorn, this is Tony Wilcox, a killer, trained and shaped by your Army."

The young man stands motionless, his eyes dead, ramrod straight, feet apart, grasping the M14, modified for a left-handed shooter.

"Shoot him, Tony. Do your duty, soldier. Blow his head off like you did the ragheads."

"Yes, Sweet Daddy." Tony shifts his weight and slowly shifts the M14 rifle into firing position.

"Tony," I say softly. "Sweet Daddy killed Sandy."

Tony's eyes flick toward me. "What about Sandy?" he mumbles. "What did you say?"

"Kill him!" Crowley yells. "Now!"

"Crowley murdered Sandy. He killed your Pollywog."

"What's he talking about, Sweet Daddy?" Tony's voice is low and shaking. "You told me Sandy was okay. You said she was safe."

"Don't listen to him," Crowley screams.

"Sandy's dead," I repeat. "Sweet Daddy killed Polly. With his bare hands. He pushed her head under water. She struggled. She wanted to live, but Sweet Daddy wouldn't let her."

"Tony, he's lying."

"I found her floating in the Pool." I keep my voice calm. Which I'm not feeling. My heart races, the adrenaline surges through me. All the muscles in my body want to move. I have to force myself not to run. If I do, I'm dead. "Tony, I found Polly. I looked into her blue eyes and she asked me for help. Listen to Polly. Sweet Daddy killed your little sister."

"Pay no attention." Sweet Daddy's almost beseeching now. He must sense he's losing Tony.

"Tony, remember what Sandy told you? She told you Sweet Daddy was evil. Isn't that right, Tony? You remember. Polly warned you. That's why Sweet Daddy killed her."

"Shoot him!" Crowley screams.

"Did you hurt Sandy?" Tony looks directly at Crowley. His eyes are moist with tears. "You promised." He's looking at Crowley in a new way. Maybe seeing him for the first time.

"He caught Sandy," I say. "He dragged her to the Reflecting Pool."

"That wasn't me. That was somebody else." Crowley's voice trembles with fear.

"Sweet Daddy pushed Polly's head under water. He held her head while she struggled. She was frightened. So scared. Sandy died for you."

Tony's face is covered with tears. He pivots, the M14 held tightly under his left arm. "You promised me she was safe. You promised, Daddy." Tony fires. The round hits Crowley in his chest and he's flung back, slamming him, sprawling, to the ground.

"Holy crap!" Floyd shouts, raising his AK47. His head explodes from the second round from Tony's M14.

I know what's coming and I sprint toward Tony. I'm too late.

Tony Wilcox lowers the M14, and, in a single, fluid motion places the muzzle under his chin and pulls the trigger.

Behind me I hear Kenneth vomiting.

CHAPTER FORTY-FOUR

KENNETH LEANS AGAINST the Oldsmobile's left front wheel. "You okay?" I kneel beside him. I have five minutes.

His face is ashen. "Those men—are they dead?"

"I'm calling an ambulance. The medics will be here soon."

"I don't need a doctor, sir."

No slurring in his speech. A good sign. "Don't call me 'sir.' I have to go away for a few minutes. Will you be okay?"

I don't think Kenneth hears me. He's in shock.

I leave Kenneth, retrieve the cell phone I gave Crowley, and put it into the tote bag, along with my tools. I leave the warehouse by the back door.

Cloud is dead. Lamont is badly wounded but is still clutching a Ruger. I don't know what happened to the other gun he was using. I pull the Ruger from his grip and throw it to the far end of the alley. Lamont is still wearing his Rolex. I expect it will be stolen when he gets to the hospital.

I reach into Lamont's pocket, take out a cell phone, and call 911. "I want to report a shooting."

"Name?"

"Lamont Jones."

"Please spell that."

"The shooting took place . . ." I give the dispatcher the address of the warehouse. "There are multiple dead and wounded. One police officer needs urgent medical attention. Send ambulances."

"Please stay on the line, sir."

I cut the connection, wipe the phone clean of my fingerprints, and go to work. I maybe have two minutes left. I sprint to the front of the building where what remains of Lamont's van is standing, riddled with bullet holes, the driver slumped over the steering wheel. There are four bodies lying on the pavement, two motionless. One twitches and seems to be reaching for a shotgun lying a few inches from his right hand. I kick the shotgun away.

I search the van and quickly find a black garbage bag. I dive into Cloud's black sedan parked a few yards away. It's dark inside and at first I find nothing except expended shell casings.

In the distance I hear a siren, and for a second, consider abandoning my search. Then I see a black attaché case in the back, jammed behind the driver's seat. I yank it free and hurry away just as the headlights of an approaching car appear a block away. I walk quickly, careful not to run, to my parked Jag, pop the trunk, dump in the attaché case, the plastic bag, the tote bag with my tools and slam the trunk shut.

I walk briskly back to the warehouse in time to meet the arriving police cruiser. I hold out my police shield so it can be seen at a distance.

The cruiser pulls up to the warehouse entrance and two uniformed officers jump out, weapons drawn. The driver is young, maybe twenty, and is very nervous. "Jesus H. Christ!" he gasps, staring open-mouthed at the carnage around him.

The second is a man I know slightly, a Sergeant West or something, from an outlying precinct.

"There's an officer in there," I say, pointing into the warehouse. "I think he's okay, but he'll need medical attention."

"Any active shooters?" Sergeant West asks.

"Neutralized," I say. "But be careful. There are a lot of loose guns."

"You're Zorn, aren't you. You're Marko Zorn."

"I was here to make an arrest, but my suspect was killed in the gunfight. I'm going back inside and look after my partner."

"We'll wait until backup gets here," Sergeant West says.

"Good idea." I duck back into the warehouse and sit next to Kenneth putting my arm around his shoulder. Awkwardly. "You'll be fine." I take my arm away. It's making us both nervous.

The first to enter are the SWAT teams, dressed in military gear and wearing bulletproof vests and heavy headgear. They flood the warehouse and, I expect, the entire neighborhood. I sit beside Kenneth to be sure the SWAT teams don't shoot Kenneth in a fit of enthusiasm.

Finally, a lieutenant questions me, examines my credentials and calls in my ID and Kenneth's and determines neither of us is a known terrorist.

While being interrogated by the lieutenant, other forces arrive— several ambulances, sirens blaring, pull up outside the warehouse and a team of medics descends on Kenneth. I move away to give them room. They're followed almost immediately by Frank Townsend and a dozen uniformed officers. Frank looks at me from across the warehouse, shakes his head, perplexed, then rushes to Kenneth.

The atmosphere in the warehouse quickly turns chaotic. Personnel from half a dozen agencies arrive, each claiming priority. Patrick Grier, from the Secret Service, stands over the body of Tony Wilcox talking to Carl Nash, our crime scene investigator.

Carla Lowry and Arora Lovelace arrive. Carla ignores me while she speaks with the ranking FBI agent on the scene. At one point, they both look at me. Arora studies me from a distance, but we say nothing to each other. I can't read her expression.

Hal Marshal arrives at the warehouse, sees me, and makes a quick nod acknowledging my presence then speaks to Frank Townsend. I even see Captain Fletcher. What is he doing here? I wonder. I suppose the Department of the Interior must establish its presence.

I stand to one side, trying not to be noticed, until Frank Townsend appears at my side.

"What in hell happened here?"

"You still want me to turn in my service weapon and my badge."

"No. But you're still in deep shit."

"I found Kenneth."

"You fucking lost Kenneth first." Townsend shrugs. "But Kenneth tells me you saved his life."

"Is that what he says?"

"Kenneth saw the whole thing. How the shooter—how he was going to kill you and Kenneth, but you talked him down. And the shooter killed the guy in the white suit instead. Who, I'm told, is the head honcho of this terrorist group. Is that how it went down?"

"Something like that."

"And now Hal Marshal tells me you were somehow involved in putting the two most dangerous criminal thugs in DC out of business." Townsend looks disgusted. "The mayor will give another press conference, and he'll take credit for this whole business, of course. We might even get a unit citation." He stops, frowning, as if a terrible idea has crossed his mind. "Jesus, he's probably going to want to give you some kind of medal. Keep your goddamned badge. I'm taking Kenneth to the hospital."

Matt Decker, the head of the Secret Service, comes after me. He points to Tony Wilcox, now covered with a heavy cloth. "That the shooter?"

"That's right," I say

"And that other one . . . the guy in the white suit . . . ?"

"His name is Crowley."

"And he is?"

"He created the Brotherhood of the Aryan Dawn."

"How did you find them?"

"A confidential source."

"That's not a satisfactory answer."

"That's the only answer you're going to get from me. You know how these things are."

Matt Decker shrugs. "You heard Talbot was killed last night?"

"I heard."

"That pretty well confirms he was working with the terrorists."

"Look further. You'll find he's innocent."

Decker looks at me funny and walks quickly away.

I think that's it. They're finished with me. I can leave and collect my car and what's in the trunk and go home and get some sleep. No such luck. Hal Marshal stops me as I'm about to go, and we both survey the hell that's been left.

"My contacts tell me Cloud and Lamont were both planning to purchase a shipment of weapons this morning," Hal says. "What happened to the guns?"

"I think they got blown up. I expect ATF will be able to track down what's left of them."

"Cloud and Lamont have both been collecting money for their payment." He stops to see if I have anything to add. "The word I get is between them they collected almost two million dollars."

"That's a lot of money."

"Yeah. If these men were here to buy those weapons, they would have brought the money with them, don't you think?"

"You would think," I answer.

"We've looked everywhere and there's no money around. Where's the payoff money?"

"Search me."

Marshal shuffles away, not saying anything.

I leave the warehouse and stand next to an enormous command vehicle that brought the Secret Service contingent. I take out my cigarette pack and light one. By the time I'm halfway through, Carla Lowry and Arora Lovelace come out of the warehouse. "This is a fine mess," Carla says. We are silent. What is there to say?

"You found your partner?" Arora asks.

"Yes. Crowley had him."

"How is he?"

"Kenneth is shaken. He'll be fine."

"I'm glad to hear he's okay." Arora looks as if she has something more she wants to say but is silent. Maybe because Carla Lowry is there. Maybe because there is nothing more to say.

A pair of Bulgari sunglasses lies on the ground a few feet from where we stand. An EMS team pushes a gurney out of the warehouse toward one of the ambulances. An EMS blanket covers the body, excerpt for the combat boots—black and spit polished. They gleam in the morning sun.

"Stop!" Carla orders, raising her hand.

The EMS team hesitates, uncertain.

"I want to look," Carla says, softly.

We all three approach the body. Carla gently lifts the blanket from the dead man's face.

"This is the boy who was going to change the world."

Arora and I both nod.

"Poor bastard," Carla murmurs, almost reverently. "He deserved better." Carla gestures for the EMS team to continue. They cover Tony's face and place him in the ambulance, slamming the rear doors.

"Give me a cigarette," Carla tells me.

"I thought you quit smoking."

"Give me a damn cigarette!"

She takes the cigarette pack I'm holding, removes a cigarette. "I need a light."

I take my lighter from my pocket, flip it open, and hold the flame out to her. She drags on her cigarette then takes the lighter. "You still have it?" she asks. "I never thought you were such a romantic." She returns the lighter and cigarette pack to me. The touch of her hand feels nice. Like old times.

"Agent Lovelace," Carla speaks to Arora, "go to Headquarters. Write out an incident report on these events. I want it on my desk by the close of business today."

"Yes, ma'am."

Arora glances at me, her expression a combination of relief and regret, then ducks away, leaving Carla and me alone.

"What did this terrorist outfit plan to do at Arlington National Cemetery?" Carla asks.

"Probably try to infiltrate Tony Wilcox into the ranks of the honor guard. During the funeral ceremony he was supposed to shoot the President. Of course, Tony would have been shot to pieces by the Secret Service agents if he ever got close. I don't know how they thought they'd manage the infiltration."

More bodies are placed into waiting ambulances. One of them is Cloud's.

"There's nothing more for me here," Carla says. "As far as the Bureau is concerned, this case is closed. Our primary interest was in

Crowley and his Brotherhood organization and in protecting the President. The murder of Sandra Wilcox is not really our responsibility. Sandra Wilcox was murdered by Crowley to keep her quiet. End of story."

Carla takes another drag on her cigarette, tosses the smoldering butt onto the street, and crushes it with the toe of her shoe. "I'm told you convinced Tony Wilcox that Crowley murdered his sister Sandra and so Tony shot Crowley in revenge. I hope you realize that wasn't the way it actually happened. Crowley had nothing to do with the murder of Sandra Wilcox."

"Of course not."

"You just made that story up," Carla says. "About Crowley killing Sandra so that Tony Wilcox would believe Crowley was his enemy. It was all bullshit, wasn't it?"

"That's right. Bullshit."

"I suppose it's bullshit I can live with," Carla agrees. "It will be the official version for the FBI and the United States government. I'll see that Agent Lovelace writes it up properly." She looks at me intently. "But not you. You're not satisfied with the official bullshit."

"Certainly not."

"Be careful. You're on dangerous ground. You know the name of the killer. Right? I'd guess you've known all along." She holds up her hand, palm facing me. "Don't tell me. I don't want to know."

CHAPTER FORTY-FIVE

KENNETH BLAKE IS in a bright, sunny hospital room, sitting up in bed wearing one of those ridiculous gowns hospitals make you put on. Apart from that, he looks in pretty good shape. He's had a shave, somebody has combed his hair, and he looks cheerful.

Also in Kenneth's room is Frank Townsend and Nat Blake, Kenneth's father, looking more friendly than the last time I saw him. There are several bouquets of flowers and some brightly colored balloons—the kind you buy at hospital gift shops. And a large Teddy Bear. A middle-aged woman with curly gray hair and sensible shoes sits on the bed next to Kenneth.

"Detective Zorn," Nat Blake booms from across the room. "I'm glad you came. I wanted the chance to thank you." He strides around Kenneth's hospital bed and grasps my hand. "I want to thank you, personally, for saving Kenneth. I can't tell you how grateful Mrs. Blake and I are for all you've done." He waves at Frank Townsend, who stands near the window. "Frank told me all about it. How you took down that terrorist group and saved Kenneth. Great job!"

He stops and waves at the gray-haired woman. "I want you to meet Kenneth's mom, Mrs. Blake."

He kind of pushes the woman so she's standing a few feet from me. "Thank you, Mr. Zorn. Thank you for saving our boy from those awful people. Kenneth told us about how you saved him. I don't know how we can ever thank you enough."

"Just doing my job, Mrs. Blake,"

"It's Lucille. Please call me Lucille."

"Would you like a doughnut, Detective Zorn?" she asks.

"No thank you, I'm on a diet." I disengage myself from Lucille and go to Kenneth's bed. "How are you doing?"

"Pretty good, now that I've had a shower and a square meal. And I'm with my family." He looks at me. "Family and friends like Captain Townsend and you."

"Did they hurt you?"

"Not really. The scary part was they kept saying they were going to kill me. But now, here with you, it all seems like a bad dream. I can't believe it happened."

"Wasn't he brave, Detective Zorn?" Mrs. Blake chimes in. "Wasn't our Kenneth brave?"

"He certainly was, Mrs. Blake. Your son was a real hero."

"You hear that, Nat? Kenneth's a hero."

"He was key to uncovering this terror group. If it hadn't been for Kenneth's undercover detective work, we wouldn't have found the assassin. They might have succeeded in assassinating the President."

"Didn't I say?" Nat Blake announces, his face beaming. "I told you he was a hero."

"And he kept his head under the most difficult circumstances imaginable," I say, deciding to lay it on thick.

"Do you think the President will want to meet with Kenneth? Maybe give him a medal?" Mrs. Blake asks hopefully.

"I can't really say."

"Detective Zorn," Kenneth calls from his bed. "I have something I have to tell you."

"What's that?"

"I've been thinking . . . today . . ."

"Kenneth's been offered a position in the Richardton sheriff's department," Kenneth's father explains. "A real good position. With good prospects. And medical. He'd be in charge of the anti-terrorism section. He certainly has the experience."

"I'm seriously considering the offer," Kenneth says. "I hope you aren't too disappointed, my leaving you like this."

"You have to do what's right for you, Kenneth," I say.

"In point of fact, I'm not sure I really fit in with the DC police homicide squad."

"Sure you did."

"You think so, sir?"

"But you've got to do what's best for you," I add hastily.

"I'd be near my parents. You know."

"I'm sure you'll do the right thing, Kenneth. You keep in touch. Don't be a stranger." I move toward the door. "It was a pleasure to meet you, Mrs. Blake."

"Lucille."

"Lucille. Mr. Blake. You should be proud of your son."

"Detective Zorn," Kenneth calls from across the room. "Thank you for saving my life. I never had any doubts you'd find me. Not for a moment."

"How could you be so sure?"

"Because we're partners. I trusted you."

"See you at the office," Frank Townsend says. "You need to write up the Sandra Wilcox case."

"I'm not quite ready for that. I need to arrest someone first."

CHAPTER FORTY-SIX

IT'S TWO IN the afternoon before I'm able to reach Miss Shaw through the White House communications center.

"Good afternoon, Detective. The President and First Lady want to thank you for your help in putting an end to this terrorist threat. They just returned from Arlington National Cemetery. The ceremony went without incident. Thanks to you. How may I help you?"

"I need to talk to the First Lady."

"Can I tell her what you wish to speak with her about?"

"The murder of Sandra Wilcox."

There is a long silence at the other end. "I thought that case was closed. I understand Agent Wilcox was killed by the leader of the terrorist group."

"That's the official version."

"And you don't accept the official version?"

"That's right, I don't. But I do expect to close the case today."

There is a long silence. "You've found the note, then."

"Yes, Miss Shaw, I found the note."

"The First Lady is engaged until six this evening. I will arrange for you to see her then."

Miss Shaw must have made very special arrangements for me this time. When I arrive at the 15th Street security entrance, a uniformed

Secret Service agent meets me in front. He exams my police ID then informs me I've been cleared to drive directly to the East Wing entrance. Somebody opens the security barriers, and I drive straight through. No armed, suspicious agents accompany me. When I arrive at the East Wing entrance a young man I've never seen before is waiting for me. He shows me where to park my Jag. The space is almost directly in front of the entrance.

"My name is Samuel Price. Please follow me."

"Where is Miss Shaw?" I ask.

"Miss Shaw? Who is Miss Shaw?"

"She's on the White House staff."

"I'm afraid I don't know her."

"She's the one who usually escorts me."

"I'm handling the First Lady's appointments today. Please follow me. She is expecting you."

Price leads me through the West Wing, which seems all but deserted, into the East Wing and up the elevator to the private quarters of the President and First Lady. A few Secret Service agents stand at their posts, watching me without interest as I pass. There are no signs of Miss Shaw or her security detail.

The young man taps gently on the door to the First Lady's sitting room. I hear a faint voice from within: "Come in."

Price opens the door and I enter. Mrs. Reynolds is sitting on the same couch I'd seen her on during my first visit. She is dressed in dark clothes, suitable for a memorial ceremony, and wears two large diamond earrings. Her face is drawn, almost haggard. Was that the way she looked when I last saw her? I try to remember. She's grown old in the last few days.

"That will be all, Samuel. You may shut the door." The young man silently leaves the room, closing the door behind him.

Mrs. Reynolds looks at me with an expression I can't read. "Sit down, Detective Zorn. I understand you have something to tell me."

I take a seat opposite her. "Yes, Mrs. Reynolds. I thought you should know; I plan to close the Sandra Wilcox case today."

Mrs. Reynolds pinches the bridge of her nose. "Matt Decker told me Sandra was murdered by this terrorist militia group."

"Mr. Decker is mistaken. As you know very well."

The pearl-gray phone on the side table next to the couch rings gently. "Excuse me. I must take this. A call I've been expecting."

Mrs. Reynolds carefully removes an earring from her left ear, placing it carefully on a side table, and lifts the receiver. "Yes," she says softly. She listens for a long time. "I see," she says at last. "Have Ken prepare a statement. Show it to me before it is released. The usual: our hearts and prayers go out to the family, etcetera, etcetera . . . No, I don't think we need to trouble the President about this. Leave it to me." She replaces the receiver on the hook.

"Sorry, Mr. Zorn. You were saying."

"From the very first day of my investigation, I've been lied to."

"You're a policeman. You should be used to that by now."

"Sandra Wilcox's death had nothing to do with the assassination plot. It was a simple act of murder. It was murder about love gone wrong. Not all that different from hundreds of other murders that happen every day."

"I see."

"Except that . . ."

"Except for what?"

"Sandra Wilcox was murdered on orders from someone here in the White House."

Mrs. Reynolds is on her feet, staring down at me, trembling. She is shorter than I remembered, but that does not diminish the power of her anger.

"Are you accusing someone of murder? Someone here in the White House?"

"Yes, ma'am."

"I was at dinner with a dozen friends the night Sandra was killed. All of whom will vouch for me. Among my guests were the British ambassador and Lady Charles. Do you propose to haul them to your police station and beat them with rubber truncheons?"

"That won't be necessary. I'm not accusing you of murder, Mrs. Reynolds. I'm sure you have ensured that your alibi is solid. But we both know who the killer is."

"It's time you left, Detective Zorn."

"I'm not finished."

"Who are you accusing?"

"I'm accusing Miss Shaw."

Mrs. Reynolds turns away from me. She snatches up the diamond earring she left on the side table and nervously attaches it to her ear. Playing for time, I suppose. "Hogwash!"

"On the night of the murder, Miss Shaw managed to get Sandra Wilcox to leave the White House and go onto the Mall. Only a senior member of the White House staff could enter and leave the White House without being logged in and out. She forced Sandra, I assume at gunpoint, to go to the Reflecting Pool. There she was murdered."

"How could Miss Shaw have done that?"

"Miss Shaw certainly had help. I'd guess from her private security detail."

"Why on earth would Miss Shaw want to murder Agent Wilcox? They barely knew one another."

I remove from my pocket the note I'd found hidden in the lampshade in Sandra Wilcox's bedroom. Mrs. Reynolds stares at it and abruptly sits on the couch as if her knees had given way. "May I?" she holds out her hand.

I pass her the note.

"What do the words '*The moon has set, and the Pleiades; it is midnight, and time passes, and I sleep alone*' mean to you?" I ask

"They mean everything to me."

"Did you send Sandra that note?"

"Why should I answer your questions? And on what do you base your speculation that I sent that note?"

"Your perfume. I recognize the scent. The scent on the note is the same you're wearing this evening."

"That's pretty thin."

"The handwriting on the note is yours."

"How could you know that?"

"You were kind enough to inscribe a copy of your book for me. The handwriting on the inscription and on the note is undoubtedly the same hand. It also seemed unlikely to me that a man would quote the Greek poet Sappho about a woman longing for her woman lover."

"Where did you find the note?" she asks, after a long silence, holding it against her breast.

"Sandra hid it in her apartment."

"She kept it?" Mrs. Reynolds whispers, barely audible. "She kept it after all. How very wonderful." She turns the note over a few times. "It was foolish of me, wasn't it?"

"Why did you send the note to Sandra, Mrs. Reynolds?"

"I was desperately in love and love makes fools of us all."

"So I've noticed. Did your husband know about your affair with Sandra?"

"Eliot is oblivious."

"I thought at first the President himself might have ordered Sandra's murder. I suspected he was jealous of your relationship with Sandra."

"He could not have cared less about me and who I loved. Understand, my husband is a sexual predator. He wanted Sandra on his security detail for one reason only, to fuck her brains out."

"I suppose you hoped eventually he'd tire of Sandra and go on to some new victim. And she would return to you."

Mrs. Reynolds is silent.

"But she didn't, did she? Instead, she fell in love with your husband."

"Being pursued by the most powerful man in the world is irresistible, it seems. A middle-aged woman is no competition. It all came to a head one evening about a week ago. I called Sandy here to my quarters to have it out with her. I told her to give up Eliot. I begged her. But Sandy was lost to me. She believed Eliot loved her. I told her Eliot knows nothing about love, but she wouldn't listen. She became angry and said things . . . hurtful, hateful things. It was the end. I was furious and I suppose I lost my mind."

"So you decided to get rid of her."

"I'm certainly not going to answer that."

"But you told Miss Shaw, I imagine, how hurt and desperate you were and, in an act of fealty and devotion, she did what she knew you wanted."

"Imagine what you please. Our conversation here is at an end."

I make no move to leave.

"Must I call my Secret Service detail?" She reaches for the phone, but her hand hangs suspended above the instrument.

"When I told Miss Shaw this afternoon I had to see you, she realized I'd found the note you sent. You both knew then it was all over. You and the President would be disgraced. Lives lost to a moment of jealousy and rage."

"May I keep the note?"

"I will need it for the prosecution."

Mrs. Reynolds shakes her head, a sad smile on her lips. "I don't think so."

"Miss Shaw will tell me what I need to know to bring charges."

"I don't think so." She sits back in her couch, arms crossed. "You're too late. That phone call I just received—that was my personal assistant passing along a report from the Maryland State Police. About thirty minutes ago the Maryland Highway Patrol found a car parked on the side of a highway. Inside was a body of a woman."

I take a deep, painful breath "Who was it?" I dread the answer.

"The victim was carrying a White House pass." Mrs. Reynolds pinches the bridge of her nose. "The pass identified the victim as Miss Shaw."

My throat is constricted and I have a hard time breathing. We sit in silence for a moment while I try to take in what she has said. "Did they give the cause of death?"

"The police reported that it looked like a massive drug overdose." Mrs. Reynolds sighs. "A long time ago Miss Shaw was an addict. I thought she was cured. But you never know about these things."

Maybe I've been in this job too long. There was a time, not so long ago, when I would be hard charging to fix this. I'd have told the Maryland police that Miss Shaw's death was no accidental overdose or a suicide. I would insist they investigate Miss Shaw's death as murder, that they search for members of her security detail. But I won't do that. What would be the point? Her security guards will have long since vanished. Any investigation into Miss Shaw's murder will be quickly shut down, just like the investigation into Sandra Wilcox's murder.

"Miss Shaw's death is the end of the road for you," Mrs. Reynolds very quietly interrupts my reverie. "I hope you're satisfied. You realize, if you'd not been so stubborn in finding the truth about Sandra's murder, Miss Shaw would still be alive. Was it really worth that price for the truth?"

I have no answer to that. That question will haunt me for a long time.

"May I keep my note?" she asks. "I don't think you'll be needing it anymore."

She's right. This is the end of the Sandra Wilcox investigation so why not let her have the note? It may give her some comfort. Or maybe grief. I don't know. In either case it's of no further use to me.

"I have one last question, Mrs. Reynolds. What was Miss Shaw's first name?"

"I'm not sure. Allison maybe. I don't really remember. Does it matter?"

CHAPTER FORTY-SEVEN

IT's EARLY EVENING and traffic in Georgetown is heavy and I check up and down the street before going into Le Zink.

"Hey there, Moon Man," a familiar voice calls. Otis stands next to a UPS delivery truck. A big smile on his face. He holds a leather satchel in one hand.

"Your mama know you're out this late, Otis?"

The smile fades and Otis looks at me with contempt. "You don' know nothin', Moon Man." Otis sidles up to me, looking furtively around. "I got somethin' for you."

"What's that?"

"You gon' pay me something?"

Another time I'd argue with Otis. Or tell him to get lost. Today, I don't have the heart. I'm still shaken from the news about Allison Shaw so I give Otis a twenty.

"Sister Grace sent me," Otis announces. "She say you did good." He presses the leather satchel into my hands. "Sister Grace say you and she square now."

The satchel feels heavy. Filled, I assume, with $25,000 in small bills.

"See you around, Moon Man."

"That depends on what you do when you grow up."

"I am grown up."

"What about when you're really grown?"

"I'm gonna be a gangsta."

"You don't want to be a doctor? Or a lawyer?"

Otis makes a disgusted face.

"How about an astronaut? Astronauts are cool."

"They losers. I'm gon' be a gangsta."

"Then you're going to end up just like Cloud and Lamont."

"No way. I'm too smart for that. You have somethin' to do with what happened to Cloud and Lamont?"

"None of your business."

"See you 'round, Moon Man." Otis runs up Wisconsin Avenue, disappearing into the evening crowd.

Inside Le Zink there are only a few customers. A couple of bored waiters stand at the entrance to the dining room. Edith Piaf is back on the sound system. A woman sits alone at the bar watching me as I approach, her eyes blazing with fury.

"You killed my Cloud," Mariana says.

"I didn't kill him. Lamont killed him."

"You set him up. You might as well have pulled the trigger on him yourself. You shouldn't have killed Cloud."

"I was trying to save you." That sounds pretty lame, even to me.

"Cloud was my man. I loved him. He loved me."

"He was going to kill you."

"That was between me and Cloud. You should have stayed out of it. You had no business interfering."

"My friend was killed last night. The man there to protect you and he was murdered." I don't know why I'm talking to Mariana. This is not a real conversation. She doesn't register a thing I say. Instead she looks away from me.

"Did you open the door to your apartment to Cloud?" I demand. I'm losing it. The anger boiling up inside me. "Was your story just an invention to get me to your apartment so Cloud could get to me?"

It's as if she doesn't hear me. She hears only the angry voices shouting in her head, drowning out everything.

"There's nothing here for me," she whispers. "I'm going home. Your police are after me. Thanks to you, I'm a fugitive."

I press the leather satchel Otis gave me into her hands. "This will get you as far as Buenos Aires." Her face shows no expression.

Why am I doing this? Why should I help this woman? Part of me hates her for what she did to Talbot, for her betrayal of me. And there's another part of me that wants her. It mystifies me why I do what I do.

"I imagine this is money." She slips off the barstool and stands facing me. "This is supposed to make you feel better? You think your money makes any difference to me? You killed my baby. It should have been you killed last night."

She walks to the door. "Burn in hell, Marko."

"You look like crap," Roberta says to me as I sit at the bar. She goes off to pour me an extra-large Van Winkle bourbon.

I'm on my second glass when Arora Lovelace takes the seat next to me.

"You get your report into Carla on time?"

"Of course."

"Did you include everything?"

Arora reflects a moment. "Certainly not."

"Can I buy you a drink?"

She shakes her head. "I'm catching a seven thirty flight out of Reagan National tomorrow morning. I just came to say goodbye."

"Where are you going?"

"It doesn't matter. Carla has given me a special assignment. To find the FBI mole—the person who told the Brotherhood about my informant in Denver and had him and one of our agents killed."

"Where will you be stationed?"

"Somewhere far from here. Carla wants me away from Washington. She thinks you're a bad influence."

"She's probably right."

Arora fiddles with a paper napkin. "Have you closed the Sandra Wilcox case?"

"I'm at a dead end."

"Carla tells me you know who the killer is."

I nod.

"She also told me not to ask you who it was." She pauses. "You must be angry that you can't close the case."

"These things happen."

Arora turns in her seat and looks directly at me. "Who are you, Marko? Who the fuck are you?"

"How would I know?"

"Never mind. I wouldn't believe you even if you told me."

She stands up. "We could have made a great team."

And she's gone.